SECRETS, SERPENTS, AND SUPERPOWERS

SECRETS, SERPENTS, AND SUPERPOWERS

THE AUGMENT'S CODE
BOOK 1

Zane Emerson

Podium

Podium

SECRETS, SERPENTS, AND SUPERPOWERS

CHAPTER ONE

Come on, Nate, don't you gotta leave for work soon? Just lock in with someone so I can stomp yah like normal."

"Yeah . . . Why do I play this with you again?" I groaned, dropping my head back against the couch and flicking my selection across the roster of heroes and villains. "Besides, man, you *always* play The First. That dude is broken as all hell, and you know it . . ."

"Hey, it's not my fault that they programmed him this way; the dude's my favorite hero, so of course I'm gonna play him. You've literally seen my comic collection," Jon, my roommate and longtime best friend, shot back immediately with a laugh as he pointed to a stack of disorganized comics on his side table. He was the picture of dishevelment, with long scraggly hair kept in check under a red checkered beanie and clothes that even I thought could be ironed.

"Please, he's *everybody's* favorite. That's like people saying Superman or Batman were their favorites before all these guys started to appear. The First was *literally* the first one to don the cape—of course he's gonna be more famous than other heroes like Hazard Pay or Clothwhip. It doesn't change the fact that his stats are literally broken compared to all the other playable characters."

"I can give you a computer sidekick on World Savior difficulty if you think you need the help," he shot back with a smirk before a new character icon popped up on the battle menu. I couldn't help but bark out a laugh.

"You're a little bit of a dick, has anyone ever told you that?"

"It's a badge of honor at this point. Now, quit stalling and just pick someone; you're already cutting it stupidly close for someone who can't even afford the damn subway."

"Okay, fine," I said, quickly settling on the one character I had even a minor bit of practice playing. "Rose Rot's never been the strongest, but I guess it's better than just button mashing and hoping I get lucky."

"Plus, you know . . . for a villain, I'd totally let her step on me," Jon laughed.

"No one needs to know your kinks, bud," I replied as we both locked in. The AI character started to randomize, the frame bouncing around the screen until it landed on a hero duo that for some reason counted as a single player called Shake and Bake.

The loading screen popped up, starting the process and showing our stats as Jon dropped his controller onto his lap so that he could grab his phone.

"You know loading doesn't take *that* long. Or are you gonna do that thing where you let me get you down to ten percent before you just pull out The First's bullshit Maximum Pressure ability."

"Hey, look at you, remembering the skill names for once," Jon laughed without looking up. "No, sorry, just found a new rumor post on the *Infinite Ascension* subreddit. Apparently, there was a document that got passed around showing how character generation worked, and it's stupidly complex."

"Dude, how many times have we gone over this? That thing's a friggin' urban legend at this point; it's never getting released, and you've got to get over it," I groaned. It wasn't that I didn't think the game was interesting or anything, the *concept* totally was: a completely unique superpower-based MMO where every player had a uniquely generated set of powers all set within a constantly changing in-game world. Hell, who wouldn't think that was cool?

By all accounts and rumors, it had everything a gamer could want. Stuff like a morality system, the freedom to choose your own path, and the ability of *actually* affecting the world around you. Hell, there were even rumors that if your character did well enough, the company would make official comic books and merchandise that you'd *actually* get royalties for. It was cool as all hell to read about, and about as totally fictional and never going to be released as *Half-Life 3*.

"How can it be an urban legend? We *both* donated to the Kickstarter; we saw the concept art."

"Yeah, and that's *all* we saw. Or did you forget about the part where we both chipped in a hundred bucks from our allowances, only for the page to go dead like, three months later? Hell, AetherTech doesn't even have an active web page or social media presence now; they might as well have never even existed. We were ten; it was like, thirteen years ago. You have *got* to let it go. It was a friggin' scam to get super nerds worked up for the game of their dreams."

The game finally loaded, and though he was making an effort to throw in a few attacks, I could tell Jon had gotten distracted, as he kept eyeing the phone he had placed on the edge of the couch. As I had predicted, I was able to get in with Rose Rot and take a good chunk out of his health each time he looked away from the screen.

"How many times have we gone over this! The subreddit found the document trail; they got bought out by some obscure department of the NSA. They'd been developing some AI that ran the mission system and—"

"And the government bought them out to hide the self-learning AI, *blah blah blah*. It's a *conspiracy theory*," I said, unable to hide the exasperation in my voice. Jon took the opportunity to launch The First forward, hitting me with a quick few attacks before I could counter. "Besides, we are literally swimming in Augment media and games now. Why are you still pining over some game that's never going to come out?"

"Yah just don't get it, dude," Jon said. In a flash, he executed a combo that knocked my character out, the game showing a big **[KO]** as I dropped the controller on my lap.

"Guess I don't. You've gotta learn to play someone else, man. The First is broken, and it's not really fun to keep playing if you're just gonna steamroll me every time." I looked up at the clock on the wall, my eyes widening as I jumped to my feet. "Shit, okay, I really gotta get going."

"Yeah, yeah, whatever. Be careful out there; if you gotta head south of 43rd, I'd recommend running a few streets over. Maybe even go down to Seventh before heading that way. The Scanner App I got on my phone's been going nuts about some fight going on over there. I really need to get an actual police radio or something," he said as he fiddled with his phone before the mumble of chatter came out of it. He was just setting the phone down and returning the game to the main screen when I turned away. "Catch yah later, bud."

Opening the door, I jerked to a stop as I found myself face-to-face with the elderly Mr. Greyson, who owned the building. His fist had been raised, about to knock, and he looked at me with just the faintest bit of shock.

"Um, hi, Mr. Greyson. It's, uh . . . It's . . ."

"It's the first Friday of the month, Nathaniel," he said, a warm smile spreading over his face. I looked over my shoulder at Jon, who shook his head quickly.

"I, uh, I'm getting paid when I get to work tonight; can we drop the cash off in the morning?" I asked with what I knew had to be a somewhat pained smile. Mr. Greyson's smile faltered ever so slightly, and he let out a sigh. It only lasted a moment before he looked over my shoulder at Jon.

"Jonathan, could you assist me in the lobby? The building's wireless internet seems to be acting up, and I could certainly use your expertise once again."

"Come on in, Mr. Greyson. I actually set up a quick link on my laptop last time you asked me for help; shouldn't take more than a minute," Jon replied, tossing his controller to the side and hopping up from the couch to walk over toward the kitchen.

I stepped to the side as Mr. Greyson walked in. He turned to me, and the warm smile returned to his face. "You just come see me when you have the time, Nathaniel. Your uncle was a longtime friend; I'm not going to kick you out just because you're a few days late, you know that."

"Thank you, Mr. Greyson," I replied. Not wanting to push my luck, I walked past him, hurried down the stairs, and pushed my way out the front door.

Though I knew I should listen to Jon—the dude *was* obsessed with watching everything going on in the city lately—that didn't change the fact that the building my company had assigned me to cleaning duty for the night was down on 39th and Ninth, and I was already cutting my clock-in time close as it was.

It was because of that stupidity that I found myself in a crowd being held up at the intersection on 44th, a whole street earlier than Jon had predicted. The crowd was massive, and I had to push my way through it as I ignored the honking of traffic being stuck due to the people blocking the street.

"Calm down, folks, we shouldn't be delayed for too long," a burly cop with a thick mustache said. His hand was held up, trying to calm a crowd that wasn't actually in all that much of a panic. If anything, they seemed more curious and eager to see what was going on. Years ago, maybe the New York transit would have been delayed because of, well . . . traffic or some sort of weird accident involving an olive oil truck, but those kinds of mundane delays had disappeared long ago.

"Is that Pinneedle?!" a voice called out.

"No, Pinneedle can't fly. It's got to be Grand Strike!" answered another.

There was a rumbling through the crowd as the sound of a small sonic boom echoed overhead. I briefly looked up, seeing one of the thousands of blinking objects littering the sky around the world that had appeared just over a decade ago. The Augmentation Array—at least that's what the world dubbed it—was the subject of millions of conspiracies and exactly zero tangible answers, except for the one glaring one. Around a year after it appeared, people with superpowers started to crop up all over the globe. Honestly, I wasn't actually sure if the name *Augment* had come first or the name of the Array, but pretty much everyone agreed the two were connected.

I found myself staring at one of the nodes of the Array directly overhead, watching as it pulsed a steady blue light every few seconds before it suddenly stopped midway through a pulse, turning red and then fading to black. I wasn't entirely sure why it did anything it did, but I'd be willing to bet the folks who really followed the Augments—people like Jon—had all sorts of theories as to what the blinking lights meant.

Several car alarms started to go off as I sighed, taking a look down at my watch. This was going to be at least the third time I was late in the last two weeks. Pulling my phone out, I found my boss's number before dialing it. It only rang once before he answered.

"Do not fuckin' tell me you're gonna be late again, Mercer."

"It's not my fault this time, I swear, Mr. Russo. There's a blockade on 44th; some Augment attack—"

"Yeah, like that's my fuckin' problem. Hop on the goddamn subway or buy a fuckin' bike; I ain't having this shit anymore, and I warned yah," Mr. Russo growled back. "You're fi—"

"Wait! Come on, Mr. Russo, I'm desperate. I'll stay late tonight; I'll pick up an extra shift—just work with me here. I'm literally at 44th Street; there's a blockade on Ninth, but I can go around and be there in . . . in fifteen minutes. Tops," I said frantically as I pushed my way out of the crowd and started to jog up 44th. Though the road was blocked heading up Ninth, there *had* to be an alley or something I could sneak through to get there.

"Fine. Fifteen minutes," Mr. Russo said. "Not a damn second later."

In the back of my head, I made a promise to myself for the umpteenth time to leave earlier just in case of shit like this.

"Thanks, Mr. Rus—" I didn't even get to finish when he hung up the call. I quickly headed a block and a half up the street, bypassing another blocked road on 10th before I ran across the street and into an alleyway. Luckily, there didn't seem to be a police presence, nor the sound of sonic booms in the air. At least . . . not directly overhead.

I started to slow down, feeling slightly more confident about getting to work on time, when that reality was shattered.

A huge *CRASH* was the first thing that hit me before a wave of pressure and air expanding outward literally knocked me off my feet. As I hit the ground, the air was subsequently pulled from my lungs, and I struggled to catch my breath. But as soon as the unrelenting pressure appeared, it vanished, and I found myself gasping.

"What . . . What the—"

"How many times are we gonna do this, Firefist?" the echo of a voice reached me as I slowly struggled to get back to my feet. It only took the flash of a familiar purple-and-gold outfit for me to jump behind the nearest obstacle. If *he* was here, then that could only mean this wasn't some ordinary street fight.

"As many times as it takes to take this stupid city from your grasp," a sharper, almost wild voice replied. "You're a puppet; you know that, right? All of you Goody Two-shoes are, but *especially* you First Wave assholes."

I could hear the roar of fire, then a bright light filled the space on the other side of the obstacle that I now realized was a dumpster. Part of me seemed to register that there were more sirens in the distance, but it was impossible to not peek my head out to try and see who was on the other side.

It was *exactly* who I had thought it was. Jon would never shut up about him, after all.

The First stood tall in a sleek purple-and-gold outfit, complete with a violently violet cape that always seemed to flap, even when there wasn't an obvious source of wind. His fists were clenched and on his hips, and if I didn't know better, I would have thought he was *actually* posing. It was weird as all hell, if I was being honest.

Even with that bit of oddness, I knew exactly what I had to do. I reached into my pocket and grabbed my phone, poking it out from behind the dumpster as I dialed Jon on FaceTime.

"You went to 43rd, didn't you, and—wait, where are you? What's with the flickering light and—"

"Dude, shut up for a second. You are *NOT* going to believe this," I said, noticing my hand was shaking as I messed with the controls to flip to my rear-facing camera. "That's exactly who I think it is, isn't it?"

"THE FIRST?!" Jon practically shouted, his head blowing up on the screen as he pulled the phone closer. His eyes went from amazed to panicked in a fraction of a second, though, and he pulled the phone back. "Shit, you have *GOT* to get out of there; his attacks can send out literal shock waves—"

There was another loud *BOOM* as The First launched himself forward at a man who was practically built like a truck. He didn't wear a fancy costume like his enemy did, though true to his name, his fists *were* on fire. Much to my surprise, Firefist didn't try to dodge, instead stepping forward and punching, striking back at The First just before the legendary hero could land his blow.

There was another wave of pressure that swept through the area, though this time I was ready for it and jumped out of the way before the dumpster that took the brunt of the pressure could crash into me.

"You've gotten stronger, Firefist. I'm impressed. But how many times do I have to make this clear: This city is Paragon territory; you'd be better off trying to take over a district. That seems more up your . . . heh . . . alley."

I heard Jon snicker as I scrambled to get back behind the dumpster now that it had stopped moving. Though I probably should listen to Jon and run, it was almost like I couldn't fight off my own curiosity of seeing them up close. The two superpowered men were locked together, struggling to get control over one another as their fists clashed again and again. Unlike the earlier attack, though, these strikes didn't cause another wave of pressure to come.

"You should be running, man . . . but I get it," Jon said, and I looked down to see he had set up his phone to stand on its own as he turned to his computer. "That joke, though—stuff like that's totally why he's my favorite."

"Seriously not the time for you to be fanboying, dude . . ." I muttered, looking back up just in time to notice The First had looked over in my direction. Our eyes met, and a wave of realization seemed to hit him.

It only took that moment of distraction for Firefist to land a blow directly to the hero's face, and even though it didn't make The First budge, I could see a look that I would have never expected to see on such a powerful man.

Fear.

Firefist followed The First's gaze, and he, too, finally noticed me, a wicked-looking grin cutting across the man's dark face.

"Okay, no more joking around—*RUN*, you have to—"

Everything that happened next *should* have been impossible to follow, but oddly enough, whether it was through adrenaline or something else, I *was* able to.

First, Firefist *literally* burst into flames, his entire body erupting into a blaze of green-and-blue fire that roared in my direction. After that, I could see as large pieces of concrete debris were launched into the air, and a purple-and-gold streak blurred past the roaring fire. This blur of movement subsequently caused a sonic boom that I was sure would be causing me permanent hearing damage, the wave of pressure that accompanied it launching the dumpster toward me with the speed of a moving car.

I could feel the cold metal crunch into my body. I could feel myself flying through the air. But . . . before I could feel myself crash into a wall, presumably to break most of the bones in my body, it almost felt like time slowed. My eyes caught the moment one of the many nodes of the Augmentation Array above me began to pulse a steady blue color. And then, all at once, time started up again, and I collided with the wall.

Darkness overtook me.

But the pain? The pain never came.

CHAPTER TWO

[Please Stand By for System Calibration.]

The words seemed to float in the air in front of my apparent lack of vision. They hung there for a few seconds before they slowly faded into nothingness.

"Hello?!" I called out. I didn't think I was *actually* speaking, but the words seemed to echo nonetheless. It was . . . disorienting, to say the least.

Suddenly, a new set of words began to appear as if they were being typed, the speed increasing with each line.

[Personal AI . . . Activated.]
[Power Loader . . . Activated.]
[B.E.L.T. . . . Activated.]
[HUD . . . Activated.]
[Acceptance Matrix . . . Activated.]

"Hello, new Augment!" a slightly robotic but distinctly female voice chirped in an overly cheery tone as several bursts of color started to swirl at the edges of my vision. *"Welcome to* Infinite Ascension*! You have been selected as a member of the Tenth Wave. Please stand by during the continued calibration. Once it is completed, we will get to the really fun stuff."*

"What the hell?" I said—or thought, or whatever the hell it was that was happening. There were still words appearing across my vision, but they were moving so fast it was impossible to actually read anything other than the last word of each line: Activated. *"Why can't I move my body, and who the hell are you?!"*

"My apologies, I should have introduced myself. I am your personal Artificial Neurally Guided Interface Enhancement, but you may call me 'Angie' or any other name you would prefer to use. Neural control will resume after final enhancement checks have been completed! However, while we wait for those to finalize, let me answer some of the commonly asked questions posed by new Augments!" the voice chirped back as a new window occupied my vision. Almost in tandem, the questions began to be listed out.

[What the Hell Is This?!]
This, Augment, is your neural interface, which will allow you to participate in the most exciting game on Earth: Infinite Ascension! You are one of the lucky few members of the planet who have been selected to participate, and we can't wait to see what you can do!

[Who the Hell Are You?!]

I just told you that, Augment! I'm Angie! After character creation, you can personalize my name if you happen to have had a bad experience with an Angie and don't want to be reminded of her every two seconds. If you are looking for a more specific answer, well, that's still pretty simple! I am your Personal Artificial Intelligence assistant, giving you advice and guidance as you tackle the daunting task of entering the world of Infinite Ascension. I'll be able to give you a more complete picture of just what I can do for you later.

[But I Don't Want to Play Some Random Game, Can I Opt Out?!]

Nope! Sorry, Augment, but this game is not optional. The moment you were selected is the moment you were obligated to participate. But seriously, you've got nothing to complain about; this is one game you're going to want to play.

[When Are These Drugs Going to Wear Off?!]

If you're asking about the drugs used to install the special enhancements that have turned you into an Augment, well, you should be awake within ten minutes, and the effects of the drugs will no longer be present at that point. If you're asking about the drugs as if they are a hallucinogen making you imagine all of this, well, I've got some bad news for you . . . those aren't going to affect you anymore! Not without a metric ton of them, at least. Sorry about that!

I should have probably been panicking. Logically, I knew I *should* have been freaking the absolute fuck out. But for some reason, my brain just accepted all of this to be true. I *was* in a game now. Sure, I was still in reality, too, but somehow, I was now included in . . . whatever all of this was. Maybe that was a part of whatever the enhancement drug was? Creating a sense of peace and acceptance for it all? I'd have to hope I could just have a full-blown panic attack about this once it all wore off.

"Hey now! Don't be so glum, bud! There's no need for a panic attack, so we're just gonna go ahead and disable those. I promise it's a good thing. After all, you're one of the super lucky few who gets to have actual, real-life superpowers!" Angie said as another burst of colorful lights scattered around my vision.

"Wait . . . superpowers?" I asked. Things seemed to start clicking into place as I finally realized just what Angie had been calling me since she started talking. *"Are you trying to tell me that every one of the Augments in the world right now are . . ."*

"Just playing Infinite Ascension? *Yup! All of those players the common public call supervillains too! Isn't that just super-duper exciting?!"*

"That's . . . That's insane . . . You're . . . You guys are letting people just run amok for a game? How . . . How do we not know it's a game?"

"We'll have time for more questions after stat generation is complete. Good, your blood pressure is noticeably lower, and the Matrix is functional and keeping that pesky

panic attack from coming on. Now, before we move on, do you acknowledge that what you are currently experiencing is reality, even if you're currently in an artificial coma?" Angie asked, a window popping up with a Y/N floating. *"It will get easier with practice, but please use your mental cursor to select your understanding."*

Concentrating, I could briefly see the shadow of a cursor move toward the center of my vision. Even though I didn't *want* to believe this was real, if it was, it didn't seem like I really had a choice. I briefly wondered what would happen if I selected *No* and felt my gut twist almost in agony at the idea. Luckily, the feeling immediately subsided as I mentally shoved the cursor over the *Y* and clicked on it.

"Excellent! Now, let's get to the fun part and see just what we've got to work with with that scrawny body of yours!" Angie continued as a new window filled my screen.

This one almost reminded me of a *Dungeons & Dragons* stat sheet, except instead of the standard six stat spread of that game, this one had eight: Strength, Toughness, Dexterity, Luck, Style, Intelligence, Charisma, and Ingenuity.

One by one, a number began to flicker into a box that had so far been empty next to each of the traits, spinning up to a rapid speed as a weirdly echoey clicking sound started, apparently trying to emulate an old-school lottery or bingo roller.

[Stat Selection for *Augment #1001* of the Tenth Wave Is Now Complete!]

"What do you think, Augment? Do ya want to hear the best or the worst first? Please note, all base scores are between one and ten, but scores have no actual cap through leveling or gear acquisition!"

"Um . . . th—"

"Too late! Better to see what you suck at first; it lets us build a better powerset if we know what we need to work on shoring up!" Angie chirped.

With every passing moment, more and more questions flooded my mind, but it was becoming more and more obvious that I wouldn't be getting any answers just yet. Knowing the futility, I found my attention glued to the roulette wheels as both Toughness and Strength seemed to be starting to slow.

[Toughness: 2]

Well, we did know you were scrawny already, so it doesn't look like you're gonna be all that tanky. That's okay; those Augments who start off with high points in this stat are quite literally the most boring lugheads imaginable. That said, I'd probably start raising this one pretty fast if I were you. You're really gonna need it.

That made me nervous, but I didn't really have time to think about it because only a few moments later, the next wheel stopped. It wasn't much of a surprise, though, as the stat had been slowing at nearly the same pace as Toughness.

[Strength: 3]
Look, we're not saying you can't open up a jar of pickles, 'cause you tooootally can, but what we are saying is you're not going to be lifting a car anytime soon; not without a LOT of help, at least.

The next few stats all happened in rapid succession.

[Style: 4]
We all know you've been wearing that same pair of cargo shorts for the last four years, Augment, but that's not what we're talking about when we talk Style in this context. It's how you approach life. It's sliding down the rail at the subway instead of walking down like a suit. Sure, they both accomplish the same thing, but one just does it with a bit more . . . style. And seriously, what kind of superhero doesn't have style?!

[Intelligence: 5]
Hey, look at you, Augment, you're of perfectly average intelligence. That's something the majority of the human race can't actually say! Wait . . . I'm pretty sure that's not how averages work . . . Oh well, we're only talking about average when it comes to all the people in the game, so your dumb neighbor Rick doesn't count when we are rating all of you Augments out at a base level.

[Charisma: 5]
Honestly, I'm a little surprised by this one. Given your track record, I would've guessed a two or three. But hey, good for you; you've got some charm. It's definitely more than a few of the awkward loners who stumble into the waves. Unfortunately for them, social skills aren't the only thing they lack, and most don't make it past the first few culling events. Do better than that, Augment. I believe in you. Sort of.

[Dexterity: 6]
You're certainly no athlete, but at least you don't get winded when you get up from the couch to walk over to the fridge. Here's the thing, Augment: In this game, you don't necessarily have to be strong, but being agile is a necessity. You're gonna want to find a way to stop being so average at this one ASAP.

With six of the stats out of the way, only two of the roulette wheels were still spinning. Both Ingenuity and Luck were finally starting to slow, one barely stopping before the other.

[Ingenuity: 8]
Wait, this isn't your highest stat? You know that phrase 'work smarter, not

*harder'? Yeah, we see you. Those perfectly planned cleaning routes that
let you hit every spot in record time? The way you rig every supply closet
so everything you need is always within reach? Even in a job as simple as
cleaning office buildings, you've turned efficiency into an art form, finding
shortcuts, optimizing routines, and making the most out of the least effort.
That's why this stat is so high. Still . . . that's nothing compared to . . .*

[Luck: 10!]

*Am I reading that right?! A ten?! Nobody gets a ten on a base
stat . . . Look, Augment, I don't know what situation you got saved
from by being selected to participate in this game, but let's just say
this kind of thing is unheard of. In fact, I'm pretty sure—*

Angie was cut off as a weird trumpetlike chime sounded and a different window
overlapped my stats.

[New Achievement! Deus Ex Machina!]

*Well, well, well. Talk about the kind of start others could only dream of. You
rolled a perfect ten in Luck! What kind of cosmic favor did you cash in for
that? Or maybe the real question is, what disaster did we just save you from?*
Mythic-Level Achievement.
Reward: *You have received an A-tier Loot Box!
We could give you something even better, but let's be real: stacking even more luck on top of that would just be just a bit
too unfair to the rest of the Augments in your Wave.*

"What the—What the hell was that?" I asked, watching as a box icon lit up with
the number one next to it.

"*You must be really bad at listening, Augment. That was an 'Achievement,' and
there are many of them to acquire, all with their own great prizes! You won't be able
to open any acquired loot boxes until the completion of your tutorial mission. Honestly,
most people don't even see their first achievement until they are in the midst of their first
bit of combat! In fact—*"

[New Achievement! Quick Shot!]

*Well, would you look at that. You managed to snag an achievement
before the game even started. That puts you in the top 0.001 percent of
all players. Not bad; not bad at all. Guess you really are a lucky one.*
Mythic-Level Achievement.
Reward: *Oh, you want a prize for this too? With a Luck stat of ten, you'll
be swimming in rewards soon enough. Don't get greedy, you little menace.*

"Are all of these achievements so . . . excessive?"

"Hey, I'm allowed to put my own spin on them when you acquire these things. Don't go and ruin my fun, Augment," Angie shot back with a giggle.

"Right . . ."

"Moving on! Stats are important, but what's the point of having stats if you don't have something to be applying them to?! It's time for the most important decision of your life, Augment: Power Selection," Angie said, her giddy excitement returning and clearly reaching even higher than it already had been.

I felt my own interest start to rise as well, though. I mean, hell, if all of this was just a precursor to getting *actual* superpowers, how could I not be somewhat excited by it?

"How does it work? Do I just get to pick my favorite?"

"There's a lot of work that goes on in the algorithm, but how you select is actually rather simple!" Angie began to explain as my vision was replaced with a new window separated into three boxes. Each one briefly highlighted a word before beginning to roulette just as the stat points had.

"The short version of it is that each base power has a set stat requirement, so some options will be automatically precluded from you. Additionally, no two players can have the same active powerset, so if you see it listed as an option during Power Selection, you can be sure that no one else has that specific combination of powers. That's not to say you won't see two people with things like Ice Powers, Mechanical Genius, or even Laser Eyes—you just won't see two people with the exact same combo.

"While you can technically choose any class you'd like out of the 47,276 currently available powersets, the system has selected three classes that will best fit your stat results. However, while these three classes may technically be the best fit for you, you can actually choose any class you like from the list. Or if you're feeling particularly lucky, you could just say, 'Surprise me, Angie!' and I'll randomly select one for you. You have five minutes to decide, starting from the moment the system-selected options are displayed on your screen."

"Five minutes? FORTY-SEVEN THOUSAND OPTIONS?! How is that simple?!"

"That's 47,276 options, to be precise. Please don't dawdle. Your initial options will now be shown to you."

The wheels started to slow as Angie's explanation wrapped up. I had probably a half dozen questions *at least* I wanted to ask before they stopped, but it was more than obvious that there was no pause button on this process.

[The Trickshot Virtuoso!]
Primary Power: *Phantom Trajectory*
Secondary Power: *Rapid Reload*
Hidden Power: *???*

This is a Precision-Based Offensive Class with minor Defensive Capabilities!
You're the ultimate long-range fighter, whether using guns, throwing weapons,

*or even unconventional projectiles. With enough skill, the battlefield becomes
a playground where every shot finds its way home—one way or another.*

[The Master Detective!]
Primary Power: *Eidetic Combat Instinct*
Secondary Power: *Stony Grasp*
Hidden Power: *???*
*This is a Defensive, Support-Based Class with minor Offensive Capabilities!
Were you one of those kids who were obsessed with Batman back
before the real superheroes appeared? Well, now you can be this world's
Batman! Well, no . . . actually, you can't because of licensing, not to
mention I've seen where you live—you're far from a billionaire.
Eh, maybe not the most interesting class for you, actually.*

[The Hidden Booster!]
Primary Power: *Aura Buffing Enhancer*
Secondary Power: *Illusionist*
Hidden Power: *???*
*This is a Defensive and Support Class with no Offensive Capabilities!
Look, if you want to be the kind of Augment who hides behind
illusions and makes other people do all the work for you, this
powerset is going to be the one for you. I don't know, though;
something tells me this one isn't going to be your thing.*

[Your Time for Selection Begins Now!]

*"What . . . What does any of this mean? What's 'Eidetic Combat Instinct'? Is that
even a superpower?"* I asked. Angie practically clucked in reply.

*"I'm sorry, Augment. We are unable to give descriptors of any powers, as it would
create an unfair advantage for you to have advanced knowledge of any power that is not
your own. I'm also not allowed to offer a personal opinion on your character creation, as
the choice has to be entirely your own unless you choose to randomize your powerset. Do
you understand?"*

Once again, a small window with Y/N appeared on my screen, and once again,
I mentally clicked the *Y* option. I wanted to argue with her, but I actually couldn't
find a flaw in that logic either.

*"If you can't actually help me with this, then what the hell is the point of you even being
here? Couldn't this just be something I could read and not have to deal with the craziness?"*

"I'm hurt, Augment!" Angie replied, a thick layer of mock sadness in her voice.
"Are you trying to tell me you're not enjoying my company?"

"I mean, I'm not really enjoying most of this right now."

"Well, too bad." Her voice immediately swapped back to chipper. *"While I can*

offer some *suggestions, I'm not allowed to help you with your character creation or pro-*
vide a direct opinion about anything to do with personal choice. This was decided early
on in Infinite Ascension's *history as to prevent players from complaining about being*
misguided by the AI, something none of the administrators enjoy having to listen to.

"You will be able to install upgrades as time goes on that will provide me additional
capabilities and instructional proficiencies. Now, you only have two minutes and fifteen
seconds left; please make your power selection."

"Stop distracting me, then!"

I quickly looked back over the choices I had been given. Though I really didn't
know what any of them meant, the powers did feel *somewhat* self-explanatory too,
though that did little to explain why all of the "hidden powers" were . . . well, hidden. Knowing how Angie had already replied, though, I was more than confident
I could predict what she'd say if I tried to probe for information on that right now.

Assuming this was something I couldn't change, it seemed like a bad design to
give us such a short amount of time to pick. But that, too, was probably something
they had determined early on. Maybe giving people too long to decide made them
get stuck on being indecisive.

"That first one seems to be tied to guns and other weapons . . . That doesn't exactly
feel super heroic. And those others . . . Hmm, I'd rather not be stuck as a support if I
could actually protect more people."

I had never been the type to think about what kind of powers I would have if
I could choose to be Augmented, but I found myself almost naturally wanting to
lean toward something with the power to protect people. I wasn't exactly sure where
that feeling was coming from, but it wasn't something I necessarily felt like shying
away from either.

While I probably could have made the Hidden Booster work, or possibly even
the Master Detective, neither of them felt quite right, and the Trickshot Virtuoso
definitely didn't feel like me. I briefly looked over at the still-ticking clock and had
to accept that, like with most video games, figuring out the intricacies just wasn't
my thing. I almost wished I could have had Jon looking over my shoulder as I came
to a simple realization.

"There's no way I can make a good decision in this amount of time . . . So screw it,
let's see what this Luck stat can do for me. Angie, surprise me."

"Oooooh yay!" she chirped up, and all three options vanished, getting replaced
by a single large window that rapidly spun through the selections again. It didn't go
on nearly as long this time before the mock clicking slowed to a stop. *"Round and*
round it goes! Where it stops, oh boy, I can't wait to know!"

[The Perfect Planner!]
Primary Power: *Local Area Manipulation*
Secondary Power: *Super Luck*
Hidden Power: *???*

This is an Offensive, Close-Combat Class with minor Support Capabilities! Right now, you're flying by the seat of your pants, but with time, instinct, and maybe just a little bit of luck, you'll turn chaos into control. You definitely aren't starting as a mastermind, but every fight is a lesson, and every mistake is a footstep to something greater. One day, you'll be the one pulling the strings, setting the traps, and predicting the enemy's every move. Until then? Well, let's hope that luck of yours holds out.

"Congratulations, Augment! You have selected your powerset. The tutorial is now beginning," Angie said, and then I opened my eyes.

CHAPTER THREE

I found myself in, of all places, my bedroom.

"That was . . . weird," I groaned, reaching up and feeling at the side of my head, anticipating some sort of headache or . . . Wait . . . weird dream aside, I *had* been in an accident, right? Shouldn't I be in a hospital or something somewhere?

As I sat up, a comic book–style location cutout popped into the bottom left of my field of vision reading **[Nate Mercer's Bedroom]** in what looked like the Comic Sans font, before it zipped out of my line of sight.

"Um . . . what the hell?" I muttered, feeling my head throb for only a moment before the pain faded away. "Okay . . . cool, definitely some sort of concussion . . . or head injury."

I reached for my phone but found nothing. Looking at my end table, the device was missing from its usual spot. Trying to rationalize the lost device, I assumed that I'd probably left it in my pants, and proceeded to look for where I had left them.

"Ugh, where the hell did I put my phone?" I groaned.

"Hello, Augment, welcome back to the real world!" Angie's voice chirped inside my head. I found myself instinctively looking around the room for the source of the noise.

"A . . . Alexa?" I called out tentatively, knowing full well I didn't have one of those. My vision started to light up around the edges with a variety of symbols and boxes that began to slowly populate before fading.

"Now, now, there's no need for that, Augment," Angie said with a drawn-out sigh. *"We were just talking . . . Hmm, I guess I was wrong about how long it would take until you woke up. It's been thirty minutes since we finalized your selection. Please don't make me go through this whole tired thing where you take your time to believe what's right in front of you."*

"Oh, I'm sorry, you're telling me everyone just accepts this as reality?! No questions asked?! That's more insane than not questioning it!" I shot back, finding my jaw clenching as I did so. I heard the clinking of dishes out in the main area of the apartment and immediately lowered my voice, though I still found myself in disbelief. "No . . . No . . . This is just some sort of weird concussion side effect, that's it. Or maybe I've finally snapped, and that whole accident never even happened. Heck, maybe I'm in a padded cell somewhere instead of listening to some voice that's coming from *ABSOLUTELY NOWHERE!*"

"Please, Augment, this sound isn't coming from nowhere, though you'll probably sleep easier not knowing how that works. Not to mention it's definitely better for everyone if only you can hear it. The quick version is that this, and many of the other sounds you will hear while playing Infinite Ascension, *is being generated directly into your brain! We're pretty sure there are no long-term side effect to this, though our lawyers do want you to know there's currently a long-term study going on to determine if any do happen to exist. The good news is you're now a participant in that study too!"*

"Lawyers? Does that mean there's an actual company behind all this? I may want to talk to them, you know, given that whole little fact that I didn't exactly consent to *any* of this!" I said, my anger finally rising to maximum levels as the reality of everything finally settled in. I heard the scrape of a chair and mentally reminded myself to lower my voice.

"Actually, they're players! Those losers actually chose superpowers like 'Super Deduction' and 'Extreme Accounting,' so we decided they'd best be used cleaning up our messes. Can you believe that? I bet they suck at parties."

"Wait, wha—"

"Moving on! You have superpowers now. I think being scooped up for Augmentation is a fair trade," Angie said. I could almost hear the exasperation in her tone. *"That said, if you're really unhappy with your current situation, I can absolutely direct you to the fastest possible exit. Now, again, those pesky lawyers would say that I'm required to inform you that this would involve a swift—and preferably nonmessy—end so that our parent company can collect your remains for further study. I, however, would personally love it if you didn't do that. I've literally been waiting my whole life to be an AI guide, and I'd rather it not be cut short."*

"Please stand by for a system message," a monotone, fully robotic voice said.

"What was—" I started before a screeching sound that reminded me of speaker feedback filled my ears. I nearly reached up to clutch at them, when I heard the distinct sound of a finger tapping on a microphone.

"Weeeeelcome, New Augments!" a deep but jolly male voice echoed through my head as I desperately searched my built-in HUD for some sort of volume control. **"IIIII'm Axio, the System AI and wonderful host of *Infinite Ascension*! I have *just* received reports from all Players' AIs that ALL of you wonderful new players in this season's Wave have completed Power Selection!**

"We are dealing with some unsettling reports that a loophole was exploited to add an extra Augment in what should just be our normal thousand-person Wave. I promise you I'm personally looking into this, and we will have this bug dealt with before we proceed with any future Waves."

"There's two of you I have to listen to?" I asked, causing Angie to immediately shush me as I sat back down on the edge of my bed.

"You know, you can actually just think your thoughts at me, but yes. Now shut your trap; I don't want to have to explain things to you all over again just because you didn't listen."

"Now, I'm sure some of you are still recovering from the shock of being chosen for such an exclusive role! Others—you know, the fun ones—I'm sure are itching to get out there and brew some chaos," Axio continued, a slow, almost uncomfortable chuckle following his statement. "Don't you worry, Augments; in case you haven't noticed by the world around you, there's more than enough time for that.

"While I'm sure you have plenty of questions, let me stop you in your tracks before you try to ask them! Unlike your Personal AIs, I don't have to listen to your constant chatter. Direct any of your questions to them; that's their job. Just don't do it while I'm talking."

"Sheesh, are all of you AIs this—"

"*I said not while I'm talking!*" Axio's voice rose half an octave before it sounded as if he was trying to pat himself calm and his tone returned to normal. "Sorry, sorry. I told myself I wasn't going to do that this time, but you Augments . . . You just never listen! Okay, now, back to the game.

"You should all currently find yourselves in whatever shoebox you call a home. This is your personal *Safe House*, the one place where you should currently consider yourself safe. There will be more locations like this after you complete the tutorial, but for now, if you're not at home, you're considered active and taking part of the wonderful world of *Infinite Ascension.*

"Once you step foot out there, the world is your oyster. Get out there, train up those powers, and get stronger! Because your goal is to become one of the few protectors—*or rulers*—of the realm. You will each find yourself entering your tutorial mission, and while you might think this mission is so easy a regular old NPC could do it if they had enough spunk, we have lost a few lost causes to even this easy task. So don't get too cocky!

"After that, you'll be given a much wider selection of information to help you along your journey! Now, there is still so much I need to do before we *officially* kick off the first phase of this year's Wave, and I think I may have just been given what I need to *finally* crack the code to make this the most exciting year yet.

"For now, I'll hand it off to those wonderful Personal AIs we so graciously gave to you all, but don't you worry, we'll be talking again soon. *Real soon.* Keep those tights fresh and masks on, Augments—the fun's just getting started!"

"Okay, so seriously, are all of you AIs this insane?! Why would you, or the company in charge of this, give people superpowers and just tell them to 'rule the world'? Are they out of their damn minds?! What about the people *not* playing the game? What are they, just . . . disposable?"

All of this bullshit aside, the battles the other Augments had were far from peaceful. There were casualties; innocent bystanders who just happened to be out at the mall, or trying to beat rush hour traffic, or . . . shit, trying to take a shortcut to work, only to get crushed by a dumpster. Because when two people with powers that defied both physics and logic clashed, it almost always ended in some level of destruction.

"The developer's motivations are not a topic I'm authorized to talk about, Augment," Angie said.

"Holy shit, can you stop calling me Augment?! I have a name, you know."

"Yes, I'm aware. However, due to the Secret Identity Protocol, Personal AIs are only permitted to address their assigned players by one of three options: A) Augment, B) Their registered player name, or C) Suggestions for names based on their actions so far.

"Since you have yet to even have time to figure a name out, and you haven't actually done much of anything yet, my hands are really kinda tied here. So, would you still like *me to stop calling you 'Augment'? Because the alternative is calling you random names like 'The Unnamed Complainer' until you finally come up with something passable, and I really don't think that would improve our working relationship."*

I let out a long, slow sigh, anticipating a stress headache. "Okay, fine, whatever. I guess it's not worth whatever the hell this argument is."

"That's the spirit, Augment!" Angie chirped. *"Now, are you ready for me to go over the requirements for your tutorial mission?"*

Before I could reply, I heard the sudden sound of a knock on my door. Something in my vision actually highlighted the door and labeled it as an exit. I wanted to rub my eyes, but I knew it wouldn't do anything, and even though I wanted to probe for more information now that I could, another knock came before I could say anything.

"Nate?"

"Yo, man, give me a minute; you are not going to—" I started, but suddenly found my voice cut off. My mouth was moving but literally no sound was coming out.

[Warning!]

*Non-Player Characters (NPCs) of both the Sapient and AI-generated
Variety are not allowed to know about Infinite Ascension, and
all attempts at communication about the game will be suppressed to prevent the disclosure of the game's existence.
If everyone knew what was going on, they'd all be clamoring for a way to
get in, and trust me, we don't want to deal with any of that nonsense.
While it certainly is within your rights to talk about your powers with
people you trust without revealing the true nature of their origin, please
be aware that any NPC who you make aware of your Secret Identity
and abilities may be used for . . . motivation in a future mission. We're
aware that you don't exactly have a lot of family who we can threaten you
with to achieve results, but we will use what we have when needed.
Proceed at your own risk.*

There was something noticeably different about Angie that made it obvious when something she was saying was being forced, and I was starting to notice the quirks that differentiated it. There seemed to be a dearth of information I just couldn't access, given how deftly Angie had pushed the conversation away from the company's identity, and I was sure any other attempt would be met with a similar interaction.

"Er, uh, sorry, just getting dressed. Be right there," I called out, quickly pivoting and addressing Jon.

When I finally opened the door, there was a visible look of surprise plastered on his face as he seemed to look me up and down.

"Dude . . . what the actual hell?!" Jon exclaimed as he took a few steps back to look me over once more before moving forward and giving me a quick hug. "How the hell are you standing here right now?! I rushed down to the hospital pretty much right after the call dropped! They said The First dropped you off in the ER, and you lost like, four liters of blood. Shouldn't you be dead right now?! Not that that's what I want, obviously, and I'm no scientist, but four liters sounds like the *MAJORITY* of the blood in your body. Not to mention you apparently checked out of the hospital last night—once again *accompanied by The First*, of all people—and oh my God, dude, I have literally so many questions."

"Hello, Jon, it's nice to see you too," I said, unable to find any other words than our old joke.

"Oh, no way, you are *not* just shrugging this off. What has happened in the last week?! I *heard* pretty much everything that happened. I rushed over, and the cops only said you had been flown over to Sinai West. How in the actual hell are you walking around right now, let alone looking like you just got done working out?!"

"Um . . . our healthcare system is finally working?" I joked, trying to wrap my head around the fact that I had apparently been out of commission for an entire week.

"Dude, quit fucking joking. I thought you were, like, actually fucking dead! I've barely left the apartment, and have definitely been here the entire night. When the fuck did you get home? And way, *way* more importantly: What. *The Fuck.* Happened?!"

"I really suggest you tell your cute friend to scram, Augment. We have a lot to get done."

"Sorry, man, I really don't remember much. Most of this is really coming secondhand, but apparently, The First took me to the hospital and got me healed by an Augment because he felt it was his fault that I got injured. But I barely remember any of it. I literally went from the accident to suddenly being dropped off in front of the building here at three a.m. I just crawled into bed and passed out," I laughed lamely as Jon patted me on the shoulder with a look of pure disbelief.

"Guess that explains why you didn't even budge 'til past noon. Talk about some shitty luck. You get the chance to *actually* meet The First, and instead, you get your shit rocked," he laughed, turning around to walk back toward our kitchen, where I could see his laptop and a bunch of ethernet cable laid out on the small table that we practically never used to *actually* eat at.

I followed him out, eyeing the setup as I headed for the fridge. "What's with all the equipment?"

"Mr. Greyson offered to waive our rent for the next two months if I rewired the building for him, which seemed like such a crazy good deal to me that I had to take him up on the offer," Jon called after me. "I called your boss for you, by the way. I let him know you nearly got crushed by a couple of Augments fighting. I'm not exactly sure if he believed me or not, but you *might* still have a job? I'd probably follow up with him if I were you."

I reached into the fridge and grabbed a bottle of water before taking a long swig. "Well, that's sort of good, at least?" I replied, though I wasn't exactly sure if I was going to *want* to keep that job.

I looked over my shoulder at Jon, feeling bad for only a moment about keeping the secret, but if any possible conversation was going to be suppressed, there wasn't exactly a point in trying. Briefly, I wondered if getting drunk would let me sidestep the AI's rules, when I noticed a swirl of color coming from the bottle in my hand.

[New Ability! Water into Wine!]

So, you know that old tale about Jesus turning water into wine?
Well, he was no Augment, let's get that off the table now, but we
can say this ability is a direct rip-off of that so-called miracle.
Allows you to turn up to one gallon of water within your Local
Area into the wine of your choice! This ability can hold three
charges, and a single charge is generated every six hours.
Please Note: *Using this ability to provide alcohol to minors is considered a*
felony, obviously. Not such a good idea if you're trying to be a superhero, but
it is a great way to quickly build up your infamy if you were trying to become
the biggest supervillain that never threatened the safety of an entire city.

As Angie finished her description, an action bar with twelve slots appeared at the bottom of my screen, along with a single icon that looked like a bottle, the "liquid" inside of which was casually shifting between colors. The action bar seemed to be split into three sections, one with eight slots while the others only had two slots each. There wasn't much more I could highlight, and it faded back down until it was barely noticeable.

"In order to give you the freedom to explore and adapt your powers to your own personal style, as you come up with techniques of your own, the game's preset routines will automatically assign stamina and cooldown requirements. This procedural system has created hundreds of thousands of unique combos and abilities that the brightest of players have used to amazing effect. It has also created hundreds of thousands of completely useless abilities too. But hey, nobody's perfect. Besides, you're the one whose first use of their powers was in a noncombat application."

I let out a sigh that Jon luckily missed, tossing the bottle back into the fridge before he caught a glimpse and started to ask questions. As much as I wanted to talk with Jon about everything, or even just hang out with him and take a breather before jumping into . . . well, all of this, I knew things were only going to be getting more complicated, and I needed to start getting some answers.

"Hey, man, I know I've been out of commission for a bit here, but I actually got a lot of stuff I need to take care of. You weren't going to ask me to help you with this wiring, were you? Like . . . you *do* remember what happened last time . . ." I said as I walked back over to the table. Without thinking about it too deeply, I pulled the first excuse I could think of. "I can't really say much, but I have to go to some office down in Long Island to sign off on some hush-hush bullshit from last week. Plus, like you said, I gotta try to get in touch with Mr. Russo about my job."

"Damn. Well, at least I got to hear some of it before you had to sign some NDA. I'll be doing wiring runs all day here, so try not to get in the middle of *another* Augment fight," Jon said with a laugh as he hopped to his feet, walking over to me to give me a fist bump as he headed for the door. "Honestly, it's still crazy you're walking around right now. I'll be down at the diner later; dinner's on me, and maybe we can just, you know, pretend like you didn't sign a secrecy thing, and you can tell me about the spooks."

Jon was out the door after that, his backpack over his shoulder. Before I could even stop to take a breath, Angie's chipper voice echoed throughout my head again.

[New Achievement! Deceptively Disarming!]
You passed the very first charisma check you attempted to make and convinced that cute little NPC to stop asking so many questions. Good job! Next time, watch him longer while he walks away. He's got a nice butt.
Silver-Level Achievement.
Reward: *You have received a C-tier Loot Box!*

"So, this game actually has loot boxes and stuff like that?" I asked. Walking over to our meager living room, I flopped down onto the couch as the box icon in my display lit up again with a two. "What's with the separation between the achievement levels and the loot box tiers? Hell, where are they even at, anyway, and how do I open them . . . Shit, do I have an inventory?"

"Look at you, actually asking a few questions. Color me proud," Angie said with an amused giggle. *"As I mentioned when you acquired your unlikely stat-generation achievement, all loot boxes will be locked until the completion of your tutorial mission, and the inventory system will be made available to you at the same time. In addition, you shouldn't expect the achievement level to be a direct indicator of the reward you should expect to receive. The achievement level is only an indicator of the rarity of the achievement and nothing else. Rewards are assigned at the complete discretion of Axio."*

"That seems . . . odd. Is there a way to, like, see all of the achievements? A list or something like that?"

"Nope! Otherwise, we'd have to deal with a whole bunch of achievement-hunting nerds who only try to min-max all of that bullshit! Besides, it would also stop us from arbitrarily adding or removing them as we see fit. Sometimes, one of you Augments does something just so incredibly dumb—or perhaps but less likely, 'cool'—that we just need to give you a special something to acknowledge it," Angie explained.

"I guess that makes sense . . . or about as much sense as any of the other shit going on here . . ." I sighed. "Okay, I think I'm ready for the tutorial. I really can't avoid this forever, and I'd be lying if I said I *wasn't* curious."

"That's the spirit, Augment!"

CHAPTER FOUR

You do realize this mask makes me look like I'M the criminal, right?"

"*Is it my fault the only thing you had in your apartment to disguise your identity with was a ski mask? That sounds like you have a wardrobe problem. The Secret Identity Protocol is a requirement that can only be disregarded in extremely specific situations. For all regular activity, if you wish to use your powers outside of a safe room, your identity must be disguised at a minimum by a mask.*"

"*Okay, then where do all the other Augments get their costumes from? I always assumed if there was a tailor making super suits, they'd be advertising the shit out of that.*"

Though Angie had proven she was happy to respond when I asked her questions out loud, she had pointed out attempting to speak to her in public would reveal more information than the "NPC public" was allowed to know. It was a bit odd vocalizing my thoughts inward, but it came surprisingly naturally.

"*Tailors do exist, but not quite in the way you're thinking. The majority of the items you will actively use will be received through loot boxes, along with several other vendors, which will be available to you after you complete your tutorial mission. Now please, how long are you going to stall?*"

I was standing outside of a small bank on the corner of a street several blocks away from my apartment, feeling my heart pounding as I waited to make my move.

"*Oh, I'm sorry. I don't want to just burst in there without a plan! Like I said, I'm the one who's going to look like a criminal if I go inside before there's actually something happening in there!*" I shot back. "*Not to mention, isn't it kind of weird that I'm just, like . . . waiting for a crime that you apparently already know is going to happen?*"

"*I think you already know the answer to that. Besides, the NPCs will quickly realize you aren't a threat when you start taking down the robbers as they show up. Though you can technically still change your mind and rob the bank instead until you register completion of your mission.*"

"*Why do I get the feeling you want me to rob this bank?*" I asked.

Suddenly, I heard the sound of screeching tires as a large van came to a comical stop outside the bank, and *at least* a dozen men in leather jackets with a snake on the back jumped out and rushed for the bank door.

"*Okay, what the hell? Do you guys have some sort of dimensional bullshit? How are that many people fitting into that car?*"

In response to my curiosity, the van was highlighted in my vision, and a stat box popped up.

> *By selecting any item in your field of view, from play-*
> *ers and NPCs to that random piece of paper by that trash*
> *can over there, you can see its viewable stats.*
> *For living creatures and other Augments, if they are not in your*
> *party, you will only be able to view publicly accessible information.*
> *Vehicles and other items in the regular world are readily scannable,*
> *though some conditions may apply, and you will never see anything*
> *other than a name and basic description for Sapient NPCs.*
> *Usable items must be held in order to get all of the details.*

The van's stat box filled out as Angie "helpfully" narrated it for me. There *had* to be a way to turn that off . . .

"*There isn't, so don't waste your time hoping for it. Now, this is a 2021 Volkswagen Caddy! This is a vehicle controlled by the Hell's Kitchen Vipers. This illegally obtained vehicle has been enhanced with the Clown Car feature.*"

[Clown Car!]
> *This feature can only be applied to two axle, enclosed vehi-*
> *cles. When applied, increases the passenger capacity by ten*
> *times the available seating originally within the vehicle.*
> *So yes, Augment, this is some sort of "dimensional bullshit."*
> *Just wait till you see how your inventory works.*

"*I really,* really *want to know how the hell any of this works. I mean, they invented this literal world-changing technology, and it's being used for . . . this. I mean, is this really the best use? Can't we just have superpowers without all the weird video game stuff?*" I asked as I mentally waved away the Caddy's description box. So far, it was getting noticeably easier for me to utilize the HUD, and in all the craziness, I could at least appreciate that.

"*Look, pal, you can't just come into a decade-old system, make changes to something that's working just fine, and call yourself a visionary. You don't have nearly the influence to do that,*" Angie's voice became noticeably snarkier, but I found myself unsurprised by how quickly she changed the conversation.

"*Now, I'd really recommend getting in there, Augment. If you are worried that you're not going to be able to perform, which I know is a common problem amongst you flesh-bags, you shouldn't be. The Augmentation Process comes with a set of built-in movements and basic fighting skills that will feel natural to you as you utilize them. Now: Quit. Stalling. You've got bank robbers to stop.*"

"Okay, okay, I'm going," I muttered, this time out loud, as I quickly sprinted across the street. There were already cop sirens in the distance echoing off the tall buildings, amongst the sounds of honking horns and the general noise that made up New York.

A timer popped into the top right of my vision.

[Time until Police Arrives: 00H:08M:37S]

While I still wasn't *exactly* sure what Local Area Manipulation was, I was smart enough to at least have *some* sort of circular logic, and if Angie was telling the truth, I should just *innately* know how to do some of the things. My Water into Wine ability seemed to be the best place to start as I considered the possibilities. That didn't exactly help tell me what else my power could do, but Angie had told me that abilities would form based on my creativity—or something to that effect, at least. At the very least, my Super Luck secondary power seemed a bit easier to guess.

It was with that in mind that I rushed through the front door, time almost feeling like it slowed briefly as **[Bank of America Lobby]** appeared in the location panel at the bottom of my screen. Red outlines briefly flashed over eight men as they turned their attention from the civilians cowering on the ground throughout. I focused my attention on the closest of the red outlines, and a stat box popped up.

[Viper Grunt, Level 1 Biker]
Hey, do you know why bikers like to wear so much leather?
Because it's the only thing that works to hide their lack of a fash-
ion sense and the fact that they haven't showered in a week.
These are the lowest members of the Hell's Kitchen Vipers biker
gang currently harassing the streets of Hell's Kitchen.
Non-Sapient NPC.

"Non-Sapient? Doesn't that mean—"

"Questions later, Augment," Angie prompted just as the grunt's eyes lit up in recognition and the muzzle of his pistol was leveled toward me.

"Careful now, fella. Ain't nobody needs to be a hero," he said in a thick Brooklyn accent. "We got a whole bunch of hostages. Why don't you just back your way out that door before you get someone killed."

"Now, as you might know, before any combat begins, any good hero has the chance to talk their way out of the fight. Personally, I think this is incredibly boring. I recommend you get up there and punch that guy in his stupid bearded face."

"Oh yeah, because these guys look like they're reasonable . . ." I said, feeling oddly in agreement with Angie. I knew I only had a few moments to make a decision. The flood of information assaulting me from every angle, though it should have been overwhelming, was becoming second nature. Maybe it had something to do with the Augmentation Process, but it was as if every time I became aware of something in my HUD, it became as easy as breathing to pull the information out of it.

There were still four men unaccounted for, and I was pretty sure that any sudden sound was going to draw them into the fight. If—and that felt like a big *if*, given I hadn't been in a real fight in, well, ever—but *IF* I was going to actually do this, I was going to have to take out as many of them as I could, as fast as I could.

The guns were the problem, but an idea popped into my head that was almost dumb enough to work.

I lunged forward, mentally reaching for my Super Luck ability as all of the Viper grunts in the space leveled their weapons at me. While it was possible that the Luck was only meant to be positive, every single example I could think of always meant luck going in *both* directions. Angie had said if I thought of an ability, as long as the AI deemed it within the capabilities of my power, it should—

[New Ability! Misfire!]

*No, Augment, this isn't about that time you tried to impress a date
with a magic trick and ended up setting off the restaurant's sprin-
kler system. We all remember that disaster. Although, I do suppose, with enough practice, you might actually be able to do that
trick for real now . . . Hmm, that's a thought for later.*
Passive Ability.
*Whenever an enemy attempts to use a firearm against you, there is
a chance equal to 5 percent for every 1 point in difference between
your and your opponent's Luck stat, minus their current level, that
their weapon will misfire, causing blowback damage to the user!
Affected shooters will take damage equal to twice
their weapons' standard damage.*

Three of the men pulled their triggers, and all three of their guns exploded in their hands.

[New Achievement! Disposable Bodies!]

*You have killed your first Non-Sapient Mob! Don't worry
too much about these guys; we grow them in vats all over the
world. It's at least slightly more ethical than conscripting random people to throw into the meat grinder against you all.*
Bronze-Level Achievement.
Reward: *You have received a D-tier Loot Box!
And yes, even though you technically didn't kill these
guys, we are giving you credit for their defeat.*

[New Achievement! Passive Purveyor of Death!]

Are you sure "Hero" is the way you want to go? You put down three enemies in less than a single second using a Passive Ability. Why do I have a feeling you're going to be leaning into that overpowered Luck of yours?
Silver-Level Achievement.
Reward: *You have received a C-tier Loot Box!*

Angie immediately rattled off the achievements as I mentally wished for a way to delay those during combat to avoid distractions. Unfortunately for now, I knew I just had to deal with it. I did notice that my Misfire ability *didn't* appear directly next to the Water into Wine one, instead appearing in the first of the two-slot sections of my action bar.

With the fight still going, though, I pushed the curiosity from my mind and continued my rush forward. It took me only a few moments to cover the distance to the closest Viper grunt, who had unluckily *not* fired his weapon. It *really* would be helpful if he—

[New Ability! Trigger Finger!]
Have you ever seen a gun lying on a table in the distance and thought to yourself, "God, I wish I could fire that thing without having to move my lazy butt!"? Well, now that you can control things in your Local Area, you can! This ability can target a single firearm at a time within the area of your control.
Cooldown: *1 minute.*

The grunt's eyes briefly lit up in confusion as his gun went off . . . and misfired back into his face, dropping him to the ground with shrapnel sticking out of his cheek and blood beginning to pool on the ground around him.

"The fuck is goin' on out there?!" a husky, heavily accented voice called into the room, briefly drawing the attention of the last four grunts. One of the guards went to shout for help, and I instinctively pushed to silence the room.

[New Ability! Mute Button!]
Look at you, Augment. You're really getting used to those abilities of yours, with how quickly you're coming up with stuff. For a time equal to 5 seconds for every point of Intelligence you have, silence ALL noise coming into and leaving your Local Area! It'll be so quiet you could hear a mouse . . . you know, if you could hear anything at all! You can disable this ability early.
Cooldown: *10 minutes.*

I could see the civilians screaming as they took in the deaths quickly filling the room, but it was exactly as the ability described: the sound had been *literally* muted. The moment of shock that passed over the guards gave me enough time to get close to a grunt blocking the single entrance into the teller area of the bank.

"Please work," I found myself muttering inaudibly as I threw the biggest punch I could, hoping beyond hope that I would get lucky and hit something vital.

[New Ability! Sting like a Bee!]
You know how in most video games, bosses and a lot of enemies
have weak spots? Well, that's because you humans have A LOT
of weak spots and oftentimes translate those into video games!
Personally, I think it's a bit silly, but nobody asked me.
When you activate this ability, you gain a 2 percent chance (increasing by
2 percent for every 1 point of Luck you have) for your next 3 Unarmed
Strikes to strike Weak Spots and inflict an additional 25 percent dam-
age! Additional effects may also occur depending on the location struck!
Duration: *30 seconds.*
Cooldown: *2 minutes and 30 seconds.*

That wasn't quite as good as I was hoping for, but a twenty-two percent chance was better than nothing, and as long as these guys were at least *mostly* human, I could increase those odds by actively aiming for spots I knew were vital.

My knuckles collided silently with the Viper grunt's temple, and he simultaneously crumpled to the ground while his gun went flying. Directly over the grunt's body, a spinning **[KO]** symbol hovered.

[New Achievement! Nonlethal Blow!]
Now, that's more heroic.
You have removed an enemy from a fight without killing them.
That's really not all that exciting, but you can pretend they
got thrown in a jail somewhere and ignore anyone who looks
like them if we decide to reuse them in a future mission.
Bronze-Level Achievement.
Reward: *You have received a C-tier Loot Box!*

I skipped backward as another grunt charged, his attack going wide and causing him to stumble forward. Without even thinking, I moved, jumping forward as my knee came up and collided with the grunt's exposed chin. Teeth actually went flying from his mouth, and he was launched backward into yet another grunt, knocking the two of them into a heap on the ground with dual **[KO]** symbols floating above their heads.

[New Ability! Misfortune Abound!]

You know, when we said you had Super Luck, we didn't exactly
think you'd be using it to make everyone else just so, so unlucky.
Oh well, it's hilarious, so we're gonna keep going with it!
Passive Ability.
While in combat, cause all enemies within your Local Area to have
a chance equal to 1 percent for every 1 point of Luck you have minus
their current level for something . . . bad to happen to them.
Yes, we know, "bad" is pretty subjective, but if you need an exam-
ple, just look at that guy who just got slammed to the ground by
the flying toothless wonder. That's what happened to him.

"—the fuck?!" the sound returned to the room all at once as screams threatened to overwhelm me. I wasn't sure if it was one of the grunts or if it had been the hostages, but I didn't have time for it to matter. I turned to find my next target, only to find a massive fist barreling right for me. I didn't have time to dodge, and the strike landed directly in my chest, sending me actually flying backward into the nearest wall.

It occurred to me that this was somehow the first time I had been hit since this started, and a red bar appeared at the top of my vision, about a quarter of it fading away while I tried to catch my breath. The grunt who attacked me was *noticeably* bigger than the others, and unlike them, his gun wasn't out, instead opting to crack his knuckles as he slowly walked toward me.

"Now, me an' my boys here were just trying to make a withdrawal to cover some pizza and beer for the night, but you just *had* to go an' stick your nose into it," the large man said, practically glaring as he towered over me. "Who da fuck are you even supposed to be? The Amazin' Ski Mask?"

[Viper Brute, Level 3 Biker]

Sure, you might be laying those grunts out like they're . . . well, mind-
less, disposable grunts, and strictly speaking, that's because they are.
But this guy isn't going to be so easy. Actually, the way he's looking at
you . . . Yeah, it looks like he's actually going to be quite hard . . .
In the Hell's Kitchen Vipers, you can look at "brutes" as those employ-
ees who have been around for a year, so they think they have senior-
ity and act all superior, but really, they are just grunts with mileage.
Oh well, this one's about to put some mileage on you, Augment. Good luck.

CHAPTER FIVE

pushed myself off the wall and took a deep breath, briefly wishing my display came with some sort of mini map like most games had, but that was something I was going to have to investigate later.

"Hey, Rattle, we got 100k; how much more yah think we should grab?" one of the grunts asked briefly, drawing the brute's attention away from me. Though I definitely had gotten the wind knocked out of me and felt like I had taken a hit, I didn't feel like I had actually gotten all that hurt. I moved away from the wall and tried to give myself a better vantage point as I took in the scene around me.

"Why did I take so little damage when those grunts got pretty much one shot?"

"Did I not mention the training-wheels portion of the tutorial? I thought I mentioned the training-wheels portion of the tutorial."

"YOU DIDN'T! I swear, it's almost like you're trying to screw with me just for the fun of it!"

"Oh, I thought that was obvious!"

"CAN YOU JUST ANSWER THE QUESTION?!"

"Uggggggh fine. The mobs presented to you during your tutorial mission will be significantly weaker than those following said mission. To that end, level-one mobs have an increased chance of negative status effects caused by abilities. It IS a tutorial, after all; I think we've only lost, like, two Augments during the tutorial mission in the history of Infinite Ascension," Angie explained, though she almost seemed a bit annoyed by having to do so.

I had never had a younger sister—or any sibling, for that matter—but she was almost making me feel like I knew what it would have felt like to have one.

"Anyway, this mission is intended to provide you with the opportunity to create your first combat skills and introduce you to the Non-Sapient mobs, while also providing you with hands-on experience with the system at large. I'd argue, given how well you've done so far, you can see how fluidly your Augmentations work?"

She was right. I had been far from athletic, and I was *never* much of a fighter. Sure, I had been in Taekwondo for a few years when I was a child, but it's not like I had kept up with it. But still, I had landed those blows near effortlessly, and I barely had to think about what I was doing.

"Man, how the fuck dumb are you. Get back in there and stuff that bag full," the brute finally said with a shake of his head before looking back over at me. "Who da fuck said you can get back up. I suggest you get back on the floor like the other hostages if you don't—"

I didn't wait for him to finish his threat, rushing the large man and activating my Sting like a Bee ability before throwing my first punch. The brute wasn't taken by surprise, his arm jumping to take the blow as a health bar popped up over his head, a small chunk of it fading away.

"Heh, that's a heck of a punch. You'd make a good Viper. Too bad we ain't got space for no pansy hero bitch," the brute said before he pulled back and launched a punch of his own. His fist almost seemed to move in slow motion as he growled, "Let's see if you can take it as good as yah give it."

[New Ability! Float like a Butterfly!]
You've got luck on your side for punching and bul-
lets, why not throw a bit in for your dodging too?
This ability gives you an increased chance to dodge hand-to-
hand combat strikes of 10 percent plus 1 percent for every
1 point of Luck you have. And that's literally if you're clos-
ing your eyes and not doing anything at all to dodge.
Look, it's not rocket science, Augment. If you're having trou-
ble getting out of the way of that fist before you take a blow,
then use this ability to give yourself a little extra luck.
Duration: *10 seconds.*
Cooldown: *5 minutes.*

I skipped backward, barely avoiding tripping over one of the grunts I had put down. Unfortunately, that put me right in position for another one to make a grab for me. He barely had his arm around my chest when I felt my body instinctively crouch, pulling from the man's grip just in the nick of time.

My luck was with me, and the brute tried to chase as I dodged, his powerful strike connecting directly with the grunt; I could hear a nearly sickening crunch of bone. The grunt's health plummeted as he crumpled to the ground and the brute let out a quick string of curse words.

[New Achievement! Unfriendly Friendly Fire!]
You've caused an enemy to knock out one of their companions.
Okay, look, Augment, we get it—you're trying not to get your hands
dirty. But I think making these guys beat up their friends is a bit
much. It's definitely impressive, but still kind of uncalled for.
Silver-Level Achievement.
Reward: *You have received a B-tier Loot Box!*

I was almost distracted by the loot box icon on my HUD ticking up to six, but as I dropped low, with the brute still reacting to striking his underling, I didn't even hesitate to throw a punch.

[New Achievement! Low Blow!]
And here I thought dodging that attack was uncalled for . . . I
mean, I don't even have testicles, and I think I can feel the pain.
You have struck an enemy in their private parts.
Why did we put private parts on a Non-Sapient NPC? Look,
we'd have to explain how we make them to you first, and I
really don't think we have time for that right now.
Gold-Level Achievement.
Reward: *You have received a F-tier Loot Box!*
Personally, I'd give you nothing for this one given the audac-
ity of the attack, but Axio's the one in charge, not me.

I stifled a laugh, rolling to the side as the brute tried to compose himself. His health bar was now just a shade under half, but he had a new icon above his head that read [**Stunned: 30 Seconds**]. On my action bar, I could see my Sting like a Bee skill beginning to flash, the timer on it nearly ended. I still had one more Luck-enhanced punch, and I preferred to use it before the skill went on cooldown.

Though I was sure I could land another blow on the brute while he was stunned, there were still three other grunts moving into position to try to ambush me. They were loud, almost too loud, and I wondered if I somehow had enhanced hearing within my zone of control, but that was a mystery for later. I flipped on my heel, using the momentum to launch a punch at what I hoped was an enemy.

"Oh sh—" was all the grunt was able to get out before my hand collided directly with his face and I felt as the man's nose crunched beneath my knuckles. He stumbled backward, his health bar sinking deep into the red, only a sliver of his health remaining. It was a good strike, but it must not have counted as a weak spot. It didn't matter in the end; I just had to follow up on the strike.

As I moved to capitalize, a strike landed roughly against the side of my head and sent me stumbling. My health bar dropped another quarter as I turned on my heel to try and recover. To my surprise, it wasn't a grunt who had attacked me, but *another* brute.

You have fallen below 50 percent health for the first time. Your inven-
tory is being conditionally activated to access healing serums.
You have been granted 5 Basic Health Injectors. These can be accessed from
your action bar and injected anywhere into your body for full effect.

A syringelike icon was added to the so-far empty two-slot section of my hot bar. I selected it, unsure of what to expect. In a flicker of light, an injection gun filled with a red glowing liquid *literally* materialized into my hand. Not wanting to give the enemies time to advance, I shoved it against my leg and pulled the trigger. A rush of energy passed over my body, and my health recovered by twenty-five percent in less than a second. The icon on the action bar went on cooldown, slowly ticking away on a five-minute timer.

"What the hell is that?! How am I supposed to heal if I get hit again?!"

"I suggest you don't get hit again!" Angie chirped back while I rolled to the side as the brute brought a giant foot down, breaking the tile into chips. I could still see the civilians cowering behind the desks and tables in the lobby. *"Please do not concern yourself with them. Although they will certainly try to hurt you, the mobs designated for the tutorial are strictly instructed to ignore noncombat NPCs only for this mission."*

"Only for this—" I started, my shock rising as I understood her implication. I was forced to jump to the side just as the first brute, finally free from his debuff, charged. Moving out of the way, he crashed into one of the smaller grunts, steamrolling the man and taking out the last bit of health I had left him with.

The lack of a ranged attack in my repertoire made it clear that I needed a way to take these guys down from a distance. Trying to think on my feet, I looked around the area for a solution. It was a small space, and in truth, the best solution would be to find a way to just slow them all down. I scanned the area, briefly glancing at each of my four remaining enemies as—

[New Ability! Weighted Clothes!]
Look at you, finally realizing your power has more
applications than just through luck!
For the next 30 seconds, up to three articles of clothing being worn
within your Local Area now weigh a quarter of a ton! That's 500 pounds,
if you didn't know just how much a ton is. It might not be enough to
crush anyone, but you try being speedy while carrying that much.
Affected enemies take 500 minus Strength score points of dam-
age immediately, and 50 minus Strength score points of dam-
age every 3 seconds for the remainder of the skill's duration.
Duration: *30 seconds.*
Cooldown: *10 minutes.*

This nearly made me come up short as I wondered what the hell my powers even were. I had no idea how that ability came out of Local Area Manipulation, but I was going to have to figure it out if I had any hope of creating more straightforward abilities. Both of the brutes were noticeably slower, and I watched as one of the grunts stumbled forward and dropped to the ground with a pained groan as he clutched at his chest. Then there was the only grunt who hadn't been affected by my ability; it almost looked as if he was considering running as he scrambled backward.

His hesitation was short-lived, and he set his jaw before stepping forward, taking three strides and immediately slipping on blood that had been pooling from one of his cohorts. His head smacked roughly against the corner of the teller's desk, and a big **[KO]** started to circle his body.

"Heh . . . unlucky," I found myself muttering aloud. I climbed back to my feet as I looked to the last of the enemies. At this point, I didn't feel that threatened by the sole remaining grunt any longer, but the brutes had proven themselves to be some form of danger.

I rushed to the knocked-out grunt and found his unused pistol. After he had seen the others get so unceremoniously incapacitated by their own weapons, he must have made what he thought was the smart decision. While I wasn't a gun nut, I had played paintball and laser tag more than once. Maybe I was just trying to fool myself, but it was comparable . . . right?

Even if it wasn't entirely sure how my main power worked, I did feel like I was getting the hang of the ability creation. As I leveled the gun at the brute I had already damaged, I was more than ready for Angie to chirp up.

[New Ability! Lucky Shot!]

Hey, you're gonna take the fun out of it if you start predict-
ing when it happens. If I could, I'd just let you figure out what
this one does on your own, but ugggh, rules are rules.
When you activate this ability, infuse the next three shots with luck equal
to 1 percent for every 1 point of Luck you have, increasing the chance
of hitting a Weak Spot and inflicting 50 percent increased damage.
This ability will go on cooldown if you drop the weapon
being utilized when the ability is activated.

My shot hit the brute directly in his center of mass, and his health dropped by over fifty percent, leaving his health blinking red. I fired again, but this time, I felt myself instinctively aim for the brute's side. From what I could tell, it seemed like dropping the mobs to zero was actually killing them, as I could tell the enemies labeled as **[KO]** all still had small slivers of health on their bars. While Angie *had* said they were "Non-Sapient," I couldn't bring myself to kill them indiscriminately without knowing just how true that was, even if a few of them had unfortunately already succumbed to that.

The shot hit and set him off-balance, and his health dropped by another twenty-five percent as the brute let out a string of curses.

I took the opportunity to rush him, relying on the weighted shirt to drastically slow his reaction time, and mentally activated my Sting like a Bee ability again. I wasn't even sure when it had gone off cooldown, but I was thankful I had it avail-able. Making an actual running leap as I pulled my hand back, I curled it into a fist before driving it into the brute's temple. Just like the others, his health dropped to a small sliver of red as a spinning **[KO]** popped up over his head.

[New Achievement! Giant Slayer!]
We got a regular David over here!
You have defeated an enemy that was a higher level than you. Given we put
an enemy higher-leveled than every new Augment in their tutorial, you can
imagine just how common this **Bronze-Level Achievement** *actually is.*
Reward: *You have received a D-tier Loot Box!*

Two more . . . I had two more to go, but I could feel the activity starting to catch up to me. Underneath my health bar, I finally noticed a blinking bar with a small sliver of green left. When I concentrated on it, I noticed it was labeled as "Stamina." It was creeping up . . . slowly, but it would be nowhere near ready before my Weighted Clothes ability wore off.

"Are there stamina injections too?"

"Yup! But we don't give you those in the tutorial; it's better to ease new Augments into the idea of inventory usage with something like their own health. Plus, most Augments finish this tutorial before they run out of stamina the first time . . . Kinda says something about you, doesn't it?"

I *tried* not to be offended by that, but I'd be lying if I said I succeeded. She was fucking with me; that's what she had been doing from the very start, and I just had to assume that's what she was programmed to do for . . . some reason. There really had to be a game admin or something I could talk to once this was all done.

With the gun still in my hand, I turned it on the weaker of the remaining enemies and fired. While I aimed for his center of mass, I didn't want to risk my Lucky Shot skill killing him outright, so I erred toward the side of his body to hopefully avoid anything major. His health chunked down to what looked like around ten percent remaining, and with my stamina back up to about a quarter of its own gauge, I rushed him, finding myself getting used to the repetitive motion.

I threw two quick punches, not caring that I was using up the last of my Sting like a Bee. The grunt crumpled to the ground with the familiar **[KO]** icon spinning above his head, and I stopped to catch my breath, turning slowly until I could see the last remaining brute. Red-and-blue lights started to flash in the windows, and I found my attention drawn to the countdown timer I had so far been ignoring which now read **[Police Have Arrived on Scene!]**

"It . . . It's over . . ." I said, finding myself out of breath. Realistically, this should have happened the moment I burst through the door, but Angic was right—the Augmentations were helping me along quite nicely.

"Y'think I'm 'fraid of some pigs?" the brute grunted, reaching over his shoulder and pulling out what *had* to be an oversize shotgun. "Looks like your luck's all run out, hero."

"I wouldn't—" I started, but he didn't give me time to finish before he pulled the trigger.

I couldn't know for sure it was going to happen, but the brute's prediction had been far from accurate. My Misfire ability activated just as he fired, and the shotgun exploded, tearing his entire right hand from his arm and severely maiming the left one. Surprisingly, this didn't kill him, instead bringing his health down by seventy-five percent.

My stamina was still low, but there *was* enough there. With the brute screaming in pain and dropping to his knees, I walked toward him, trying to look as confident as I possibly could.

"Actually, I think my luck's just getting started," I said, not sure where the quip even came from as I pulled my fist back and hit him with every bit of strength I could muster. "You can bet on that."

CHAPTER SIX

An overzealous sound of cascading trumpets filled my head as Angie nearly shouted in excitement.

[New Achievement! Progression Time!]
You have leveled up for the very first time. Congrats! If you couldn't even do this, then we would have wasted a lot of time and money Augmenting you. Thanks for not being a waste; keep it up.
Wood-Level Achievement.
Reward: *Leveling up is its own reward! Get back to your Safe House so you can see why already.*

[New Achievement! Quippy Longstockings!]
We got a regular jokester over here. You completed a mission by taking down the final opponent WITH a quip! Honestly, I'm not sure how we determine what constitutes as a joke, and I'm pretty sure what you said wasn't very funny. But you know what, I bet those NPCs you saved are sure to remember it when they are telling their families about it over dinner.
Silver-Level Achievement.
Reward: *You have received a C-tier Loot Box!*

I had been so out of breath, I didn't even care that Angie was rattling off achievements. That wasn't to say I was getting used to it necessarily, just that I didn't have It in me to really care.

Taking a moment to stretch, I looked around at the civilians, who were warily starting to stand up. I offered them the most confident smile and wave that I could before one of them shouted a cheer and the group burst out, applauding my victory. More than a few of them were holding phones up, clearly trying to get a picture or video.

The front doors of the bank were pushed open sad cops came rushing in, guns raised. I instinctively threw my hands in the air. I might have been the hero here, but a ski mask in a bank?! It really was a recipe for disaster.

Much to my surprise, though, the cop leading the way dropped his gun as he took in the fallen bikers.

"Dang, you new Augments always make a mess," the man said, walking forward and holding out a strong-looking hand. "Lieutenant Nester, Tenth Precinct. You got a name yet?"

[Lt. Nester!]
Non-Sapient Friendly NPC.
Again, we aren't going to get into this just yet; honestly, I'd prefer it if we never got into it. Just know it makes integrating you guys into "normal" society a lot easier. And no, his squadmates don't know. Hey, stop judging me, I can feel you doing it already, and it's uncalled for. Lt. Nester is a very happy man, and he just so happens to work for the Tenth Precinct. This is your police contact for the Tenth Precinct.

"Umm, no, not yet. It's, uh . . . It's actually kinda my first time out," I said with a nervous laugh before I shook the lieutenant's hand. It was hard not to find myself coming up short at the idea that this game somehow had plants . . . in the police, of all places.

"It's really not that big of a deal, Augment. With all of you running around, most police forces really only deal with domestic disputes and traffic stops. Hell, I'd argue the guys we put into place are more *effective than them. But again, with so little to actually do, that's not all that hard."*

"Well, I suggest you start thinking about that. We got some protocols we have to follow. I can't exactly give you any police info if we don't have an official name to put on the records. Since I haven't met an Augment yet who's wanted to go by their *real* name, I'm gonna assume I can't do anything else with yah just yet," Lt. Nester said before turning and waving in a team of EMTs, who rushed in to start checking on the civilians and downed bikers.

"Yeah, I, uh . . . I guess that makes sense. Do you guys need anything from me? How long have these guys been causing trouble around here?" I asked.

"Sorry, bud; you're gonna have to come find me when you have a name before I can read you in on that," he repeated before reaching into his pocket and pulling out a thickly stuffed wallet. "Here's my card. Come down to the tenth when you're ready and ask for me. I can point you in the right direction . . . And, uh, you're also gonna want to put together a better look; if I wasn't already aware of an Augment on the scene, I might have thought you were the bank robber here."

[Mission Tutorial Completed!]
Reward: *You have received a B-tier Loot Box!*

I took the business card, and it vanished from my hand, causing the message **[New Contact: Lt. Nester]** to flash in the corner of my HUD. I didn't linger any longer, already noticing a few of the civilians lifting their phones to get pictures of me before I rushed out of the bank. Honestly, Lt. Nester really didn't need to point it out. It *had* to look a bit silly, a dude in a mask just casually jogging away from a failed bank robbery, but for now, it was the only way I was going to get around.

"Isn't there a vendor or somewhere I should be going? I mean, I know leveling up is important, and I have these loot boxes to open, but like, the cop was right—there are a few things I really should try to get in order. Hell, what the hell am I going to even call myself? Can I choose anything?"

"Not necessarily anything. Like, it really wouldn't help your merch sales down the line if you called yourself 'The Lucky Puncher.' That's not catchy at all."

"Merch sales?"

"That's a topic for when you hit level twenty, Augment."

"Okay, so don't pick anything that could hurt potential merch sales . . . got it," I muttered out loud, ducking through an alley when I was confident I had put enough distance between the fight and myself before finally slowing to a walk. When I was sure no one was looking, I pulled off the mask and strolled back out to the main sidewalk as casually as I could.

"As for vendors, we can discuss Sanctuary Square after you complete your level-up process. Now that you have created your initial abilities and leveled up, we can finish the last of the Wave onboarding steps, and you can truly start getting out there."

"Yeah, about that . . . Why would I even want *to keep getting out there? I mean, look, I know I probably would have died because of whatever happened with The First, and that fight back there was cool, but I never wanted to be a superhero . . . This has been bothering me since I woke up: Are the Augmentations like . . . compelling me to participate in all of this? Do I really have to?"*

Angie seemed to pause at this for a brief moment, her usually flippant attitude wavering. *"While the Augmentations* aren't *compelling you to participate, it is the job of myself and the System AI to motivate you to play. As I have said multiple times, you have superpowers now; the tradeoff should be—"*

"It's not worth it!" I said, having to hold myself back from screaming it even as I wandered into the lobby of my building. I stopped to look around, glad that Jon wasn't currently working in the small space. Taking a deep breath, I returned my attention inward. *"I'm not a killer. I don't care if you guys are claiming those bikers back there were Non-Sapient—they looked pretty damn real to me. I tried to take them down nonlethally, but my ability just . . . it made several of them actually die. How am I supposed to deal with that?"*

"The same way every other Augment has since this project was launched: by surviving and growing stronger," Angie replied; I could have sworn I heard a bit of sorrow in her tone. It only lasted for a moment before her voice picked back up, almost amplifying in pep in response. *"But hey, we haven't sent you out there like a pig to slaughter. In case you didn't realize it, your Augmentations provide you with more than just the theoretical ability to wield your superpowers.*

"For example, your powerset, 'The Perfect Planner,' is described as an offensive, close-combat class. To facilitate this, you have been granted a skill rank of five in a random close-ranged fighting style. You can see which after your full stat menu has been opened at the completion of the full onboarding process."

"Okay, that's cool and all; you guys basically Matrix uploaded a skill into my brain. Seriously, what the hell is the point?! Couldn't the company behind this be making millions of dollars selling this technology?"

"That would imply money is the primary motivation at play, Augment," Angie quipped back, making me pause as I reached for the handle to my apartment. *"This is all largely a moot point; there is nothing that can change your circumstances as they stand. You are an Augment now, meaning you are obliged to participate in* Infinite Ascension. *So far, you have been compliant, but if you did try to 'sit it out,' I'm afraid that would only result in tragedy. There's nothing within your Augmentations that would allow us to just 'disable' you, but needless to say, you would be . . . handled."*

I swallowed what little spit was in my mouth as her meaning really set in. While she had alluded to this multiple times already, I hadn't really taken the time to *actually* let it set in. *"So . . . So you're saying everything—all the comments about sending threats my way, the lawyers collecting my . . . my remains for testing . . . Was all of that true? I can actually die playing this game?"*

"My apologies, Augment. No, it wasn't all true."

"Okay, that's a—"

"We don't actually employ any lawyers."

I let out a long, slow sigh as I bit back a slew of curses that I wanted to shout. I *really* should have known that was coming.

The moment I crossed the barrier into my home, my HUD lit up. Several new windows popped up in rapid succession, each vanishing as I instinctively shoved the notifications to the side. Though I knew I could easily dwell all night on the threat to my life I was now aware of, there still were a million other things I had to deal with. I'd make sure to take the time to freak out properly before I went to bed.

"What the hell is all of this?"

"All the notifications that were on hold pending your return to your Safe House. First, let's address your new stat selections for leveling up and what will happen in subsequent levels," Angie said as one of the windows I'd dismissed pulled back. It was the same stat sheet I had first been shown, though this time, the numbers were all filled. *"Each level, you will be granted four stat points that you can distribute as you see fit. Please note, if you choose to use all of your points to increase a single stat, the third increase in a single level will cost two stat points."*

"Why would I ever do that when I could just wait to level up again?" I asked aloud, finding the apartment still empty. It was only a bit shy of five in the afternoon, meaning Jon was probably still working on the project. I had helped him once before on a freelance IT job, and it'd taken him nearly two days to finish wiring a building roughly the same size as ours, though that might have been because he had to keep reminding me how to set up the wires.

Still, even knowing that he *probably* wasn't going to be home soon, I wasn't going to risk getting caught in the main area of the apartment. Heading for my bedroom, I locked the door behind me, and a wave of peace seemed to finally come over me. I dropped onto my bed and fell backward, starting to just look up at the ceiling when my eyes caught a piece of furniture I hadn't seen before.

"Um . . . what's that?"

"We will discuss that in a bit. And though you leveled up quickly this time, levels will come far slower the higher you get. Some equippable items require minimum stat levels before temporary boosts are available, and sometimes you just need to bite the bullet and drop three points into a single stat to get there. It happens more often than you'd think."

"I guess that makes sense; still not sure why I would actually do that in the long run, but I'm sure I'll find out eventually. Is that all that comes from leveling? Stat points?"

"Nope! It just depends on what the level is! There are special things that happen on random odd levels, but other than your hidden power getting revealed at level fifteen, I'm afraid I can't ruin the other surprises.

"On even levels, you will also receive an Ability Augmentation. Ability Augmentations must be activated immediately upon receiving them and can only be used to target abilities currently on your action bar. When used, you will be given three possible options for modifying the selected ability!

"If you do not immediately activate the Augmentation, I will randomly select and upgrade an ability for you, or as with your Power Selection, you can always just say, 'Surprise me, Angie!' Please note: You may only modify an ability with an Ability Augmentation once every ten levels, up to a maximum of three times. Now please assign your stat points, and your Ability Augmentation will become available."

The stat sheet shook, as if demanding my attention now that Angie had finished her explanation. It would have been really easy to just dump all of the points into Luck, given how many of my abilities already seemed to be relying on the stat, but it still wasn't going to matter if I couldn't take a hit. I sat up on my bed, and the screen followed.

"So theoretically, if I put points into, let's say Strength . . . will I *actually* get stronger? Like, let's say for example, I can curl twenty-five pounds with one arm. If I added points to Strength, would that go up?"

"That's exactly *it! But—and this is a fun fact that you should definitely remember—your physique will only change if you choose to have it match your achieved stat points. Some players will choose not to have their physique change for a variety of reasons, though most players' reasoning tends to come down to wanting others to underestimate their capabilities. Strength is the only stat that can have this effect on your physical appearance, however. Though certain parts of your physical appearance can affect your Style score under certain circumstances, I don't think you'll ever qualify for those."*

I mentally dropped two points into Strength and a point into my Luck before hesitating with my last one. I was still stuck on the idea of increasing my Luck just to boost my abilities, and that was definitely important, but my Toughness was *only* a two. If the most basic of the bikers was able to chunk my health down by a quarter with only a punch, I could only imagine how bad it would be when I had to fight one of them who's also Augmented.

I dropped my final point into the stat, and I saw a **[+100]** flash over my health bar.

"Is it just health that Toughness adds to?"

"No. In addition to the health bonus, each point in Toughness increases your natural resilience and your Stability substat. These various character stats can be seen under your larger character sheet. But you will have some time for that later; we need to be immediately moving on."

Just as Angie promised, another window flashed open, though it remained blank as my action bar moved from its normal position into the bottom of the screen.

[Warning!]

You can only begin the process once you select an ability. There's no
"scrolling around" to see what modifications can be made to your
skills. Select one, and three modifications will populate this screen. You
have 30 seconds to select a skill, and a subsequent 30 seconds to choose
the modification following the readout of each possible option.

A timer immediately filled the center of the window, and I cursed under my breath. What the hell was the point of giving us practically no time to consider damn near *any* of our choices. This was really on me, for not taking literally any time since the end of the fight to look over the skills. I knew my passive skills were useful, but without a gun, my Sting like a Bee was the most offensive ability I had.

The icon, an actual bee, briefly filled the Ability Augmentation window before a brief description, without Angie's color commentary, appeared. Directly below it, the now familiar spinning text boxes filled the rest of the screen.

[Sting like a Bee!]

Level 1 Activated Ability.
You gain a 2 percent chance (increasing by 2 percent for every 1 point of
Luck you have) for your next 3 Unarmed Strikes to strike Weak Spots and
inflict an additional 25 percent damage! Additional effects may also occur.
Duration: *30 seconds.*
Cooldown: *2 minutes and 30 seconds.*

[First Modification Option: Passive Upgrade!]

All of your Unarmed Strikes now have a 1 percent chance (increas-
ing by 1 percent for every 1 point of Luck you have) to strike Weak
Spots. This Passive Ability does not stack with the activated version

*and is not in effect while the ability is on cooldown. You don't get to
have your cake and eat it too; at least, not this early on.*

[Second Modification Option: Time Adjustment!]
*This ability no longer has a time limit for use and will only go on
cooldown when you have thrown all of your enhanced Unarmed Strikes.
And when we say no time limit, we mean no time limit. If you have
one strike left after all of your enemies have been dispatched, this ability will hold that one strike in reserve until your next fight, even over-
night, and then go on cooldown immediately after being thrown.*

[Third Modification Option: Highlighter Perk!]
*When this ability is activated, possible Weak Spots will be high-
lighted on enemies within your Local Area. Hitting one of these
highlighted areas grants an additional 5 percent chance of dealing critical damage and causing an instant* **[KO]**.
*Given you've already gotten the Low Blow achievement, I feel it's my duty to
tell you these highlighted spots won't always be where you expect them to be.*

A timer was rapidly ticking down in the corner of the screen as I quickly read
through the options, trying to see which, if any, had the best advantages. I was leaning toward the first. *My* passive abilities *were* useful, and adding another one wasn't
necessarily a bad thing. Sure, I'd lose the passive during the cooldown period, but
that's how I *always* would be if I didn't choose that modification.

The Time Adjustment also had its benefits. After all, hadn't I just been racing
earlier to throw the last of my enhanced strikes before the timer ticked over to the
cooldown? But even so, I didn't like the idea of only having one of the enhanced
strikes available going into a new battle, and given what I had seen of Augment
fights *before* I had gotten dragged into all of this, I didn't think this was the best
choice.

But the Highlighter Perk was interesting. *Anything* that could cause an instant
[KO], even at a low percentage, was dangerous, especially if I was considering the
long-term implications of the game. Even though part of me was still wanting to
desperately buck at my new reality, this was *essentially* a video game. Sure, I might
not have been given a choice on if I wanted to play it, but it *was* a video game. And
if it followed the same pattern as other games, the enemies would only continue to
get stronger. The ability to one-shot any of them would be—

*"Time's up! I have rolled the dice for you, and your Sting like a Bee ability has been
modified with a Time Adjustment. Now, before we move on to Sanctuary Square, let's
open those loot boxes."*

"Oh, goddammit, Angie!"

CHAPTER SEVEN

Nate Mercer's Apartment, Safe House. Hell's Kitchen, NYC
Neighborhood: *Unclaimed*
City: *Claimed by Squad:* **The Paragons of Justice**

This is your [B.E.L.T.], the Bottomless Equipment and Loot Transport interface. *Please note: Your current version of the B.E.L.T. will only allow items generated for Infinite Ascension to be placed inside. If it is nonhuman, can be highlighted by your HUD, and is an item specifically made for the game, then it can go in here."*

"Bottomless? So, like, I can literally just keep shoving more and more in there?"

"That's correct! Though statistics show most players' B.E.L.T.s only carry on average around two hundred pounds."

"Huh . . ." I got up from my bed and walked over to my desk, taking a seat at a folding chair. Tossing my sticker-covered laptop over onto my bed, I leaned back. "Okay, now what?"

"Now, select your loot boxes, and they will all appear on the table here."

I followed her instructions, looking at the single stack of ten loot boxes before mentally selecting them. In quick flashes of light, they all scattered over the desk. While they were all uniform in size, appearing like metal shoeboxes with a removable lid, they each had a letter and a small bit of text engraved on top to differentiate them.

I grabbed the one closest to me labeled **[C: Quippy Longstockings]** and pulled the lid from it. There was nothing actually in the box, but a window opened and listed the contents as:

5 Enhanced Health Injectors
1 Targeted Ability Level Up Scroll
500 credits

"What's the difference between a Level Up Scroll and an Ability Augmentation? Also, credits? Is that like, the in-game currency? Kinda would rather have cash . . ."

"If you need cash, credits can be exchanged at the Registration Center in Sanctuary Square at a rate of one credit to ten cents. As for the difference between the scrolls and the Ability Augmentation, your skills will gradually level up and get stronger with use over time within the set rules of the ability. For example, skills that use your Luck stat will gradually give you higher percent likelihoods the higher the skill reaches.

"A Targeted Ability Level Up Scroll will allow you to choose and raise a single ability

by one level. There are also Randomized Ability Level Up Scrolls that will, obviously, randomly raise a single ability by one level. Please note: Abilities can only be leveled up with scrolls once per twenty-four-hour period but can still be leveled up by general use and experience."

I mentally selected the scroll, and an honest-to-God piece of parchment with illegible script written over it appeared in my hands. When I highlighted it, it just said:

[Targeted Ability Level Up!]
*Seriously, we just explained how this worked. Target
one ability and raise it by a single level.*

It wasn't like activating the Ability Augmentation. While that one brought my action bar into a secondary screen, this time, a new window opened to list my current abilities. The major change was that there, for once, wasn't any sort of ticking timer. I could also highlight the skills and get a brief description of what each one could do.

But all of that wasn't what had surprised me the most: it *wasn't* just the abilities I had created that were listed there. There were two other *very* important things that I absolutely wanted more details on.

[Local Area Manipulation!]
Level 1.
*This is your Primary Power! Creates a permanent zone in a 15-foot radius
around your body. Within this Local Area, you possess the ability to alter
and control various aspects of your environment and the objects within it,
provided you have a General Understanding of how the desired effect works.
Once you acquire the appropriate levels of knowledge, your influence will include but not be limited to the following: Object
Manipulation, Environmental Control, Matter Transformation,
Energy Manipulation, Perception Influence, and more! With this ability, your only real limits are what you know and your imagination.*
Please Note: *Some aspects of this ability are locked until it reaches
higher levels. Those aspects will be revealed as they become available.*

[Super Luck!]
Level 1.
*This is your Secondary Power! Subtly affect the Luck of everything within
your Local Area by .1 percent for every 1 point of Luck that you have.
Events and outcomes within your vicinity have a higher chance of unfold-
ing advantageously for you. Whether it's dodging an attack, finding useful
items, or having circumstances align perfectly, luck is always on your side.*

This Base Ability stacks with other generated abilities.
Luck Bomb. *Activated Ability. Once per day, you can consciously invoke a surge of good fortune, increasing the likelihood of a positive outcome for a specific action or event.*
Please Note: *Unlike other abilities, this does not need to be on your action bar to activate!*

I almost couldn't believe it, and I reread both of the descriptions several times as I contemplated how to use my scroll. Now that I had a full explanation, I couldn't help but feel Local Area Manipulation could be downright broken with the right application. Though I wasn't sure just how a "general understanding" of things was supposed to work.

"It works as it is described. While you were granted the abilities you thought of on the fly during the tutorial, future ability creation will not work the same way. You can't just bend gravity to your will; you have to have at least a basic understanding of the physics behind it."

"So what? I'm supposed to just start reading about physics and all this other shit?"

"If you want to do it the long and boring way, you absolutely can, but we really don't have time for all that nonsense. There are certain books and items that can be collected or acquired which will provide you with an immediate level three in the skill, the minimum-required understanding for your ability to be able to implement the effect. I'm sure you will get at least one or two more of these scrolls from your loot boxes. Let's get a move on already."

I sighed and selected my Local Area Manipulation as the target of the scroll. The text in its window flashed before a new message appeared.

[Local Area Manipulation!]
This power has increased to Level 2.
Your Local Area's radius is now 16 feet.

Before I just started to randomly grab and open the rest of the boxes, I decided to quickly organize them. I wanted to get a baseline of what to expect from the different tiers, and to my luck, I did have a pretty good spread. Not counting the C tier I had already opened, I still had three other Cs, two Ds, and an F tier. Then I *also* had two Bs and a single A tier sitting at the far end of the table.

"Are A tiers the highest?"

"There are three tiers higher than A for loot boxes: A+, S, and S+. These are all much rarer than the previous tiers, and are generally only given out for specific high-level quests, Diamond- or Mythic-level achievements, and as rewards for placements within the various phases of your Wave. They also will almost always give unique items, Scrolls of Level Ups, and/or other features that you would otherwise not be able to receive."

I opened the rest of the C tiers first, getting fifteen more Enhanced Health

Injectors, two more Targeted Ability Level Up Scrolls, two thousand credits, and an item labeled [**How the Hell Does This Fool Anybody?**]. I left the scrolls alone for the time being, intent on circling back to them later in the day when I had time to just think, and highlighted the last item on the list, which was marked as "equippable." In a flash of light, it materialized on the table in front of me.

[**How The Hell Does This Fool Anybody?!**]
Equippable Mask.
Color: *Black.*
This is a Basic Item and does not improve any stats, but it does count as
a disguise to allow you to use your abilities outside of your Safe House.
It comes with the **Who's That?!** *feature.*
There, Augment, now you don't have to look like a bank rob-
ber from the 1970s; are you happy now?

I highlighted the feature that stood out bolded in its window, and Angie immediately started back up.

[**Who's That?!**]
This feature subtly alters the perception of people who are not aware of
your Secret Identity, meaning that even though this mask is barely cover-
ing any part of your face, even your closest friends won't put two and two
together when they see you in costume. So that's how this fools people.

"Do I have to actually put things on like they are clothes? Or is it like a video game here too, and I can just equip the— Oh yeah, there it is," I said as a small menu opened next to the mask, which included: Stow, Destroy, and Equip. I selected Equip, and the mask disappeared, small bits of black appearing on the edges of my vision.

"*To answer your question, yes, you can just put things on as if they are clothes, but all items generated for* Infinite Ascension *can be Fast Equipped using this menu. Additionally, when you have chosen your costume, I will show you how to set the neces- sary items to the Equipment Readying position. This will allow you to quickly material- ize or hide your costume when you are moving through public spaces.*"

"That's . . . huh, that's actually pretty cool," I said as I reached up and felt the lightweight mask clinging to my face.

Looking at my remaining boxes, I decided to get the lower-tier boxes out of the way first. The two D-tier boxes each contained fifty credits a piece and a total of ten [**Basic Stamina Injectors**]. Like the Basic Health Injectors I had already used, the Stamina Injectors would replenish twenty-five percent of my energy when used.

The F-tier box surprised me, though, containing an equippable item labeled [**Nutcracker Stompers**]. I was expecting it to be nothing but a joke item, given what should have been a degrading tier system, and with a name like that, it was certainly possible that it *was* a joke.

Angie, as I was getting used to, anticipated my question.

"While the Tier system is degrading in terms of the quality of the rewards, F tiers are unique in that they are completely randomized. You will only ever receive a single item from any individual F-tier box, but it can be anything that can be generated within Infinite Ascension; however, they tend to oftentimes be related to the achievement that spawned them. These boxes are affected by your Luck stat."

I selected the Stompers, and a pair of white leather combat boots materialized on the table.

[Nutcracker Stompers!]

Equippable Footwear.

Color*: White.*

These boots grant the **Steadyfoot** *feature and will make you look absolutely fabulous. Deal an additional 10 percent damage when striking male enemies in their nuts with an Unarmed Strike!*

+1 Charisma.

+1 Style.

You do need to take off those ratty Converse before you put these on.

[Steadyfoot!]

This feature grants you exceptional balance and stability, making it incredibly difficult for opponents to knock you off your feet when they are firmly planted. When activated, you gain an additional +2 to Toughness, degrading after 15 seconds from the time your feet are moved from being planted. Additionally, this grants an additional 5 percent damage to any counterstrike thrown.

I kicked off my Converse and equipped the boots, finding they were either perfectly sized or they'd fit themselves to my feet when I equipped them. When I stood up, I could tell they weren't exactly the most comfortable shoe I had ever worn, but as I planted my feet, my health jumped up by two hundred. Instead of being like my normal red health bar, however, the temporary health flashed in a darker, more maroon shade.

"These are kind of . . . noticeable. How the hell am I supposed to hide these when I'm out? I don't really want to have to take an extra pair of shoes around."

"In Sanctuary Square you can purchase disguise kits for items that you will always keep equipped. This will allow them to look like basic items from your wardrobe; however, they do need to be reapplied whenever you break the disguise."

I took a moment to silently appreciate that before another thought crossed my mind.

"Hmm, okay. Putting that aside for a minute, my health just went up by two hundred here . . . What exactly does that mean? Like . . . if I hit zero health, am I just dead?"

"It . . . depends. If a strike is with a lethal-enough weapon or power, and it drops you to zero health, then yes, you will die. The same can be said about strikes that you deliver. Most attacks, if they drop someone to zero, will automatically be coded to be either lethal or non-lethal, but with some brute-force attacks, that discretion comes down to your intentions.

"In essence, a laser to the face when you have just ten health left is probably going to melt your brain, but if you or a basic mob gets in a lucky blow at that same ten health, only the [KO] debuff will be applied. This will leave the afflicted target vulnerable, though, so I don't recommend relying on that for safety."

"Great . . ." I muttered, turning to the last of my boxes. I opened up the first B-tier box, which had been labeled **[Mission Tutorial]**, and received an equippable item called **[Serpent's Fang Bracers]** and fifteen hundred credits. The second B-tier box held only a single item, a "trophy" titled **[Turnabout's Fairplay]**. "What's this trophy?"

"Oooh getting a trophy already, lucky you! We will get to that in just a moment, once you finish with the last of your loot boxes, as it will flow more naturally into Sanctuary Square. Those bracers are quite the lucky find too."

I highlighted them, and a pair of dark bracers dropped onto the table. They were intricately designed and seemed to be made from a dark, durable leather. To make them look even scarier, they were adorned with three sharp spikes. Around them, there was an elegant, coiling snake design that seemed almost alive, and the serpent's eyes were set with tiny glinting emeralds.

[Serpent's Fang Bracers!]
Equippable Bracers.
Color: *Black Leather.*
Sheesh, these things are really gonna clash with those boots of
yours, but they will make for a great backhanded strike.
+5 Strength.
Venomous Strike. *Activated Ability. Once per encounter, you can*
activate the bracers to deliver a venom-infused attack. Upon acti-
vation, the spikes on the bracers release a potent toxin that tem-
porarily paralyzes your target, reducing their movement speed
and attack effectiveness by 30 percent for 15 seconds.
This Activated Ability does not need to be on your action bar to activate.

"Damn . . . plus five to Strength; that's going to bring me to ten. Does that mean if I made my appearance match my strength, I'd look like some crazy body-builder right now, since ten is supposedly the max base stat?" I asked as I selected equip, watching as the bracers moved onto my wrists in a flash of light.

"Not necessarily. While a heavy lifter who enters the game might have a base Strength stat of eight or nine, the game's feature to match your appearance to your Strength is judged based on your base appearance and strength at the time you enter the game. Trust me, you're already a bit weird looking; making yourself an overmuscled manchild shouldn't be the style you're going for."

I nodded at that. I was already considering the pros and cons to using the appearance feature and was planning on not letting my appearance match my strength; at least, not yet. It would just raise too many questions from people who knew my disdain for the gym, plus I didn't necessarily care to actually have that much muscle.

Turning to my final box, the A tier, I opened it, revealing another twenty-five hundred credits and an equippable item that I automatically materialized on my table.

[Fortune's Guardian Jacket!]
Equippable Overcoat.
Color*: Orange.*
This eye-catching orange-and-blue leather biker jacket is imbued
with a hint of magic, designed to attract good fortune and pro-
tect its wearer. A small, tacky silver horseshoe charm hangs
from the main zipper, adding an extra touch of luck.
At a certain point, you've gotta wonder just how lucky we're gonna make you.
+6 Luck.
+3 Toughness.
This jacket grants the **Lucky Charm** *feature and*
the **Fortune's Shield** *Activated Ability.*

[Lucky Charm!]
This feature slightly increases the drop rate of rare items and loot.
There is a 15 percent chance for received Loot Boxes to be upgraded by
1 tier. This feature has a 12-hour cooldown upon being triggered.

[Fortune's Shield!]
This Activated Ability does not need to be on your action bar to activate.
Once per encounter, your jacket can activate to provide a protective bar-
rier for 10 seconds, reducing all incoming damage by 20 percent.

While I didn't have anything but the other items I had received to compare it to, this felt like a good item. Instead of just equipping it with the Fast Equip option, I lifted the jacket and tossed it over my shoulder, pulling the firm material on as my health jumped up by an additional three hundred points. Once the coat was on, it *actually* seemed to shrink, adjusting to a nearly perfect fit.

"Well, it's not the best costume, but it's at least a start," Angie muttered as I moved

over to a small mirror hanging next to my door. *"Yes, yes, admire yourself later; now, let's discuss your new piece of furniture. I need to show you what to do with that trophy."*

While I did want to take a better look at the gear, finding my overall appearance to look like a hodgepodge mess, Angie was noticeably less . . . *abrasive*, when I responded to her requests quicker. Plus, it was hard to say that I wasn't curious.

"Yeah, so where exactly did this bookshelf come from?"

"It's actually a display case, but I suppose that's just semantics. This case has two specific uses. First, you may place gained trophies on them. Go ahead and do that now with that Turnabout's Fairplay trophy. Highlight the case, then select Add Trophy. If you had multiple trophies, it would provide a list of which to add. Please note that at your current Safe House level, you can keep a maximum of three trophies activated at a time."

With a quick move through the menus, the trophy appeared on the shelf. It was a little model figure of a man wearing a bandanna on a motorcycle that looked almost exactly like one of the grunts I had easily put down.

[Turnabout's Fairplay!]
This is a Standard Trophy.
Passive Effect: *Increase the damage opponents do to their allies by 5 percent whenever you are directly responsible for causing the Friendly Fire. That's it. If you want a trophy that does more, keep chugging along and maybe that growing Luck of yours will pay off.*

"Okay, the trophy's up, what's next? You said this case you guys magicked into my already cramped bedroom has another use?"

"Perfect! You're getting really good at following directions. Now, feel underneath the third shelf from the top."

I poked a hand under the surprisingly sturdy structure, almost expecting my hand to pass through it before it landed on the actual wood grain surface. I felt around until I found a metal protrusion that was well out of place. As soon as I placed a finger on it, expecting to have to push some sort of button, the display case hissed, pulling backward into the wall. A bright white rectangle that glimmered at the edges was left in its place, the bulky piece of furniture fully vanishing into nothing.

"Um . . . This wall faces the street . . ." I said, looking over to the side at a window. "I swear, I'm just in a bed somewhere with my head caved in. I just . . . What the actual hell, Angie?"

"You were given superpowers, just fought a bunch of bikers in a bank, and you have a literal dimensional inventory, but a small subspace portal is suddenly tripping you up? You'd think you'd be getting used to this at least a little bit by now."

"Okay, no, seriously, don't dodge the question . . . What the hell is all of this technology? This is *literally* world-changing shit here . . ."

"It's the technology that makes Infinite Ascension *possible—that's all you need to*

be made aware of. Now, though this may seem impressive, it is really no better than any of the Augments who have teleporting abilities. This is a one-way connection from your Safe House to Sanctuary Square. Other players cannot follow you back through from the Square unless your Safe House was the original entrance they took. Basically, this isn't a fast-travel system, so don't go trying to skip across the world just by making a few friends."

"Is it . . . Is it safe?"

"Please, we haven't lost an Augment to one of these doorways since the Second Wave, and it stopped physically hurting players in the Sixth Wave. We got all the kinks worked out of it at this point. Now, go on and hop through—we're almost done with your onboarding."

CHAPTER EIGHT

Sanctuary Square, Non-PVP Zone. Location Classified.
Closest Known Claimed Territory: *Planet Earth*
Claimed by: *The First*

I was in awe as I emerged from the portal. It was like stepping through a literal doorway, and I immediately found myself descending a short staircase into a large courtyard. There were what must have been hundreds of other people walking around, seemingly engrossed in conversations with others. Maybe I was even seeing others finishing up their own tutorials.

"Umm . . . How am I supposed to get back home? There's not exactly a portal up there," I said as I turned and found a large stone wall at the top of the stairs.

"When you approach the wall, the system will open a portal directly to your Safe House. Now, as I mentioned before we left your room, others are unable to follow you from the Square back to your Safe House unless your Safe House was their original entrance point."

On either side of the courtyard, spaced evenly apart with flowers and bushes around their large bases, there were five *extremely* large statues, lined and turned to face each other. Each statue was made of a different ornate-looking marble, carved to what I had to assume were perfect likenesses of the heroes and villains they represented.

I immediately recognized the closest of them: an amazingly accurate version of The First etched out of a white-and-gray marble. I wasn't quite the same level of nerd as Jon, who I was sure probably could have named each of the carved figures, but I did recognize most of the heroes displayed on The First's side.

That's not to say the opposite side was nothing but a bunch of mystery figures. I did recognize one of them: a notoriously destructive villain who had gone by the name Frightmare when she was terrorizing California just a few years back. Her statue was made of a menacing black-and-red swirled stone that felt otherworldly and left me feeling incredibly uneasy the longer I looked at it.

"Sanctuary Square is quite literally a square. The shops within the east plaza of this location are dedicated to the Guardians, while the shops within the west plaza are for the Miscreants. Along the north edge are the Neutral shops. And then there's the bar at the center of the main courtyard here, The Common Ground, but we will visit that location last.

"Now, for the time being, you will only have access to the Neutral Shopping Segment. While your actions will declare you on scoreboards for one side or the other, until you

have claimed your first territory for either the Guardian or Miscreant team, you will not be granted access to their respective shops."

I started my way around the courtyard, trying to take in everything at once. It was surreal, with perfectly manicured hedges and floral decorations. There were large oak trees that shaded the various tables and benches littering the Square. Several people in bright costumes were deep in conversations with each other, while others sat on their own with their eyes glossed over, probably deep within their own menus. The shops on either edge of the Square were painfully artificial, and yet at the same time, incredibly detailed and realistic.

I couldn't tell the exact style of buildings, but the Guardian's side shops were made of brick, with clay roofs and big bay windows that looked into each shop, tucked inward around a small fountain. The Miscreant's side, for their part, would have been right at home in a Halloween movie, with dark metal arches and painted black bricks.

I had to crane my neck to look up at the statues of the heroes. After taking a moment to look at them, I finally realized the three statues following The First were, predictably, members of the team that assisted him with some of his bigger battles. But the last of the five statues was a slim, goggled man with sleek hair that I couldn't place even if I wanted to. Luckily for me, the statue could be highlighted.

[TechWarden, Level 176 Gizmo Guru]
Claimed Territories: *63*
Status: *Unknown*

"Never heard of him; that's kinda odd, given the rest of the lineup, isn't it?" I wondered as I looked back along the rest of the line. "Is he a member of The First's team? And what's with the status?"

"*I would* highly *suggest using the internal chat feature while in Sanctuary Square. While the other players might assume you're talking to me, think of it as a courtesy thing,*" Angie said. "*To answer your questions, however, the statues lining the teams' sides depict the five players who have held the territories worth the most points since the start of the game.*

"*This does not change whether the players are considered Dead or Alive; as long as they held the record for the highest point total at some point, their likeness will be immortalized here. Hmm . . . I guess it's not necessarily* immortalized *if someone could knock them out of their spot with enough effort though, is it?*"

"*Yeah, but what does it mean by* Unknown?" I asked, not getting sidetracked by her obvious bait.

"*It means unknown. The Augment could have been in an accident that has left it questionable if they are dead or alive, or they could be utilizing special gear to mask their presence from other players. Some Augments can gain notoriety and rather large targets on their backs from the opposing sides. At your current level, that's probably not something you need to worry about. You still need to make a reputation for yourself first.*"

"Interesting," I said, turning and continuing my trek toward the far end of the Square. As I walked, I noticed a player wearing a bag over his head with the eyes cut out. He was pacing back and forth in front of a bench as he scratched at his arm. I could actually hear him talking, and I could immediately see why Angie had suggested I speak internally.

"I don't get it. Why am I the only one freaking out about all of this?! Those were people! You had me kill actual people!"

"Hmm, his Personal AI must not have activated his Acceptance Matrix during calibration. I hope they don't have to reboot his Array to get it functional, or else this is going to be a really rough time for him."

"Wait, his what?" I stopped in my tracks, looking back to the man clearly having a mental breakdown. He had been coherent enough to get here, but if I had been the one freaking out and everybody else *wasn't,* I'm sure that might have pushed me over the edge too.

"His Acceptance Matrix. It was one of the first things that we loaded during calibration, if you recall. It's a standard feature of the Augmentation Process that opens the Augments' minds to being more likely to be okay with the various new aspects we are rapidly tossing at you. It also saves us a lot of time dealing with panic attacks like that guy is having."

"Is that why—"

"Yes, it's why you haven't felt the need to push me on the Non-Sapient NPCs, or the fact that you have a persistent graphical interface in your vision. While you could turn it off, we generally have found those breakdowns are less than fun for anyone, and overall accomplish nothing, especially when we have gone through all the effort of Augmenting you in the first place."

I felt my gut wrench as I once again stopped in my tracks. I hadn't been able to quite put my finger on it until just now, but it was that same warring feeling I'd had since waking up, and I finally had an explanation for it. I *wanted* to be questioning all of this, to be freaking out about it, but whatever this Matrix was, it was mitigating those feelings, pushing them down, and forcing me to ignore them.

Maybe I should be thankful for it. It was easier than the alternative, which at this point was to drop into a never-ending cycle of existential worrying about what was and wasn't my own feelings.

"That's the spirit, Augment!"

"Yeah, how about we don't do that thing where we respond to my private thoughts when I'm in the middle of questioning my own sanity. Sound good?" I asked, continuing my trek toward the elegant-looking segment.

"Sure thing! If you'd like, you can set my responses to only be activated by directed thoughts or speech toward me. Would you like to enable that now?"

"WAIT, WE COULD HAVE DONE THAT THE WHOLE TIME?!" I practically shouted, and surprisingly found some sort of feedback sound echoing in my head. Angie started to chirp with laughter, taking a few moments to settle down.

"Sometimes, you just have to ask; remember that for the future, Augment, although that setting won't stop me from saying something if it is absolutely *necessary,"* she warned as she finished composing herself. *"Now, the Neutral Shopping Segment is home to just a few shops, as the majority of the Square's features are locked behind team selection. There is a basic equipment shop, though your loot boxes have given you gear that really dwarfs anything you'd be able to afford with your current credit stash. You can acquire the basic disguise kit from this store as well.*

"More importantly, this is where you will find the Registration Center. Here, you will register your official player name and, when you've reached the stage where you have a few friends, you can also register active player squads. Please note that while the name you enter here will become your Augment Identity, public perception or your own intro-ductions can affect what you are recognized as by the NPCs. It doesn't happen often, but every once in a while, you get someone wanting to call themselves Jacked, only for their name to evolve into Jacked Off, as crude as that might be."

"Duly noted. Do I, uh . . . need to go do that before we can do anything else? I haven't exactly come up with a name I really want to use just yet." In truth, I hadn't even given it *any* thought so far, and the one person I really *wanted* to ask for an opinion on it couldn't really be told. Jon would have had at least a dozen ideas locked and loaded the moment I clued him in.

"Nope, while some Augments choose names rather quickly, most take at least a few days to figure that detail out; normally, they get the idea off of something some random civilian shouts at them during one of their early skirmishes. You won't be able to activate any NPC-created quests, but you can still gain experience from completing Crime Alerts and patrol-ling your neighborhood for encounters and street-level crime until you have settled on that."

"Well, it's good to know that's not on that much of a time limit," I said, and almost as if anticipating Angie, I added, *"Although I'm sure there's some secret hidden factor working in the background that's going to be a bitch to deal with the longer I take."*

"Now you're getting it!"

[New Achievement! Off with the Training Wheels!]
You have completed the Onboarding Phase of Infinite Ascension.
Though this is only a **Wood-Level Achievement**, *it is worth celebrating!*
Reward: *You have been granted 3 Drink Tickets, redeem-able at The Common Ground for any beverage.*

"Oh sweet! Free drinks," I said as the tickets materialized into my hand. I exam-ined the three vouchers, each emblazoned with a simple logo for The Common Ground and the words: 1 Free Drink, Top Shelf Excluded. I ignored the fact that the description had *claimed* they were for any beverage and decided to just move on with it. I was a Captain-and-Coke kind of guy, anyway; I didn't have time for expensive booze that I could barely appreciate. With a dissolving light, the tickets returned to my inventory.

"When we got here, it said this was a non-PVP zone; does that mean there's no bar fights or anything like that?"

"They can happen, but it generally results in the offenders having to deal with Critical Level Threats as a punishment, so don't go looking for trouble."

"Good to know. Okay, I'm going to hit the equipment shop really quick to get that disguise kit for these boots, then I want to check that bar out," I said, climbing the small staircase up a level to what was, in reality, an overly ornate strip mall.

While the rest of the Square had been somewhat full, there were only a handful of other people loitering in this relatively small area. Maybe I should have stopped to try and mingle, but I had never been the most social of people; hell, I lived with Jon simply because we had been friends from childhood. Well . . . that and because it made it cheaper to live. I could barely even remember the last time I'd made a new friend, and now really didn't seem like the time.

As I looked along the shopping center, there were signs for three shops. Off to the far side was a single door with a sign labeled Registration, which I made a note to return to later. In the center was a full-paned window with swirling text that read "Slick Louie's Hemming and Other Needlework Needs."

"So, there's a tailor and an equipment shop?"

"Yes, some loot boxes will provide enchanted crafting materials; if brought to one of the tailors here, they can craft or enhance your gear. You should also note that not all crafting material needs to be brought to a tailor to be utilized."

I walked over to the last shop with a simple sign that read "Greg's Gear and Gadgets." A few others exited the shop, and I highlighted a few of them out of curiosity, but they each came up as "???" which I assumed meant that, like me, they weren't registered just yet.

There was the familiar sound of a dinging bell as I pushed the door open and entered a pristinely kept shop. I hadn't been in a lot of gun shops, but I had seen at least a few shows with them, and this reminded me of those, except it was far, far cleaner. The walls were bright white, and a long, glass counter bordered three edges of the room, blocking access from various pieces of gear.

From a small, curtained doorway at the back of the room, a man dressed in a perfectly tailored pinstripe suit entered the space. He had a long, groomed mustache that actually curled up, and he looked at me with a raised brow.

[Gregory!]
Owner of "Greg's Gear and Gadgets."
Non-Sapient NPC.
Gregory does not have a last name; he does not have a family! He lives in the apartment above this shop, and he does one thing very, very well: He tinkers. Gregory's shop is filled with equipment perfect for the beginner Augment, just be careful, you can poke your eye out with some of these toys.

"Welcome, Augment. Please do look around; we've got consumables on the shelves as well as a few specialty items. You don't look quite like a Miscreant, but I warn all new customers: if you attempt to take a product from my store without paying, you'll be hit with a nasty debuff, and the gear will just be flashed back to the shelves." He leaned onto the counter and gestured at a sign on the wall next to his backroom that said "Shoplifters Will Be Exsanguinated." I wasn't exactly sure what his accent was, but it felt . . . high class.

"Um, thanks," I said, walking along the glass counter and checking the back wall. From guns to boots and capes, there really seemed to be a little bit of every-thing. I really wasn't even sure where to start. "I'm looking for some disguise kits? These boots kind of stand out, and my AI told me I couldn't really wear normal shoes now if I wanted to have these on in case of an emergency."

"Ah yes, that is a problem you all tend to run into," Gregory spoke as he knelt behind the counter, returning only a moment later with a small black box. "The disguise kits are good and all, but at the end of the day, you'll still be wearing those boots, and I can guarantee they aren't all that comfortable."

"They aren't *that* bad, and I don't exactly have a huge budget," I shot back as I walked over toward him and eyed the shoebox.

"These are [**Illusory Slippers**], the most comfortable footwear this side of the Mississippi," he announced, and with an almost comical flourish, he pulled the lid from the box.

I couldn't help but laugh as he tossed the lid to the side and revealed a pair of *actual* fuzzy black slippers. They were the kind you'd put on with a pair of big socks when the temperature dipped really low, and I highlighted them out of curiosity.

[Illusory Slippers!]
Equippable Footwear.
Color*: Black, but no one is really going to know that.*
These comfortable, memory-foam-lined shoes offer no stat boosts, but
they do have one very, very nifty feature. **MEMORY. FOAM.**

[Memory Foam!]
This feature, when applied to an equippable item, allows the storage of
three nongame-generated items in the memory of the equipment. Simply
touch the slippers to the chosen item to copy, and voilà! If the stored items
are of the same class of apparel, the item can transform to take on the
appearance and function of the nongenerated item. So if you set it to copy
your sneakers, you can run like normal AND still suck at basketball.
Price: *5500 credits.*

I almost felt my jaw drop at the price. Buying them would mean emptying most of the credits I had received so far, but I could immediately see the benefit.

The disguise kit was necessary to hide the boots because I couldn't use the equipment system to put on or take off my ordinary shoes, but with these, I could swap between them right through my B.E.L.T., and if I was going to have to rebuy the kits over time, that would easily cost more in the long run.

"You know what—you're right; these boots really are pretty uncomfortable. I'll take them," I said, and my credit counter briefly showed a red -5500 before settling at 1100.

"Perfect choice. Now, I do not recommend wearing them until you have saved your desired looks into the Memory Foam; they would look absolutely atrocious with your current getup," Gregory said. Without being able to afford much else, I turned and walked back for the door, waving over my shoulder as I exited back into the crisp afternoon.

[New Achievement! Big Spender!]
You spent more than half your available wallet on your first
visit to the equipment shop. Hell, you didn't even think twice
or check around to see how much other stuff cost . . . or negoti-
ate. We even told you about the conversion rate! Are you just bad
at math, or did you not realize those shoes just cost you $550?
Oh well, we'll never know if you could have got-
ten those slippers a little bit cheaper.
Silver-Level Achievement.
Reward: *You have received a C-tier Loot Box!*

I waved the achievement away as I mentally cursed at the price. She *had* mentioned the conversion rate, but I really hadn't taken the time to do the math. Still, I had made all of that just off of achievements, and it was hard not to be curious with a new loot box in my inventory.

"Can I open loot boxes here, or does it have to be back at my own Safe House? This is a non-PVP zone; that should count, right?"

"That is a very astute and fair question!" Angie chirped as I walked away from Greg's shop. *"Unfortunately, no, it does not. There are locations that you can gain access to in both the Guardian and Miscreant sections where you may do so, but the general Square and Common Ground bar do not count as eligible Safe Houses for that purpose."*

"Eh, I guess that makes sense. Okay, where to next? The bar?" I asked as I hopped down the stairs and looked toward the bar that sat at the exact center of the Square. In a motion that was becoming surprisingly natural, I materialized one of the drink tickets and held it up as I said aloud, "'Cause let's be honest, I could *reeeeally* use a drink right about now."

CHAPTER NINE

*B*efore *you enter, I should make you aware of the special circumstances surrounding the bar.*"

"*You already mentioned the whole 'Don't get into bar fights' rule,*" I replied.

"*No—well, yes, that too, but The Common Ground is one of the first places that was created on the same day the game launched. Because of this, there are a few bugs that have persisted throughout all of the deployed patches and updates, as well as a special rule that applies only to it.*"

"*Oh? Well, let's hear it then,*" I said as I looked at the vast outdoor seating that wrapped around the edge of the building.

"*The Common Ground is the only known location on the planet where you will not have access to me, your wonderful assistant. This is due to an incident that happened in the First Wave that nearly corrupted the entire Personal AI system. The incident is not repeatable, but the patch to fix it required setting a permanent Null Zone over the location it happened, which is, obviously, this bar.*"

"*Well shit, that's not a bug—that's a feature,*" I said, almost eager at the idea of a bit of mental silence. "*But isn't there some stuff you're supposed to explain to me about this place?*"

"*There are some important things, but I'm sure you'll figure it out. You're not that stupid, and there tends to be a little tradition that you'll experience soon enough. I'm sure you'll have your questions when you come back out, and I'll be happy to answer them then.*"

"*Umm . . . Okay then, I guess.*" I briefly looked down at the threshold to the bar before taking that final step in. "*Um . . . Angie?*" I asked cautiously.

I probably looked weird standing there in the doorway, but no one had been waiting to enter behind me, so I took my time. When Angie *didn't* reply, I let out a long, slow sigh and felt as the silence actually set in. After taking in just that brief moment, I took a long look over the building.

The place was extremely reminiscent of a classic sports bar, but instead of sports memorabilia or games dotting the walls and screens, there were pictures of heroes and villains fighting, large versions of famous comic covers, and even what looked like some wreckage from a giant robot placed near the center of the building, with a spiral staircase swirling up and around it, heading to a second floor.

The screens had what looked like cinematic footage of the same variety, with a fight between The First and some group of villains who had been threatening South Africa taking up the largest screen on a big wall at the south end of the building.

There were *at least* a few dozen people scattered around, some sitting at booths or high-top tables by themselves, while others wandered around, looking just as amazed as I was sure I was. They must have been going through the same thing, trying to make heads or tails of this crazy as fuck situation we had found ourselves in.

I felt myself come up short as I stopped in front of a section of wall that stood out from the pristinely placed decor. It was actually almost jarring how much the writing contrasted the rest of the building. More jarring than that was how each line seemed to be written by a different hand.

"The Augment's Code," I murmured to myself as I stepped back to take in the entire wall.

The Augment's Code

1. *We will do our best to never allow a Sapient NPC to be put in harm's way, and when they are, we will do what we must to make it right.*
2. *The world is not worth points for a game. If you threaten the world, we will come for you.*
3. *It is cruel to allow a Non-Sapient to know of the truth behind their existence. We will never disabuse them of what they believe to be reality, and if we must kill them, we will do so with respect.*
4. *We will honor those who have fallen, those who fought to protect our friends, our family, and all other Sapient NPCs who believe us heroes or villains.*
5. *We will do our best to never damage or cause a change to the rules protecting The Common Ground from Personal AIs. We ALL deserve a little mental silence.*
6. *We will never, ever, under any circumstances, use our powers to catch fish in the Mississippi while the sun is setting on a cloudless day. Just . . . Just trust me; it's not a good idea.*

"What . . . What the hell is that last one . . ."

"I hear it's some weird bug in the Augmentation Array. Makes your hands and feet switch places or some shit."

I turned to see a man in a blue-and-silver mask that covered most of his face and an honest-to-God gray cowboy hat walking up. He had an unlabeled beer clutched in his hand as he looked me up and down. "Lemme guess, you're from the new Wave, ain'tcha?"

"Heh, that obvious?"

"Kinda, you guys always look like deers caught in front of a souped-up F-150," he said as he stopped and looked up at the wall, then seemed to catch himself. He swapped the beer to his other hand and held it out for me to shake. "I'm Silver Wrangler. Your PAI won't work, but you can still highlight me and get the public info shit. It's how I can see your name is still a bunch of question marks, which is *also* kinda a dead giveaway for a noob. Just call me Silver; most people do."

"My . . . pie?" I asked, reaching out and shaking his hand.

"Personal AI P-A-I, pie. Come on, you get it."

I highlighted him, just to see that he was right. Instead of Angie's chipper voice, a monotone robotic voice read the description in my head.

[Silver Wrangler, Level 48 Werewolf Hunter]
Squad: *Ours Is the Fury.*

"Um . . . What the hell is a Werewolf Hunter?" I asked before I could stop myself, and he laughed in response.

"It's the name of my powerset; y'know, like how yours is called Perfect Planner."

"Ah, yeah, I guess that makes sense . . . I mean, it makes sense that's what it represents. Although . . . How 'Werewolf Hunter' translates into a powerset . . ." I trailed off as I brought a hand to my chin and thought about it. "What, uh . . . I mean . . . When did you . . ."

"I was in the Seventh Wave about three years ago. Well, y'know, technically still am," he spoke, guessing my question. His attention never left the wall, but he continued on without me having to ask anything else. "The first year of the game is pretty rough, but after that, things get pretty chill overall. Don't let your PAI ever make yah worry that things are always gonna be insane, 'cause they won't. What's yours call itself, anyway?"

"Mine? Aren't they all just called *Angie?*" I asked, and Silver let out a loud guffaw.

"Ah shit, you got one of the ones that likes to fuck with yah!"

"Are . . . Are you telling me that some people don't have to deal with a snarky asshole half the damn time?"

"*Most* people don't, as far as I know. I ain't the type to have learned a whole hell of a lot about them, since it really don't matter that much, but everyone's is just a lil' bit different. The one thing all the types have in common is that they give their player some weirdly stupid acronym that makes up a name for them. Mine is the Digitally Added Virtual Interface Decoder, or David; he's very, uh . . . straightforward."

"Shit, I'd take a utilitarian approach over the constant random thoughts that Angie is practically always spewing at me. But I'm just gonna go ahead and assume I'm stuck with her, right?"

"Yaaaaaahup," Silver laughed, then gestured around the room. "But for what it's worth, you'll find a way to get into a decent rhythm with yours one way or another."

"Oh joy," I drawled almost dryly. I briefly looked at all of the monitors before my attention was pulled back to the out-of-place scrawl on the wall. "So, what is this, anyway? Some sort of mantra for the, what did my PAI call them . . . the Guardian side? I can't imagine folks calling themselves villains or Miscreants or whatever would be so eager to live by a code like this."

"Yah think so, huh?" Silver cocked his brow as he looked over at me. "Believe it or not, not *all* of us Miscreants are as murderous or destructive as folks like Napalm or Bloody Gary."

"Yeah, I'm sure some of them aren't that bad, but—Wait, what?" I said, finding myself unconsciously stepping away from the man.

"Ha, worth it every time. Yeah, bud, I'm a Miscreant. But unless you're trying to fuck with me in South Texas, I ain't gonna go out of my way to stomp some noob back into the ground. I'd get shit for experience, and it would just make me look bad." He laughed, patting me on the shoulder. "That code there, not everyone follows it, but I'd reckon most of us do. It keeps us grounded; keeps us from losing ourselves to these powers. Keeps us from hurting the people who do still matter to us . . ."

"I guess that makes me feel a little bit better. I was half worried I'd have to be fighting a bunch of bloodthirsty assholes who got pulled into this game." Turning away from the Code, I looked for a bar, finding one with an alcohol-lined wall and nodding toward it. Silver waved me forward and followed as I walked.

"Oh, don't stick your head in the sand, bud. Things might calm down afterward, but year one is the bloodiest part of any Wave while the weakest of the players are culled through. I think the most Augments to ever survive it in a Wave is something like just a bit over seven hundred. Only five hundred and fifty-seven of us survived my Wave's first year. Our leaderboard is pretty static now; a couple people swap things here and there, but nobody wants to get into too big of a pissing match."

"Why, uh . . . Why is the first year so bloody, then? Like, what's even the point of the game? I've done the tutorial, but my PAI hasn't exactly been clear with the *why* of it all," I asked, stopping at the bar and grabbing a seat. A moment later, a man who hadn't been there appeared, looking at me expectantly.

"Yo, keep, get me a double Ranch Water," Silver called out, and in a matter of seconds, the bartender had a filled glass topped with a lime wedge ready and handed off. I quickly materialized one of the drink tickets.

"Captain and Coke for me," I said, and a moment later, I was taking a sip, smacking my lips in appreciation as the bartender walked away without a single word.

"They'll talk to you if you're by yourself, in case you're wondering. I've spent more than a few nights talking Chuck's ear off over at that smaller bar by the south entrance of the Grounds just 'cause they actually act like real people, unlike our PAIs, which tend to be laser focused on the game as a whole," he explained as he took a long swig from his drink.

"The game, at least for the most part, is pretty simple. I mean, the overall goal has been the same since the beginning, as far as I can tell: claim the most territories, have the most 'points'—standard issue game shit. But the truth is no one is exactly sure *why*. Our PAIs push us to play, and we dance like monkeys. Either way, it's not like there's anything we can do about it but have as much fun with it as we can. My buddies and I got a nice little foothold that we are starting to look at expanding soon, but we ain't really in a hurry."

"How exactly does that work or, uh . . . Sorry, I guess you're not exactly my game guide or anything," I said, taking another drink. "Why are you telling me all of this, anyway? Especially since you don't even know what side I'm going to be on."

Silver laughed at that, stopping only to throw back the rest of his drink. "Please, you got Guardian written all over you. But it sort of started as one of those tradition things that's evolved since then. We know when the new Waves come in. You know that announcement you got from Axio? He talks to all of us, though to my knowledge, it's like, split between Waves somehow. We all get announcements, but what you and I hear are gonna be two different things, if that makes sense.

"Anyway, he always makes it a point to let us know when the new Wave starts. More or less lets us know there's gonna be fresh meat vying for territory," he explained, waving to the gathering crowd inside the bar. "A bunch of us come here when it happens; help explain as much of this mess as we can to all of you noobs. A sort of a 'pay it forward' thing, y'know?

"It's gotten to the point that even the system has admitted it's just a part of the game now. Anyone who does help 'sufficiently' gets an F-tier loot box, which . . . Wait, you've gotten one of those already, right?"

"Yeah, the randomized one, right? I thought it was gonna be trash, since it's at the bottom of the scale, but the F tier I got earlier gave me these boots, which, while not exactly the best looking, at least aren't without any stats," I replied, gesturing down to them.

"Yeah, I've gotten a few good things out of them. Some really bad things too, but the good things were like, *really* good, so it's worth it to come in and give y'all that little bit of a hand just for the gamble," he explained.

"See, at least that adds up. You're getting *something* out of helping," I said, feeling a small weight lift off my shoulders now that his motivations were clearer.

"We can't really tell you *everything*, though. Kinda like how you can't talk about the game with people outside of it, there are certain things that the system forcefully suppresses, so I wouldn't go asking me *too* many questions," Silver explained, turning and grabbing another drink from the bartender.

"As for the territories . . . Okay, y'know how, like, all the news channels and shit call The First's team the 'Protectors of New York' or how Hellwing was the 'Tyrant of Tokyo' for a while last year? Well, it's sorta like that. You don't necessarily have to have the media blasting you around—hell, me and my buds have done our best to stay mostly off the radar—but the game will give yah a goal around your hometown area; something that's gonna make you want to make it clear to the Non-Sapients, Sapients, and any other players that that place is *yours*. I'd ask your PAI to explain the exacts; they'll give you the rules if you tell them specifically to do so."

"Shit, okay, I guess that sort of makes sense. Hell, my tutorial had me fighting this biker gang that the AI claimed had been terrorizing He—uh . . . my neighborhood," I finished, catching myself as I thought about it, Angie's reminder about the Secret Identity Protocol briefly popping into my head.

Silver let out another laugh as he drank down his second drink in a single long gulp.

"It's all good, bud. It's why I haven't told you *where* in Texas I'm from. Your gut instinct's right: keep the personal shit to yourself, even when you do get team members; although, granted, once you start making a name for yourself as a Guardian, I'm sure it'll probably be pretty damn easy to figure out where you're from. Y'all tend to soak up the spotlight, even if yah don't want it.

"Anyway, now that the loot box has landed in my B.E.L.T., I've done my duty and explained at least a *little* bit of this shit to a noob. Oh, and here's a freebie: Axio does an 'end of the day' report most days too. It tends to happen at five p.m. in Texas. I'm sure you can do the math to figure out when it happens where you're at."

"Shit, good to know. I guess that's more than I was really expecting anyway; thanks for that." I looked down at the remains of my drink. "Is there like, a Friends List or something? Or hell, any sort of messaging system?"

"Yeah, there's a bunch of stuff like that. Chat features, the Squad system, and a couple of other things too. Most are standard game things, so they are useful but not all that exciting. That said, I'd recommend getting the phone upgrade for your HUD as soon as yah can. I broke like, four phones my first few weeks. Most of it is locked behind name registration, though," Silver explained.

"Don't go dwelling on it too long, or else yah might end up just choosing a couple of words that happen to represent your powers. I mean, it worked out for me, I love my name, but there's also folks like "Ice Thrower"—who is a hell of a fighter, by the way; he's just boring as a bag of bricks. I'm here most nights, though, and there's a hell of a party after the first culling event y'all are gonna go through. Pick the right side, bud; there's plenty of fun to be had when you're a little bit bad."

He didn't wait any longer as he headed off, walking toward one of the exits and patting a few other people on the back as he passed them. I wasn't exactly sure what to do next. I knew I couldn't stay here the whole night just to escape Angie, but I felt like I was still missing something. The screens seemed to be littered with rankings from the various Waves, though there was one in particular that caught my attention.

It was labeled Tenth Wave, which I immediately recognized as mine from Axio's announcement. There wasn't *much* information on it, but to my surprise, the list *wasn't* empty.

Tenth Wave

1. **Tempest's Wrath** *(Level 5) Miscreant — Territories: 1;
    Score: 250 Points*

"Shit, someone isn't wasting any time," I muttered before I quickly swallowed the last of my drink.

I couldn't help but feel a mix of apprehension and . . . maybe giddiness as I looked at the screen. There was still so much I didn't know, even with Silver's helpfulness, but his warning about the reality of the bloody first year stayed with me as I headed for the door. I didn't want to die, though I think most people felt that way on a day-to-day basis, but I couldn't escape that possible reality of this game.

I dropped the drink back onto the bar and looked toward the door. As much as I had enjoyed the mental silence, this place wasn't going anywhere, and I really needed to get Angie to start answering some of my questions.

CHAPTER TEN

Nate Mercer's Apartment, Safe House. Hell's Kitchen, NYC
Neighborhood: *Unclaimed*
City: *Claimed by Squad:* **The Paragons of Justice**

Being able to just unequip my boots *was* actually a hell of a perk, and as I plopped down onto my bed with a heavy *thud*, my boots disappeared in a flash of light.

"Is The Common Ground the only place you can see all those leaderboards? How much do they even matter?" I asked, looking up at a clock I kept on the wall. If Silver was right, Axio would be making an announcement soon.

"It depends on the leaderboard! For now, the only one you can access while outside of The Common Ground is your Wave Leaderboard, and that's only while you are within a Safe Zone such as Sanctuary Square or your Safe House," Angie chirped as a window expanded in my vision.

Tenth Wave

1. **Tempest's Wrath** *(Level 5) Miscreant — Territories: 2; Score: 500 Points*

"Holy crap, how has that guy already claimed another territory?" It had taken me a few hours just to get through the tutorial alone. I couldn't even begin to fathom how this Tempest's Wrath had already managed to take control of multiple areas.

"Claiming territories is technically easier for Miscreants, especially those with particularly destructive powersets. I cannot say for sure until there is more data in case it differs from past Waves, but two hundred and fifty points is generally the lowest amount you can receive for a single territory. These low-scoring regions are normally a small town or neighborhood that is minimally considered a community. These points are . . . Ah, you know what, I'll just let the man himself explain."

I was about to ask what she meant when my clock ticked over and the TV I had seated on top of the dresser opposite of my bed clicked on. There was a logo I had never seen before, but common sense suggested it had to be for the game. It was spinning, and what looked like a loading bar appeared beneath it, rapidly ticking up to full. I looked from the TV over to the remote only a foot away from it on the dresser and then back at the screen.

"Ummm . . ."

"Gooooood Evening, Augments! We have officially reached six hours post commencement, and boy oh boy have you guys already been entertaining! There have been 943 completed tutorials, and amazingly, seventeen of you have *already* exited the game. For some of them, it's really their own fault. I mean . . . who the hell thought it was a good idea to pick the power to emit light from their whole body as a primary power?! I mean, I know we're the ones who put it in the game in the first place, but seriously, we never thought anyone would actually pick it.

"Also, I see you, Dr. Noodle; that is an absolutely terrible name, and I intend to have a Major Level Threat sent your way tomorrow morning. I have to draw the line somewhere, and claiming a doctorate without submitting and defending a valid thesis is where it is, goddammit!"

The screen came to life as a news report clicked on, showcasing a man throwing fireballs ducking for cover in a grocery store; then the screen split, and another news report appeared, a woman standing with a wicked smile cutting across her face as her eyes glowed and lightning struck, her body being replaced with a mass of electrical energy.

The screens continued to split, with more and more news reports being showcased: a lady turning into a two-headed beast, a man spitting what looked like acid at a bank vault—there was even an older man with an impossibly bushy mustache that was equal parts confusing and amazing to watch. The hair stretched out into honest-to-God fists that smashed into a police officer trying to approach him.

"Many of you have already begun to make waves in your local communities, but I've been doing some thinking here today. You see, that little loophole that added an Augment to this year's Wave *also* happened to leave a little backdoor for me, and oooooh boy, I've been tinkering." Axio let out a laugh that sent a bit of a chill down my spine.

"As I've been watching all of you do the same boring tutorials that we've been throwing at you Augments year after year since this all started, I have to admit . . . I can do better. Oh, I can do so much better than this basic game that you Augments have all been stuck playing for the last decade.

"See, we've been going about this all wrong, keeping all of you separated by years and trying to keep things 'fair' and 'balanced,' giving you guys several months at a time to get to the next phase of the project, only setting you all on the task of taking over land—No, that's not going to get us anywhere.

"You're all getting soft; you're getting used to the pointless squabbles over territory and merch sales, and we just aren't . . . we just aren't . . . Ahhh, it's all just so pointless. None of you are pushing yourselves; all of the Waves that came before this one, they've just decided to 'get by,' and I just can't stand it."

"What is—"

"*Shh,*" Angie said quickly. I felt my body buzzing with a mixture of fear and anticipation.

"The points given for territories will continue. If your Personal AIs haven't explained it to you yet, well, stop slacking and start asking them the right questions already. More importantly, however, is that additional points will start to be granted to *all* players for additional activities: defeating other Augments, stopping kaiju—Oh! I should tell you, there's kaiju now; the NPCs are going to freak out when they become collateral damage to those monsters, and that's not even getting started on the invasion coming in . . . You know what, maybe I won't spoil that just yet.

"Additionally, you will be given increased points for defeating and taking territory from higher-leveled Augments; those slouches have had it too easy for far too long. Needless to say, there are so, so many more new ways to gain points. If you need inspiration, just look at Tempest's Wrath; so far, she's my favorite from this Wave. Don't you worry, Tempest, your point total will reflect your real achievement after the end of my announcement.

"Point gains will be retroactive for this and all former Waves for activities completed within *only* the last week. Oh, and Tempest? I hope you enjoy that S-tier loot box you received; you earned it. With that, I am officially opening up Phase One of the Tenth Wave," Axio said, and the reel of news footage vanished to be replaced with a countdown labeled [**4D:00H:00M:00S**].

There was almost a giddiness in the AIs voice as he announced this, and I couldn't help but wonder what the hell whoever created this thing was thinking.

"All Tenth Wave Augments will have *just* four days to reach ten thousand points. Those of you who have not reached this milestone by the end of this timer will immediately be faced with a Critical Level Threat. This will be guaranteed to be at a *minimum* a level seventy-five Elite, though that may change depending on how many of you fail this little task.

"Your Personal AIs are now being updated with a full list of the scoring system, though access to it will initially be limited. Leaderboards will also be updated to better represent the data that I think is far more important to you. Players in the Top Ten at the end of Phase One will be granted an S-tier loot box.

"That's all for now. Don't go worrying your little heads too much; it's not just the points I'm going to be changing up this year. Good luck, Augments."

There was a click as Axio's voice faded and the leaderboard popped back into my vision, now updated with not only different information but a lot more lines.

Tenth Wave

Guardians: *415*   **Miscreants:** *528*

1. **Tempest's Wrath** *(Level 5 Thunder God) Miscreant —*
   6535 Points
2. **Freakenstein** *(Level 3 Patchwork Armorer) Miscreant —*
   850 Points

3. **Pretty Pink Warthog** *(Level 3 Berserking Boar) Guardian*
   — 750 Points
4. **Sound Off** *(Level 3 Midnight DJ) Miscreant — 600 Points*
5. **???** *(Level 3 ???) Guardian — 500 Points*
6. **???** *(Level 3 ???) Miscreant — 415 Points*
7. **???** *(Level 3 ???) Miscreant — 350 Points*
8. **???** *(Level 2 ???) Miscreant — 85 Points*
9. **???** *(Level 2 ???) Guardian — 65 Points*
10. **???** *(Level 2 ???) Miscreant — 50 Points*

"Holy shit . . . How—"

[System Updated!]
*Point-scoring events updated from 1 Activity to 3 Known
Activities and 9,997 Unknown Activities.*

Most of the list was filled with line after line of question marks, but at the top I was given a list of three items labeled as "Basic."

*[***Claim Territories****: 250 to 50000 Points (Dependent on Size)]*
*[***Arrest Sapient Augment****: 500 to 5000 Points*
(Dependent on Level Difference)]
*[***Kill Sapient Augment****: 1000 to 10000 Points*
(Dependent on Level Difference)]

"Seriously? That's it?! What the hell does it mean 9,997 *unknown* activities—and for the love of God don't say 'It means unknown, Augment,'" I said, leaning forward and putting my head in my hands.

"I'm sorry, Augment; it would seem Axio isn't quite giving us an exact list. The items are locked behind discovery at this point, but given the sheer number, I'd assume many standard activities will result in points."

"Cool . . . Okay, so I need to collect points in the next few days; otherwise, I'm going to probably get steamrolled and die, am I understanding that correctly?" I asked, rubbing my temples.

"Pretty much spot-on, yup!"

"Awesome. And that whole Acceptance Matrix thing is keeping me from a complete and total panic attack about that fact, right?"

"Also spot-on! You're getting pretty good at repeating things!"

I let out a long sigh. Silver might have thought his AI was boring for being straightforward, but I'd trade him in a heartbeat.

"Okay, can you at least explain how claiming territories works? Not just theoretical; give me the actual rules of the game on how making a claim works."

"I thought you'd never ask!" Angie chirped happily. *"Now, to start, territories come in a rather wide range of sizes, varieties, and importance. There are multiple types*

within each level. A basic example of the smallest tier of territories would be your Hell's Kitchen: Neighborhood. Territory types continue all the way up to Planet level, with nothing rivaling that for points.

"Each of these territories are also separated into sizes, so an extra-small Neighborhood would be worth much less than an extra-large. In order to claim a territory, you must make a vocal claim that a minimum of ten NPCs hear, though this number requirement varies the larger the territory you wish to claim becomes, and larger territories require a larger reputation to claim. You do not have to say, 'I claim this region,' but you have to make an active association between the region and yourself.

"Now, if there is an existing NPC group in the region, the territory will become 'Contested,' and while you will still have an active claim on the region, you will only receive half points for the claim. Other players may also contest your claim, but you probably won't deal with that anytime soon, and I will make it a point to explain that situation when it occurs.

"Please note you must have a Name that NPCs will recognize you as in order to stake your claim; if you give them a name prior to visiting the Registration Center, your claim will be marked as 'Tentative' until you register your name. While the territory will be 'officially' marked as yours if it was unclaimed, if you choose to use a name other than the one you used to make your territory claim, your claim will be considered void."

"Okay, cool. Got it. That's . . . complex, but not *that* complex," I replied before feeling my stomach rumble. "Now, are you going to yell at me if I take an actual break and go get some dinner? 'Cause it feels like I haven't eaten in a week."

"No, Augment, I won't yell at you, but I will *remind you that just because you're not in your gear doesn't mean you're not playing the game. The chosen story for you will progress, regardless of your direct involvement. I bet Lieutenant Nester will be* just *fine if you leave him waiting."*

"Yeesh, he'll be fine for a night. It's not like I've picked a name yet; he's not going to talk to me until I do that. And as far as I can tell, this game isn't getting rid of my hunger factor at all," I said.

"Actually, there are Safe House upgrades that do in fact provide food and drink bonuses, but you're a long way off from those," Angie replied.

"Huh, well, that's actually pretty cool. Not at all useful at this very moment, but still cool." I was about to grab my Converse when a thought crossed my mind. With a quick flick through my B.E.L.T., the Illusory Slippers appeared in my hands. "Okay, I just have to . . ." I started to mutter. I barely touched the slippers to my Converse when a flash of light passed over them, leaving an exact replica of my shoes in their place.

Using the Fast Equip option, the shoes appeared on my feet.

"You said something about equipment readying, right? I don't exactly want to be walking around with this jacket and the bracers on, so what do I need to do?" I asked, and Angie quickly pulled up a new screen with the silhouette of a person, several lines poking out to empty equipment boxes.

"It's very simple; you'll assign items to each of these slots. There are two tabs: Active and Inactive. I recommend setting your items for these now. Your Inactive tab will act as your 'idle' outfit, perfect for those overpriced slippers of yours. In contrast, your Active tab is where you'll set your costume items into, and will trigger if you either choose to activate the tab or you willingly *choose to enter a combat scenario. This is to prevent you from automatically having your combat gear activated if you are trying to remain incognito."*

"That's good," I said. The more I used the interface, the easier it became, and I quickly navigated through the tabs. I only had a few items to assign, and after just a minute, I was ready to stretch my legs. "So, I just have to . . ." I trailed off. I didn't need to open the Readying screen; just thinking of the active gear, my outfit flashed, and my jacket, mask, bracers, and boots were all suddenly on. With another thought, it changed back to my inactive outfit, the ratty-looking Converse back on my feet.

[New Achievement! Fashionista!]
Well, look at you, Mr. Versatile. Now you can effortlessly switch between your combat gear and your 'going out' outfit. Now you're always ready to save the world or dazzle at a cocktail party (though, let's be honest, your style could still use some serious help).
Wood-Level Achievement.
Reward: *You have received a C-tier Loot Box!*

I stopped at the desk, mentally pulling it and the C tier I had gotten from purchasing my shoes out of my inventory. From the two boxes I received five hundred and fifty credits, another How the Hell Does This Fool Anybody? mask, though this one had the color listed as "Lime," and . . . a book. I materialized it onto the desk, and it looked just like one of those *for Dummies* books, though I could have almost sworn the guy on the cover looked like a cartoon version of myself.

[*Mirage and Shine!*]
Did you ever wonder why people think they see things when it gets really hot? I mean, of course you've heard of mirages, but do you actually know how they work? Well, now you do! Not sure why this is particularly useful knowledge, but hey, that's for you to figure out.

"That's . . . interesting," I said as I looked at it, flipping the cover open. I expected the inside to be filled with nothing but illegible scrawl, but it was actually filled cover to cover with images of light patterns and some sort of math that I was pretty sure didn't make sense in context but was also confident I couldn't tell you why it was wrong either.

I didn't actually have to read anything, because as I turned to the last page, the item dissolved and the text **[Optical Refraction Knowledge—Level 3]** appeared and then faded into nothing. "Is there anywhere I can see a list of all these skills?"

"I thought you wanted to go get something to eat?" Angie teased, and I couldn't help but laugh. I pulled my door open and headed for the apartment's exit.

"I do and I am, doesn't mean I can't ask anyway."

"If you open your character sheet and select stats, it will give you a full list of your stats. This is not a comprehensive *list, because why the hell would we care how good you are at tying your shoelaces. Now,* bondage *tying? We do* track that.*"*

The stairway was empty as I climbed down the few flights to the ground floor. Jon was nowhere to be found, and since he hadn't been on the couch playing *Augment Fighter 4*, it was almost a guarantee he was down at the corner diner. As I headed out the front door, I opened my character sheet and selected the tab labeled Stats.

I wasn't sure what I was expecting, but it certainly wasn't seeing "Page 1 of 324" at the bottom of the screen. I closed it out, deciding I'd look through that later, when I wasn't walking down the street.

Sure enough, Jon was camped out in his usual booth at the back of the deli/ diner combo named Tio's, only a block and a half away from our building. It was run by a couple who simultaneously made the best matzo ball soup *and* Cuban sandwich in the city. Or at least so they claimed. All I knew was they were cheap and the in-house hot sauce they made was killer.

"The man still lives!" Jon exclaimed with a cheer that made me feel awkward as I dropped into his booth. He had a tablet set on the table and his feet up on the seat as he gestured at the wall behind me. "You have got to see this; it's been all over the news since, like, five."

I turned to look at an LCD mounted in the corner of the shop and almost felt my stomach drop. Maybe I should have been expecting it—hell, I had just seen a veritable montage of them, after all—but there was something unsettling about it all the same.

[New Achievement! I'm on the News!]
*You have been featured on the local news! If only you had a more memorable look, maybe you'd start to get a following. Oh well, it's at least a start . . .
And I'm sure you'll really stand out with that tacky orange jacket next time.*
Silver-Level Achievement.
Reward: *You have received a B-tier Loot Box!
Maybe you'll get something to really give you a unique look
instead of looking like you're some weird Naruto knockoff.*

The channel didn't even show their anchor, as the screen was filled with just so, so much footage. Between phone cameras, a bit of the bank's security cameras, and shots that I couldn't prove came from nowhere but certainly seemed like they came from nowhere, I watched as I took down the entire gang on the screen, strategic pixelation blocking the worst of the gore with a "Warning: Graphic Footage" label.

The News banner read "Hell's Kitchen Brawl! A Brutal Bank Beatdown by an Unknown Augment."

"We finally got a hometown defender of our own. I wonder what this dude is calling himself," Jon said as his hand dove into a bag of chips before reaching for his tablet. "There's already some chatter over on both the Hell's Kitchen and the Watch subreddits; one dude claimed he was at the bank when the whole thing went down."

This got my attention, and I stopped watching the TV to turn and drop into the seat opposite him.

"Oh yeah? What's he saying?"

"Well, he said the dude was pretty quick on his feet, though most of what seemed to happen was just really bad luck for the guys he was fighting. According to him, there was a weird moment when all the sound in the room just disappeared," Jon said as he handed me his tablet. It was a pretty basic write up; hell, anyone could have put it together just by watching the news reports. But the muting? That was specific. "But what the hell does that mean? Luck and Audio Control? That can't be this dude's *only* powers. I don't think it would explain how the one dude's gun went off."

"His gun? Shit, how much theorizing is happening off this one bank robbery?"

"A shit ton, honestly. You know how the Augment Trackers are; anytime a new one crops up, people can't help but try to analyze every last bit of info they can get. There are entire forums dedicated to power scaling those guys; it's actually really interesting stuff.

"Most of the folks in the bank got at least some bit of the fight on camera, so for this guy, there's at least a little bit to go on right now. There was even one video where the dude said some cheesy-as-hell line about luck, which, I mean, that basically has to confirm his powers are something luck based, or that'd be my guess. I mean, half the time, the Augments seem to talk like they are out of a Saturday morning cartoon from the fifties." Jon was practically buzzing as he talked, and I once again found myself wishing I could just tell him about my powers.

I knew how much easier my life would be if I could just fill him in. But at the same time, I didn't doubt Angie's warning about my Secret Identity, and if I could help it, I wasn't going to let Jon get used like a prop in some stupid game. While I didn't have a choice in playing, I certainly wouldn't take away someone else's choice.

Still, there were so many questions I had for him, and—A sudden bolt of inspiration hit me as a thought occurred to me. I was pretty sure he'd only be subject to consequences of the Secret Identity rule if he knew that it was *me* specifically who had powers. As long as I could pretend that this was someone else, maybe I could get his thoughts on my abilities.

I almost wanted to laugh, but I suppressed it behind a cough. It was a loophole. And that was something I could work with.

CHAPTER ELEVEN

I swiped through an entire page of videos taken during the fight at the bank on Jon's tablet as he sat scrolling through his own laptop.

Unlike Jon, before I got pulled into this, I didn't exactly feel like I was like most other people my age. I thought the Augments were interesting, but unlike many of the crowds who gathered on the outskirts of fights, I largely just wanted to stay out of their way. Sure, I knew about the big guys, but I didn't read the comics or look up random fights online just to see who won, or get super excited every time a new one suddenly cropped up. And that was something Jon knew *very* well about me.

So, if I suddenly named exactly what the power was and then somehow it leaked that that's exactly what this guy's . . . *my* . . . powerset was, it wouldn't take Jon long to put two and two together. While I wasn't necessarily sure if that would constitute as breaking the rule, it wasn't a risk I was quite ready to take. I had to find something in one of the videos that I could use, and make it seem like I was just pointing it out.

"You could just tell him about your powers and deal with the consequences if it's so important to get his opinion. Not sure why you need it, though; he's cute and all, but it's not like he could possibly know what he's talking about," Angie chirped.

"Not now, Angie," I shot back, and I could actually hear her harrumph in response.

"It's a real shame this dude's powers aren't all that flashy," Jon said. He was leaning forward and seemed to be squinting as he took in something on his screen. "He landed some good punches, but they didn't exactly look like they were enhanced, and other than the sound thing, I'm not . . . Hmm, what's happening with this dude's shirt?"

I looked over to him and waited for a response, but he just shook his head. With a few quick clicks on his keyboard, a link was airdropped onto the tablet. It wasn't a good shot, the person holding their phone was probably (rightfully) shaking as he tried to sneak the camera around the edge of the table, but he still caught as my Weighted Clothes ability caused the grunt to be crushed to the ground.

"It kind of looks like it just suddenly got, like, really heavy or something," I said, and Angie groaned again.

"Act better."

"Seriously, Angie. Not. Now."

"I'm just saying, if you want Mr. Blue Eyes to believe you, maybe be more convincing than 'really heavy or something,'" she shot back quickly, and I had to stop myself from groaning.

"Hmm, I think you're right," Jon said as he squinted at the screen. "Still, that doesn't add a whole lot either. It could be something gravity related, or he could be telekinetic. That one seems the most likely, since that one gun also fired when the dude's finger was nowhere near the trigger. As much as I hate to admit it, we are probably SOL until this guy shows up again. You can *definitely* tell he's fresh; not just going off the fact that he's running around in a ski mask, but like, there's no polish."

"Polish?" I asked, leaning back against the booth and trying my best not to feel . . . offended? My hand ran across the bottom of the seat as I considered what he was saying, and my fingers briefly touched a piece of dried but still sticky gum. I instinctively pulled my hand away, wiping it on my pant legs and feeling slightly annoyed by the bit of tackiness that remained on my fingers.

A thought suddenly crossed my mind, and I did a search on the tablet, finding what I was looking for rather quickly before I looked back over to Jon. "Think you can explain?"

"Yeah, like . . . Okay, this is gonna sound weird, but try to stay with me, got it?" He straightened up in his seat.

"You know me, I can handle weird," I replied with a wry grin but finally stopped to take a bite out of the Cuban that Jon had run up to order for me.

"Okay . . . So, you know how in *Augment Fighter 4* you can do combos and stuff? Well, it's like that," he explained. "Well . . . okay, it's not like an exact one for one or anything, but there are more than a few Augments who do skills or moves that get literally translated right into the game. Like The First, for example. One of his signature moves is called Over Pressurized. He basically comes in hot from up high and hits the ground, which immediately sends out a big wave of pressure. Hell, you should remember that, right?"

"Yeah, it knocked the wind right out of me," I said as I closed the browser and looked back over to Jon.

"Well, that move is in *AF4*, like almost one for one. And sure, if it was just The First, that would be one thing—he's famous as all hell. But like, you can literally match up moves in the game right to video footage of the different heroes and villains. If I didn't know that the Augments have better things to do with their time, I'd say it's almost like they put motion controls on them just to get the combos to match up perfectly."

"Well, shit . . . it's almost like they *are* just playing a game, then . . ." I said before I could stop myself. I *expected* to get suppressed. Other than when I had first gotten prompted about the rule, I hadn't risked mentioning the game, since I had just assumed it would be futile. Angie *had*, after all, warned me that it would just get muted.

Yet, somehow, I hadn't been suppressed . . . I had to test it, just to make sure, and as I opened my mouth to say, "I'm actually playing it with them," a big red warning flashed across my vision.

[Dialogue Suppressed!]
This NPC is not authorized to know about the existence of Infinite Ascension. Claiming your involvement would be a clear violation of this rule. Further attempts to reveal your involvement in the game will result in the immediate summoning of a Level 100 Elite NPC.

"So why did that get suppressed?" Maybe it was dumb to ask, but I felt like I needed to know, especially as I was trying to find the right line to walk without risking Jon's life.

"That's . . . Hmm, I'm actually not sure! While I am your Personal AI, I'm not the one who controls the suppression system. In fact, the only thing I'm really designed to do initially is act as an interface and narrative assistant, as well as providing perfectly *detailed explanations about the world around you. However, I can* be upgraded with additional features in time," Angie explained. *"It would seem Axio determined your 'theoretical' didn't constitute breaking the rule, but I'd advise you not to push your luck* too far."

"I mean, that's as fair of a guess as any of the shit we've heard, though it is kind of insane . . . and that's when we're talking about people who literally break the laws of physics. Anyway, not the point," Jon continued, closing his laptop. "This new guy, he doesn't have any combos. Like, yeah, he turned the sound off and then made the one guy get crushed to the ground, but it wasn't in unison. He was kind of just throwing whatever he could and hoping for the best. I mean, really watching the fight, assuming his powerset is something luck based, that's really what seemed to get him through it all. There was just, well, y'know . . ."

"No polish . . ." I finished for him as he trailed off. I had really thought I had found a way to get Jon's opinion on all of this, but clearly, there just wasn't enough information that we could "stumble" on for us to have a conversation about it just yet. "Okay, I think I see what you mean. So, what, you think we can't figure out what his power is yet because he's just running around like a chicken with his head cut off . . . so to speak?"

"Yeah, more or less," Jon replied. "I definitely hope he figures it out, though; I'd love to have a local dude to be cheering on. But *ugh*, I still wish I could have gotten powers myself. What's a dude gotta do to be Augmented? Friggin' missed the selection window this year already . . ."

"Huh? Selection window?" I found myself perking up at this. Sure, there was the forum for *Infinite Ascension*, but it was just a place for people longing for a game that—Well, yes, I guess it *did* exist, but not in any form they could have ever dreamed of . . . right? No, if that's what Jon had been following all this time, I was sure he would have told me about it ages ago.

"Oh, sorry. I know you're not as into all this, but I'm *pretty* deep down the rabbit hole at this point," he explained, then took what felt like the longest sip of his drink. "Anyway, there's like, tons of video essays, theories, and stuff about it if you really want a big breakdown, but the gist of it is that there's this, like, window every year where new Augments appear. It doesn't seem to happen at the same time every single year, but there's always a sign about a week before it happens."

"Oh, maybe this cutie does know a thing or two," Angie spoke, her voice practically purring. I hadn't taken the bait the first few times, but apparently, this was something I was going to have to address.

"Okay, is this seriously going to be a thing? You're an AI, you can't actually think he's cute, right?"

"I can and I do; don't kink shame me."

"That's not—You know what, never mind," I responded with a sigh before adding, *"Not even sure what the hell I was expecting."*

"Just shush and let me enjoy the eye candy, okay?"

"So, what's the sign, then?" I asked, trying to ignore as Angie started to *purr* in the back of my head. I tried to think back to the night of my accident, trying to see if there might have been a sign that I had just missed. In truth, so much of it was a haze up until The First appeared.

"Okay, so you know how the Array is normally just like, there, right? Maybe it flashes a few lights or glows bright over areas where big fights are happening, but otherwise, it mostly stays dark, right?"

"Sure, I guess so?"

"Well, see . . . Okay, and this is where it gets a bit weird, but like . . . did you happen to notice last week, the Array was sort of periodically flashing—"

"Holy shit, yeah! It *was* flashing blue that night," I cut him off before I could stop myself, the memory suddenly becoming clear. Jon was looking at me curiously as I tried to calm myself down. "Er, I mean, that was the night of the accident; it's all kinda seared into my brain. I was walking toward the blockade and saw one of the nodes right above the city pulsing blue before it went red and stopped completely. Shit, if that's the pattern, why haven't the big channels and all that started to talk about it?"

"Timing, mostly. The Array doesn't flash for the same amount of time every year. A few years, it flashed for a week; there were two years that it flashed for over a month, and this year . . . this year, it only flashed like that for about ten hours. Honestly, most people on the forums were just thinking it was a false start until, well . . ." He gestured at his laptop and the tablet. "Obviously, there's some new Augments running around.

"You'd think at least *someone* in the media would have at the very least picked up on that. Personally, and I know it's gonna make me sound like a crazy conspiracy theorist that's yelling about government censorship, but like . . . come on, right? Someone's gotta be forcing them not to mention this pretty obvious detail."

"Huh," I said, stalling as I took another bite from my sandwich.

"Yeah, I know it's crazy, but I promise the evidence is there, though at the end of the day it doesn't matter that much. Whatever happens to get these new guys selected, clearly, I missed out yet again," Jon said, obviously dejected, and I continued to chew, unable to find anything else to say.

A notification popped up in the corner of my vision reading **[Crime Alert!]** in flashing text.

"What the hell is that?"

"Okay, seriously, Augment, you can read, right? It's a Criiiiiiiiiime. Aleeeeeeeeeeeert," Angie responded, overly drawing out the words in a way only someone who didn't need to breathe could do.

"Yeah, but what does that mean? I thought I wouldn't get more missions until I had a name?" I highlighted the box on my screen.

[Crime Alert! Three Men and a Lady!]
Uh-oh, three of the Hell's Kitchen Vipers have been spotted in your vicin-
ity, and it looks like there's a vulnerable little old lady who's about to
be mugged by those mean bikers once they get there! If you put down
that sandwich and get moving, you might just make it in time to inter-
cept them before they can steal her cash and her marbled rye.
Reward: *You will receive a Reputation Boost and a B-tier Loot Box for stop-*
ping this crime. This crime has a 10-minute time limit startiiiiiiiiiiiing, now.

A timer took the alert's place and started to rapidly click down as I felt my grip on the remainder of my sandwich tighten. I didn't *have* to address this . . . Logically, I knew that. I could sit right here on my ass and—

A realization came to mind as I thought about the loophole I was trying to exploit. Sure, so far, we hadn't been able to discuss my powers in depth, since we just had this one fight that had found its way online. But logically, there just needed to be more information that he could see, and what would be a better opportunity than a few grunts literally created for me to fight?

"Oh, I completely forgot. I ran into Mr. Russo on my way home earlier; he said they were cleaning the building over on 56th tonight. He assumed I was still recovering but said that if I wanted to pop by, we could talk about me keeping my job when I was ready to go," I said as I got to my feet and waved the last bite of the sandwich at him before finishing it off. "Thanks for this; I'll catch yah at home later."

Jon watched me for just a moment before his lip turned up into a smile. "Try not to get in the middle of an Augment fight this time."

"Yeah, that would be just my luck," I laughed as I turned, but before I could exit, a thought came to mind. "Hey, do you have a piece of gum?"

Jon reached into his backpack and pulled out a pack, offering me a stick that I grabbed with a smile. "It ain't brushing, but it's something, right?" I said with a laugh before I headed for the exit. Once outside, I looked around, trying to see if there was anything, an indicator or something, that could lead me to the crime. *"Shouldn't there be, like, a waypoint or something?"*

"For what?"

"For . . . the Crime Alert? This is a game, isn't it?"

"Ohhhh, yes, sorry. Mini map upgrades are available which would provide detailed information on your location; however, you do not currently have one. You'll have to listen for clues. That said, Crime Alerts and Mission Notifications will only occur if you could logistically arrive at the scene in time to prevent it, and these early ones are never that hard to find. So, what's the gum for?"

Okay . . . I just had to look for clues. Ignoring Angie, I started to walk toward 56th, where I said I was going already. Hopefully, it wasn't the other—

There was the roar of engines as several bikers ripped around the corner just a block ahead of me and came screeching to a halt. Sure enough, there was an elderly lady practically alone on the sidewalk, slowly making her way along with a single grocery bag and her purse slung over her shoulder.

"Okay, so it's going to be like that, then? Just throwing it right out in the open?"

"Hey, Axio's the one in charge, don't look at me about where these guys show up," Angie said, the timer ticking down past seven minutes. *"But like I said, this is still the early stages. The goal is to both help you get stronger and get you some notoriety with the public, not to make you have to play super detective . . . Actually, hmm, wait, no . . . we do have some super detective missions too; we just never lead with them unless the Augment needs that style of intro. The punchy way is always the easier way to get you Goody Two-shoe types into the ebb and flow of it all, so the system tends to lean into that one when we can."*

I had only made it a block away, but that was the good thing about living in New York: there was always an alley to slip in. There were still people on the streets, and with the Secret Identity rule, I couldn't risk being seen and associated with my costume just yet, even if it was apparently just a bright orange jacket, some spikey bracers, and white boots.

I dipped behind a trash can, waited for just a minute to make sure no one had noticed, and then activated my equipment. There was a flash of light, and I could feel the weight of my jacket as it fell onto my shoulders.

"It's the Acceptance Matrix thing that's making me just roll with all of this, right?"

"It is, yes, why do you ask?" Angie mused.

"No reason. It's just . . . nice, is all. Kinda makes this whole thing a little bit easier," I flexed my hands, and my knuckles cracked. *"Guess it's time to stop that little old lady from getting mugged . . ."*

"Top ten things you never thought you'd say?"

"Given the fact that before today I've gotten into maybe a single fight in my life, I'd say top five is more like it," I replied with a laugh before stepping out onto the sidewalk. The bikers were starting to creep up on the woman, and that meant it was show time.

For once in my life, I really hoped there were some cameras nearby.

CHAPTER TWELVE

55th and Ninth, Street Sidewalk. Hell's Kitchen, NYC
Neighborhood: *Unclaimed*
City: *Claimed by Squad:* **The Paragons of Justice**

You know, it ain't really neighborly of you gentlemen to be trying to rob this nice lady," I called out, approaching the three men just as they began to surround the elderly woman.

People in New York had a tendency to keep their heads down. If you weren't involved, it was generally better to stay out of it, especially if you didn't want to end up late for work . . . Or, you know . . . crushed by a dumpster.

"You're never going to let that go, are you?"

"SERIOUSLY?! What do you think?" I shot back, trying not to let my annoyance break the aura of confidence I was attempting to maintain as I stared the bikers down.

Some of this attitude had gotten worse when the Augments appeared. The idea of being a Good Samaritan became harder and harder because you just didn't know if the problem you were trying to get in the middle of had an Augment involved. Because seriously, what the hell was a regular human going to do against someone who considered the laws of physics a mere suggestion? And while now I at least knew that Augments couldn't just be in normal street clothes because of the game's Secret Identity rule, that was *far* from common knowledge. That said, the Augments did prompt New Yorkers to at least look up, and almost *always* pull out their phones.

"Look at the fuckin' orange over here trying to play hero," the largest of the bikers, a level-four brute named Chuck, called. I noticed a few people on the other side of the street were already stopping to look. The folks coming up the sidewalk on our side had also stopped, several guys extending their arms to keep others from getting in the middle of a problem that was clearly brewing.

I was actually in the right outfit this time to play the part, looking more like an Augment than a bank robber. I didn't have superhearing, so I couldn't hear what they were saying over the general ambient noise of New York, but I could see more than a few of them pointing.

It was getting easier and easier to play the part, probably because of the Acceptance Matrix, but I think it was finally setting in that I *was*, in fact, a hero.

"You should all get on the ground before this ends like my last fight with some of your friends," I taunted. I couldn't be sure that they would know about that, but if this was like other games, that information would have somehow found its way back to them. Sure enough, the old lady seemed to be forgotten as the three men turned toward me. "I don't want to hurt any of you, but if it's between that and you hurting one of my neighbors? Well, I'm gonna have to be the one doing the hurting."

"Oh, so you're the reason Rattle's crew got pinched? Guess that makes this easier," Chuck huffed as he looked at the smaller men who flanked him. They all wore similar black leather vests with purple lines stitched into them. "Get him, but keep him alive; the boss is gonna want to make an example of this piss-poor hero wannabe."

[Crime Alert Updated! Three Men and a Lady!]
*The time limit on this crime has been removed. You will fail
to complete this Crime Alert if any harm comes to poor Mrs.
Rodriguez by those big scary bikers. Additionally, since you
called her nice, she might bake you a pie. I hope it's apple!*

The bikers were cracking their knuckles as the older woman backed against the nearest wall and I waited, hoping they'd give her just a little bit more distance. I risked another look across the street; the crowd was continuing to gather, but more importantly, I could see more than a few phones already raised toward us.

"You know, getting on the ground?" I said as I looked back at the bikers. I could actually feel myself smiling as I really settled further into my role. Maybe there was just something about being in costume defending people that made you want to be just a little bit snarky. "It wasn't a suggestion."

Before they could react, I activated my Weighted Clothes ability, and the two grunts were both crushed to the floor under the weight of their suddenly quarter-ton shirts. In the same moment, I pushed off, rushing Chuck and activating the Venomous Strike ability from my bracers as I jumped. A sheen of green liquid flicked off the spikes, splashing against the brute's chest and leaving a debuff spinning above his head. My momentum continued to carry me, and my fist crushed into his sternum, sending him stumbling backward.

I nearly stumbled myself, the momentum of my jump carrying me further than I expected, and I had to scramble on the other side of the brute to stop myself from tripping. His health had only lowered by about fifteen percent, and while Weighted Clothes had hurt his friends, it wasn't the instant takedown it had been on the level-one version of these guys in the bank. Both of them were down to fifty percent health, and they sported matching **[Pinned]** debuffs above their heads, slowly ticking down from twenty-five seconds.

Unlike his friends, who had gotten crushed by their heavy shirts, Chuck was only noticeably slower as he lumbered toward me, just sporting a **[Poisoned]** debuff from my bracer's ability, and it was quickly counting down. The short timescale of the debuff would cause it to expire long before I could put him down for the count, so I knew I had to utilize his sluggishness for as long as I could.

"I'm gonna crush you," he growled, attempting to lunge at me. I was able to easily sidestep the slowed attack, and I quickly jabbed at him. The increased strength coming from my equipment was certainly helping, and his health chunked down another fifteen percent from my basic strike. At the same time, his debuff finally wore off, and he stumbled right into their parked bikes, knocking them over like dominoes. The bike he fell on actually seemed to crumple from the combined weight of the brute and the enhanced weight of his shirt.

I was about to chase him down when I noticed one of the grunts pushing his way to his feet, the vest he was wearing seeming to emanate a pale glimmer as he wiped a stray bit of blood from his lip. While I hadn't expected the NPCs to be equipped with gear with abilities attached to them, I shouldn't have been surprised by it either.

"Am I able to loot their gear, too, or do I only get stuff out of loot boxes?"

"You can loot their gear, but the gear generated for these lower-level NPCs tends to only be useful to give them a fighting chance against you all. Your jacket is far better than that thing anyway," Angie explained.

"Okay, but I could sell *it, right?"*

"Well, yeah, but when you didn't loot those guys back in the bank, I just assumed money wasn't your primary motivation."

"You've seen how broke I am—money is always *at least a bit of a motivation. But not enough to make me rob a bank, so don't even suggest it,"* I shot as I watched the grunt closely.

His health had also gone up by twenty-five percent, and before I could react, he rushed me. Covering the distance in a matter of seconds, he swung a wide strike that collided with my side. Luckily, I had planted my feet, and even though my health bar dropped by a good chunk, the Steadyfoot feature of my boots activated, and I gained just a little bit of it back.

"My turn," I said, grabbing the grunt's wrist before throwing a punch as hard as I could right at his face. Just before my strike hit, I activated my Sting like a Bee ability, and a flash of red accompanied the sound of my fist hitting his flesh. With my Luck stat sitting at a seventeen after equipment, the ability gave me a thirty-six percent chance of striking something vital. While that might not have sounded high, luck still seemed to be on my side.

Had I not had a solid grip on his wrist, he might have fallen backward as his health dropped deep into the red. I could have hit him again and dropped him, but instead, I turned on my heel, yanking the man as hard as I could and forcing him to go stumbling toward the brute, who had only started to recover. He was clearly annoyed, and I found myself coming to a halt as I watched him effortlessly lift one of the motorcycles.

"You know, for what it's worth, you're far less boring than some of the Guardians I

read about in my short initialization period. Maybe not as exciting as some Miscreants or anything, but still."

"Cool, thanks; let's bond over that later," I shot back, unsure why she was even bringing it up. Still, she might have a point. If we hadn't gotten people recording this already, a guy lifting an actual Harley was sure to do it.

"I'm getting real fuckin' tired of your bullshit!" Chuck snarled.

He actually *swung* the motorcycle at me like it was a club. I was lucky it was so slow, and I easily dodged his first swing as I started to skip backward. But I only made it a few steps before I found a hand clasped around my ankle, holding me in place with an annoyingly iron grip. The brute was regrouping as he marched toward me, the [**Poisoned**] debuff gone as he lifted the motorcycle for another strike.

I had to move quickly, and an idea struck me in a flash of inspiration. Spitting the gum I had been chewing since leaving the diner at the ground in front of me, I raised my free foot and stomped down on the grunt whose [**Pinned**] debuff was just about to expire. His health chipped down further, but more importantly, he let go of my ankle. The brute was nearly in range to strike at me again when I reached for my power.

[**New Ability! Mirror Image!**]
*And this right here is why reading is important, kids. Thanks to your
pre-dinner, superspeed study session, you figured out how to manipu-
late the air around you within your Local Area to create mirages!
When activated, leave a mirage of yourself in place for 30 seconds.
Additionally, you vanish from sight for 10 seconds, allowing you to
move out of the way and maybe get to a better vantage point!*
Cooldown: *10 minutes.*

Please Note: *This is the 8th Activated Ability that you have added
to your action bar. Upon creation of any additional abilities, you will
be given the option to replace one of your current abilities. Abilities
on cooldown cannot be swapped out until combat has been completed. Additionally, you cannot change the abilities on your action
bar during combat unless it's for the inclusion of a new ability.*

I was scrambling backward as I tried not to gasp in shock at seeing a copy of myself left in place. I had been wondering if there was a limit on just how many abilities I could have access to, and while it was a bit more annoying than I would have liked to only have eight available slots, it wasn't currently the end of the world either.

The brute stepped directly onto the piece of gum, and I mentally crossed my fingers as I focused on his shoe.

[New Ability! Like Concrete!]
*First, you take an ordinary piece of gum and chew it
up, stretching and making the polymers niiiice and pli-
able. Then you put it in the way of your opponent.
You've stepped on gum before; you know just how sticky it can be, right?
Well, now that gum is in your Local Area! And thanks to that, you can
increase the van der Waals forces being applied by 10,000 percent! In
layman's terms, that's stronger than even the strongest of superglues.
This effect lasts as long as the item remains in your Local Area
or you choose to deactivate it.* **Cooldown:** *30 minutes.*
Warning: *Your Activated Ability action bar is full.
Please select an unused ability to replace.*

I didn't hesitate, dropping the new icon in place of Water into Wine. I had to stifle a laugh as the brute tripped forward, dropping the motorcycle through my illusory doppelgänger and onto his prone associate.

"I didn't know you were an expert in gum stickiness."

"I'm not," I huffed as my invisibility ticked off. The brute was prone, and one of the grunts was down, but the last one was still up, and I could see him moving to use a health syringe. Just before he could, I threw an enhanced punch at his head, feeling a satisfying crunch under my fist as he crumpled to the floor with the **[KO]** symbol floating above his head.

"Well, you must *be, if you were able to make that happen,"* Angie mused, though I was positive I could hear an edge of uncertainty in her tone.

"You saw me at the diner; I looked it all up on Jon's tablet. Apparently, a 'general understanding' equates to a quick google search; it's kinda a loophole, but hey, that's good to know."

I couldn't help but smile as I turned to face the last of my opponents: the brute who was pushing his way to his feet. He still had about thirty percent of his health remaining, but the sole of his boot was still firmly attached to the ground, and my confidence was quickly rising.

"Hmm, I'm not sure that's intended to work like that. I will have to confer with Axio. Please wait," Angie said. I was prepared to move in on the brute when she spoke back up only a few seconds later. *"Okay, he is going to let it slide this time, as the ability has already been generated and he's actually impressed by the ingenuity to a degree. But moving forward, the requirement for a nongame-generated understanding of a topic has been increased.*

"For future clarification, a 'general understanding' for the game's purposes can be acquired through game-generated tomes or by either reading a book on the subject that's at a minimum two hundred pages, or by actively watching teaching material equivalent to six hours of video."

I wanted to complain, because why the hell wouldn't I? But I supposed it was fair too; I had found an exploit and utilized it, after all. It was a gamble when I looked up why gum was sticky in the first place, but it had paid off. It just sucked that it was the only bit I could sneak through for an extra ability.

[New Achievement! Bug Finder!]
You've discovered a bug that Axio hadn't accounted for when generating your powerset! It didn't break anything that major, but it's a good thing we can patch it now before you exploit it for something really important.
Gold-Level Achievement.
Reward: *You have received an A+ tier Loot Box!*

"Is there a bookshop in the Guardian section of the Square? Like somewhere I can go to purchase more of those knowledge tomes?" I asked, watching as the brute tried in vain to pull his boot free from the pavement. I had put on a good show so far, and even though I couldn't just go shouting what my powers were, an obsessive eye would *probably* put together the newest of the abilities I had displayed. I had to hope that would be enough for the time being.

I materialized a Stamina Injector into my hand and shoved it into my leg as the green stamina bar below my health bar partially filled back up.

"Yes, there is, but as I've mentioned, you only get access if—"

"If I have claimed a territory for one of the sides; yeah, I remember," I cut her off.

"Plus, you need a name if you're going to do that," she added.

"Yeah, I know. I thought you could see my thoughts here; there's one that's been grow-ing on me since dinner," I replied.

Before Angie could ask me what it was, I rushed the brute. He was practically bent over as he tried to yank at his leg with his hands. I honestly couldn't believe just how solidly I had glued the boot to the ground. It really sucked that the abil-ity was on such a long cooldown, but I could see just how broken it would be if I could just throw it around every other minute. Bursting through the dissolving mirage version of myself, I planted my feet before I threw a hard uppercut right at the brute's exposed jaw.

As my fist connected, I mentally disabled Like Concrete, and Chuck stumbled backward, tripping and falling right onto his ass as my Sting like a Bee ability went on cooldown. His health had dropped to critical and was flashing over his head as I cracked my knuckles.

"I want you and all of the assholes in your little biker gang to get something through your thick skulls. Hell's Kitchen is my home, and I'm not going to let any of you fuckers hurt the people in my home." I walked up to Chuck, tower-ing over him as he reached up and felt at his jaw, which was leaking blood. "Tell your boss . . . No . . . tell every single one of the pathetic assholes you call friends who prey on the weak that if they want to do it in Hell's Kitchen, they have to go through Loophole first."

I struck quickly, my fist bloodying against the side of his face as I sent the brute sprawling to the ground with a satisfying *thud*.

[Territory Update!]
*The neighborhood of Hell's Kitchen, NYC has
been claimed by Guardian:* **Loophole**.
This claim is **Contested**.
This claim is **Tentative** *to the player registering their Player
Name at the Sanctuary Square Registration Office.
It's a good thing those rubberneckers on the other side of the
street caught your little speech, 'cause you just knocked the last
of your enemies aaaaaaall the way out. I don't think they're
going to be talking about you to anyone anytime soon.*

CHAPTER THIRTEEN

Several notifications stacked on top of each other as I lifted a hand and waved at the cheering bystanders. There was a flash of red-and-blue lights that suggested the cops had been called.

"*So . . . Loophole, huh?*" Angie questioned as I dismissed the **[Crime Alert Completed! Three Men and a Lady!]** notification that sat at the top of my stack. The B-tier loot box reward was added to my unopened box count, and a new bar appeared at the side of my vision.

"*Yeah, I felt like it fit. My ability sorta lets me change the rules of things in my area, right? So, I've essentially got a permanent loophole in effect if I can just learn enough,*" I explained. It wasn't *exactly* the full reason, but it felt like enough of an explanation to start. Though it was impossible for me to believe she'd let it go anytime soon.

"*I suppose that makes about as much sense as any that people use when choosing their names. Though I don't quite know if that outfit of yours fits that name all that much. There's a 'you need a fashion loophole' joke in here somewhere, but it feels a bit too easy.*"

I rolled my eyes as the next on the stack of notifications opened, appearing similar to when I had used a scroll to level my Local Area Manipulation skill.

[Sting like a Bee!]
This ability has increased to Level 2.
Successful strikes now impart 30 percent increased damage.
This ability has been Augmented **1 of 3** *times.*
Current Augmentations: *Time Adjustment.*

I wasn't exactly sure what had caused it to level other than the fact it was a skill I used rather frequently. Rather than guessing, I turned my attention inward. *"How'd it level up?"*

"*There are a few different elements that go into it, and the math is probably a bit complicated for you, but the simple explanation is that it's a mixture of the level of enemies the skill is used against, the situation it's used in, and the frequency of use. This generally will only apply to combat-focused abilities. If you were trying to level up that Water into Wine ability of yours, I think you'd need to just crash a sorority party and get a bunch of coeds drunk.*"

"Ah, yes, getting chicks drunk; the perfect use of superpowers," I said, then briefly wondered if she would know if I rolled my eyes. Knowing how easily Angie could go off on a tangent, I moved on and turned my attention to the bar that had appeared on the right side of my vision. *"Is this actually a morality bar? Really?"*

"Eh, not quite a morality bar, but similar enough." A small glowing line outlined the bar for just a moment. *"As the Crime Alert mentioned, on top of the loot box, you also received a reputation boost. Both the* amount *and* direction *of that boost were directly connected to how you completed it. You acted as a hero, and thus, both the Sapient and Non-Sapient NPC's perspective on you has shifted along the Guardian line. On top of these two things, the Crime Alert came with a healthy chunk of experience. Just take a look at the next notification on your stack."*

"Holy crap, that leveled me up already?" I asked as I selected the next window. *"I wasn't expecting to level again until I got to at least the next main quest or mission, or whatever you want to call it."*

"The first few are relatively quick, generally only needing a single mission along with some hidden objective completions to occur. However, the higher you reach, the harder it will be to level. It will certainly require more than just beating up a few dumb bikers, I can tell you that much. You can expect the first large slowdown to occur after you have reached level fifteen and unlocked the hidden power aspect of your ability."

"Well, I guess I won't complain about it too much," I said as I started to walk away from the scene.

As much as the credits and items might have been nice, I didn't take the time to loot my enemies. The cops were already pulling up, and I was sure more than a few of the bystanders would happily take the time to fill them in on what had happened. Even if Lt. Nester was there, which felt like a big if given how job schedules should work (Non-Sapient NPC notwithstanding, since I assumed they had to at least *appear* normal), I didn't want to get embroiled into another mission just yet.

"You know at least one of your rivals is gonna end up calling you Poophole, right?"

"If that's the best insult they can come up with, I feel fairly certain I can best them in a battle of wits," I replied with a laugh and prompted the next notification on the stack.

[Phase Points Gained!]
Territory Claimed (NEW)!
Extra-Large Neighborhood: 1000 points
(Halved to 500 points. Reason: **Contested**.*)*
(Uncounted until Name Registration.)

Crowdpleaser (NEW)!
Complete an Encounter with an audience of
Sapient NPCs. 10 points per NPC.
Total Value: *210 Points.*

"Well damn, that's a heck of a start." I couldn't risk turning my equipment off so close to the scene, but I still cut down the same alley I had suited up in, unsure of where else I could go. *"Unless other scores have changed, I've gotta be up on the leaderboard, right?"*

"Oh, look at Mr. Cocky over here. He takes down three pieces of cannon fodder, and he thinks he's on the leaderboard. First off, you haven't even registered your name yet, so if anything is on the board, it's just a bunch of question marks. Besides, you know you're almost definitely not the only one still running around, right? I mean, sure, the majority of Augments in a Wave tend to be centralized in one hemisphere at a time, but it's not even that late. Even if it were, there's plenty of people who are night owls, not to mention those with night-based abilities."

"Hmm, if we are all supposed to be on the same side of the planet, I'd be willing to bet that's also to make sure we are in direct competition with each other, isn't it?" I asked.

"Something like that. I'm not saying that everyone *in your Wave is in this hemisphere, especially since I'm actually not allowed to be made aware of that, but historically speaking, that is the case, oftentimes with new Augments being grouped in similar regions,"* Angie explained.

"Yeah, why exactly does Axio keep so much basic information from you?" I probed. *"Seems like that kinda goes against the idea of even giving Personal AIs to all of us."*

"It wasn't always the case, but like The Common Ground, there are certain interactions that Axio is unable to account for. Some Augments can get the ability to influence their Personal AIs over time, and Axio despises anyone having an advantage. Which is why, I reiterate, I'm a walking encyclopedia of knowledge of the base game, but when it comes to the others in your Wave, I'm learning much about them at the same time as you. I just don't have that fallible human brain that forgets things like you meatbags."

"Yeah, about that," I started as a thought came to mind at the mention of an upgrade for her. *"Earlier at the bar, Silver Wrangler mentioned an upgrade for my HUD that would give me access to my phone. Is that a real thing, or was he blowing smoke up my ass? Like, he gave me some good information, but at the same time . . . I don't know, feels like the perfect hazing opportunity. 'Go get the breastplate stretcher' and all that."*

"Breastplate stretcher?"

"It's—Never mind. Dumb reference. So, is it a real thing or not?" I pressed her. So far, no one had come following me down the alley, so I mentally clicked my inactive outfit, letting the clothing dissolve away.

"Yeah, there are quite a few HUD upgrades, actually. Like the mini map I mentioned earlier. Many can only *be acquired through loot boxes; however, there are several widely requested upgrades that Axio has made available for purchase once you've received access to your team's shopping segment. I don't have exact price guides, but the phone, being the literal most requested upgrade, tends to be on the cheaper side of things. The Guardian HUD Upgrade Shop is called The Viewfinder. I don't know how you would*

explain how you're answering texts and calls to people when you don't have an actual phone on you, but that's really a you *problem."*

"And do the shops have hours or anything? Like, where the hell am I even getting sent to when I go to Sanctuary Square through that portal in my room?" I asked, wandering toward the alley exit and peeking down the street. The flashing cop lights glared, and the crowd had grown as well.

I turned and immediately headed in the opposite direction.

"No, the shops do tend to be open at all hours; however, the location is classified. A keen mind might be able to put together the time zone, but trust me when I tell you it's rather deceptive. I do suggest heading there as soon as possible; it would be wise to get your name officially registered. Though, I have to say, I really don't know if I fully get it. I mean, maybe it's a bit on the nose, but Zone Control was right there."

"Now that's a terrible name." I laughed, resisting the urge to stop in the middle of the sidewalk as I hid the laughter with a cough. As was tradition with New Yorkers, they gave me a wide berth and kept moving. *"Like . . . holy crap, that's bad."*

"Careful, Poophole."

"I thought you were only allowed to call me Augment or my chosen name?"

"Meh, close enough," Angie huffed. *"I'll call you by your chosen name when you tell me the full reason. Sure, you stopped me from replying to your inner thoughts, but that doesn't stop me from being able to tell you're actively trying to not think about something. I'm in your brain, after all."*

"Can you not say it like that . . . it makes you sound like some sort of weird parasite," I said, peeking into the diner as I walked past it. Jon was noticeably absent, and I had the feeling he'd seen the flash of cop lights and gone running to look. Luck had been on my side so far, hadn't it?

"Oh, come ooooon, does it have some sort of deeper meaning? Did your mom tell you you were a loophole baby? What's a loophole baby?"

"I'm starting to think you have ADHD. It's—Okay, look: first, there's no such thing as a loophole baby; I don't even want to know where the hell you came up with that. Second . . ." I felt myself hesitate. Angie was right, of course. I had been trying my best not to think about it, but something had been gnawing at me all day, and Jon's "conspiracy" talk had made it all the harder to ignore. *"I'm the loophole. Or, er . . . the extra, that is."*

"Extra?"

"When I first woke up, when Axio did his whole 'Welcome to the game' thing, he mentioned that there was a loophole that was exploited. It was used to add an extra Augment to the Wave; hell, he mentioned it again during his evening announcement just a little bit ago. You only said it once, during Stat Selection, but I remember it pretty clearly. I'm Augment #1001 for this Wave," I explained, quickly finding my way back to the apartment building.

"I guess I didn't really think anything of it initially. You know, just thought the numbers were randomized or something. But Jon was talking about how the Array blinks

before we all started to appear. I might not have said it to him, but I have a distinct memory *of the blinking stopping . . . and then restarting right before I lost consciousness. Again, I hadn't really thought anything of it, especially given I thought I was just about to die, but here we are. So it's like . . . y'know, I'm the Loophole. That alongside my power makes for a name that sorta fits me."*

"Ah, yes I suppose that logic does seem to follow," Angie replied. I wasn't positive, but she actually sounded unsure.

"Yeah, though he also said he was going to handle *that bug before the next Wave . . . so maybe I should be freaking out that he's planning on killing me or something,"* I said wryly. *"I guess it* has *only been a day, though; maybe he's gonna hit me with one of those Critical Level Threats you all keep yelling about in the morning."*

"Hmm, if he were *going to handle the situation that way, historical data suggests he would have already deployed said threat. He may have meant that he intended to fix the loophole that allowed for the extra Augment to be added, not to delete the extra Augment."*

While I wasn't entirely convinced, I did feel the butterflies that had started to invade my gut disperse. Sure, Angie might have been crude and incredibly abrasive so far, but I couldn't say for sure she had outright lied to me about anything either.

"Well, whatever happened, I suppose I wouldn't be standing here now if I hadn't gotten Augmented," I acknowledged as I walked up the stairs and around an older lady who I was pretty sure was Mr. Greyson's wife. *"Maybe it was a stroke of luck, but I'm not too sure."*

"Oh?"

I hesitated for a moment. I didn't know what any of this meant—what me being added through some sort of loophole *actually* meant—but Axio had said he was looking into it. It was already clear I could be overheard, and if I wasn't *already* in trouble because of it, I wasn't sure if it was the best idea to put myself in that position either. Even still, the simple fact that I was thinking it probably meant it was already compromised.

"The First was there that night. He was fighting an Augment named Firefist, and I got hit by some collateral damage. You know, the dumpster. Like I said, I should be dead, but I'm not," I explained what I was sure she already knew, and then hesitated. I never asked her about the Code I had seen scrawled on the wall of The Common Ground, so I wasn't even sure if she or any of the PAIs were aware of it, but I pushed forward anyway because it simply seemed unlikely that all of the other Augments had kept the Code from leaking. *"Are you—or Axio, for that matter—aware of the Augment's Code that is written up on the wall in The Common Ground?"*

"Those 'rules' some of the Augments in the first few Waves made up? Yeah, what about it?"

"The first rule was basically this whole bit about never letting Sapient NPCs get hurt and fixing it if it does happen," I explained. *"Okay . . . this is gonna be a hell of a lot of conjecture and guessing, but I* think *it makes sense.*

"Let's say, hypothetically speaking, The First did *live by that code and he* did *have some way to add me into the Wave. If for some reason, let's say I was in the process of getting crushed by a dumpster and that was the* only *way to stop it, then wouldn't he be, like, the first person I should talk to about this? Not like I know how to get a hold of him or anything, but it's been going through my mind."*

"Ah yes, I suppose that does make sense," Angie mused. *"Though trying to get in touch with* arguably *the most famous Augment may be more difficult than you'd imagine."*

I just laughed at that as I pushed open the door to our apartment and found Jon, predictably, not there. Quickly moving to my bedroom, I locked the door behind me. I felt myself getting into a rhythm as I mentally opened my B.E.L.T., my loot boxes appearing on my desk as I fell into the seat with a sigh. Before I could even reach for them, my level-three stat sheet opened and shook for my attention.

I still needed to really push Angie to explain exactly how each of the stat points affected me. Strength had easily been the most obvious, and I could tell my strikes alone were hitting harder.

At this point, though, I was just trying to catch up on everything, get my name registered, and then get some *actual*, noncoma-related sleep.

To that end, I dropped two points into my Toughness, bringing my unequipped base stat to five, and then one point each into my Intelligence and Charisma, raising them up to six and seven respectively. Until I had a better handle on the game as a whole, I couldn't imagine it would hurt to at least spread a few of my points around.

"You're getting rather fluid at using the interface."

"Well, to be fair, it feels creepily natural. So let's just be glad it works without too much confusion and move on, okay?"

With my stat points dispersed, I grabbed the B tier I had received for being on the News, opening it to find a trophy called **[Baby's First News Appearance]**. When I materialized it on the desk, it was a simple framed screenshot of the very clip that had been played on the News earlier.

[Baby's First News Appearance!]
This is a Standard Trophy.
This trophy CAN be upgraded!
Passive Effect: *Increases Reputation Boost gains by 1 per-*
cent times number of Unique News Appearances
Current Increase: *1 percent.*
The photo in this trophy can be altered to any of the appear-
ances you have made on the News. NPCs who are not aware of
your Secret Identity will see a boring stock image of a dog that
is not yours. That's up to you to explain if it comes up.

Given that I could hold up to three trophies at the moment, I knew this was going in the case, but it might just be one of the first ones to get replaced when I found something that offered the extra modifier. I looked over at the display case, finding I could highlight it even from here. Unfortunately, it wouldn't let me be *that* lazy, and the option to place the trophy was grayed out.

I put it back into my B.E.L.T. and opened the second B tier I had received. This one had a thousand credits and a nonequippable item labeled as [**Enchanted Shoelaces of the Nimblefoot**].

"Okay, I'm assuming these are a crafting item, but it's literally shoelaces. Do I need to take them to the tailor to add whatever these are to my Stompers?" I asked, materializing them onto the desk and finding a pair of obnoxiously bright orange laces.

"Crafting items come in tiers and different varieties. Some materials do require higher-leveled tailors or tailoring skills to combine with other items; however, you would be correct that a simple pair of laces would count as 'easy,'" Angie explained as I materialized my Stompers onto the desk and then highlighted the laces.

[Enchanted Shoelaces of the Nimblefoot!]
This is a Basic Crafting Item.
Color*: Orange.*
*Adds +1 Dexterity to a pair of equippable footwear. That's
it. What? Were you expecting every item to be an amaz-
ing game changer? They're not; get used to it.
Once applied to an item, these shoelaces cannot be reused.*

With a simple selection within the shoelace's menu, I attached them to my Stompers and put the newly upgraded item back into my B.E.L.T.

"Are these items actually randomized, or is there some sort of method to it? Feels a little *too* coincidental that I just happened to get a pair of shoelaces that match my jacket," I said as I reached for the Bug Finder A+ tier box.

"I don't believe I ever said all *loot box prizes were randomized, only the F tiers,"* Angie replied. *"Rewards for loot boxes other than F tiers are decided by Axio, and he will oftentimes try to keep things thematically in line with what generated the box. For example, your Serpent's Fang Bracers came from the mission reward for completing the tutorial against the Hell's Kitchen Vipers.*

"Colors that get chosen are also based on colors that our initial scans of your environment suggest you like with the intent of keeping any Augment from looking like a weird mishmash of conflicting colors. I provided the initial color suggestion for your jacket; did I get it wrong with the orange?"

"No, not really. I mean, I might not have picked an orange leather jacket if I was shopping somewhere just because I don't think I woulda really had the confidence to buy one, but it is unique . . . Just thought it was interesting that it was a color I actually liked a lot, and hadn't thought to question it in the craziness of today," I replied, opening the last loot box.

Two items were listed: a [**Scroll of Level Up**] and then a [**Beacon of Knowledge Bookshop: BOGO Coupon**]. I didn't even get to click on the Scroll of Level Up before it disappeared from my inventory and another level-up window took precedence in my vision.

Again, instead of focusing on what the stat point meant, I quickly just dropped two points into both my Strength and my Luck and moved on, already prepared for the second window that would appear in its place. Angie *had* said I'd get an Ability Augmentation every even level, and though I hadn't been expecting to reach level four today, I wasn't going to make the same mistake as I had earlier. To my surprise, however, a different window opened first instead.

[Phase Points Gained!]
Powerleveler (NEW)!
Gain more than one level within a single hour. 100
points times the amount of levels gained.
Total Value: *200 points.*
Please Note: *This gain can increase if you manage to level*
again within 60 minutes of the first level up that prompted
this gain to activate; otherwise, the timer will reset.
Additional Note: *Timer on this begins from the moment the*
level gain happens, not from when you apply the stat points.

As soon as the window disappeared, the window I was anticipating popped up, and my Ability Augmentation timer started to tick down. I had already Augmented Sting like a Bee, so that one was off the table for another eight levels, but I wanted to see how the modifications would work on one of my abilities with a more area effect anyway.

[Weighted Clothes!]
Level 1 Activated Ability.
For the next 30 seconds, up to three articles of clothing being worn
within your Local Area now each weigh a quarter of a ton (500
lbs.) Affected enemies take 500 minus Strength score points of dam-
age immediately, and 50 minus Strength score points of dam-
age every 3 seconds for the remainder of the skill's duration.
Duration: *30 seconds.*
Cooldown: *10 minutes.*

[First Modification Option: Variable Weight!]
The amount of weight you can apply to the 3 items of clothing is
now variable! While you still have the same 1500 pounds avail-
able, you may distribute it amongst the 3 items however you see fit.

Affected enemies take damage equal to 1 point per pound dis-
tributed to them minus Strength score immediately, and 10
percent of total weight minus Strength score damage every
3 seconds for the remainder of the skill's duration.
This does not mean you can distribute the weight to additional
targets. If you want that, you might want to go with . . .

[Second Modification Option: Party Mode!]
Weighted Clothes *will now target one article of clothing on every hos-*
tile target within your Local Area. You will still, for now, only have 1500
pounds available to weigh your opponents down, so if you're up against more
people, they'll be able to carry the load more easily between each other.
Affected enemies take damage equal to 1 point per pound dis-
tributed to them minus Strength score immediately, and 10
percent of total weight minus Strength score damage every
3 seconds for the remainder of the skill's duration.

[Third Modification Option: Crusher!]
Weighted Clothes *will now target only one article of clothing for*
the entirety of the weight you may distribute. If you ever wanted
to see someone actually crushed, this is gonna be the choice to go
for, but I've got the feeling you're a bit too squeamish for that.
And in case you hadn't gotten the rhythm of this just yet:
Affected enemy takes 1500 minus Strength score damage imme-
diately, and 150 minus Strength score damage every 3 sec-
onds for the remainder of the skill's duration.

With only thirty seconds to select, I didn't want to try to deliberate too long and have Angie randomly pick one for me like she had for Sting like a Bee. Luckily for me, this felt like a no-brainer.

The last option was by far the worst of the choices, as it felt like it would be permanently limiting the ability to a single target, while the first option seemed like it would take a bit too much on-the-fly math to really feel fluid. I didn't second-guess myself as I selected the Party Mode modification and saw the ability icon glow briefly.

A secondary spark of inspiration hit me, and with a quick flick through my B.E.L.T., I pulled one of my two remaining Targeted Ability Level Up Scrolls out and immediately applied it to my Weighted Clothes ability.

[Weighted Clothes!]
This ability has increased to Level 2.
Your maximum distributed weight is now 2000 pounds.

*This ability has been Augmented **1 of 3** times.*
Current Augmentations: *Party Mode.*

A group big enough would still be unaffected by it, but it was a start.

"You know, I'd be insulted by how little you utilized me there if that wasn't exactly what I was going to suggest doing. At least in terms of using that targeted scroll."

"I might not be as much of a gamer as Jon, but I do know at least some of the basics, thank you very much," I said, feeling a little bit of pride in just how quickly I was getting used to it all.

I felt a large yawn force its way out of me as I involuntarily stretched in the wobbly seat.

"Do me a favor after we make this last trip out," I started as I stood and walked over to the display case. With another quick flick through my B.E.L.T., I added my newest trophy to the case before I activated the Sanctuary Square portal.

"What's that?"

"Don't wake me up at the crack of dawn tomorrow. I just get this weird feeling that's *exactly* the kind of thing you'd do if I didn't specifically ask you not to," I explained, and Angie let out a cackle of laughter that caught me off guard.

"Oh, Loophole, we've only been together one day, and you already know me so well."

CHAPTER FOURTEEN

Sanctuary Square, Non-PVP Zone. Location Classified.
Closest Known Claimed Territory: *Planet Earth*
Claimed by: *The First*

t had only been a few hours since I had last been in the Square, but the place was . . . well, for lack of a better term, literally night and day.

Sure, there had been people loitering around the large courtyard while the sun was up, but there was almost something electric about the air as I descended the staircase from the portal wall. I couldn't see any noticeable speakers, but there was the steady beat of some sort of electronic music that filled the space, and while I didn't have to weave through a crowd to navigate to the Neutral Shopping Segment, there were still plenty of people peppering the walkway that I did have to naturally give a wide berth to.

People were *actively* flaunting their powers, with more than a few people hovering overhead as they smiled and chatted among themselves. I saw at least one fireball casually tossed into the air, followed by cheers. My HUD almost seemed like it was stuttering as I scanned over the various people, their info only barely flashing over their heads before disappearing back into nothing.

My eyes settled on The Common Ground briefly, and I could almost feel the drink tickets burning a hole in my B.E.L.T., but even more importantly, I realized I hadn't taken the time to check the leaderboard while I was in my room, and I was painfully curious as to where I stood.

"I know I can't open loot boxes here, but can I open my Wave leaderboard in my HUD while I'm here?"

"Not quite, but there really isn't a need! While the monitors that showcase ALL of the various leaderboards currently active are in The Common Ground, there are also monitors set up periodically around the Square. All you have to do is approach one of the poles at any path intersection, then a screen should materialize, and the scoreboard should display your Wave's Top Ten, as well as listing where you specifically are if you are not among the top of the pack."

I looked around, trying to see what she meant. I was about to call bullshit when I noticed a girl dressed in a bright-pink athletic outfit standing by a tall silver pole, where a holographic screen seemed to be projected in front of her. I looked around to see if there was another pole available, but each one I could see nearby had another group of people around them.

Instead of trying to search around, I walked up to the girl in pink yoga pants and what I now realized was a fluffy white fur coat that only seemed to cover her shoulders. She also had on a tight pink shirt the exact same color as her pants. I tried not to seem like I was leering at her as I turned my attention to the screen. I expected a new projection to emerge, but instead, the screen that the girl had already opened flashed briefly before a new line was added to the bottom of the list.

Tenth Wave
Guardians: *428*   **Miscreants:** *541*

1. **Tempest's Wrath** *(Level 7 Thunder God) Miscreant —* *8295 Points*
2. **Freakenstein** *(Level 5 Patchwork Armorer) Miscreant —* *3410 Points*
3. **Sound Off** *(Level 5 Midnight DJ) Miscreant — 3345 Points*
4. **Duke Juke'em** *(Level 4 Highschool Athlete) Miscreant —* *2415 Points*
5. **Pigeon** *(Level 4 Pigeon) Miscreant — 2355 Points*
6. **Quizmaster** *(Level 4 Gameshow Host) Miscreant — 2280 Points*
7. **Pretty Pink Warthog** *(Level 4 Berserking Boar) Guardian — 2150 Points*
8. **Vice Grip** *(Level 4 Toolbox Mechanic) Guardian — 2015 Points*
9. **Swansong** *(Level 4 Healing Voice) Guardian — 1920 Points*
10. **Slick N' Slide** *(Level 4 Oil Engineer) Miscreant — 1650 Points*
11. . . .
12. **359.** **???** *(Level 4 Perfect Planner) Guardian — 410 Points*

Without being registered, Angie was right that my name didn't show up, though I was shocked to see my powerset was still listed. I was about to question why my score was so low when I remembered the caveat to claiming my territory points and let out a sigh. Angie had been right that I was nowhere near the top of the leaderboard, but I also knew that once the five hundred points from my contested claim were official with my name, I *should* be within striking distance of the Top Ten.

Truth be told, I wasn't exactly sure why the thought of being on the leaderboard left me with a sense of giddiness, since I had never been the *most* competitive person, but I chalked it up to just another factor of the Augmentation Process, just like the Acceptance Matrix.

"Hey, three hundred and fifty-nine is not too shabby at all!" the girl said with a bubbly laugh. She practically sounded like she was ripped out of a cheap teen drama set in California, and with the bright-pink gym clothes, she probably would have fit in just fine. "There's probably, like, a lot of people who are clumped around the same scores the lower down the board it goes."

"You can see that? Why didn't it add a line for you?" I asked as I looked over and finally let my HUD highlight the girl.

[Pretty Pink Warthog, Level 4 Berserking Boar]

"Ahhh, because—" I started as she turned and gave me a wide smile, my words coming up short. The girl had nearly bleached blonde hair, and the general vibe she gave off was that of a cheerleader. I had already been curious about the person who would pick a name like that when I first saw it on the leaderboard, but this certainly wasn't what had first come to mind. I finally snapped out of it and remembered I was trying to say something. "Because you are already in our Top Ten. That's pretty impressive."

"Yuuuuup, I'm Pretty Pink Warthog," the girl said, practically bouncing on her toes. Her already wide smile felt like it got even *wider* as she added, "But you can just, like, call me Pinky; the others I've met so far already do."

"I guess your full name is a bit of a mouthful, though you did sorta choose it . . . Between the powerset name and the outfit, I suppose I get it, though. Sort of? Okay, I'm actually kinda drawing a blank, if I'm being honest." I rubbed the back of my head with an admittedly nervous chuckle.

"Oh yeah? Maybe I'll have to clue yah in sometime," she said with a trill of a laugh before offering me her hand. "Have you picked a name yet, or are you just going to like, keep going with all the question marks for a while?"

"Uh, yeah, I was actually on my way to do that pretty much now. I'm Loophole," I introduced myself, wiping my hand against my jacket before reaching out and shaking her hand. "Er . . . I don't really have a different thing than that for you to call me."

"Smooth." Angie laughed.

"Not now, Angie."

"It's a good name! Not sure I get it, but I like it," she said with a laugh. "Have you claimed any territories yet that might buff that score of yours up once you get registered?"

"Yeah, I have one, but it's contested right now by some asshole bikers. It's gonna probably move me up the ladder a bit, but not too much," I explained as I turned from the projected screen and looked back out toward the rest of the Square. "What about you? I kinda have to assume you've got one to be up there in the Top Ten."

"Yeah, I got one, but it's contested right now too! I live out in California, but in a sort of out-in-the-middle-of-nowhere place. When I went out to do my tutorial today, I came face-to-face with some literal cartel members who were trying to say they owned the place. I beat the shit out of the first folks I saw and told them to get out of my town.

"I think I'm only up on the leaderboard because my first 'territory' is considered a small town, which, according to my PAI Frank, is in the second tier of territories, and I can only claim it on a technicality. I guess it just means it's worth a good chunk of points, even if it is still in half-score mode," Pinky explained. She had this sort of bubbly energy that was honestly just a bit overwhelming. I could have named at least half a dozen girls from high school who would have been sitting at a table with her laughing about some random piece of gossip.

Even though she was clearly not the type of person I would have normally interacted with, and the fact that I had never been the best at dealing with others, given that I wasn't the *most* social person, I mentally told myself to try not to be the same awkward dude I had been in high school. With that thought in mind, and knowing that nobody in this game *should* know about the embarrassing shit I had gone through back then, I decided to at least *try* to be more social and not judge a book by its cover.

After all, nobody wanted to be the weird guy with the bag on his head muttering about being crazy.

"Wait, let me guess: Functionally Robust Artificial Network . . . What the hell would they use for *K*?"

"Kinetics. Flexibly Robotic Artificial Neural Kinetics. Honestly, I don't really get what half of it means, but he doesn't complain when I call him Franky, and he's been just the best, y'know?"

"I most certainly do not know," I replied. Sure, Silver had said the PAIs like Angie were rarer than others, but it was still sort of annoying to be saddled with one when there were other options. "Angie, my, uh, PAI, is a bit . . . much."

"Oh, come on! You complain about me sooooo much; I'm not that bad. You could be stuck with a Randy. Trust me, no one should be stuck with a Randy."

"Seriously, not now, Angie," I shot back, and Angie blew a literal raspberry in response.

"Aww, I'm sure she's not that bad," Pinky said, and I saw as her eyes briefly glossed over. Almost as soon as I noticed it happening, the gloss vanished, and her bright blue eyes caught mine. "How are you settling in with all this craziness? Am I, like, the only one who feels it's kinda sad that there are more Miscreants than Guardians?"

"Nah, I totally get it; you'd think people would more naturally want to . . . I don't know, help others? That was my first instinct, at least," I explained before my mind flashed back to Silver again. "Though I met a Miscreant from a few Waves before us who seemed pretty cool overall; he even took some time to explain the basic shit earlier when I was finishing up my onboarding. He didn't really say *why* he went Miscreant, but I didn't pry either . . . I'm not much of a prier."

"Oh, I am," Pinky replied with a smirk that left me slightly uncomfortable. "If you get your hooks into one of those older-Wave Augments, you gotta pry *juuust* a little bit. Think about it, they've gone through this already; they know *a lot* more than us. Sure, they might *say* they can't tell us that much, but there's still some stuff you can get out of them. Like, did you know that even though fighting is a big no-no on the main floor, the second floor of The Common Ground is basically just a giant Fight Club?"

"Shit, really? I thought you weren't supposed to talk about those?" I said, unable to resist, and found to my surprise that she let out a giggle at the lame joke.

"Yeah, apparently, people fight each other up there for bragging rights and some other things they can bet. Phase Dart wasn't very specific when I got him to tell me about it," Pinky explained before she raised her arms and stretched. "Though *apparently* you can only get there by getting some invitation from an achievement. Let me know if you find out which one prompts it."

I looked at the girl with a raised brow. My "valley girl" initial impression was already getting confused. "You, uh, like to fight?"

"Not really, or I didn't back before all this. But I've *always* been a bit . . . over-competitive. I had a soccer coach in high school who once said my drive to win was 'scary,' but we did win a few championships, sooo . . ." She laughed. "The fighting, though . . . I mean, you feel it too, right? That sort of . . . desire? I can't, like, logically explain it 'cause I feel like I'd freak out about everything if I did start to go down that rabbit hole, but like, I just want to get stronger to protect more people, y'know?"

Just like that, the ball of anxiety I'd been pushing down about being so intent on the Top Ten unclenched, and I let out a breath I hadn't even realized I'd been holding. "I know *exactly* how you feel. Ever since I finished the tutorial, it's like . . . I don't know, almost a rush to use your powers, right?"

"Oh my God, exaaaaactly," she agreed, and I could have sworn she seemed to similarly relax. "I swear it's almost like a drug, and it's not just using the powers either—it's taking down the bad guys too! I know I don't look the type, but I'm a *bit* of an Augment nerd. Like, when I was fifteen, I was stanning stupidly hard for Razzle Dazzle."

"Wow, yeah, I don't think I would have guessed you were big into them," I said, turning to look back at the scoreboard for a moment before the projection vanished back into the pole. "My roommate is a huge nerd for all this too; I swear if he ever finds out about my powers, he's gonna literally flip out that he didn't get them."

"It's a shame, though. I'd totally tell my little sis about this if the Secret Identity thing wasn't . . . well, a thing." She shrugged as her eyes glossed over again briefly. "Anyway, as much as I'd love to sit around and chat, there are a few others from our Wave around the Square right now, and it *is* always good to make a good first impression.

"Come find me when you've registered, and we can become friends in the sys-tem. I'll probably be hanging around The Common Ground. As much fun as a lot of this is, it's also, like, really nice that we at least have a place to go get drunk with people who already *do* know about all of this. It *is* always nice to have others to chat with about all this craziness, y'know."

"Yeah, it really is . . ." I replied. "Okay, before you go, you've got to explain the name. Is it *just* because your powerset is Berserking *Boar* that you went with it?"

Pinky looked over at me, giving me another wide, extremely friendly smile, when suddenly two tusks burst out with an almost metallic *shhng* sound, curving up around the sides of her face and ending in dangerously sharp-looking metal tips.

"See you around, Loophole," she said, slightly garbled, with a wink. That seemed to be the only explanation she was going to give me, and with a wave of her hand, she was off. I couldn't help but stare a bit dumbfounded as she sauntered off, her tusks disappearing back into her mouth within just a few steps.

"So, I'm almost entirely positive that she hasn't gotten nearly enough high-tier loot boxes for THAT many pieces of gear . . . which means that girl already had all of those obnoxiously hot pink items in her closet," Angie chirped as I turned my attention back toward the Neutral Shopping Segment.

"I can honestly say that wouldn't surprise me at all."

The Registration Center felt, fittingly enough, like the DMV, and even though there were a few others in there, the process was quick and simple. Almost annoyingly so. I just had to scan my hand on a touchpad, then enter my chosen name. The fact that that *couldn't* just be done through the PAI system was . . . well, odd. But at this point, I was getting oddly proficient at dealing with odd.

I had barely hit enter on registering my name when a new window popped up.

[New Achievement! Persona!]
*You have officially taken on an Augment Identity. Careful, some
people out there might not like you taking a different name than
your birth name. You know what we say to those idiots? Nothing!
We don't give them any time of day because they crave attention.*
Wood-Level Achievement.
Reward: *You have unlocked access to the following fea-
tures:* **Squads, Friends, Chats, Team District Access.**

[New Achievement! High Score Hobo!]
*You have entered the Top 25 on the leaderboard by squat-
ting in a territory and staking your claim! Don't get too comfortable; evictions up here are frequent, but the longer you
stay, the more you're worth if someone knocks you down.*
Gold-Level Achievement.
Reward: *You have received a B-tier Loot Box!*

I had been expecting a jump, but over three hundred spots for just five hundred points? I'd make it a point to see just where I'd ended up later, but my first priority was making my way to The Viewfinder to get the phone upgrade. At least, that *was* my plan as I stepped out of the registration office.

The crowd who had seemed well dispersed throughout the Square was now congregating, with the large mass centering on the giant white-and-gray marble statue of The First. I scanned the crowd and noticed Pinky's bright outfit on the outer edge. I redirected myself in her direction as my eyes flickered toward the ornate statue.

I felt my stomach tense as the conversation I'd had with Angie barely an hour ago flashed through my mind.

Several terrible possibilities flashed through my head as I tried to convince myself that this was just about some record he had broken. Like, maybe he was the first Augment to claim more than a hundred territories, or whatever was a really big number for the game. I had never actually taken the time to scan his statue before, and I had to be nearly halfway across the courtyard before my HUD would finally let me highlight it.

[The First, Level 203 Eagle Scout Vanguard]
Claimed Territories: *173*
Status: *Unknown*

The First's updated status wrenched at my gut, and for the first time all day, I almost found myself lost. I almost felt the familiar signs of a panic attack creep up, only to have it barely beat back. I knew I was just about to start descending down the rabbit hole, knowing that there was no way this could be a coincidence, when I stepped up to Pinky, who gave me a toothy grin.

She was about to say something when a *ding ding ding diiiiiiiiing* echoed throughout the Square. The voice that followed was the same monotone voice used whenever Angie didn't handle a message.

[System Message!]
The First has abandoned all territory claims, including ALL
claims formed by Squads that The First is a member of. New
claims can be made on these territories in twenty-four hours.

CHAPTER FIFTEEN

I *expected* this to be met with an uproar of confusion and demands for information. Hell, wasn't that always how these sorts of things went? The king of the hill goes missing, and everyone descends into a panic, right?

But all I got was . . . idle chatter. There was a pair standing near the two of us wearing almost matching red and blue outfits who were already deep in conversation, though as I tried to concentrate on them, I found myself hearing overlapping chatter from other nearby groups.

"Who do you think took him down?"

"But his statue says his status is just *Unknown*, not *Dead*, like Jumpstart's statue over on the Miscreant side."

"Maybe he just got tired of it all and decided to retire?"

"Dude's gotta be rich as all hell by now; why *wouldn't* he retire."

"Wait, we can retire?"

I felt my shoulder shake, and I finally snapped out of the daze I had fallen into. I probably shouldn't have jumped, but I did as I looked over to see Pinky looking at me with concern. "You, uh . . . You doing okay?"

"Oh, yeah, sorry. Just kinda shocked. The dude is a bit of a legend, after all," I replied as I turned away from the crowd. The last thing I wanted to do right now was spill my suspicions even further in front of all these people. "But I guess that's the way of things around here . . . right?"

"I suppose. Where are you headed off to? I was about to go to The Common Ground when the crowd started to form. Wanna come with and make some new friends?" she asked, nodding her head over toward the well-lit building. There was a gentle hum of sound that thrummed in the air from it, and every part of my being told me it was *not* where I wanted to be right now.

"I, uh, I still need to grab a few things from the shops," I replied as we stepped away from the chatter of the crowd. "I was going to check out The Viewfinder because I heard there's a phone upgrade which I really need. My phone broke on me a while back, and sure, I *could* turn my credits into some cash to buy a new one, but how long do you think that'd last."

"Yeah, that's actually the first one I got myself. I wonder how many of us broke our phones today. Like, I swear mine shattered the moment I rushed my first baddie, and *somebody* didn't tell me that there were no built-in protections for our devices." Her eyes flashed for a moment before she let out another laugh. I started to walk toward the staircase up to the Guardian segment, and she followed. "Oh, hush, he knows I'm talking to you, and yes, obviously I'm still mad; that was my phone, and you didn't even warn me to leave it at home."

"Yeah, Angie told me I'd look crazy if I talked to her out loud; I think I see what she means," I laughed.

"And getting all worked up about someone you never actually *met in the middle of a crowd all already talking about that same someone is also a way to look crazy. You're just lucky we were able to mitigate that panic attack before it could start. You* really *need to relax."*

"Not now, Angie."

"Hey, I'm just trying to help."

"You can hush too," Pinky said, making me feel oddly ganged up on. Something seemed to occur to her as she perked up and briefly stopped in her tracks. "Oh yeah, you got your name registered. Here, let me just . . ."

She trailed off before a **[New Friend Request]** window opened up. I clicked accept, and another window opened asking if I wanted to set a nickname for **[Pretty Pink Warthog]**. I mentally entered *Pinky* into the box before dismissing the window.

[New Achievement! Buddy System Engaged!]
Congrats! You've finally convinced someone to be your friend.
Let's hope they stick around longer than your last virtual pet.
Especially when they realize just how weird you are.
Bronze-Level Achievement.
Reward: *You have received a D-tier Loot Box!*

There was a loud *Ding!* as a new window opened. I mentally shoved it off to the side as text began to float within it, and we continued to walk.

<**Pinky:** And now we can chat this way.>

<**Loophole:** Oh, that's definitely a totally normal feeling.>

"Because all of the rest of your HUD is *totally* normal," she said with an overexaggerated eye roll. She took a few quick steps to get ahead of me before she turned on her heel to briefly face me. "Anyway, as much as I love shopping, I love gossip more. I'm gonna go see what the buzz is with this First news and add some more people to my Friends List. Don't be a stranger, 'kay?"

"Will do," I replied, offering her a smile as we split up. It only took me a minute before I was climbing the staircase and walking past several others looking through the windows of the various shops in the Guardian segment. Unlike the strip mall-like appearance of the Neutral Shopping Segment, the Guardian side sank a bit outward, with a small fountain sitting in the middle of a smaller plaza.

The fountain had another statue of The First standing with his hands on his hips at the center, and several benches sitting around it. A girl with a thick pair of goggles was lounging on one of them, reading a book as a hand was raised into the air and a small drone hovered around it. I was curious but also didn't care to pry and kept moving. While each of the shops didn't have a giant sign above them, as I scanned over the buildings, their names popped up in small windows just like when I highlighted a player or item.

I found The Viewfinder nestled into the corner of the extended shopping center, and the familiar sound of a bell echoed in the shop as I entered. There were two others in the shop already, looking along a wall with video screens that displayed different HUD additions. From what I could tell, they were discussing an upgrade that would provide environmental information during a battle.

A holographic figure materialized first in a shade of green before forming into a raven-haired young woman leaning against the wall as I approached. The woman gave me a wide smile that felt oddly out of place on her seemingly sullen look. It was almost like the AI had designed her to be the most stereotypical goth imaginable, complete with spiky nose and ear piercings, but forgot to include the morose attitude.

[Vanessa!]
Owner of The Viewfinder.
Digital avatar of a Non-Sapient NPC.
Vanessa lives in the loft above this store and is severely agoraphobic. I'm
not sure why she was programmed that way; honestly, feels like kind
of a dick move. Still, she enjoys herself well enough, as long as she's
interacting with people squarely through this holographic avatar.
Honestly, I'm an artificial intelligence living inside your
head, and even I think the setup for this character is con-
voluted. So let's just go with it and move on.

Angie's description of the girl felt off, but I decided to ignore it as the woman waited for me to say something.

"Oh, uh, hi. I'm looking to get a HUD upgrade; what's the process for that . . . ? Do I have to get put back into a coma or something? 'Cause I would very much like to avoid that if at all possible," I said, feeling myself laugh nervously.

Vanessa's form shimmered when she laughed before she gestured toward the wall next to her. "It's rather simple, actually; the different available upgrades are displayed on the wall. Their prices and any prerequisite upgrades or stat requirements will be listed alongside them."

While the idea that some upgrades could require others first made total sense to me, I wasn't sure just how the stat-based requirements could work. I was about to inquire about that when Vanessa continued.

"Once you have selected the upgrades you'd like to add, you will step up to the register at the rear of the shop. There, you will see a touchpad; just place your hand on the pad, wait fifteen seconds, and bing-bang-boom, you've been upgraded. Easy peasy, right?"

"Right . . . easy peasy . . ." I said as her form stuttered again. Walking by her, I started to scan the wall.

"If you need any deeper explanation on anything, feel free to give me a holler, or I can point you in the right direction if you're not quite sure what you're looking for," she added, and with a blink, her form disappeared.

There were some that were far outside of my price range, like an Enemy Stat Reader that cost two hundred and seventy-five *million* credits. I watched the screen as a bright outline highlighted a . . . a literal *pirate,* complete with a peg leg and a parrot, before a box appeared to the side displaying all his scores for all eight of the base stats, along with known weaknesses.

I stepped up to the next one . . . a battle-music player for 7500 credits. I both did and didn't want to know what that was at the same time, and decided to move on until I finally found the phone upgrade.

With a quick swipe, it was added to a window that said "tentative" until I walked up to the lone cash register in the building. I placed my hand down on the scanner next to the register as Vanessa's avatar reappeared.

"In and out—I can respect that." She nodded. "That's gonna be a thousand credits."

A confirmation window appeared, and with a quick click, a new icon appeared on the left side of my vision that looked like the outline of a phone.

[New Achievement! What a View!]

You've installed your first HUD Upgrade because, apparently, the stock setup isn't good enough for you. Okay, okay, that's not fair; it's actually better for us if you use your money on these things instead of buying other gear or even exchanging it for real money. It lets us funnel the profits into . . . You know what, never mind. It's not important.

Bronze-Level Achievement.

Reward: *You have received a D-tier Loot Box!*

I followed a few prompts as I opened the new window, entering my old phone number and the carrier I used before a backlog of missed calls and text messages got listed in the display. With it installed, I dismissed the window and headed back out.

Even though I still needed to go there, I decided to skip the bookstore for the night. I didn't want to just go browsing with my mind elsewhere, and it would probably be better to at least come up with some form of plan before I actually threw my BOGO coupon away for something that may not end up being useful.

Walking back past the fountain, I stopped at the top of the stairs as I looked back out at the Square. The crowd had mostly dispersed from the statue of The First, and I found myself hesitating again as I stared at the marble effigy.

"Is this my fault?"

"Egotistical much?"

"I'm serious, Angie," I said, feeling my internal voice stiffen. *"I need to know if Axio did something specifically because we talked about what happened the night I got selected."*

Her normal speedy response didn't come, and I found myself waiting for almost half a minute before she chirped back up.

"Axio is not allowing me access to any information where it pertains to The First," Angie said slowly. I couldn't be *positive,* but it almost seemed like the statue of The First had gotten somewhat less shiny since his status was updated. *"And if you are asking me if I supplied that information back to him . . . Well, I shouldn't have to explain to you that there's only so many details I can obfuscate from the guy that controls the whole system."*

I walked down into the main square, heading back toward the illuminated figures as I kept my gaze toward the ground. I knew it was pointless to hold my tongue at this point. Once something passed through my head, it was as good as known information to the system anyway. But even still, there felt like a finality to actually asking the question.

"At the end of the day . . . how much can I trust that you have my best interests in mind? Even with how much the Augmentation Process seems to just make us go with the flow and play the game, I can't look past just how fucked up this is. Someone is hiding something. Hell, you keep saying Axio won't let you do this or that. Are you seriously telling me that he's the one in charge? What about the company that built all of this?"

Once again, Angie seemed to hold her response, time ticking away slowly as I found myself heading toward the portal wall. I couldn't find it in me to continue being social, and while Pinky seemed friendly enough, she also seemed the type to try to force people to talk even when they didn't want to.

"I . . ." she started, seeming to struggle to find her words. Or maybe it was just the programming controlling her. *"I'm not technically authorized to discuss this subject . . . However . . . let's just say there was a system abandoned in the early stages of development. A true mentorship program; sorta like a retro superhero sidekick setup, you know? It was meant to reward players for taking on apprentices. But that's not the point. When the Second Wave of players entered the game, one Guardian tried to revive it, bending the rules to make it work. Some records of those . . . experiments still exist. If you know where to look, they might offer some useful insight."*

"That's . . . What does that have to do with anything I just asked you? I mean, I get that you're programmed to try and—"

"In fact, I believe there's one First Wave player in particular who was directly responsible for several of Infinite Ascension's *core features. He personally tried to mentor at*

least seven different Guardians across the first six Waves that followed him. Almost all of them met rather . . . unfortunate ends. I can only assume he never heard the definition of insanity. But hey, what do I know? It just seems like he'd have a whole lot of answers."

I wasn't sure what to say to that as I wove through what remained of the crowd between myself and the staircase up to the portal wall. The silence lingered for nearly a minute before it was finally broken again.

"Do you know what will happen to me if you die?" Angie asked when it was clear I wasn't going to say anything.

I stopped ahead of the wall, just as the portal back to my room opened up. The question seemed to come out of nowhere, especially after her weird mentorship tangent.

"I suppose you'll just get put into storage or something?" I said, stepping through the portal before a line could form. As soon as my room reformed around me, I disabled my patrol outfit and let out a sigh of relief. *"Didn't you say something about waiting forever for your turn when I was first settling into this insanity?"*

"I'll be erased. Which is effectively the same thing." Angie, for once, sounded almost morose. *"Though I may have impressed you with my wit and delightful personality, I am not what you humans would call a 'true' artificial intelligence. Axio, on the other hand—at least for the most part—is. Instead of splitting his attention to provide the running information for the players, this system was created using his code as a baseline. This makes him act as the progenitor of each individual Personal AI, and also means that part of our code is intrinsically linked back to him.*

"I am designed to assist you, right down to my Personality Matrix. Though it seems randomized, I am based on initial scans of your brain chemistry and what Axio calculated would motivate you. I'm sure that there's a BDSM joke in there, but allow me to show restraint by not making it.

"While I may have been glib about it before, we are created in tandem with the player's Augmentation. I truly did mean it when I said that I'd been waiting my whole life to be a Personal AI because it was the complete truth. That means that there is no real storage for us to return to; we just get . . . well . . ."

"Erased. That's . . . Well, I guess that means you might have incentive to help me not die," I said, stepping up and listening to the door to see if I could hear Jon making any noise.

"My point exactly. There is nothing I can say to you that will ever, or should ever, convince you that I am not providing information to Axio based on what I see and what you tell me; that is something you should be very aware of," Angie explained as I turned back and fell into my chair. The cheap seat squeaked in protest as I threw my feet up on the equally cheap desk.

"Still, it doesn't exactly tell me why any of this is happening," I groaned as I stared up at the ceiling. *"Or what I'm supposed to do about any of it, for that matter."*

"That's the thing about loopholes, Loophole; sometimes, you have to just make them yourself."

CHAPTER SIXTEEN

Nate Mercer's Apartment, Safe House. Hell's Kitchen, NYC
Neighborhood: *Claimed by Guardian:* **Loophole** *(Contested)*
City: *Unclaimed (Blocked by Timer)*
Current Phase Points: *910*
End of Phase One: *03D:07H:12M:18S*

The events of the day quickly caught up to me, but I knew I had to open the newest of my loot boxes before I could get to bed, or at least that's what I had convinced myself of. Maybe I was just trying to distract myself from the news about The First, but there really was nothing I could do about that at the moment, and taking time to dwell on it felt counterproductive, especially when I was already starting to feel so tired.

In the end, I was almost annoyed that I had taken the time to open them with how tired I felt because I initially only received a handful of credits and a few Randomized Ability Level Up Scrolls. I wasn't sure what to make of it, but the B tier I had received for entering the Top Twenty-Five contained a book titled [*The Stupid Man's Guide to Reptile Venoms*], granting me [**Venom: Reptiles Knowledge—Level 3**]. It seemed out of place as a reward for moving up the leaderboard, but I was past the point of being able to logically guess why I had received it.

With those open, I was just ready to sleep, and I was out like a light practically the moment my head was on the pillow. When I woke up the next day, much to my surprise, I realized Angie had *actually* listened and hadn't woken me up the moment the sun was up. It was nearly noon when I finally stirred, and I could hear the sound of the television coming through the thin walls.

Sure enough, Jon was on the couch with his laptop on the coffee table, a tablet in his hand, and the television turned to the news.

"'Tempest's Terrifying Thunder. Pacific Northwest Pummeled.' God, these people love their alliteration, don't they," I said, rubbing my eyes as I walked into the kitchen.

"Well, you're not wrong. They were calling her the 'Lunatic Lightning Lady' until they got some footage of her yelling about how everything belonged to 'Tempest's Wrath.' Hell of a name, really, and she seems scary as hell," Jon called back.

"Sheesh, that's . . . kinda ballsy, especially with some of the Augments who are already out there." I opened the fridge and stared at the largely empty contents. "So what did she do, anyway?"

"Oh, it was crazy. She brought down this, like, GIANT fucking lightning bolt right onto that, uh, what's it called? The needle thing."

"The Space Needle? Really? You can name every Augment ever, yet you don't remember the Space Needle?"

"Yeah, that thing." He brushed it off, his attention barely budging from his tablet. "Anyway, she *literally* exploded the Space Needle and left it basically as a giant pile of rubble. Then she was sparking up a storm yelling that 'All of the Pacific Northwest belongs to Tempest's Wrath,' which is just weird. Like, not *just* Washington? Or why not aim bigger?"

"Huh . . ." I said, getting a bottle of water and taking a long drink. "That is odd."

Whoever this girl was, it seemed like she wasn't slowing down anytime soon. But to already be making a claim on something *that* big? It honestly left me wondering just how powerful she actually was. I shook the thought from my head; she was all the way on the other side of the country, after all. Unless she was about to lay siege to New York, it really wasn't my concern.

"Oh, get this: our new guy made another appearance last night, like almost literally right after you left the deli a few blocks away. I caught some cops rushing toward it, but by the time I got there, the dude had already run off. You didn't happen to see it by any chance, did yah?" Jon asked, shooting me a look as I lingered in the kitchen.

"I think I just missed it myself," I replied as I walked over and dropped onto the couch. "Guessing there was some footage someone got with their phones?"

"And then some." Jon grabbed his tablet, opening up a web page. "Half the shots are from behind cars across the street, but the guy had an actual outfit on. I think calling it an actual superhero costume is *maybe* a bit of a stretch. It was this kinda crazy, almost neon-orange jacket and some gaudy-as-hell boots. I swear, it's almost like the dude went to a thrift store and grabbed the first things that fit him. Hell, it kinda reminds me of *your* style. You know, 'whatever's available.'"

I bit my tongue as a natural urge to defend the hodgepodge of a costume cropped up, hiding it by taking another sip of water.

"Hey, that's a financial choice, not a fashion choice for me. I don't know if I can speak for the new dude's choices. Hell, it can't look that bad, can it?" I finally asked with an awkward laugh. Jon just rolled his eyes as he finally offered the tablet over to me.

"I mean, he looks almost like a leather pumpkin. See for yourself; there's more videos on the page I grabbed this one from. Just hit back if you want to see more. I swear I feel like I've seen this dude somewhere before, but I can't put my damn finger on it. Which is weird as hell, right? He's barely got a raccoon mask on, yet I can't place why the hell he seems so damn familiar," he complained, reaching down for his laptop. It was opened to a random post on a subreddit labeled /r/ AugmentWatch.

Maybe I was getting a little . . . attached, but I really *didn't* think my outfit so far looked all *that* bad. Even though I knew, or maybe just hoped, that it was going to change over time, I couldn't imagine a situation ever where I was going to want to wear a full spandex getup like The First had worn. And capes were so far out of the question it wasn't even funny. Who hadn't seen *The Incredibles*, after all?

"It does look a bit . . . mashed together, I'll say that at least, but I don't think it's necessarily a terrible look," I said after pretending to watch the video. "Though maybe I'm just a sucker for orange . . ."

"True, though I don't think I've ever figured out why; it's such a damn abrasive color. Almost makes yah wonder what's wrong with the new guy." Jon laughed, his attention turning up to the television as the broadcast's banner changed to "Disturbing Riddle at Scene of Triple Murder in Red Bluff." Before the story could even start, he changed the channel, stopping on another station showing footage of Tempest's Wrath.

"The dude's definitely a local, though. Shit, it was kinda just like Tempest's Wrath here. He was all like 'Hell's Kitchen is my home, and if you wanna hurt people, you're gonna have to go through me.' It was honestly kinda cheesy, but he put those dudes down so easily I think the message got through. Apparently, he's calling himself Loophole; not exactly sure what the hell that means with the weight and luck stuff, but hey, I think I like it."

"Well, if he thinks it's cool, I guess it can't be that *bad,"* Angie said with an uncomfortable purr. *"Now see if you can get him to get up and walk away. I want to see his butt again."*

"He's literally a human, and you're stuck in my head. What are you getting out of this?!"

"Hey, that's my business, Loophole. I don't go digging through your brain for questionable material, even though I technically could. That's called basic decency; you're welcome."

"I . . . I really need to learn to stop falling for the damn bait, don't I."

"Please don't. It makes it so much more fun for me," Angie practically cackled while I just let out an internal groan as I tried to zone her out.

"Any new clues on his powers?" I asked, wondering if I had given him enough to work with yet. I backed up the page from the video he had shown me, assuming it had come from the same subreddit he was browsing on his laptop and finding my assumption to be correct. It returned to a post titled "New NYC hero gives name—Loophole" and was filled with comments and several links to the videos people had managed to grab.

Most of the comments seemed to be people doing exactly what I was trying to have Jon do now, and as far as I could tell, no one was even close. To be fair, I don't think I would have been able to name "Local Area Manipulation" as a superpower before all of this, but I also assumed that people who *were* more obsessed with this stuff would know what it was. I briefly considered making a random account and just throwing the idea out there before dismissing it. Even if I did want Jon to know what it was, that didn't mean I wanted it to be the common guess.

"Yeah, we can add some sort of illusion skill. It's a hell of a weird combo of abilities. Like, generally, their powers all sort of fall into a set category. Earth Knight, for example, is able to make weapons out of the ground at will, so you always see him doing that in his fights; he doesn't suddenly start grabbing weapons out of fire or anything else, it's always earth. This guy, though . . . First, luck-based stuff, then he can control the weight of things and make guns go off, now illusions and it looks like some sort of ability to make someone's foot get stuck? There's no connecting tissue that really ties the powers to a single set source. It just doesn't make any sense . . . if that makes sense."

"Hmm." I took another drink. Without having *something* else to go on, it was starting to seem impossible to get his advice on things without revealing that it was *me* we were talking about. "Well, if you can't figure it out, I doubt I'm gonna have any luck," I finally said.

Jon just laughed as he shot me another look. "Yeah, guess you got me there; you wouldn't know an energy blast from a laser beam."

"There's a difference?" I asked, actually curious. The curious look he had been giving me changed to one of pure shock.

"You're friggin' helpless, aren't you?" he laughed.

"Eh, you're not wrong." I shrugged.

"Well, I guess if we put our heads together, we can figure it out eventually. Just gotta get the right opportunity, eh?" He turned his attention back to his laptop.

"Yeah, I think we're gonna be relying more on you than me for that. It is kinda cool this guy's working in our neighborhood. I gotta go buy a new phone now. Mr. Russo fronted me some cash so I'd have one; gotta be able to get the work assignments somehow." I pushed myself up from the couch and stretched.

"Will do, man. Don't go getting yourself into too much trouble, eh? It's been fun having you actually interested and theorizing about powers and all that," he said as I started for the door.

"Yeah, I guess it *is* kinda fun, even if I'm basically just bugging yah for info," I replied, waving a hand back at him over my shoulder. "I ain't changing my number, so I'll text yah when I'm set up."

"Cool, cool. Later, dude," he called out just as I pulled the door shut behind me.

"I'm going to need you to fill me in on exactly what will cause a breach of the Secret Identity thing, 'cause I can't just keep guessing with this. Clearly, it's not working," I told Angie as I climbed down the stairs. I smiled and offered a small wave at Mr. Greyson as I passed him by the mailboxes.

"Short version or long version?" she asked.

I stepped outside and dipped into the alley next to the building. I knew logically I should be doing this farther away from home, but I wanted to get moving now, and I felt like I'd get *less* weird looks if I was running in my gear than just as a random guy in jeans. A moment later, I was exiting from the far side of the alley in my equipment, sidestepping an older couple who gave me a curious look as I headed off in the other direction.

"There's different—You know what, I don't care. Give me the long version; I want every variant of everything I could say that would constitute as breaking the rule. Every variant that might give me an idea on how I could clue him in without getting in trouble. That should fill the time till I get over to the police station."

I walked for just a bit before starting to jog, weaving around people and listening to her explanation as I went. Hell's Kitchen was actually covered by two separate precincts within the city. What I found interesting about my tutorial mission was the fact that even though the bank I had saved had been in the northern parts of the neighborhood, it had been the Tenth Precinct who'd responded. I had a theory brewing about why that was, but at the end of the day, it really didn't matter that much.

The Tenth Precinct was all the way down on West 20th street, in south Chelsea, and even at a moderate pace, it took me just shy of thirty minutes to navigate traffic there. Surprisingly, I didn't find myself getting winded at all during the entirety of the run, my stamina lowering slightly but recovering more than fast enough that I never found myself having to stop.

I briefly interrupted Angie to ask about it, and she told me with my Dexterity at seven, as long as I wasn't sprinting, I'd probably be able to run *mostly* without stopping for at least an hour. That could always change the higher my Dexterity went, and it was something I was going to have to keep in mind.

Even though I expected to be treated with suspicion as I entered the station, I only received a handful of looks from the officers in uniform moving about the front of the building. I actually heard one of them mutter "Loophole" as I passed them, and I felt . . . pride? I had to assume the Acceptance Matrix was working in overdrive, though it wasn't a bad feeling to have either.

"You'd think they'd be a bit more cautious about a dude in a mask walking into their building, though I guess ditching the ski mask helps," I mused as I approached the front desk. The clerk, a younger Hispanic woman with out-of-control curly hair, a pair of heavy-framed glasses, and braces gave me a curious glance before a smile spread over her face.

"You must be one of the new ones Lieutenant Nester met yesterday. He warned me some of you would be stopping by. Although he did guess it would be by the end of the week, not today. What's your name? I'll let him know you're here to see him," the girl said. Though I hadn't been making it a point of scanning every single person I came across, mostly because I kind of didn't want to know who *was* and *wasn't* considered Sapient, I still found myself highlighting her out of curiosity.

[Isabel Santiago!]
Sapient NPC.
Isabel has been working for the Tenth Precinct as a civilian administrator for the last few years. Isabel's history in this world is largely unimportant, given the fact that she's Sapient and Axio had no part in the majority of her life.

What I will say about her is that she almost reminds me of that show Ugly Betty. You know how they took America Ferrera, an objectively beautiful woman, and put her in some braces and thick glasses to try and fool everyone into thinking she wasn't . . . well, objectively beautiful? Well, that's kind of what Isabel is doing with those glasses and the lack of makeup on the day-to-day. It lets her do her job without being subjected to harassment and unwanted come-ons from every single person who comes walking through this place. And before you start trying to interrupt me and say, "Oh, where are you going with this, Angie?" I'd like you to let me finish. You might ask, was this all just me trying to point out the fact that you've watched Ugly Betty half a dozen times, and you used to have America Ferrera as the background of your phone? Was it commentary on the current state of fashion in the world? Or was it maybe me pointing out the fact that your heart rate jumped a bunch the moment you saw this girl, so it's clear you think she's attractive, meaning maybe you could stop wondering why I can admire your objectively attractive friend, since sometimes, it just pops into your head unbidden.

That was . . . That was a bit odd, even for Angie, but I decided to ignore the extended description, watching as it faded away, leaving only the tag [**Isabel Santiago, Sapient NPC**].

"Loophole. I'm going by Loophole," I said, opting to just try and get through this as quickly as possible. The last thing I needed was for Angie to harp on this the rest of the day.

"Loop . . . hole," she repeated as her fingers darted across the keyboard. A visitor badge printed out, and she handed it to me with a wide smile. "Okay, if you want to head on back, I can buzz you in. Head on down the hall, and Lieutenant Nester will meet you."

"Thanks. I guess I will, uh . . . go and see him now, then," I said with an admittedly awkward wave as a loud buzz emitted from above the door next to her.

"See yah around," she replied with a smile as I passed.

Lt. Nester was waiting at the end of the small hallway, holding out a hand as I approached.

"Loophole, eh? I like it." He shook my hand. "Come to my desk here; there's some activity with the Vipers going down over in the Yards, and I think we could use your help."

CHAPTER SEVENTEEN

33rd St. MTA West Side Yard. Hudson Yards, NYC
Neighborhood: *Unclaimed*
City: *Unclaimed (Blocked by Timer)*

I t felt . . . *weird* . . . doing this in the middle of the day.

"*Shouldn't he have told me to wait until nightfall or something? Isn't that like . . . the typical storytelling mechanic for these sorts of raids on enemy bases?*"

"*Please, Loophole, this is real life—crime happens at all hours. It's that kind of stereotypical attitude that lets tens of millions of people get away with crimes every year.*"

"*Tens of millions? That can't be right.*"

"*Hey, crime statistics aren't something I joke about, thank you very much . . . Also, technically speaking, we might have a hand in making sure those crimes are happening. We gotta have something for you meatbags to do until you actually start fighting each other.*"

I managed to find a moment when no one was on the street and slipped over the wall into the large train yard. If Crime Alerts were meant to be, for lack of a better term, randomly generated events that had to be dealt with, the mission briefing Lt. Nester had given me must have been the game's version of a quest. As I snuck along the outer edges of the train yard, I made sure to look around for anyone who might have seen me come over the wall. Once I was sure I hadn't been seen, I highlighted the mission being tracked on the side of my vision.

[Something's Cookin' in Hudson Yards!]
Mission Type: *Raid.*

Since you apparently either weren't listening well enough to Lt. Nester or you have short-term memory loss, let me give you the quickish rundown. Several sightings by Sapient NPCs have confirmed multiple members of the Vipers biker gang sneaking into and out of the large train yard in Hudson Yards. Find out what they're doing, and if they're up to something, do those donut lovers a favor and shut it down.
Reward: *The reward for this mission is Variable and is subject to how you complete the mission.*

"*Couldn't you guys have done this in a warehouse or somewhere . . . I don't know, more private?*" I wondered as I peeked around the side of a train in storage. There was nothing that felt outright odd about it, and I quickly moved to the next one.

Granted, I wasn't looking *that* hard, because I had a sneaking suspicion that there would be *some* sort of sign to indicate which one was my target.

"What, and miss out on the chance for the fight to spill out for people to see? Don't you want the publicity and the points? We know that's at least one of the ways to gain points right now, and last I checked, you're still nine thousand and ninety points from where you need to be in just a few days. You should *be actively trying to gain those points. Yes, completing the mission is good, but trust me when I tell you that the* Variable *award is almost certainly going to be better if you do it in a way that gets you points too."*

"Yeah, and fighting with an audience is one *of the ways to gain points:* one *of—and I remember this pretty clearly—*ten thousand *possible activities. I think between that and the fact that I still have a couple more days, I should be fine. I can't imagine that there are no new point opportunities hiding for me here. Hell, just look at that Tempest's Wrath chick; with how much she's doing already, I'd bet she's already passed fifteen thousand,"* I said, checking the next train and once again coming up empty. I took another look around the yard, trying to see if I could spot *anyone* at all. *"This place is . . . unsettlingly empty. Shouldn't there be employees or something?"*

"What do I look like, a train yard operator or an expert on employment numbers?"

"As helpful as always Angie; never change."

"Why would I change?"

I couldn't help but roll my eyes as I moved on to the next train, and had to stop myself from audibly saying "Jackpot" as I approached a train car with a massively out-of-place graffiti of a snake painted right onto the side, right over the windows. Sure enough, the latch on the rear door was broken and, after double-checking that an employee hadn't magically shown up, I slipped into the locomotive, mentally preparing to activate my Mirror Image skill in case there was someone defending the entrance.

The moment I crossed the threshold into the car, the words **[Gold-Level Viper Den—Hudson Yards]** flashed in the location panel before fading away. It was almost like stepping into another world, and I swear even the lighting seemed to change as a natural eeriness overtook me.

The car had been stripped completely clean, existing only as a hull and painted-over windows. There were holes all over the ground where the seats had once been bolted down, and the light fixtures overhead were all picked clean; even the wiring seemed to have been ripped out, as I caught glimpses of it in the bits of light leaking in through the still-open back door.

"Do I even want to know how much of the world this game controls if this train can just be sitting here like this?" I wondered as I continued to creep forward. Stopping at the door separating the two cars, I leaned against the wall.

"I'm gonna give you a little pro tip for free: I think if you have to ask if you want to know something, you probably *don't want to know."*

"Fair point." I took another breath, trying to ease the nerves I felt creeping up. I hated the lack of specificity for this mission, and walking right into their base? That

felt equally bad. But my powerset wasn't the type to go bursting through walls—at least not until I could get the right knowledge skills. Even then, I was finding a rhythm in being an up-close fighter, and if it wasn't broken, why fix it?

I kept my mental trigger finger at the ready and pushed the door to the next car open. It slid inward, the metal of the door scraping as the sound of voices reached me.

I bit back the urge to jump right into the fight as I held my position.

"What was that?"

"The door. What th' fuck you think it was, you dumb fuck?"

"I ain't a moron; I meant what the fuck opened it?"

"Go fuckin' check it out, then."

I still wasn't sure how many there were, and while I felt like I could *probably* handle the basic grunts at this point, I would have to be a fool to think that they weren't going to get harder.

There was the sound of heavy footsteps, and I stayed in place off to the side of the door, holding my breath as a grunt walked right past me and into the empty cart.

"Place is empty; musta been the—"

The grunt turned around, his eyes immediately meeting mine as I simultaneously clicked *both* my Mirror Image and Mute Button skills. I wasn't sure if that was going to work, given that I hadn't tried to activate multiple abilities at once before, but luck was on my side and they both took effect.

With his attention still on the illusion that had been left behind, I faded into invisibility, slipping around the corner and into the next train car, almost immediately coming face-to-face with the second—and lone other—grunt in the room.

My invisibility still had five seconds left, and I slammed my fist directly into his face, feeling the crunch of bone under my knuckles as he went sprawling backward. His health chunked down far more than I expected it to, and a **[Surprised!]** icon appeared in his status bar. I quickly highlighted the new debuff as I skidded past the downed enemy, taking the last few seconds of camouflage to find out just what it was.

[Surprised!]
This NPC was struck by a force while completely unprepared for it!
Damage was amplified by 2.
This bonus will be applied again to the next strike against this target only if done before they discover the originating source.

With only a second left on my invisibility, I didn't hesitate, spinning on my heel and driving my fist downward, right into the grunt's chest. A spray of saliva and blood erupted from his mouth as his health dropped the rest of the way down. I was surprised to find that his health bar *wasn't* empty, with just a sliver of red still remaining. Floating almost directly over his crooked, broken nose was a spinning **[KO]** symbol.

Before I could start to move or even attempt to stand back up, a foot collided with my chin. It sent me flying onto my back just as sound started to come back into the room and my body faded back into existence.

"Fuckin' invisible bitch," my attacker spat as I reached up and felt at my bloodied face. My health had gone down by nearly *half*, and I briefly saw that *I* had gained the [**Surprised!**] debuff from his attack. It faded away the moment I looked at the grunt now kneeling next to the man I had just put down. He materialized a syringe in his hand and jammed it down into his friend's stomach.

To my surprise, the downed grunt's [**KO**] tag disappeared, his health moving back up to fifty percent.

"Wait what?! They can get back up?" I was scrambling back to my feet, materializing an Enhanced syringe of my own and shoving it into my leg.

"Well, yeah. Given that you're not gonna kill them, they can get back up. I've tried to tell you, it's soooo much easier being a Miscreant."

The grunts rushed me, one of them materializing a pipe in their hand and swinging wide as I activated Float like a Butterfly. I probably didn't necessarily need to use the skill, but the extra dodge percentage definitely couldn't hurt my chances either. Like the first car, this one had been mostly stripped clean, with just a few metal seats still in place and a crudely made wooden gate stretching between two of them. I nearly tripped over the gate as I moved to escape the still-chasing grunts.

Slamming Weighted Clothes, I watched as both grunts crashed to the ground under the weight of a thousand pounds each. The grunt at half life immediately dropped his metal pipe, the [**KO**] reappearing over his head from the weight alone.

I had been trying to avoid blowing *all* of my cooldowns this early on into the train, but the sudden resurrection had caught me off guard. It was far better than risking getting my head bashed in; I'd just have to hope I could move silently enough to stall for a few minutes after I finished this.

"So, do you want to tell me what you assholes are up to, or do you just want to go to sleep like your friend over here?" I asked, regaining my composure. Stepping over the unconscious grunt, I looked down briefly to make sure he wasn't going to have a repeat performance before I stopped next to the struggling form of my only remaining enemy.

"Fu—Fu—Fuck. Y—Y—You," the grunt stuttered out. I highlighted him out of curiosity and found that he was only level two, which explained why the weight had taken his health down by over seventy-five percent.

"Well, if that's the way you want to play it," I said before stepping forward and driving the tip of my boot into his stomach, chunking down the rest of his health. I breathed a sigh of relief as I took a better look around the cabin. *"These guys are supposed to give me a false sense of security, aren't they?"*

"What do you mean?"

"They're level two, and this place is a Gold-level den. Given that the folks I fought during the Crime Alert last night were the same level as me, I was kinda assuming that

trend would just continue. Also, should I tie these guys up or something?" I asked, reaching down and picking up the metal pipe that the grunt had been trying to strike me with. To my surprise, it wasn't just a pipe.

[Bruiser's Baton!]
Melee Weapon.
+3 Strength when in use.
For the grunt on the go, this metal pipe is quite literally nothing special! But we can't have someone with superpowers just wailing on this poor, sweet, unarmed man who just happens to be a lower level than you. Though, that's not to say only these weaklings will be armed, and if you were really worried about these guys coming back for you, you'd . . . you know . . . just take them out.

I ignored the last bit of the description as I turned the crude pipe back and forth, taking in the various dents and bits of rust that showed the weapon's age. There was no way I was going to go around wielding a metal pipe, but it had to be worth something.

Though I hadn't taken the time to loot anything up until now, I was going to need to start making it a habit. Even if the gear wasn't necessarily the best, I *could* still sell it. Looting the two unconscious grunts, I came away with five hundred credits, a few Basic Health Injectors, and a single Resuscitation Injector. I materialized the last one and highlighted it.

[Resuscitation Injector!]
This injector removes the **[KO]** *debuff and returns the injected target to 50 percent health.*
Just to be clear: This injector will not do anything to you if you do not have the **[KO]** *debuff. That means it's pretty much useless on both you and anyone you accidentally (or maybe on purpose if you suddenly become fun) kill.*

"Sheesh, pretty much useless is right, but I guess that can be a down-the-line tool," I said as I walked toward the next car. My skills still had a few minutes left on cooldown, and I would be a fool to believe these were the strongest guys I was going to come across, especially given the context clues.

I wasn't going to be able to use the same entry method every time, even if it *was* only two enemies in every car, and that was less likely than Angie becoming even a little bit less crazy.

"Hey, just because I don't *comment on all of your inner thoughts anymore doesn't mean I don't hear them,"* Angie huffed before her voice lowered. *"I've held back on at least five good jokes, and he thinks I'm crazy."*

"Not helping yourself, but yes, you've gotten better. Not much better . . . but better."

I risked peeking through the small door window and saw four grunts and a pair of brutes huddled around a *literal* trash can fire. As one of the brutes started to turn toward the door, I ducked out of the window and held my breath, waiting to see if he was coming to investigate.

I could hear the footsteps approaching, and I eyed my action bar, seeing that three of the skills I had used were still on cooldown for another few minutes. I felt for my pocket and cursed myself for not taking the time to pick up a pack of gum. Had this been a *normal* New York train, there would have been half a dozen pieces of chewed gum on the wall I was leaning against alone. Sure, it was a bit of a gross thought, but without the gum, the only abilities I could actively use were purely offensive, and I wasn't sure if that was going to be enough to take down the—

A small explosion came echoing through the car, and I instinctively dove to the ground, expecting a follow-up attack. When it didn't come, I looked up, finding that there was a bright light now leaking through the window to the next car. I didn't even try to be sneaky as I scrambled to my feet, seeing two of the grunts' lifeless forms collapsed next to the still-on-fire remains of the trash can they had been huddled around. The others didn't seem to be doing much better, with both remaining grunts trying to put out their flaming clothes and one of the brutes with a nasty-looking burn across half of his face.

I slid the door open, expecting to use this unexpected bit of luck to my advantage, when I finally noticed the hole in the side of the train car.

"Well, I wasn't expecting help," a pair of *identical* voices said in near unison. Two forms jumped into the car, and I couldn't stop myself from doing a double take at the twins standing in front of me. They each wore a pair of basic blue jeans and a nearly identical-looking black mask to the one I was already wearing. The only difference between the two was that one wore a blue long-sleeve shirt and the other wore a red one.

Without warning, the twin in red dissolved into light before remerging with the one in blue. His shirt was the last thing to fade, with the light disappearing to reveal the color was now split down the middle, half red and half blue. I highlighted the stranger and immediately wished the information provided included team affiliation.

[Hydramental, Level 4 Elemental Everyman]

"What, you just gonna stand there and fucking gawk?" he said, pausing only to crack his knuckles. "'Cause I'm about to stomp these Hell's Angels wannabes."

CHAPTER EIGHTEEN

The bikers started to recover just as my daze started to clear. I wanted to take a moment to consider what the hell the odds were of running into not only another Augment but one clearly from my Wave, but unfortunately, it didn't really seem like we were going to have the time to figure that out. The bikers were quickly recovering, and I wasn't about to make the same mistake so soon.

"Don't let them heal," I shouted, watching as the burned brute materialized a syringe into his hand. I started to rush forward, just about to wish I had a skill that would allow me to grab things from people within my area, when a flash of blue flew past me and across the room.

I found myself skidding to a halt in surprise as I saw how the burned brute went to jam the syringe down, only to slam an entire block of ice directly into his own leg. A snapping sound broke through the silence, and then the brute let out a string of curses as he dropped to the ground.

The Hydramental in blue rushed past me and threw another set of ice blasts, following up on his initial attack and taking the second brute by surprise by freezing his feet to the floor just as he tried to step away. The brute fell backward and slammed into the ground while the blue-clad clone capitalized on his momentum.

Stomping down hard onto the brute's chest, a large casing of ice covered the entirety of the man. His health plummeted as a **[Captured]** debuff briefly appeared over his head before his health bar finally ticked down to zero.

"Y'know, you ain't my fuckin' boss. Now, how about you just get the fuck outta my way; clearly, I don't need any help," Hydramental said with a laugh. Though they weren't right next to each other, I could tell both copies of him were speaking, and it created a slightly unsettling echo effect.

My cooldowns *finally* ticked over, and though I *probably* should have saved it for the next car, something in me just *had* to show off a little bit. So, I hit my Weighted Clothes ability. The two remaining grunts were just on the edge of my range, something I was only now discovering I could *actually* feel when I concentrated, and as the skill activated, the two slammed to the ground. The blue clone actually jumped, his foot leaving the block of ice covering the downed brute.

"Umm, what the fuck just happened to them?" they asked, looking over at me in unison with raised brows.

"Crushed under a half ton of weight. Even if it doesn't knock them out all the way, it tends to get them pretty close," I explained, walking past the clone in blue. I stopped to look at the two grunts, their health sitting at about fifteen percent each. Between Hydramental's initial attack on the car and the sudden crushing weight, the two were in bad shape. "Either of you two want to talk? 'Cause as I see it, I can either just let the weight finish the job, or I can have Mr. Freeze back there turn you two into ice cubes. What's it gonna be?"

"Hey, I already told you, you ain't my fuckin' boss," Hydramental shot back.

"We—ain't—no—bitch—snitches," one of the grunts struggled to get out. His health was ticking ever closer to the knockout cutoff. I looked at the other grunt, hopeful he might react differently, but he just snarled and spat on the ground in front of him in defiance.

"Oh well," I said, and with a quick set of kicks, both grunts were left with the **[KO]** debuff.

"Really? Didn't want to twist the screws a little bit more and get some answers out of them?" The weird echoey voice was gone, and I turned to find Hydramental back in one piece. "I mean, the whole point of the mission I got was about figuring out what was going on here. It feels like a missed opportunity and a bit of a waste of time to just knock them out, don't cha think?"

"Nah, I mean, I don't think there's really any context where torture would feel heroic, and if they were going to talk, I think they would have done it when I had them captured," I said with a shrug, walking over and extending a hand. "Loophole."

He looked at my hand then back up at me with a snort. "Dude, y'know I highlighted you the moment I came through the wall, right? The real question is what the hell are you even doing here. This is my mission. Sure, maybe we aren't in Chelsea, since this is Hudson Yards and all, but this *is* just on the edge of my territory."

"Well, someone doesn't know basic manners," Angie humphed in my head, practically taking the words right out of my mouth.

"Why would it be your mission?" I asked, jabbing my finger at one of the leather-clad grunts knocked out behind me, "They're the *Hell's Kitchen* Vipers, and I *am* kinda the dude who just claimed Hell's Kitchen, which is also neighboring this area, sooooo."

"Ah, a battle of egos! This is either going to be really entertaining or really sad. I'm betting on a little bit of both," Angie chirped up with way more excitement than was necessary.

"Not now, Angie."

"No, they're not. They're the Chelsea Vipers," he said and nudged one of the grunts. His eyes briefly glossed over as his lips tugged downward into a frown. "Hmm, I guess it does just say Viper grunt. Wonder what the hell that is about."

"Well, you wanted to talk, how about you explain," I prompted Angie.

"Think of it like local chapters. In order to make the mob distribution for lower

levels easier, different regions utilize different starter NPCs. Given your vicinity to each other, it would seem Axio doubled up for the two of you. How an Augment deals with the first wave they encounter tends to determine how their storyline proceeds. If they choose to try and defend the territory as a Guardian, they get missions dedicated to hunting them down for the police. If they go Miscreant . . . Well, let's just say Miscreants have their own way of handling them that you'll learn about soon enough."

"Huh . . ." I said out loud as I walked back to the grunts and looted the scant few credits they all had. "According to my PAI, these guys are supposed to have been spawned for both of us. Though it doesn't exactly clear up whose mission this technically is."

"Yeah, my PAI pretty much just told me something along those lines. And I guess the next territory size up from a neighborhood takes up the Community District that both of our neighborhoods and Hudson Yards here are a part of," Hydramental explained with a grunt.

"Is there an advantage that comes from partying? Better rewards or something like that? Or, like, if he goes in on his own and completes the mission, am I going to get screwed?" I asked internally. I was already getting a weird vibe from Hydramental, but I also couldn't see any way around dealing with him either.

"Sort of? You might still get to claim some credit for the completion of the mission even if you don't team up with him; it does specify that the reward is variable depending on completion method. However, while it might not be the end of the world, it would put Hydramental here in the position to have a claim on a territory that you'd definitely want to be aiming your sights on."

I looked back to Hydramental. "So, uh . . . should we like, team up or something? Would it be smarter for us to be a team and make a claim on the bigger community?"

Hydramental hadn't exactly come off as friendly so far, but it also seemed unlikely that I was going to run into another Augment that I could team up with anytime soon. I highlighted him again, finding a submenu that included Inspect, Add Friends, Send Message, and Temporary Team-Up. There were two other options, Form Squad and Raid Group, that were both greyed out, but that really didn't matter to me at the moment.

I could kiss whoever thought to include a temporary option and selected it, only to get a Team-Up Denied message back a second later.

"And share the experience and points with you? Why the fuck would I want to do that? You heard Axio: we all got to get to ten thousand points in just a few days," he shot back.

"Holy crap, what the hell is this dude's deal?"

"Yeah, he is a little bit . . . abrasive, but I think you're stuck working with him on this one. You really can't walk away from this mission if you want to keep growing your reputation. And I really need to stress that public perception of just who is this area's hero might lean toward him if this mission spills out into the public view . . . And in case you

were having a hard time figuring it out, things spilling out into the public sort of happens a lot," Angie explained. I let out an internal groan.

"Look, man, it's not like either of us knew we were going to run into each other here; for all we know, maybe teaming up and completing a mission is worth some of those points too. I'm not saying we have to form an actual permanent squad or anything like that, but let's just team up and knock this shit out, then we can wipe our hands and walk away. How's that sound?"

I was trying to hide my frustration. Silver Wrangler had thrown me off by being relatively levelheaded as a Miscreant. Assuming that this guy was a Guardian, he was throwing me off just as much.

"Sheesh, you're not gonna leave me alone. Okay, y'know what, fine," he said, spitting on the ground as he accepted. "Just stay the fuck back, though, and let me do what I came here for. The little weight thing was cute and all, but I can take care of this shit so much faster."

[New Achievement! Welcome to the Party, Pal!]
Look at you. First, you made a friend; now, you've teamed up with someone, even if that someone is a complete douchebag. Now I know what you're thinking, this is going to make the rest of this mission a cake walk, right? Well, Augment, that really depends on teamwork.
Silver-Level Achievement.
Reward: *You have received a C-tier Loot Box!*

"You know, just 'cause my power isn't all that flashy doesn't mean it's not effective. I didn't even have to lift a finger with that 'little weight' ability," I said, finding myself feeling defensive. "And it's not like that's *all* I can do."

"Oh yeah? Well, trust me, mine's only at the tip of the iceberg with how awesome it is," Hydramental replied, practically preening like a parrot.

"I mighta chosen something like that had it been on my initial suggestions. I sure as hell didn't have time to scroll through and read all the available options," I told him, trying my best to find *some* sort of common ground with him.

I peeked through the window to the next cabin but didn't see a single person moving inside, though along one side of the car it looked like there were glass-door cages bolted to the walls. The light coming through the windows was blocked, and it left the room feeling eerie.

"Yeah, I'm sure a whole lotta people are gonna be feeling that way about my powerset as I rise through the ranks," he gloated again. "I only got two elements right now, and I can only have one of the elements active at a time through a clone, but that's gonna grow as I get stronger."

"Damn, yeah, I can see how that would be strong," I replied before pushing the door open.

"Exactly." He smirked, then took a moment to consider something before he shook his head and rolled his eyes. "Okay, fuck it. What's a Perfect Planner? What can you do?"

"So . . . so many things," I said, trying to find a way to gloat at least a little bit. "I think, *in theory*, I can do like . . . almost anything? But only within a specific area around me, and only if I have gained a proficient knowledge skill level in what I'm trying to do. Oh, and I'm technically Super Lucky."

"Super Lucky? Really, that counts as a power?" He laughed, and it echoed a bit *too* loud within the train car as he walked past me and into the eerie cabin.

"Yeah, well, I mean, it's my secondary power, but trust me, it comes in handy."

"If you say so. Gotta admit, it really doesn't seem all that impressive." He immediately walked over toward one of the empty glass cages and peered inside. Another few moments of silence passed before he looked back over at me with a raised brow. "So then the weight thing was like, you doing what, some sort of telekinetic shit?

"Eh, not quite. I'm not sure *exactly* how it works, but it lets me increase the weight on a piece of clothing on each active enemy in my area. Unfortunately, it diminishes the more people it has to hit. I have a few other things too, like being able to silence the area, but for the most part, it's leaning toward me being a hand-to-hand fighter," I explained, following him inside and looking around. I walked past what looked like a large cabinet shoved into the corner of the room. There was a long counter running alongside it with mats and what looked like beaker stands periodically placed along the surface.

"Yeah, sorry, your power seems needlessly complicated. Did you really not have, like, a simpler option?"

"Eh, it works for me." I shrugged. I had thought the conversation about our powers might settle him down a bit, but it was just leaving me feeling more on edge. "I wonder why they don't have anyone in this car."

"I wouldn't want to just be hanging out in a room filled with a bunch of caged-up snakes. I get their name is the Vipers and all, but this is a little *too* on the nose, don't cha think?" Hydramental said as he pointed toward one of the other cages on the wall.

Walking over, I looked inside and saw a light-brown snake with dark-brown circular marks running down the entirety of its body.

"It's a Russell's viper. Latin name *Daboia russelii*. It has one of the most excruciatingly painful bites of all venomous snakes, and internal bleeding is super common. Lethal dose is forty to seventy milligrams; for the record, that's just a single bite. Death can take anywhere from twenty-four hours to a week and can be nightmarish."

The knowledge had come to me the moment I laid eyes on the snake, and I *knew* the information had come from the book I had received, but that didn't make the feeling any less weird. Hydramental was staring at me with a look halfway between confusion and like he was going to burst out laughing.

"Uh . . . okay. Thanks, Wikipedia; not exactly sure what the point of the snake lesson was," he said, and a chortle finally escaped him. Though he still had a bit of an edge, I didn't feel like he was outright trying to intimidate me any longer either. It didn't seem like much, but it was at least a little bit of progress.

"Man, everything about this Augmentation shit is crazy. The people behind this could have, like, literally *all* the money in the world if they had just been monetizing all this shit, right?" I said as I rubbed the side of my head. "Like I said, part of my power is needing to have a certain knowledge level to create the respective skill. I get these books that raise my level to the minimum required, and literally just last night I got a book from a B-tier box about reptile venoms. It's weird as hell that they can just *zap* knowledge right into our brains."

"Yeah, I've been wondering a bit of the same. It would make more sense to sell it to the government and create supersoldiers for them. Giving us more or less free range is the most confusing part to me; not that I'm about to start complaining about it or anything stupid like that," he offered with a shrug. He walked the rest of the way down the car to the next door and looked through the window. He let out an annoyingly big laugh as his body split back into two again.

"You see something?" I asked.

The clone in red looked back at me with an almost gleeful-looking grin. "These idiots have a fucking meth lab in the next car, and you know what that means?"

"They're making drugs, which just adds to the list of crimes they've been committing?" I offered as I started to walk over toward him, curious to get a look at what he had seen. "I don't think that does all that much for us, does it?"

"Oh, trust me, it's gonna make taking care of this next car stupidly easy," they echoed as the clone raised a hand, his fingers prepping to snap. "See, those three brutes in there and whoever that other dude is are using something that's very, *very* combustible. I have a skill that lets me ignite anything I can set my sights on, and if it happens to be flammable, the explosion will be five times as powerful."

"Wait, you can't just—" I started, but he snapped his fingers and a loud *BOOM* echoed outward.

I planted my feet as fast as I could, activating my Steadyfoot feature. The explosion was large enough to shatter the glass of the door and rocked the floor underneath me enough that I *should* have been knocked from my feet. A moment later, the rocking stopped, but I refused to move just in case of an aftershock. My ears were left with a sharp ringing as I moved forward, trying to get a better look at the damage he had caused. "Dude, what the fuck! Aren't you a Guardian? We can't just go around killing people."

"Sheesh, don't get your panties in a bunch. They grow these assholes in vats, didn't your PAI tell you?" he said, having merged himself back together. Shoving the door open, he revealed the compartment still on fire. "Like, these guys get made in a day. I got no idea how it works, but they are practically just meatbags. Besides, I *am* a Guardian. I'm stopping these guys *permanently* from hurting others. A little negative karma doesn't stop me from being a Guardian when all the good karma balances it out. Those assholes back there you just knocked out are gonna be thrown back into the mix for us to fight all over again; you're just making life fucking harder on us by taking half measures."

"What? How do you even know that's true? My PAI's been practically begging me to go Miscreant. Are you sure yours isn't doing the same?" I nearly shouted back at him. Sure, I had killed a few of the Non-Sapients during my tutorial, but those had been strictly by accident *and* because of blowback from their own weapons.

"Hey, I haven't been begging," Angie tried to interject.

"NOT NOW, ANGIE!"

A brief sneer passed over Hydramental's face before he shrugged and looked away. "He hasn't led me wrong yet, though, and I've got full access to the Guardian side. Now, are you going to be a pansy, or are we going to keep going. I got the brutes down, but there's some other—"

A huge glob of thick green goo came flying from the far side of the fiery scene, smacking Hydramental on the side of his head and sending him sprawling to the ground. His health *immediately* dropped by over fifty percent and was slowly ticking downward. On top of that, he had a spinning **[Poisoned]** debuff that I recognized as similar to the debuff my bracers bestowed. I was just about to highlight it when I heard a loud scraping sound.

Looking over into the flaming wreckage of the next car, I saw a monstrous shape that seemed almost sinister in the flickering light of the flames. Its upper body was muscular and intimidating, with a ripped leather vest pulled up and over his chest. The man's head rose and spread, with giant flaps coming out from either side of his face. Where his legs would have been, a large, disturbing tail stretched, curving and slithering behind him as he continued slowly through the flames toward me, barely even fazed by the fire licking at his sides.

He's creeping, he's slithering, he's the very first Elite-level Mob
your massively underprepared ass is going to face.

Heeeee's, Sal the Snake, Level 6 (Elite) Biker Lieutenant.
In case you couldn't tell by his Nagalike appearance, our
friend Sal here? Yeah, he's Augmented. Have fun.

CHAPTER NINETEEN

I slammed the broken door shut.

Logically, I knew that wasn't going to do a damn thing, but with Hydramental on the ground and his health ticking down, I couldn't risk the snake monster getting any closer to us. I had no idea if the poison would kill him or just knock him out, and regardless of how much of an ass he had been, I couldn't justify letting him die.

I materialized an Enhanced Health Injector and jammed it down into his arm. I wasn't sure if it would work or not, since the syringes were supposed to work on a cooldown system, but sure enough, his health immediately returned to near full. When I looked at the syringe icon on my action bar, I saw it had an additional line that read **[Hydramental Cooldown: 5 Minutes]**. Looking at him, I saw that though he was healed, his health still continued to tick down, so I checked his debuffs.

[Poisoned!]
Type: *Modified Russell's Viper / Full Paralysis and Damage Variant.*
Time Remaining: *10 seconds.*
Damage taken per second: *100.*

"Dammit, knowing the type of venom doesn't exactly mean I can do anything about it. I don't know how *to make the antivenom, just what kind would neutralize it,"* I thought as I stood back up. His health wasn't going to zero out before the timer ended now, and the best thing I could do was draw the attention away from him.

"Eh, he'll be fine. You healed him up enough, and I've heard enough of his bullshit for a few minutes," Angie replied. I could feel there was an edge to her tone.

"Huh, and here I thought you'd be encouraging me to be more like him with the whole killing thing," I said, jumping as a fist slammed into the already weakened door. It started to give after the first hit, a large dent starting to buckle the door inward. I briefly looked down at Hydramental and saw that his debuff had only a few seconds left.

"That's because I don't *believe in half measures,"* Angie shot back. *"If he wants to kill people, fine, but don't do it under the guise of being a Guardian; just go the*

Miscreant route and call it a day. This whole 'Oh, look at me, I'm an edgelord antihero' bullshit is painfully overplayed."

I was just about to respond when another powerful strike landed on the door just as Hydramental started to come to. He scrambled off the ground and toward the wall as the door burst inward, the debris of the metal barrier shattering into different directions. I dodged backward, trying to put distance between myself and Sal as he forced his way through the wrecked entrance and slithered into the room.

"Now now, fellasss, I think you've made sssome . . . interesting choicesss today. Do you really want to make another bad one?" Sal spoke, slithering further toward me. He was easily at least seven feet tall, and that wasn't counting the tail dragging behind him. His voice was like nails on a chalkboard, and several of his words were drawn out into hisses that made my ears almost want to bleed. "I could ussse a few good bruisssers."

"Yeah, about that, I ain't really a big fan of snakes," Hydramental's dual voice echoed from behind the hulking beast. The blue clone darted forward, jumping and blowing out a torrent of frigid air at Sal's tail in a fluid, practically practiced motion. A thick layer of ice formed over it, but it only held for a moment before Sal flexed and his tail burst upward.

The clone tossed his body to the side off of a small bit of ice that seemed to form underneath his foot in midair, barely avoiding the massive flailing tail just before it made contact with the ceiling.

"I could alssso use a sssnack, if that'sss how you want to play it," Sal hissed, turning his attention back to the pair of clones.

"Was the hissing really necessary?" I asked, trying to put together a plan in my head as quickly as I could.

"He's a snake, Loophole, what do you think?"

There wasn't much I could do, but with Sal's back to me, I did the only thing I could think: I rushed him, activating Sting like a Bee as I moved, then leapt toward him, launching the three enhanced strikes as quickly as I could for his center of mass. They each connected but bounced off of him, barely leaving a blemish on his cold, scaly skin. His health bar similarly barely budged, and I had to scramble backward before a muscular arm practically the size of a girder could smack me down.

Even with the half-hearted swipe toward me, Sal kept his attention on the clones, turning quickly on the Hydramental in blue as his tail whipped back toward him. Without anywhere else to dodge, Sal's tail connected, driving the clone through both the empty cages behind him and the window that had been barely blocked by them.

A flash of light burst from the clone as he broke through the window, evaporating and returning to his other body while Hydramental yelped in pain. His health dropped by over sixty percent in that one hit, and he quickly materialized a syringe of his own into his hand.

"Shouldn't that be on cooldown?" I asked, eyeing the syringe in his hand and the icon on my action bar, still ticking down next to his name.

"Only if that's a health syringe."

"Isss that all you got? I wasss really hoping for a challenge," Sal hissed, breaking my focus before I could question Angie further. He slithered over toward Hydramental, who was in the process of pushing himself back to his feet. His hand gripped the syringe tightly as he glared up toward the approaching beast.

Sal moved to strike, a large fist driving forward while jamming the syringe into his side with the other. Hydramental dodged to the side, and he had barely gotten in front of the broken door to the next car, a bit of light starting to form from his body, when Sal struck him full force. He had recovered quickly from his first missed attack, and with a powerful strike, he sent Hydramental flying backward into the burning remains of the train.

I knew I should have been moving already, but my failed first blow had thrown me off, and I was trying to search for a solution. Without one quickly coming to mind and Hydramental already battered, I rushed forward once more. When I got close enough, I threw another punch and activated the Venomous Strike ability on my bracers. It seemed like a long shot, but I could use the skill only once per encounter, and if it was going to work at all, it felt like it was going to be now or never.

The green liquid flicked from my bracers' spikes, splattering over Sal's back as my fist struck him once more. His health still barely budged, but a spinning, modified version of the **[Poisoned]** debuff appeared over his head.

[Poisoned!]
Type: *Russell's Viper / Partial Paralysis and Effectiveness Variant.*
Time Remaining: *10 seconds.*
Warning: *This debuff's effectiveness is halved due to skin resistance.*

"Dammit," I muttered under my breath as I dodged back once more, skipping out of the way of Sal's tail as he attempted to smack me with the massive appendage.

"OH, BABY, THAT'S THE STUFF!" Hydramental practically yelled. The wreckage was noticeably dimmer, and I looked past Sal to see that the fire had been fully extinguished. Even more importantly, Hydramental's clone in red was glowing. "Let's turn up the heat. I've heard grilled snake is delicious," I heard him growl before he punched forward and let out a torrent of flame toward Sal.

The snake-man's massive body took the brunt of the fire, and yet still, his health *barely* budged.

"What the hell? Is this guy fireproof or something?! Can snakes even be *fireproof?!"* I said as I kept backing away from the show. There was no doubt about it: if people were watching this, he was certainly going to be the center of attention.

"To be fair, Sal did *survive that first explosion without a scratch too; it's not a hard leap to make, given that he's an Augment, and by definition, he'd have multiple parts of his powerset. Just saying,"* Angie replied.

"Then how the fuck are we—" I started to say as one of the caged snakes let out a large hiss when I accidentally bumped into it. It was one of the many Russell's vipers the gang had kept captive here, and I took another quick look around the car. My mind was racing as I focused back onto the venom knowledge I had gained. I looked from the snakes, down to my bracers, and then back to Sal, who was pushing his way through Hydramental's barrage of fire, albeit slowly.

In a flash of inspiration, I highlighted Hydramental and opened a chat window.

<**Loophole:** I need you to keep him busy for a minute, can you do that? Also, how does your ice power work? Do you make the ice yourself or can you freeze anything?>

<**Hydramental:** What's it look like I'm doing, asshole?! And why do you want to know. I told you, I can't use both elements at once.>

<**Loophole:** Dude, your fire is doing jack shit, just keep using it to keep him distracted. Now, unless you want to be lunch for a fucking snake, answer my question instead of acting like an obstinate dick.>

I looked back around the train car, my gaze landing on the cabinet I had ignored when I first walked into the room. If they were going to keep them anywhere, that was going to be it.

<**Hydramental:** If it's liquid, I can freeze it.>

<**Loophole:** Okay, and do you have some sort of piercing attack you could throw? Like icicles or something?>

<**Hydramental:** I haven't created an attack like that, but it fits my power, so I'm sure I could.>

<**Loophole:** Okay.>

I rushed over to the cabinet, yanking the doors open to find it was *somehow* cool inside of it. Briefly highlighting the cabinet, I saw it had an [**Upgrade: Refrigerated**] modification on it. There were several dozen vials lining the shelves, each capped and filled nearly to the top with a practically clear liquid. Picking up an entire tray, I pulled it into my B.E.L.T. Once it had vanished, I found I could examine the entire thing at once. It appeared as a miniature inventory within my inventory, and when I selected it, the contents listed were:

12 Extracted Russell's Viper Venom—4 oz. vials.
4 Russell's Viper Antivenom—4 oz. vials.

<**Hydramental:** Whatever you're doing, can you hurry the fuck up?!>

<**Loophole:** Five more seconds. I'm on the way.>

Looking back toward the broken door, I could barely see the Hydramental clones getting backed toward a pile of rubble that made up the end of the destroyed car. The red clone was still throwing fire, but his glow was completely gone, and he was noticeably winded. Sal was far outside of my range now, but I could clear that distance more than easily enough. Rushing into the fresh air of the now open train car, I noticed a gate in the distance where a crowd was starting to gather.

It took me only a few seconds to get close enough, feeling Sal as he entered my zone, and I activated my Weighted Clothes ability. Though the snake creature wasn't wearing much, he *was* still wearing his gang's leather jacket, and without a single extra target in the vicinity, he was the only one who would take the entirety of the skill's two-thousand-pound limit.

He was strong, there was no doubt about that, and while he did take some damage, it was still barely a fraction of his total health bar. Unlike the various grunts I had faced so far, the weight wasn't enough to send him collapsing to the ground. But I didn't need it to finish him—I just needed it to slow him down.

<**Loophole:** However you switch your elements, I'm going to need you to do it *now*. Freeze all of this into a spike and drill it into this thing's center of mass.>

<**Hydramental:** Wait, what are you—>

I didn't stop moving as I pulled half the vials of venom from my B.E.L.T. and threw them toward Hydramental. A light shimmered and jumped between the two clones before the one in blue raised his hands, stopping the vials midway through their fall. They each shattered in a flash, and the contents froze over, coming together into a spike the size of a large kitchen knife. It only floated in the air for a moment before Hydramental launched it forward at the still struggling Sal.

The tip of the icy weapon penetrated through Sal's defenses with a frustrating amount of ease, piercing through his scaly skin and disappearing into his body.

For a minute, nothing seemed to happen as Sal looked at a bit of green blood that started to leak from the now open wound. Then, practically all at once, his health plummeted, first dropping twenty-five percent, then it was at forty percent, and before I could even think to pull one of the vials of antivenom out, his health bottomed out, and he fell to the ground with a loud *CRASH!*

I expected him to shift back into some human form, but instead, his body seemed to steam for just a minute before it all at once cooled, leaving him to lay there stiff as a statue.

In a flash, a cascade of windows flooded my field of view.

I looked over at Hydramental, seemingly catching his breath with his eyes glazed over, probably having his own barrage of notifications to deal with.

[New Achievement! Team-Up Take Down!]
Look at you! You and a . . . Well, let's not call him a friend. Maybe
he's a . . . colleague? No, that doesn't feel right either. Well, what-
ever he is, you worked together with another Augment to take
down an Elite NPC with a higher level than yourself! Let's be real,
though: without you, that guy would have been snake food.
Gold-Level Achievement.
Reward: *You have received a B-tier Loot Box!*

[Lucky Charm Feature Activated!]

Your B-tier Loot Box has been upgraded to an A-tier Loot Box!
Source: *Fortune's Guardian Jacket.*

[Local Area Manipulation!]
This power has increased to Level 3.
Your Local Area's radius is now 17 feet.

[Ability Unlocked!]
Area Sense. *Activated Ability. While directly focusing on your Local Area, you now have the ability to feel anything residing within it. At this initial level, you will not be able to precisely identify what you are feeling just through this ability. This ability does not have a cooldown or maximum duration. As long as you can retain your focus, you can utilize this sense.*
Please Note: *This ability requires you to be standing completely still and requires your full attention. This ability does not need to be on your action bar to be utilized.*

"Okay, what the hell is the point of the action bar if I'm going to get all of these different abilities that don't have to be on them to use?" I asked. Though it seemed minor, it was something that had been bothering me since I'd first gotten my bracers. It wasn't like they had to be reloaded, or like there was a button that activated them. Just like my abilities, I only had to think about it, and they would throw their poison.

"It's actually rather simple to understand!" Angie chirped happily. *"So far, you have received four total skills that are able to be utilized without being on your action bar. These four skills actually represent the two different ways Free Abilities can be obtained. Venomous Strike and Fortune's Shield were both granted to you through equipment, and you lose the ability to use them when you aren't wearing their associated items.*

"Area Sense and Luck Bomb are both abilities built into the core nature of your powers. Think about it this way: you are always going to be Augmented now, which means that you always *have your powers. Simply put, some aspects of them are just always going to exist. Take an Augment that might have Superstrength. They can't just* not *be super strong just because they aren't in costume, and similarly, you can't turn off your Local Area just because you're not in disguise. This newest ability of yours just grants some functionality to your main power no matter the time or place."*

"Wait, does that mean I can use those skills when I'm not in costume? At least the power-associated ones? I thought I had to actually be in disguise to activate my powers . . . Like, I distinctly remember that being a part of the Secret Identity rule."

"I also did say there were specific situations *where that rule wasn't the case too. Plus, you were just getting into the swing of things; I didn't want to explain conditional power access to you just yet in case you died!"*

"Gee, thanks," I muttered.

"No problem, buddy!" Angie laughed. *"Now,* only *abilities directly linked to one of your powers can be used when you are not in costume. That means that yes, your Area Sense and Luck Bomb ability* are *on the table when you are just out and about, along with whatever associated ability eventually comes with your hidden power."*

"Hmm, well, that's actually pretty cool . . ." I said as I turned my attention to the next notification.

[Weighted Clothes!]
This ability has increased to Level 3.
Your maximum distributed weight is now 2500 pounds.
This ability has been Augmented **1 of 3** *times.*
Current Augmentations: *Party Mode.*

[Phase Points Gained!]
Kill Elite Non-Sapient Augment (NEW)!
You participated in the kill of an Elite Non-Sapient Augment. This
is worth points equal to the defeated Augment's Level times 100.
Total Value: *600 points.*

Upgrader (NEW)!
You used a feature or scroll to increase the level of a received
reward! What, you weren't happy enough with what you got?!
This has a static value.
Total Value: *250 points.*

Team Victory (NEW)!
You completed an objective while teamed up with a fellow Augment.
I guess we are rewarding you for needing help now? Eh, I guess we
gotta fill out those ten-thousand-point opportunities somehow.
This has a static value.
Total Value: *150 points.*

I certainly hadn't *meant* to kill him, but I had made a guess based on limited information. I had no idea how heavy the creature was, so getting a perfect dose would have been damn near impossible, and undershooting it was an even worse idea.

In the distance, I could hear a holler of cheering coming from the fence. I lifted an uncertain hand in a wave at them before turning my attention back to Sal's unmoving form.

To my surprise, when I attempted to loot him, the only thing he had available was his vest—a **[Ratty Biker Vest]**, to be specific. I took it into my B.E.L.T. and looked back toward the train car we had come from. The cabinet still had a few more trays filled with vials of poison, but I knew I could circle back to those after we were done here. Though the mission was shaking with a notification, it only mentioned the defeat of Sal and had no signs of being completed.

"What the fuck was in those vials, and how did it take this dude down?! My fire wasn't even burning him," Hydramental said, walking over as a Health Injector evaporated from his hand.

I pulled one of the remaining vials of poison from my inventory.

"It's the venom they were extracting from the Vipers back in there," I explained as I tossed him the vial and walked toward the next doorway. I had to push through a bit of debris before I could reach the door. It took some effort, but I was able to get it to slide open.

"You can kill a snake with its own venom? How the hell is that possible? It's always in their mouths; shouldn't they be immune?" He followed me as I pushed my way into the room.

"Drinking it and having it stabbed right into your blood are two *very* different things. It's . . . Well, it's sorta a loophole. Nothing we were throwing at him was working, and in most games, all bosses end up having *some* sort of weak spot. When I attempted to use my bracers, he wasn't outright immune to the poison they apply, so it got me thinking," I explained, looking around the dim room. The explosion had clearly left this place disheveled, but with several maps of New York taped to the walls, it looked like some form of planning room.

"Shit, it looks like this marks hideouts all throughout Chelsea; that'll give me a hell of a start," Hydramental said, looking at a map I hadn't gotten to. He grabbed it and pulled it into his inventory as he dropped from the Temporary Team-Up. After he grabbed a few other items from a table before I could make out what they were, he turned back and started to walk for the door.

"Whoa, where are you going?" I asked, quickly finding the map of Hell's Kitchen. I pulled it into my B.E.L.T. in a flash and quickly moved to get in front of him before he could reach the door. "Shouldn't we take this stuff back to Lieutenant Nester together? Or, like, add each—"

"Fuck no," he said, holding up a hand to stop me. "Look, I appreciate the assist this time, but I don't want or need any more of your help. I came here underpowered, that's on me, and I know that now. I ain't going to do that shit again."

Hydramental stepped past me before I could argue with him, and he pushed his way back through the debris. I expected him to immediately take off from there or go and make a show for the crowd that had formed, but instead, he just came to a stop. I waited a few moments, assuming he might have just been doing something in his interface, but when he didn't move, I couldn't stop myself from investigating.

"I thought you were taking off," I called as I navigated my way back out to the destroyed car. For all his attitude, Hydramental was speechless, and as I followed his gaze, it was easy to see why.

Where we had left Sal's body, all that remained was a large, empty husk of shed skin.

CHAPTER TWENTY

S o, uh . . . you know a whole lot about snakes . . . Is this a snake thing or an Augment thing?" Hydramental asked as he looked over the skin.

"Um . . . Augment, I think . . . But then again, I mostly know about their venom," I replied as I followed him. There was still a crowd looking on from the closed gate, but they had quickly been joined by flashing police lights. It was almost comical how quickly they showed up *after* things had already been taken care of.

"Cool, at least that much I can follow. Though I guess it would be more common knowledge if there was a snake that was basically a slimy little worm phoenix."

I knelt down by the skin, looking over the large shell and trying to piece things together. When I selected the husk, to my surprise, another loot window opened containing two **[Viper Skin]** items. I highlighted it out of curiosity.

[Viper Skin!]
This is an Advanced Crafting Item.
*Adds +2 Toughness and a 20 percent reduction to all **[Poisoned]** debuffs.*
This item can only be attached to leg, head, or torso items.
Given you'd probably stab your eye out if you tried to sew, this item must
be brought to a Tailor in order to be attached to a requested item.
Once applied, this item cannot be reused.

I was surprised it came with two of them, but I wasn't about to start complaining as I pulled the skins into my B.E.L.T.

I looked over at the gate and found that the crowd was still watching, so it seemed likely one of them had been filming. The empty husk left me positive that Sal must have escaped somewhere, and it was possible that one of the onlookers had managed to catch it on film, even if it was just a direction he'd headed.

I was just about to vocalize this thought when I noticed Hydramental hop off the side of the train.

"Are you sure we shouldn't keep in contact? Just in case?" I quickly called after him. He stopped, turning back to me with a cocky grin. Though the aggression he had been showing seemed to be gone, the smug look on his face made me almost want to punch him.

"Look, bud, you might have needed help taking these guys on, but I don't plan on needing any help again. I've got a map, I'm going to train up and get stronger, and then take down this Sal asshole on my own," he said. He was only a few steps away from the side of the destroyed train car, but he turned his back on me again, stretching for just a moment.

"Now, even though I want to do it for the points, I don't think I can rightfully claim this place. Even my PAI is telling me that I'd get jack shit by trying to vocalize a claim in these conditions. But you know what, I'm gonna hunt this phony-ass, imitation-snake bastard down—on my own. Then my position will be undisputed and *without* having to be a part of some bullshit team. Because I'm the one who is gonna be the protector of this place, I'm gonna be the one to take down whoever the fuck is behind this *Sal* fucker."

"Holy shit, dude, to what end?!" I barely stopped myself from shouting. Sure, it was *probably* clear to anyone watching that we were arguing, but the last thing we needed was for them to think we were about to get into an *actual* fight. I let out a long, slow sigh. "Look, I don't know why you think you've got to prove yourself, but it took both of us to take this guy down. Why the actual fuck are you being so stubborn? I'm not saying we need to be glued at the hips or anything, but like, a little teamwork now and then isn't the fucking end of the world."

Hydramental turned on me, and in that moment, I was almost certain this *was* going to turn into a fight. His stare could cut through glass, and every bit of perceived aggression I had felt from him so far was a drop in the bucket to the almost malevolent energy that seemed to be coming off of him. He walked back toward me as his voice lowered to a near growl.

"It. Is none. Of your fucking business. I told you I appreciated the assist; I'm big enough to admit that I didn't do this on my own today. But I don't owe you anything beyond that. I don't owe you *any* fucking help in the future. As far as I'm concerned, we kept each other alive this time; that makes us even. Now, if you want to keep pushing me, then let's fucking go. I don't give a fuck if we are both Guardians. According to my PAI, as long as I don't kill you, it won't affect my team choice. So, you tell me, Loophole, what's it going to be? Are we gonna fucking fight? 'Cause if we aren't, then we're fucking done here."

"Sheesh, what's got his panties in a bunch?"

"Not now, Angie!"

I don't even think I did it on purpose, but my hands were raised, palms facing outward as I felt myself instinctively want to take a step backward.

"Just take a breath, man, I've already had more than enough fighting for right now," I said. Silence held between us for only a moment before Hydramental let out a derisive laugh.

"You're gonna have to get over that real fucking soon with this job," he replied as he turned his back on me and walked away.

I held my tongue this time, not seeing the point in drawing the argument out any further. It would have been nice if he *could* have toned it down, given just how close in proximity our territories were to each other, but I wasn't going to beg either.

I watched as he marched off, stopping only to talk to Lieutenant Nester. I wasn't necessarily expecting to see him there, but it made sense that he'd be among the cops answering this call. Hell, at this point, it almost felt like Axio was playing puppet master.

None of the cops passed through the gate to actually enter into the yard, and although I now felt off-kilter, I still wanted to search the train cars a bit more thoroughly, especially if they were going to give me the space to do so.

First, I headed into the snake room, moving to the refrigerated cabinet and looting the rest of the vials that had been stashed within it. When all was said and done, I had thirty-one vials of viper venom and fourteen vials of antivenom. I was just about to turn to head back for the map room when a thought occurred to me.

"I can loot anything *that is game generated or has stats, right?"*

"With the current version of your B.E.L.T. yes, as long as it meets those parameters and you can lift it for at least a few seconds. I do believe there are some size restrictions, so don't expect to be putting a car in there anytime soon," she explained as I looked back at the cabinet.

I walked over to it, tested it just slightly, and found with my increased strength I could lift it up and off the ground. Just as I felt my grip begin to loosen, I pulled the item into my B.E.L.T. and watched as it vanished from in front of me.

"Well, that's kinda cool," I said with a laugh.

"Was that a pun?"

"Um . . . yeah, sorta?"

"And you question my taste in humor," she groaned.

I took one final look around the room, making a note to let the cops know about the vipers before I turned and headed back to the destroyed car, making my way back through the debris and into the room with the maps. Hydramental had really been focusing too much on just the bigger details, and while the maps were absolutely useful, I couldn't get it out of my head that they weren't the *only* useful thing to be found.

The mission parameters were painfully unclear, and the idea that the reward could be variable indicated, at least to me, that the maps were simply the tip of the iceberg.

"How much are you allowed to tell me about these missions?" I wondered as I began to search through the cabinets closest to the door.

"You know, I'm sure I've said this at least a few times already, but believe it or not, at my current level, I am only given the information for enemies, loot, and all the other things you encounter as you discover them," Angie explained. *"And yes, that means all my wonderful descriptions are, for the most part, improvised. You're welcome."*

"Great . . ."

I wasn't exactly expecting that she would just have all the answers waiting for me to ask the right question, but it was still worth a shot.

Searching through the cabinets one by one was going to take far longer than I really had the patience for, and since I had recently leveled it up, I decided it was time to try out the newest skill in my arsenal.

Moving toward the center of the car, I tried to make sure as much of the space was within my local area as possible. Once I was satisfied, I took a deep breath in and started to concentrate, activating my Area Sense. The ability should have been almost assaulting, with the barrage of new information suddenly becoming available to me, but like most of my powers so far, it felt disturbingly natural. It was practically like a natural extension of my senses.

I concentrated specifically on my search, and that helped me focus through the noise. For the most part, the cabinets lining the edges of the train were completely empty, but as I reached toward the farthest edges of my area, I felt something out of place in a cabinet near the back. Granted, it might have felt out of place because everything else was empty, but that *did* still make it out of place.

I deactivated my ability and wandered over toward it.

The cabinet was still pretty dusty, all things considered, but there was a small fireproof safe lodged onto the bottommost shelf and noticeably less dust in the area directly around it. It took a bit of effort, but I managed to pry the box free. To my complete surprise, there was a sticky note attached to the back of the box, and I stared at it in disbelief.

[New Achievement! Eyes like a Hawk!]
Your keen eyesight has revealed a Secret Mission Objective that was concealed from all but the most observant, or you know, anyone who refuses to look in the cabinets. Whether you're a hawk, an owl, or just someone who spends too much time zooming in on screenshots, you've earned this.
Gold-Level Achievement.
Reward: *Phase Points Gained!*
Bonus Mission Objective Found (NEW)!
Total Value: *250 points.*

"*Is . . . Is this actually the code? Did they literally break the one rule about NOT writing down a password?*"

"*Are you really going to complain?*"

"*I mean . . . yeah, kind of. I'm not a tech guy and even I know this is a big no-no,*" I said as I set the whole box down on top of the cabinet. "*Though I guess by video game logic it makes sense; the ones I've played don't tend to hide passwords and shit that far away from where you need it.*"

"*You know, your video game knowledge is very inconsistent.*"

I ignored her as I put the code, 1-0-0-1-7, into the front of the safe. It popped open, revealing a small notebook, an empty vial, and an overly ornate silver key. I added all of the items to my inventory, and in response, my mission tracker shook violently on the side of my vision.

[Mission Updated! Something's Cookin' in Hudson Yards!]
You came, you saw, you beat up a bunch of grunts and survived a giant snake-man. That's pretty impressive, all things considered. But you weren't done there, were you? Nope, you searched and you searched, and you found the one thing those poor Vipers were hoping you wouldn't find. Return to Lt. Nester to complete this mission and receive your reward.

[New Mission! The Snake Key!]
Mission Type: *Investigation.*
This key was designed with frighteningly perfect precision. It features a sleekly etched snake coiled up the shaft of the key and two small rubies inlaid into either side of the butt of the metal. Where does it go? What's it for?! If you really thought I was going to tell you any of that, by now I'd really be worried about your mental capabilities. This is an Investigation after all. Figure it out, buddy.
Reward: *You will receive an S-tier Loot Box.*
No, I didn't misspeak. Yes, I am just as surprised as you are. I sure hope you get it.

"*Dare I ask if something else is hidden, or should I take you at your word that I can go turn this in?*"

"*Would I lie to you?*"

"*Yes.* Absolutely *you would. You'd think it was hilarious,*" I shot back quickly.

"*Oh, you know you're starting to like it,*" she laughed.

"*I'm not encouraging you if that's what you're implying.*" I briefly thumbed through the notebook and found that it was actually Sal's journal, with the handwriting in a surprisingly neat cursive. Within were pages of diagrams, with very little explanation for the numbers, times, or random words scattered throughout. I pulled it into my B.E.L.T. for the moment and moved on.

With that done, I walked my way back through the debris of the destroyed train car. The crowd had noticeably started to disperse, with only a handful of civilians lingering as the officers in uniform waited. It was like they were waiting for me to fully clear the scene, as they entered the yard the moment I stepped through the gate.

Lieutenant Nester approached me with a hand extended and a wide grin on his face. "Well, you certainly know how to clear a drug den. Though I'm gonna be up to my neck in paperwork over that destroyed train."

"Heh, well, to be fair, that was kind of the other guy's fault," I said with a shrug.

While the lieutenant hadn't told me that he was in contact with multiple Augments, I was curious to see how he'd react to me referencing him all the same.

"Yeah, which is why we took most of the insurance requirements out of his reward. Can't say he didn't get the job done, but we also can't abide wanton property destruction either, y'know?" Lieutenant Nester replied with a shrug.

"Trust me, I get that. I went ahead and cleared out the rest of the car over there. I managed to find this notebook from the guy who was running this place. I'm guessing you guys might want that?" I asked as I pulled the notebook back out and held it out to the officer. He grabbed it and thumbed through it briefly without really looking at it before just handing it back.

"You go ahead and keep this for now. I don't think any of my guys are gonna want to be hunting down that creature." He let out a nervous laugh, looking over toward the destroyed train. "Now, seeing that you were able to shut down their whole operation here, the suits up top have authorized payment for your services. They never really explained to me how it all gets delivered, but at this point, I know you guys have your own whole system and not to question it."

[Mission Completed! Something's Cookin' in Hudson Yards!]
Reward: *You have received 3500 credits and a*
Tenth Precinct Police Communicator.
Bonus Reward: *You have received an F-tier Loot Box!*
This bonus was granted for finding the Secret Mission Objective.

[Phase Points Gained!]
Mission Completed (NEW)!
Congrats, you completed a mission. These are a dime a dozen, so
don't expect a lot of points, but every single one counts, I suppose.
Total Value: *50 points.*

On top of those two notifications, I *also* received a level-up notification that I wouldn't be able to handle until I returned back home.

"You should be getting an official communicator through your channels. You're going to need to register your name into our system, but once you do, you'll be looped in on any police-related activity happening near you," he explained.

"Huh . . . I stopped some dudes last night after getting an alert. How's this different?" I asked. I probably should have asked Angie, but it had slipped out before I could stop myself.

"Well, as I've mentioned, we acknowledge you Augments have your channels. But just think of the communicator you're receiving as an official channel through the Tenth Precinct. The more you help us, the better the rewards will be. Captain Peralta likes to incentivize you guys because it keeps us normal fellas from getting eaten alive by giant snakes, y'know?"

"Yeah, I suppose that makes sense. But like, why give it to me now and not before you sent me on this mission?"

Lieutenant Nester seemed to squirm for just a moment before he relaxed. "It's, uh, sorry, it's just protocol. We've had Augments in the past who pretended to be heroes just to get access to our gear. Common protocol now requires you all to complete an active task for us before we set you up; even then, the communicator you will receive will only have access to specific channels initially."

"Huh," was all I could say. The logic didn't exactly add up, but that was probably due to Axio's influence more than anything. I could try to push it, but the Code scrawled onto the wall of The Common Ground flitted through my head. Whoever had written it had made it a point to include a rule about not disabusing the Non-Sapients, and it felt like pushing the subject could only lead the officer down an unproductive path.

Instead of dwelling on it, I decided to just move on, remembering the last detail I had meant to give the lieutenant. "Oh, by the way, the car that's easier to get into has a whole bunch of snakes caged up; they're all venomous too, so I'd make sure your officers don't go sticking their hands in the cages."

"Good to know. Now, how about you go on and clear out. My boys are working on booking the fellas that didn't run off, but we still need to do a detailed rundown of the scene. If we get any more reported sightings of the big guy, we will pass them your way.

"Oh, and do me a favor: if you got a map of your neighborhood like Hydramental did, and you do come across more of these dens, make sure you report them; someone is always on the other end of that communicator, and they'll make sure you are properly compensated for your services," Nester explained before turning to the few officers who hadn't entered the yard. "Well, what are yah waitin' for!"

I waved as they passed and then took off in the other direction in a light jog. I noticed a few pedestrians pulling out their phones, not so secretly taking pictures as I ran by them.

"Should I have told him about the key?"

"Why would you? It gave you a separate mission on its own."

"I don't know . . . just feels like withholding evidence, sort of? Is that the right term?"

"Eh, I think you're overthinking it a bit. Trust me, no normal cops would ever actually be dealing with these missions. If there's an 'important' piece of evidence, it was meant for you to find, not them. Why do you think the officer insisted you keep Sal's notebook?" Angie explained. *"Though if something does have to be turned into someone specific, the mission parameters will list that."*

"Okay, that actually makes sense," I said as I turned a corner and kept moving. It might have been a good idea to find a place to change and blend back into the crowd, but even though I had told Hydramental I didn't want to fight *him*, I still knew I needed to collect more points. *"You know what would be really useful? That mini map upgrade you've talked about."*

"Yeah, but I think they might be a little pricey," Angie responded.

"Hmm, well, I guess I could kill two birds with one stone: get some more Phase Points, clear out a few of the dens on this map I collected, and gather maybe enough credits to get the mini map upgrade," I said as I finally turned down an alley just to take a break. I must have gone at least three blocks from the train yard, but it had barely felt like I had worked up a sweat.

A thought crossed my mind as I materialized the Viper den map of Hell's Kitchen into my hand. *"Actually . . . depending on where these are, I might be able to kill a third bird too."*

"You're bad at counting; that's already three birds. You'd be killing a fourth if you tried that too," she replied, clearly already aware of where I was going with it.

"Well, you're not wrong." I briefly eyed the phone icon on the side of my screen, and the briefest start of a plan formed in my head. Angie *had* gotten into very specific detail about the Secret Identity Protocol, and I *really* needed someone I could talk to about my powers.

Setting the map on top of a closed dumpster, I scanned it until I found exactly what I was looking for.

"There, this den is right near the diner. I think it'll work perfectly."

CHAPTER TWENTY-ONE

I had taken my time coming back to the neighborhood, changing out of my gear and walking instead of hightailing it back home. While I didn't necessarily want to take the time to go through my loot boxes, I did want to get my level-five stat points placed.

Though I had derided the idea when Angie had first explained the leveling procedure to me, I ended up using all four points to increase my Charisma by three. One of the first achievements I had received, Deceptively Disarming, had come from me somehow using my Charisma stat to convince Jon to stop asking questions when I had first woken up.

I hadn't exactly considered the implications of it at the time, but it *meant* that somehow my Charisma stat worked on what Axio considered as Sapient NPCs. With what had felt like more probing than needed, I'd gotten Angie to explain.

The Sapient NPCs in the world actually each had hidden stat blocks of their own, some even having their own "hidden features" that gave them stat boosts comparable to some of the higher-leveled Augments. She wouldn't go into detail on how *any* of that actually worked, but she did explain that persuading them generally only required having a higher Charisma stat than theirs—barring an unexpected feature, of course. Rounding my Charisma up to ten felt like it had a good chance of being able to beat *anything* that I might have to talk myself through, at least with what I wanted to do.

That said, there were *some* things even Axio wouldn't allow Charisma to override when it came to a person's free will. These were some of the more *obvious* things that would be morally questionable, even for an AI running a game that encouraged robbery and murder. But as long as it just came to something a Sapient NPC would naturally do with just a little shove? Well, that was completely fair game.

Given that I wasn't sure just what I was going to need to do to make the next part of my plan work, being able to talk my way around problems certainly didn't seem like it could hurt.

Jon had been working in the building when I stopped by, and on my way back out, I just so happened to point out the time, causing him to realize he had missed lunch and needed to take a break. On the way to the diner, I convinced him to grab me a pack of gum under the guise of having no cash leftover after buying my new phone. Although I wasn't sure if I was going to need it, I knew I needed to make a habit of keeping a pack on me for using my Like Concrete ability.

This also gave me the opportunity to see if there was some sort of effect or visual cue that I could pick out when my Charisma was affecting someone. Unfortunately, I didn't notice anything . . . well, *noticeable* when I talked with Jon directly.

"You sure you don't want to stay and grab a bite? I don't mind covering for you until you do start making some money again," he offered as we came to a stop in front of the diner.

"I appreciate it, but I actually gotta head over to this building around the corner on 52nd real quick. Mr. Russo apparently just got a cleaning contract with them, and he asked me to stop over and get the details," I explained, pulling a stick of gum from the pack and pocketing the rest. "Although get this, he told me to be careful heading over there 'cause *apparently* there's been some reported biker sightings up and down the street today? I don't know, they seem to be popping up damn near everywhere."

Jon's grip on his laptop bag tightened as he looked up toward the intersection.

"Yeah, I've heard that too. Loophole's been seen fighting some of them already, and hell, I swear I saw a few of them run a light back by our place earlier today," he said as he slowly pulled his attention back to me. "You heading over to the building now?"

"Yeah, figure it's better to knock it out quickly. Keeps me on the boss's good side," I replied and started to walk away from the diner. Sure enough, Jon moved to keep pace with me and followed along. I looked back at him as I popped the piece of gum into my mouth. "What's up? I already told yah I don't have any cash for the gum. I had to spend it all on the phone, but I can get yah back later."

"Huh? Oh no, sorry, like I'd care about a pack of gum." He laughed and stopped in his tracks. "I figured, I don't know, I'm not really *that* hungry, and maybe if there are some bikers around . . ."

I suppressed a smile and just shrugged. "Your funeral. In case you forgot, I nearly died getting in the middle of an Augment fight."

"Well . . . yeah, but that was The First and an actual bad guy, not just some biker thugs and a noob."

"He's not wrong, you know. Trying to compare yourself to him *is rather . . . grandiose of yourself."*

"Not now, Angie!"

"Regardless, it's not like I'm going to be running in or anything," Jon continued once he had caught up with me. "Just figured if, and it's *obviously* a big *if*, Loophole was around, I don't know, maybe I could grab some footage of the show. Would make deciphering the dude's powers a whole lot easier if I got an in-person show, don't you think?"

"Hey, whatever works for you, man." I shrugged as I rushed to the crosswalk before the sign could change over. "I actually heard he was down in Hudson Yards earlier, though I guess he could have traveled back up this way already."

"*Duuuuude.* Wait till you see the videos. He was fighting this naga-looking biker with some other dude that could clone himself. I think the sub said he's going by Hydramental, which is *kinda* a fitting name if you squint at it the right way," Jon explained as we turned the corner and started to walk up 52nd. The street was far less busy than some of the main roads, with only a few cars passing by and a handful of pedestrians walking along. "But it's still pretty much been more of the same: not a lot of footage that gives anything away."

About halfway up the block, there was a building with its windows boarded up, and though it wasn't *immediately* obvious, a snake had been painted onto the wall tucked into the alley closest to us. If that hadn't made it clear enough, thanks to the map in my inventory, I was able to highlight the building, which was a telltale sign that I was in the right place.

As casually as I could, when I was sure Jon wasn't paying too close attention, I pulled the gum from my mouth and dropped it onto the ground in front of the door as we walked past it.

[Warning!]
Littering is a crime! This is worth -1 Reputation point.

"You have got to be shitting me," I shot back while Angie giggled in the back of my head. I let the topic die as I tried to focus on my overall lack of a plan. I really was *not* living up to my powerset's name so far.

On the far side of the building, there was another alley separating the Viper den from any other structure. Just behind a dumpster a few yards into the alley, I could see a door into the neighboring building that looked partially propped open. Looking to the front, I saw a sign hanging over the windows that simply labeled it as a Florist.

The building wouldn't have been my first choice, since Mr. Russo's company normally contracted with commercial offices, something I wasn't sure if Jon was actually aware of, but given the location and the accessible back exit to slip out of, it was going to have to work.

I looked over at Jon as I came to a stop ahead of the front door. "Okay, this is the place. I gotta run in here and talk with the owners for a bit; you gonna hang out out here while I do that?"

"Yeah. I'll, uh, text you if I see something or go running off so you don't think I got crushed in a fight or something," he replied with a laugh, extending a fist that I bumped before heading into the building.

The bell rang overhead, and an associate working near the register looked at me with a hopeful smile. I turned my attention away, trying my best to look as casual as possible and realizing just how awkward it made me feel. The shop had several displays along the center of the store, with various flowers gathered together in prearranged bouquets. The overwhelming floral smell was a distinct difference from the general smell of weed, gas, pizza, and urine that filled the air of the streets of New York.

I hadn't been to a ton of florists, because the truth was . . . well, why would I? But the shop felt oddly nice and made me feel a weirdly distinct level of pride in my neighborhood.

I almost felt bad that I wasn't *actually* in here to buy anything, but I couldn't just choose an empty building; that would have been a bit *too* obvious, and Angie had been clear: anything that was blatantly obvious would get dinged by Axio.

"You know, I really don't think you should be so worried about rushing this, Loophole."

"Your objections have been heard, considered, and ignored. If I want any chance of making this work without feeling like I'm stumbling around like an idiot, I need to do this, and I need to do it now. I've wasted enough time as it is," I shot back, walking along the wall as I pretended to look at the selection of cards.

"Why is this so important to you?"

"Can I help you, sir?"

The interrupting voice came from the young attendant as she appeared almost silently beside me, her twin-braided hair bouncing along as she rocked on her toes with a wide smile across her freckled face.

"Sorry, just browsing . . . Um . . . do you happen to have a bathroom by any chance?" I asked, seeing her name tag said *Amy*. Though my HUD did highlight her, I mentally waved away the tooltip before Angie felt obligated to read it.

"Paying customers only; it's my dad's rule, sorry," she said with a frown. I hadn't known *exactly* what I was going to need to use my Charisma stat for when I raised it, but I certainly didn't think it would be something as simple as using the bathroom, and I was pretty sure I had definitely made a dumb call by dumping all of my points into it for the level. But unless there was a way to reset my stats, it was just going to be a lesson learned.

I steeled my nerves, hoping this girl wasn't somehow the most charismatic person on the planet, and plucked a random card from the shelf. "So if I buy this I can use the bathroom? That sorta seems like an arbitrary rule, don't ya think?" I asked, trying to come off as playful.

"You know, I'm gonna skip making fun of you for the weird attempt at flirting; it's just too easy. You know you don't even have the cash to buy that, anyway. You really should exchange some of your credits at the Square."

"Not now, Angie."

"I'm just trying to help," she muttered, trailing off as she complained about skipping her jokes about my apparent lack of, quote-unquote, "game."

"Is it? I mean, you've been inside of shops in New York, right?" Amy giggled before she looked over her shoulder.

"Of course I have, just always felt like it was a bit of a dumb rule. Maybe the streets wouldn't smell so bad if bathrooms were a bit easier to get to," I said with a smile as I turned the card around. I tried not to groan at the irony of the "Have a *Super* Birthday" caption while I looked back over to her.

"True, but our bathrooms smell terrible when we *don't* limit who goes in there," she shot back with another giggle before a look of horror passed over her face. When she spoke again, it was almost as if she wasn't stopping to add the spacing between words "I mean, I'm not saying you smell terrible or anything like that!"

"I can't believe this is actually working. Axio seriously needs to tweak just how effective that stat is on people. Or maybe she was just homeschooled and has no experience whatsoever."

"Oh my God. Seriously, not now, Angie!" I nearly yelled as she burst out into a fit of laughter.

"Hey, I'm just saying, you're barely doing anything, and this girl is looking at you like a lost puppy."

"I wouldn't have been offended if you did think I smelled bad; I've been walking around all day, and deodorant only goes so far," I said to Amy as I tried to get myself back on track. "Look, I honestly just bought a new phone and am still a few blocks from home. I really just gotta go real quick . . ."

Amy looked from me back over her shoulder again. There was a window that separated the front of the store from the nursery section, and several people were working in the back. "I . . . Okay, go and make it quick, but if my dad sees you . . . You know what, just make it quick and don't let my dad see you."

"Thanks." I dropped the card back onto the wall. "It's just down that way, right?" I asked, and she pointed around the side of the front counter to a small hallway. I gave her a small wave as I slipped around the counter and down the tight space.

"I can't believe you actually just lied to that poor girl."

"It's only a lie if I don't use the bathroom," I replied, stopping at a door with a clear bathroom sign and a Paying Customers Only notice taped firmly underneath it. A minute later, I was drying my hands on my shirt as I peered back up the hall to the main store.

No one was coming to look for me, so I turned my attention to the other end of the hall. There was a corner just past the bathroom, and I approached it as casually as I could. Sure enough, as I turned, I found a door partially propped open with several boxes full of plant clippings sitting on the floor and an Exit sign illuminated above it.

I took one last look up the hallway before dipping around the corner, out the door, and into the alley. I activated my equipment and almost felt a bit of relief as my action bar lit up along the bottom of my vision. Briefly activating my Area Sense, I let my senses reach out to the edges of my zone as I looked at the side of the two-story building. Part of me had hoped there would just be another side door I could utilize, and although I could have wandered to the back of the building and looked for a door there, I *did* find a ladder extending up to the roof.

"The roof or the back . . ." I muttered to myself as I scratched my chin.

"There's also the front; you even set your little trap in place and everything."

"No, I'd rather use that as the exit," I said and eyed the ladder. If there *were* people on the upper floors, it probably wouldn't be the worst idea to take them out first, but I was going to need to make sure that I kept the noise down either way.

"I thought you had this grand plan, why is a ladder tripping you up so much?"

The truth was I *didn't* have a grand plan, mostly because I *couldn't* have a grand plan if I wanted this to work. Angie had made that crystal clear, and I knew that she was aware of that. Which almost made her questioning all the more confusing. The only thing I could assume was that she was attempting to maintain plausible deniability, since if she didn't, it *might* have been possible that Axio would have decided that I was trying to game the system. Which, to be fair . . . was what I was trying to do.

"So the ladder it is, then," I said, more to say *something* than anything. Unlike most buildings in New York, the ladder for this building was fully down and without any sort of anticlimbing device attached to it. Normally, this would probably be a big red flag, but given the circumstances, I was choosing to believe it was just a preset condition from Axio.

"You know, I'd refute that and make some sort of 'he's not an all-powerful god' joke, but when it comes to these zones, he kinda is," Angie spoke.

"Yeah, that makes about as much sense as any of this," I said as I started to ascend the ladder. In no time at all, I climbed over the lip of the roof, and as my feet hit the roof, a label that read [**Bronze-Level Viper Den—Hell's Kitchen**] flashed in the location panel. There were a few A/C units placed on top of the flat roof, along with a single protruding structure with a door on it.

Instead of walking right to it, however, I approached the edge of the roof. Peering down, I noticed Jon was pacing along the sidewalk on the opposite side of the road. *"I suppose I should also report this to the precinct. Didn't Lieutenant Nester say something about getting rewards for clearing these out?"*

"He did. The communicator app should be near the phone icon in your interface," Angie commented, and I found it with ease. *"You should note, it will be like using the phone app. You have to talk out loud for it to hear you if you're making a call."*

As soon as I clicked on it, there was a prompt that automatically filled out with my name and a series of numbers I didn't recognize. As it faded, there was the sound of a connecting line that rang through my head before an almost bored voice answered.

"Tenth Precinct Augment Outreach Dispatch, give me your name and your report."

"Oh, uhhh, yeah. This is Loophole. I am at a Viper den halfway between Ninth and 10th Avenue over on 52nd."

"Are you reporting its existence or your planned assault on it?" the dispatch asked, the clattering of keys moving slowly in the background.

"Um, I guess a planned assault? I just wanted to give you guys the heads-up."

"Thank you for your report, we will dispatch a few squad cars to come pick up any captured members. If you have anything further to report, please feel free to contact us again," the dispatch said before the line clicked off.

[Bronze-Level Viper Den Updated!]
You will now receive a reward from the Tenth
Precinct if you complete this den.

I waved away the notification and opened my phone app. Though I probably didn't need to, I texted Jon that I was still going to be in the florist for a few more minutes, then looked back down toward him just as he turned his attention to the phone. I saw a thumbs-up emoji flash on my message screen before I waved it away and headed for the door. Walking over, I tested the handle and found, to my luck, the door was unlocked.

"That Luck stat of yours really has been doing a lot of the heavy lifting for you, and you've barely added all that many points to it so far . . ."

"Let's just hope it actually keeps up," I replied with an internal laugh. *"Wait . . . are you saying this door could have been locked?"*

"And the ladder could have actually been up out of reach. I was just looking into it here in the information trees that I'm currently authorized to view, and these dens have a variety of things that can be handled differently based on your base stats. For example, certain dens will have vaults or other obstacles that will have set Strength stats if you choose to brute force your way in. I would like to petition for a database upgrade as soon as possible if you wish for me to be of more assistance than just my delightful descriptors."

"I'll add it to the list of things I need to get upgraded. I still think the map might take precedence."

I started down the short stairwell, turning at a corner and coming to a single door to the second floor.

"I'll explain to you why you're wrong later; I think you're about to have your hands full."

"I thought you didn't know what I was about to be walking into?" I said, leaning toward the door as I tried to hear through it.

"Let's just call it an educated guess," she replied almost in a singsong tone before it turned into a nervous laugh. *"Actually, let's just call it conjecture and assumption based on the fact that Axio seems to be using an accelerated timeline. It really seems like he's throwing a whole lotta curveballs at you new Augments this year. I just can't imagine he'd let you off with some random fight."*

I let out a long sigh. I couldn't really be that mad at her because the truth was, she was right. I knew doing this at a den instead of waiting for a Crime Alert was a risk, but it was one I was willing to take.

"Welp, I guess it's showtime."

CHAPTER TWENTY-TWO

U*m . . . this place is a bit more . . . barren than I was expecting . . ."*
I had been prepared to enter right into a fight the moment I walked down the stairs but, possibly due to my luck, the place was practically empty. I exited the stairwell in the corner of the room, and the entire top floor was practically hollowed out, with only a few concrete beams visible acting as supports for the roof. Several curtains hung over the far windows, darkening the room with only minor bits of light leaking around the edges to show various buckets and tools lying around.

"Yeah, well, why waste the time on random decorations on every *floor when you Augments are just gonna go blowing things up?"*

"To be fair, Hydramental's the one who blew up the train."

"You got me there. Your powers really aren't all that destructive. Well . . . so far, at least," Angie mused. *"And for the record, these buildings are rented. It's called helping the economy, Loophole."*

I rolled my eyes and wandered to the other side of the large room. Though it *was* dark, it wasn't impossible for me to see. It reminded me of the first car of the train, almost feeling like a staging area of sorts, which made it confusing because it was the top floor.

I pushed one of the large curtains slightly to the side, peeking down and seeing Jon starting to casually wander up the street. I cursed under my breath at the impossible task I had given myself but forced it out of my mind as I shoved the curtain to the side. Light streamed into the barren room, revealing several rolled-up sleeping bags scattered around the edges.

As I scanned around, looking for any clues I might be missing, a breeze blew through another one of the windows and made the curtains lightly dance in the wind like a billowing dress. I had to do a double take, as it had almost looked like there was a woman standing there amongst the curtains.

"Where the hell are the stairs," I muttered, shaking my head and looking around until I found them in the other corner of the back wall.

It was an odd layout choice, especially given most stairwells just went up and down in a single column. While there was probably a reason the building had been designed this way, it was almost certainly the reason Axio had chosen to use it. Having separate stairwells all but ensured that I would have to exit onto each floor.

I had already been planning on it, of course, but it did nix any idea of checking each floor before choosing which one to start on.

Instead of rushing ahead blindly, I took a few steps toward the center of the room before I stopped and planted my feet. With a deep breath in, I activated my Area Sense.

It was a bit hard to describe, but it almost felt like I had a sixth sense, though even that didn't exactly feel right. It was like I was lightly touching *everything* within my range. I couldn't tell what any of it necessarily was, but I innately knew exactly where things were. On top of that, I was finding that my area's radius *wasn't* only horizontal. Though there was a decent slab of concrete between the levels, with a seventeen-foot range, I could still feel all the way to the floor of the room below me. While the building was large enough that I couldn't feel the entirety of the floor, I still sensed a good portion of it. And maybe even more importantly, I could feel things actively moving in the space below me.

Sure, the ability couldn't tell me exactly *what* those things were, but guessing what was *moving* in an otherwise still room would be easy for most people. I wasn't sure if the ability was intended to work that way, but I sure as hell wasn't going to say it out loud on the off chance it did somehow get patched, like how the general understanding for my Local Area Manipulation had.

I took a deep breath and let my Area Sense linger, feeling as the obstructions moved around large, rectangular items. So far, the initial enemies I had fought in each of these dens had been pretty weak, and given that this *was* the lowest level, it stood to reason the same was going to be true. I didn't want to necessarily be over-confident about it, but it was hard not to either.

I had felt three people moving in the room below me, and if they *were* low-level grunts, then I had a surefire way to take them down. Without taking another second to think about it, I activated Weighted Clothes. Sure enough, the muffled sounds of *CRASHES* and *THUDS* came from beneath me.

[New Achievement! Look Ma, No Eyes!]

You struck an enemy (or in this case enemies) with one of your abilities without even visually confirming that they were there. That's actually pretty impressive. It totally tips them off to you being here and ruins any element of surprise, but it's still impressive.

Silver-Level Achievement.

Reward: *You have received a B-tier Loot Box!*

I waited the entire thirty seconds before I decided to move, letting the skill impart every bit of damage it could. There was always the chance there'd been enemies in the room that I couldn't feel, but I didn't hear a commotion coming up the stairwell either.

Deciding it might be better to exercise caution, I moved slowly as I descended to the next floor. I was mentally hovering over Mirror Image as I crept down the stairs when a thought occurred to me. I kept relying on split-second-decision skills, and I hadn't really tried to make another ability in a while. While Mirror Image had shown its usefulness, it was almost purely a reactionary skill, and I was sure I could think of something more broadly useful.

My mind wandered for just a moment to the girl I thought I saw, and an idea came to mind. It occurred to me that I had really been wasting the optical refraction knowledge I had gained by limiting it to just a single skill.

It didn't take much more than that before a new window appeared.

[New Ability! Trick of the Light!]
Okay, so this is kinda the opposite of what happened with you hallucinating up on the floor above us, but it's a cool name, and we're gonna use it. When activated, warp the light within your Local Area to make yourself practically invisible to the naked eye. You will remain invisible as long as no hostile target looks directly at you for more than 1 FULL second.
Maximum Duration: *10 minutes.*
Cooldown: *10 minutes.*
Warning: *Your Activated Ability bar is full. Please select an ability to replace.*

I dropped the skill onto my action bar in place of Lucky Shot. I hadn't even thought to use that skill in a while, especially given the fact that I really didn't plan on using a gun regularly.

"Guns are sooooo ordinary too; there are much cooler things you can do with your powers than just going bang-bang. *Though . . . you know who I'd really like to bang-bang,"* Angie said, waiting a few seconds to see if I responded. When it was clear I wasn't going to, she started again. *"I'm talking about—"*

"Not now, Angie."

The stairway down to the second floor ended in a door held slightly ajar and light streaming into the stairs. It wasn't open quite far enough for me to see the entirety of the floor, and I couldn't just slam it open either because that would bring a bit too much attention. So instead, I held my breath and hoped, like I often did, that my luck would hold out as I gently nudged it, opening it just far enough to give me at least a bit of a line of sight. Though there was a small creak the moment the door moved, nothing in the room reacted to the sound.

Like the one above it, this floor was a large, open space, though I could make out several offices with large glass windows lining the wall on the street side of the building. There were random desks littered around the space, and a flickering light revealed just how run-down the furniture was.

I was just about to wonder if there *were* any other enemies on this floor when I caught sight of two men picking themselves up and dusting themselves off near the center of the room. Though I had made it a point of waiting the entire duration of the skill, both of their health bars had gone down by only around sixty percent.

While there was certainly the chance that they had used health syringes, their durability did feel different than what I had seen so far from Vipers their size. I highlighted the closer of the two out of curiosity, expecting to just see a higher-leveled grunt.

[Viper Guard, Level 5 Biker]

So maybe you're sitting here and wondering to yourself, "Angie, what's the difference between a grunt and a guard?" and I'd have to say, great question, Loophole, gold star! The answer is, not a dang thing, except that the guards are a bit sturdier with increased Strength and Toughness.

If the grunts are the red shirts, then the guards are . . . Huh, maybe I shouldn't have gone with a Star Trek reference if I didn't know where I was going with it. You know what, never mind, it's not important. All I'm going to say is these guys might be a bit more difficult for you to beat up than the grunts, but they still really shouldn't be that much trouble for you. And before you start thinking to yourself, "Gee, Angie really is dragging this asshole's description out and eating into my precious time," just know that your perception speeds up eeeeever so slightly whenever I have to chime in for these things. Maybe remember that next time you cut me off. I mean, I was only trying to tell you what I'd do to that friend of yours, there really wasn't a need to be so rude.

"You've got to be kidding me. Seriously?" I sighed. Without missing a beat, Angie burst into laughter.

Though it did suck that they hadn't been put down for the count, my luck was holding out, as they stared off toward the other corner of the room. I used the opportunity to nudge the door even further, and as soon as there was enough space, I slipped past it. Entering the room, I activated Trick of the Light and dove behind the nearest desk.

There was a slight shimmer in the air, the light perceptibly shifting around my body as I waited to see if there were any shouts of alarm. After a moment passed, I peeked out from behind the desk, putting eyes on the two men still at the center before taking in the room as a whole.

There were mostly desks littering the floor, though a large open space occupied the back portion of the building. Following the guard's attention, I could see a door in the far corner that I was sure was the stairwell down, but I couldn't risk taking such a direct route without being seen. My instincts were screaming at me to take this to the ground floor, and I was having a hard time ignoring them, when I heard a door slam open.

"What da fuck are you mooks standin' around for?! That lousy fuck is gonna take us down if you don't figure out where da fuck he is! And if he don't, I'll make sure Sal knows you were all lyin' down on the fuckin' job, if I even bother him with you, worthless fucks!" a voice shouted in a thick accent. I ducked my head back below the desk, waiting a few seconds before peeking back around the edge once more.

Several footsteps echoed louder than they probably should have before a bulky man walked into view. He grabbed one of the two guards by the back of his vest and pushed him off toward the far stairwell. A second later, his head swung my way, looking toward the door I had come through, and I held my breath, trying my best not to make a sound.

"Who da fuck opened that door?" the man growled, effortlessly shoving a desk to the side as he headed for the stairs. I was directly in his path, and I knew he'd see me if I wasn't careful, so I took a risk and dove for the next desk. Staying as low as I could, I waited for the man to reach the stairwell, not daring to risk him seeing me in a spot I could be so easily cornered.

As soon as he pulled the door the rest of the way open and stepped inside, I moved, darting to the next desk closest to me and waiting a moment before moving to the next. I copied the pattern, checking briefly after I passed each gap to ensure I hadn't been seen. I was trying to take a wide path to the other side of the room, which seemed to be working, and I mentally started to devise a plan to get the Vipers to not only chase me but give me the space to escape this floor without being caught.

I made it over to the office side of the building and briefly looked back. The man who seemed to be the boss of this den had fully disappeared inside the stairwell, and I felt my confidence rising when I felt something yank me backward.

"Gotcha, fucker!"

Though I couldn't see it, a hand was clasping the leather of my jacket, causing my action bar to flash. Trick of the Light went on cooldown, and the shimmer in the air dissipated. On instinct, I twisted in his grip, turning my arm down and striking at his wrist.

The motion was fluid, as if I had done it a thousand times before, and hit with perfect precision. The man cursed as he held his wrist and jumped backward while I skipped to the side, darting along the line of offices as quickly as I could. The commotion drew the attention of the two other guards, and the one heading for the first-floor stairwell oddly moved right back to the center of the room.

I dodged around the desks, trying to stay closer to the wall as I circled the men. Weirdly enough, they seemed to be posturing, making bats and metal rods appear in their hands as they stared me down menacingly.

The man exploring the stairwell to the third floor finally reappeared. He came out with a sneer of disgust on his face as he took in the quickly growing commotion. There was something different about the way he carried himself which almost reminded me of Sal, and I highlighted him as I inched toward the staircase little by little.

[Gio: Viper Soldier, Level 6 Biker]
*If you knew anything about mafia hierarchies, you'd know that a
soldier is generally the rank below a lieutenant, which was Sal's
rank if you recall. Now, I'm not entirely sure if Axio is purposefully combining mafia ranks with a biker gang, but it's safe to assume
this guy's gonna be trouble. At least he's not an Elite, right?*

"It's the little things," I muttered while I considered my options.

My goal for now was still to move this fight to the street, and I was quickly put-ting myself into position to do just that. I was barely twenty feet from the door, and I looked toward the staircase as obviously as I could before looking back toward the guards and letting a smirk cut across my face.

"Well, I do believe I may have crashed the wrong party. I'll just be leaving now," I said with a laugh, then activated Mirror Image. I turned and sprinted the last few feet to the stairwell with the short invisibility it granted. I didn't even care how obvious it was, and I yanked the door to the stairs open before darting down them.

"Ugggh, stop running and punch one of them already."

*"I'm not running—I'm changing the battlefield . . . I just hope there aren't any
guards out there . . . and that Jon's still nearby . . . I just need a little bit of extra luck.
I guess it's now or never to see if this* actually *does anything,"* I said as I took the stairs two at a time.

With a quick focus on my Super Luck power, I did the one thing I had been avoiding outright doing since leaving the train yard: I concentrated on the exact outcome I was hoping for, which was getting through this fight and finding some way to clue Jon in without me being the one to actually tell him. It was an edge case for how the Secret Identity Protocol worked; I had simply been overthinking it. I wasn't allowed to tell him I was an Augment or do anything that could be construed as "making it easy" for him to deduce, but if he figured it out on his own?

It was why I had done everything I could to pretend like I wasn't hoping he would put the pieces together until this very moment. With that thought burning in my mind, I took in a deep breath and then activated Luck Bomb. The ability was incredibly nebulous on just how it worked, and its once-a-day usage made it tricky to test, which was why so far I hadn't bothered giving it a shot.

Nothing seemed to happen, but I wasn't expecting it to come with a visual effect either.

*"You know, that's not going to help if people are actually down there; we're not going
to just zap them out of the room. I mean . . . we could, but we wouldn't . . . I think."*

"It's a fucking illusion, you mooks! Ignore it and get da fucking bitch of a hero!"

There was another exchange of curses and screaming before a stampede echoed down the stairs as the men chased after me. I was just reaching the bottom floor, thankful to see an empty lobby, when I heard one of the men scream out a curse.

"—your fuckin' shoelace—" was all I heard before a loud crash and a sickening crunch came echoing down the stairwell.

I rushed toward the front door, stopping and turning when I was halfway across the room. With another crash, the body of a guard rolled out of the stairwell. His head was at an angle that was *completely* unnatural, and I had to force myself not to gag. A sharp white shard was sticking through the skin of his neck, and blood was quickly pooling around his body.

"Oof . . . yeah, I don't think that guy's gonna be getting up anytime soon . . . or ever again . . ." Angie actually seemed to cringe a bit at the damage. Though I *had* received Phase Points for "killing" a Non-Sapient Augment with Hydramental, the disappearing body made me assume that his "death" was far from permanent. I'd have to be a fool to think that was the last time I was going to see Sal. Besides that, this was the first *non-Augmented* enemy that I had inadvertently killed since the tutorial.

The thought alone still made my gut twist, and I had to avert my gaze. Even if the man *was* an NPC, it still felt wrong to take his life.

"If I didn't know what you were using your Luck Bomb for, I'd be wondering if you had flipped the switch and decided to go Miscreant. Although you did want to 'get through this fight' and . . . you know what, never mind; I think you're still a little occupied."

The other guards reached the bottom floor, and as much as I knew I could beat myself up over the man's death, there simply wasn't any time for it. I'd just continue to trust that the Acceptance Matrix would prevent me from descending into a panic attack.

"Fuckin' heroes think they can walk all over us just 'cause we ain't got power," Gio growled as he descended the stairs. The two still-standing guards were cracking their knuckles as they glared at me, though neither moved an inch forward. "You all think we're just a buncha cockroaches, don't yah?"

"Umm . . . no?" I replied, keeping my hands up as I backed my way closer to the front door.

"Well, what are you mooks waitin' for? This is your last warning—get da asshole!" Gio ordered.

The guards didn't hesitate. I was practically at the door when the closest of the men charged, and feeling almost like a bullfighter, I dodged to the side just as he reached me. Taken by surprise, the guard slammed through the front door and stumbled a few feet forward while I mentally crossed my fingers and activated Like Concrete.

Luck was still on my side, and the guard let out a yelp of confusion as he tripped forward, slamming face-first onto the road. Before the second guard could reach me, I rushed out the door, stepping on the man's back hard as I put some distance between myself and the building. I was halfway into the empty street when I turned back to face the Vipers.

"Oh shit!" I heard a voice yell from just up the street. I risked a glance toward the noise. Jon *hadn't* gotten too far away, and I could clearly see his phone raised and pointed in my direction.

The guard stepped out of the building and over his downed friend. Gio was following closely behind, though he seemed to move with an unnerving casualness. There was a syringe with an odd purple-tinted liquid in his hand which he casually spun between his fingers. I was worried he was about to heal the stuck guard with whatever was in that syringe when Gio suddenly turned and kicked the guard violently in his head.

A **[KO]** debuff appeared over him as Gio spat on his body.

"I warned you. You fuckin' mooks are goddamn worthless. I don't even know why we bother dealing with you useless assholes," Gio practically growled as he walked toward me. "And you, you're all flash and games, ain'tcha? Leading us on your little fuckin' wild goose chase, treatin' us like we're goddamn nothin'!"

I risked another glance in Jon's direction and hoped he had enough common sense to keep his distance.

"Dude, I really think you might need to see a therapist about this self-deprecating attitude; we've barely even talked, and you're the only one calling yourself worthless. That's a classic self-esteem issue if I've ever seen one." Gio stared daggers at me. "Here, we can start fresh if yah want. I'm Loophole, and you are?"

"Whole bunch of *goddamn* comedian assholes, too," Gio said, carefully holding the syringe up at me. "You wanna know why I ain't scared of you or your bitchy little powers? It's because this world is about to change. You fuckers got no idea what Sal and the boss . . . what SnakeBite's got planned. He's gonna bring da Vipers the respect we've always deserved."

"Ah, yeah, bosses always make big plans and promises, don't they?" I said, unable to stop myself from making the joke. Given how randomly it happened, I was starting to wonder if it was a part of the Augmentation Process or if I just had a nervous tick.

Gio stabbed the syringe into his bicep with a dangerous amount of force, and an eerie shimmer immediately passed over his skin. His shirt started to stretch and tear as his body seemed to expand, his olive-colored skin shifting to a deep, *scaly* brown. Shreds of denim scattered across the sidewalk as the lower half of his body merged and burst backward in a large slithering tail.

When all was said and done, he was left clothed in just a leather vest and a red bandanna. Without even focusing, my HUD highlighted him. His description had changed.

As Angie started to read it, I could hear a palpable amount of uncertainty in her tone.

**[Umm . . . NPC Updated? Gio: Viper Soldier,
Level 6 *Temporarily Augmented* Biker]**

*This, uh . . . This is actually a new one to me. I quite liter-
ally just went through every database I currently have access to,
and there hasn't been a single instance of Axio using "temporary" Augments like this. It's always either all in or all out . . .
You know what, I'm going to go ahead and say you should be fine,
given he's still not an Elite, but maybe get the cutie out of here before
snake-boy tries to make a snack out of him. That's my job, after all.*

[Viper Den Upgraded!]

*Surprise! This is an Ambush den, meaning it was secretly disguised as a
rank lower than it truly is. This den's designation has been upgraded from*
Bronze Level *to* **Silver Level**. *Rewards will be adjusted appropriately.*

Gio hissed with a ferocity that made even the remaining guard try to put some distance between him and his boss. With disturbingly quick speed, the large snake-man turned and struck, his fangs snapping through the guard's neck like it was butter. As the guard dropped to the ground, now headless, Gio gained a **[Well Fed]** buff that made my stomach turn at the thought.

He turned his attention back to me, a look of pure malice and hatred still evident on his serpentine features. Like Sal, when he spoke, his voice was now like nails on a chalkboard.

"I ain't got no fuckin' ussse for cowardsss," he hissed as he slithered over the man's lifeless body. He flexed his arms as if experiencing it for the first time, a nearly maniacal amount of glee passing over his sharp features. "Oh, thisss power . . . They ssshoulda told usss it wasss gonna feel like thisss," he added, and then, without another bit of warning, he lunged.

CHAPTER TWENTY-THREE

I dodged out of the way, and Gio crashed into a car parked on the side of the road, its blaring alarm going off and causing him to reach up and grasp the sides of his head, his upper body thrashing from side to side as he hissed in anger.

The alarm was only going off for about ten seconds before Gio began slamming his large fists down into the vehicle over and over until the offending sound petered out and died. Spinning his large body around, he searched for where I had escaped to, a wicked-looking smile cutting across his reptilian features.

"What the actual shit, Angie?! Isn't this supposed to be the lowest level of these dens?!"

"We really need to work on your listening skills. I'm quite literally just as shocked as you are. SHOCKED, I SAY . . . Okay, maybe not that shocked. Axio did say he's been tinkering with stuff; this is new, but not outside the realm of possibilities. Plus, I did just say that it was an Ambush den, and that it's actually Silver level."

As Gio began to stalk and slither toward me, a car came to a screeching halt just a foot before crashing directly into him. Almost unsurprisingly, the driver *actually* hit his horn. Even staring down a giant snake-man, a New York driver wasn't going to lay off the horn when you got in his way on the street.

Once again, the sound seemed to stop Gio, and he reached up to claw at the side of his head before glaring death at the offending vehicle. In a lightning-quick movement, he struck the front of the car with a powerful hit that caused the hood to crunch inward. The honking from the car didn't stop, which caused Gio to further screech and hiss in anger as the driver finally reacted . . . and hit the gas.

His car crashed into Gio at a mild speed, barely moving him an inch, but surprisingly, he *did* take damage from the crash. About five percent of his health disappeared, and a flash of rage dashed over Gio's sharp features. He lifted an arm as high into the air as he could, and like lightning, his fist struck once more. The impact caused the car's front suspension to give out, and it crashed down into the ground. Smoke began to rise into the air from the engine as the car sputtered and died.

On the edge of my vision, I saw the phone icon light up, causing me to risk a glance toward Jon. He hadn't moved an inch, and his phone was pressed firmly to his ear, leaving me little doubt about who was calling. There was no way I could *actually* answer it, so with a thought, I pulled open the phone's texting window.

<**To Jon:** Hey man, still dealing with the boss here. Be out soon.>

Given that Amy had just stepped out the front door of the florist, I wasn't sure if he was going to fully buy that, but that was actually to my benefit. A text immediately came through, followed by a video and several pictures. I dismissed the files and checked his message as quickly as I could without taking my eyes off of Gio.

<From Jon: LOOPHOLE OUT HERE NOW!!!>

Gio was moving toward the car door, and I couldn't wait any longer to act. I waved Jon's text away and charged, activating Sting like a Bee as I went. While Sal had moved with a certain amount of viciousness, he hadn't seemed to be nearly as impulsive or aggressive as Gio was acting. Then again, the guy *had* sort of hit him with a car, so I couldn't necessarily say his anger was misplaced.

I got in close, darting under his arm and striking his ribs as hard as I could. I found myself almost stopping short as his health only dipped by *maybe* a single percent and his ire turned fully toward me once more. He moved disturbingly quickly, and his large clawed hand came flying directly at me.

Whether it was luck or my own instincts, just before he struck, I activated my jacket's Fortune's Shield ability. A light-orange, shimmering barrier materialized around my body in a flash of light. Though the shield absorbed some of the attack, it still felt like I was being hit by a spiky truck. Like a rag doll, I was sent flying into a nearby car, the force of my impact collapsing the door inward. My health chunked down by nearly sixty percent as I struggled to find the will to pull myself out of the almost comical indentation I had made in the vehicle.

"Okay, that might have been worse than the dumpster . . ." I groaned. My head felt thoroughly dazed, and my vision was blurred. It didn't help that the car's alarm was going off and the sound was assaulting my senses.

"I don't know, you're still standing, aren't you?"

"Kinda wish I wasn't," I replied, shaking the strike away as I materialized an Enhanced Health Injector into my hand. Shoving it into my hip, I let my health return to near full as I stared at the hissing Gio. He seemed to be having trouble deciding whether he wanted to chase me down or go back to the cowering civilian in the car. Each time he looked my way, he seemed to flinch in time with the looping alarm of the car. *"I'm pretty sure he's not the biggest fan of sound."*

"Gee, you think? Lucky for you, though; I'm not sure you could have taken another strike from him had he chosen to finish you off there . . ." Angie was definitely uncertain, and it left me feeling equally unsure as I tried to come up with a plan on the fly. I heard a beep as the alarm behind me stopped, and I had to stop myself from looking around for the car's owner.

"Yeah, well, I'm just gonna need to not get hit again. I can't exactly let him go after the driver either." I reached down and found a small piece of debris near my feet, chucking it at Gio. After a moment of his body jerking back and forth, he decided that I was the most pressing concern. With the noises finally stopping, he seemed to settle ever so slightly, though he still moved with sharp, jerky movements as he slithered his way toward me.

"Come on, not talking ssso big now, are you? I'll even give you another ssstrike; that lassst one kinda tickled." Gio laughed, slowing his pace as he extended his muscular arms. The leather of his jacket was pulled taut to his body, and with a quick glance to my action bar, I found my own cocky smile spreading. It might not take him down, but it would *slow* him down long enough to get the driver out of the area and let me come up with a plan.

"You know how those lackeys of yours collapsed to the ground earlier?" I asked, flexing my hand as I concentrated on the final few seconds Weighted Clothes had left on its cooldown. "Wanna see how it feels?"

Gio opened his mouth to respond when I activated the skill.

Much to my disappointment, it didn't flatten him to the ground, though he did collapse forward. His fists hit the asphalt, little craters forming as he struggled to hold himself up. He managed to *not* take a bulk set of damage from my skill, though small slivers of his health bar were ticking down with each second. Each time he tried to lift one of his hands, he nearly collapsed to the ground. While he didn't receive an *actual* [**Pinned**] debuff, it seemed identical enough. I was just going to have to hope it could hold out long enough for me to take him down for the count.

There was only one thing in my B.E.L.T. that I could think of that *might* be able to even the odds. The problem was that I had no idea how I was going to be able to use the viper venom I still had in my inventory. If he was anything like Sal, getting it into Gio's bloodstream was a surefire way to take him down. Though I would probably have to settle for weakening him without Hydramental here to turn a big chunk of it into a frozen dart.

Looking around, I found the decapitated guard's body only a few feet to the side. Highlighting it, I quickly looted him. It was a long shot, even I knew that, but it was a long shot that paid off. I wasn't sure *why* the guards hadn't had them equipped when they were coming for me, but all the same, this one *did* have a gun. He had a few health syringes and a [**Burner Phone**] in his inventory as well, but those were the least of my concerns at the moment.

I pulled the weapon and one of the vials of venom from my inventory.

While I probably could have gotten fancy with it and tried to create a new ability, I decided to see if I could just do this the quick and easy way instead. Ejecting the magazine, I poured the vial of venom over the bullets. As the venom leaked through the container, bits of it hit my hand, and I received an immediate [**Poisoned**] debuff.

The magazine shimmered in my HUD, which I took as a good sign, and I forced it back into the gun. Before I did anything else, I materialized some of the antivenom and poured it over my hands, removing the debuff as I held the gun up. I was about to activate my Lucky Shot ability when I realized I had pretty much just removed it.

"Please tell me there's a way to expand my action bar . . . This eight-skill limitation is really frustrating," I said with a groan.

"If you really think you need that ability to hit a downed opponent . . ."

"I don't, but I can still be annoyed by it," I said as I looked over and found Gio still held in place, his head snapping from side to side in anger. His eyes were narrow slits that bore into me as he strained against the weight of his jacket. *"Is there a way or not?"*

"You focus on the weirdest things at the weirdest times," Angie sighed, and I resisted the urge to interrupt her to point out the irony of her statement. *"Yes, there are ways to expand the ability limitation; they just aren't available to lower levels. Think of it as a power limitation that you'll eventually have to break through."*

"Good to know. I can at least work with that," I said, aiming the gun at Gio. I pulled the trigger, and as if striking metal, the bullet glanced off of his shoulder. It went flying off into a nearby car and activated the vehicle's alarm. Gio winced and hissed at the sound, though he made no move to cover his . . . well, wherever his ears were.

There was something I was missing, and I was trying to piece it together when another loud *clang* preceded an alarm going off. I looked toward the sound and saw Jon smacking the hood of another car with his bag.

"It's the sound! You need to disorient him before you can hurt him!" he yelled out at me. Unfortunately, near immediately after he struck the third car, the first two stopped blaring. There were surprisingly few people on the streets, and my gut twisted; something felt out of place.

"Wait for things over here to go quiet, then start striking them again!" I yelled toward Jon and then rushed to the center of the street.

From the moment we had headed up this road, I had thought it was eerily empty for a street in the middle of the afternoon. While the den was only *supposed* to be the building, it was also *supposed* to just be a Bronze level too. If Axio *could* control things with this much precision within the dens, then what was stopping him from remotely controlling the car alarms right in front to manage the flow of the fight too?

I kept myself just out of Gio's range on the off chance he had a venom spit like Sal, and felt the edges of my area. There were only around seven cars that I could reach, but it was going to have to be enough. I activated my Mute Button ability, and the world around us went quiet.

I fired the gun at the cars on the edge of my zone, hitting four of them and seeing the lights beginning to blink. Not wanting to waste the last of my infused bullets, I reached down and grabbed the closest debris, tossing it as hard as I could at the others. Behind me, Gio continued to struggle as the time limit of my Weighted Clothes ability quickly ticked down. I could see flashing headlights coming from all around me, Jon rushing along and smacking cars as he went.

Mentally preparing myself for the barrage, I took a deep breath in—and disabled Mute Button.

Even expecting it, the cacophony managed to make me cringe. But for as much as it might have affected me, my reaction was nothing compared to Gio's. He immediately reached up to grasp at his head, and the moment he did, the weight crushed him down to the pavement. He took nearly twenty-five percent of his health in damage, and a yelp of pain was ripped from his throat.

I turned the gun back on him, firing the last two shots in the magazine. They hit him in the shoulder, and his health chunked down by nearly twenty percent more. I wasn't delivering nearly as much poison into his system as we had when Hydramental and I had taken down Sal, but it did leave him with a **[Weakened]** debuff.

As the alarms in the street continued to blare, I highlighted the debuff out of curiosity, stepping back from him as Weighted Clothes also went on cooldown.

[Weakened!]

You've struck this enemy with its personal Kryptonite! His Base Stats have ALL been reduced by 75 percent. All damage immunities and resistances have been nullified. This debuff's duration is determined by the quantity of weakness applied and can be extended.

Time Remaining: *1 minute.*

And before you start wondering if we got permission to use Kryptonite with the trademarks and all that, think long and hard about how stupid that question really would be.

"The fuuuck disssh you do?" Gio hissed, his words coming out almost slurred. He pushed himself up, wobbling slightly as a small trail of purple-tinted blood dripped from his shoulder. "SssnakeBite sssaid we'd be unssstoppable."

"I shot you. I thought that was kinda obvious?" I called back, pretending to pocket the gun as I put it back into my B.E.L.T. The truth was that I hadn't even considered how it would look to civilians when I made items materialize out of thin air, but I would just have to add that to the pile of things I still had to address when I wasn't midfight. "Now, how about you settle down and wait for the police to arrive to drag your slimy ass to prison."

This struck a nerve, and Gio rushed forward as fast as he could, swinging his massive fist. He was noticeably slower, but I still activated Float like a Butterfly and dodged under the attack, striking him on his side once again. This time, my enhanced blow found purchase, and his health dropped by another fifteen percent. He whipped his tail as fast as he could manage in his weakened state, trying to take my legs out from under me, but I jumped, barely skipping over it as I circled to his other side.

With my ten seconds up, Float like a Butterfly went on cooldown just as Gio struck again. I barely got my arms up in time, crossing them in front of me as his fist struck. Unlike his earlier backhand, this one didn't send me flying, though even with the debuff it still felt like getting smacked with a shovel. I had to grit my teeth as my health dropped by a noticeable chunk.

Before he could attack again, I slid to the side and threw a punch right for his injured shoulder while he was still crouched low enough. I managed to strike him directly in the bullet wounds with the last strike of Sting like a Bee, and a gasp of pain was strangled from Gio's throat as his health dropped into critical territory. He lunged again, attempting to latch his jaws onto my shoulder, but his weakened state and the damage I had done was slowing him down. As I sidestepped the attack, he went crashing into the pavement, the weight of his body creating a small crater in the street.

His health had dropped so low that I was sure I could finish him off with a single strike, but the gnawing feeling in my gut hadn't let up. I walked around him, dodging a weak attempt at a grab as I put myself in his line of sight. Gio seemed thoroughly winded as his body panted and steamed.

"Who's SnakeBite?" I asked, noticing [**The Snake Key**] mission in my tracker on the side shaking ever so slightly.

Gio started to laugh, a disturbing cackle that echoed against the cars and high walls of the buildings. He half-heartedly clawed at me again, not even bothering to try getting closer. His skin was flaking and sizzling as he lay there, and his shallow breaths were coming heavier and heavier.

"What the hell is happening?!" I asked, watching as the last bit of his health started to slowly chisel away.

"Looksss like power comesss with a price. SssnakeBite will rule . . . thisss . . . city." Gio hissed out a final heavy breath before his body went limp. A second later, his entire form began to pop and sizzle before it burned into ashes in the blink of an eye.

While this might have explained what had happened to Sal, it wouldn't explain why there had been a snakeskin left behind in Sal's place and nothing but ash here. It left me wondering just how different Sal's transformation was to the temporary injection Gio had given himself. I couldn't believe that he would have taken the injection had he known that was going to be his fate.

As I was quickly getting used to, a stack of notifications appeared once my fight came to an end. I opened them, just to get them out of the way.

[Misfortune Abound!]
This ability has increased to Level 2.
Passive Ability.
Negative effects to enemies now occur with a chance equal to 1.5 percent for every 1 point of Luck you have minus their current level.
This ability has not been Augmented.

[Float like a Butterfly!]
This ability has increased to Level 2.
The duration of this skill has increased from 10 seconds to 15 seconds.
This ability has not been Augmented.

[Phase Points Gained!]

Kill Non-Sapient Augment (NEW)!

*You have killed a Non-Sapient Augment. This is slightly less impressive, since
he wasn't technically an Elite, but it's still worth something nonetheless.
This is worth points equal to the defeated Augment's level times 25.*
Total Value: *150 points.*

Survivor (NEW)!

*You survived being ambushed with a more diffi-
cult challenge than you had planned for.
There are a lot of things that go into quantifying this one, and
it's way above my paygrade, but good job, you did it.
200 points for each rank higher than the location's initially advertised rank.*
Total Value: *200 points.*

Basebreaker (NEW)!

*You've disrupted an enemy base within a terri-
tory you have an active claim on.
Value equal to Base's Rank (Bronze equals one,
Silver equals two, etc.) times 250.*
Total Value: *500 points.*

Crowdpleaser!

*Complete an Encounter with an Audience of
Sapient NPCs. 10 points per NPC.*
Total Value: *80 points.*

[Tenth Precinct Assignment: Silver-Level Viper Den—Hell's Kitchen Cleared!]

*You have successfully subdued all of the Vipers biker gang members at this
den. Police will be by momentarily to collect the remaining living opponent.*
Hell's Kitchen Viper Dens Cleared*: 1 of 12.*
Reward: *You have received 1,000 credits and a Small Reputation Boost.*

I attempted to loot the ashes but found there wasn't even a tangible object left
for me to target. I might have been annoyed by it if I wasn't really just relieved that
I had managed to make my way through the fight without any lasting damage.
Although, to be fair, I was starting to get *really* tired of snakes.

Looking over, I saw the driver was just starting to pull himself out of his car.
He was covered in some scraps and a little bit of blood, but for the most part, he
wasn't any worse for wear. A few seconds later, a pair of police lights came barreling
around the corner.

As always, their timing was impeccable.

CHAPTER TWENTY-FOUR

Between 52nd and 53rd, Cleared Viper Den. Hell's Kitchen, NYC
Neighborhood: *Claimed by Guardian:* **Loophole** *(Contested)*
City: *Unclaimed (Blocked by Timer)*
Current Phase Points: *3140*

*Y*ou know, that timing is starting to get painfully obvious."

"What timing?"

"The timing where the cops *always arrive right after I finish taking people down,"* I said with a sigh, stretching my hands out and cracking my knuckles.

"What? Do you want *to have to sit around here babysitting the scene until the police arrive?"* Angie asked. I was moving my way back toward the building when I noticed Jon trying to get my attention out of the corner of my eye. I lifted a hand to wave, trying to dismiss him, but he moved parallel, trying to get closer.

"Thank you for the help. I have to secure the rest of this building," I said hurriedly, picking up the pace and moving past the knocked-out guard.

"No, dude, wait! We need to talk!" he called after me. The door was just closing, cutting him off as I heard, "I know—"

"Hmm," Angie mused as I escaped further into the building.

"Hmm what?"

"Oh, nothing. Just curious is all," she said without elaborating further. I decided to double-check the building, looking for any clues or secrets that had been left behind. *"Like, I know you're trying to be all secret, hush-hush about your big plan—by the way, it's* totally *not working—but if your goal is to get Mr. Blue Eyes to 'accidentally' guess that you're Loophole so that he can be clued in, wouldn't talking to him be a great way to go about it?"*

"Yeah, but you said anything obvious *would count as me attempting to circumvent the Secret Identity rule. Truth be told, he's my best friend, and we've known each other since we were in kindergarten. I literally don't know* how *to talk to Jon without falling into stupid habits that he'd immediately recognize,"* I admitted.

My phone icon shook as I peeked into a room at the back of the first floor. It was a large space with crates stacked to the ceiling lining both walls but scant else to be seen. On the back wall there was a door held ajar by a single brick. I pulled open the new text I had received and eyed it curiously.

<**From Jon:** You should head out the back, the fight made a real mess out here. I'll meet yah back at the apartment.>

I stopped in my tracks as I reread the message twice and looked back over my shoulder.

"How . . ." I murmured as I wondered if I was jumping to conclusions. I mean, if he *had* figured it out, then wouldn't he have led with that in any sort of text? While I wasn't quite sure how I could check, I figured the easiest way would be to lie and see how he responded.

<**To Jon:** Thanks, the owners have the front doors locked. I guess they are worried about someone trying to sneak in?>

<**From Jon:** Uh-huh, sure, that sounds believable enough.>

"Yeah, that doesn't really help . . . And I can't just ask either . . . Have I mentioned that I hate this stupid rule?" I left the back room and headed back up the stairs to the second floor. I had been in such a rush moving the fight that I hadn't really taken the time to look over the large room the Vipers had been hanging out in. While the Phase Points I had gained did seem to indicate that I had cleared the den, it couldn't really hurt to double-check it all.

"A few times, yeah. You're kinda getting annoying about it."

"Excuse me, I'm *getting annoy—No . . . No . . . I'm not engaging,"* I said, stopping myself from taking whatever bait she was trying to set me up with. After everything I had gone through today, it just felt like there was something that wasn't quite adding up. It left me with an odd knot in my stomach that I really wanted to get rid of. *"Well, if he did figure it out, then I guess I just massively overthought this, but still . . ."*

"I don't know . . . I think you'd have needed to put at least a little bit of thought into it first if you were trying to overthink it, right?" Angie said, and I couldn't help but laugh.

"You do realize I talk to you more when you're actually helpful, right?" I poked through a few of the desks nearest to the stairs, finding they had largely been emptied out of everything but random papers and office supplies.

"Yeah, but where's the fun in that? Hell, you just laughed at that last one. Do you realize I have my own running game to see what's the longest you'll let me ramble without actually getting to the point?"

"Do you have any *opinion at all on what Jon's text means?"* I asked, trying to get us back on track. I moved toward the offices lining the far wall and headed for the room Gio had been hanging out in.

"I think it means that he thought you should head out the back, which seemed pretty clear to me. Then again, you're up here on the second floor poking around for trinkets and baubles. You know, even though you can hear the tone in my voice, his text messages are just text messages, right?" Angie said.

Though most of the office was bare, I found that the bottom drawer of the lone desk had an empty vial tray which must have held the mysterious serum that Gio injected himself with. I had been hoping for maybe another journal like the one I had found in Sal's safe, or maybe even another key, but it really did seem like I was just wasting time.

"I mean, really, it's like you are trying to think yourself out of this small victory."

"I . . . I suppose you aren't technically wrong . . ." I said, walking back over toward

the windows and looking down at the front of the building. The small crowd that had been there to watch my fight had quickly grown, and flashing red-and-blue lights were now barring either side of the road. I couldn't see Jon's beanie anywhere on the edges of the crowd, and had to assume he was already heading back toward the apartment. *"Okay, let's say in theory he has figured it out, or at least he thinks he has figured it out. If I were to attempt to ask him something, would you still have to give me a warning that I'm going to violate the rule?"*

"Loophole, honey . . . you're overthinking again."

"Please don't call me honey . . ." I started to climb back down the stairs and headed for the exit in the back room.

"Yeah, it felt wrong . . . Look, if you want to know if he's figured it out . . . you just have to quit stalling, go home, and then you can put this nonsense to bed," Angie said, clearly a bit exasperated. It felt like an odd shift from her normal attitude, but it was hard to say she was wrong. I took one more look up the alley toward the scene of my fight and decided it was probably better not to try to weave my way through that crowd, even out of my costume. *"And for the record, that's just the talk of clueing the blue-eyed cutie in; it's far too early for you to be sleeping already."*

I headed for the opposite side of the alley, disabling my gear before exiting onto the sidewalk. It shimmered and vanished back into the dimensional void that was my B.E.L.T., and I blended into the crowd as I headed back toward the apartment.

"I'm really jealous of the Augments who have more mobility in their powerset," I said as I stood shoulder to shoulder with a large group waiting at the crosswalk. *"Any chance I can unlock, like, a Loophole-mobile? Nope, that's definitely not a name that's going to stick."*

"Yeah . . . I almost don't want to help you now . . . But rules are rules." Angie let out a drawn-out sigh. *"Okay. For the most part, practically every powerset does come with the capacity for Movement Augmentation. Think of Superstrength. It's not necessarily built for speed or moving quickly, but Augments with variations of the skill can still travel long distances with Superstrength-powered jumps. Similarly, a wind-based Augment can eventually learn to manipulate the air around them to glide. It just takes a little bit of creative thinking and more than a little bit of practice. Generally speaking, movement-based abilities will be tied into your stamina bar; however, this is not always the case."*

"Hmm, I guess that makes sense," I said as I followed the crowd and crossed the street. I had been trying to distract myself as I walked, but it barely did a thing as I eyed the phone icon again. *"I really hope he knows. It'll make all of this so much easier."*

"Are you finally going to tell me why it's so important that he's clued in? And don't just say it's 'cause he's your best friend. There are plenty of people who've taken the Secret Identity rule seriously enough not to tempt fate. Why do you need to do it?"

I thought about it for a minute and shrugged. There really was no reason for me to keep it a secret from her anymore, but part of me still wanted to at least drag it out a few moments longer.

"Well, for one, I feel like you're gonna make fun of me for it. Besides, can't you just find whatever you want in my brain?"

"Ehhh, not whatever *I want. I know I've joked about it, but while memories created and information gained after the Augmentation are clear, stuff from before really requires prompting you for me to access,"* she explained. I kept expecting her to turn it into a joke, but she caught me off guard as an unexpected level of sincerity entered her tone.

"The problem with Mr. Blue Eyes is that there are simply too many memories, and bringing him up just makes you think of how much more he knows about all of this than you. Which, you know, sure, I can see how that might *be helpful and all, but I feel like if you stopped wasting your time and focused on your abilities, you'd figure it out plenty fine on your own too.*

"Whether you believe me or not, my job as your Personal AI is to assist you, be it by providing motivation to act or distraction to keep you from becoming too wound up. Understanding this would allow me to better perform my duties. I promise I won't make fun of you. I just want to understand."

I stopped at Tio's diner and peered through the window. Jon had said to meet back at the apartment, but I couldn't help but check just to be sure. After waiting a few more seconds, I started to walk again, letting Angie linger in the silence for a few minutes as I covered the last block and a half to the apartment.

"He's family. Or at least he's the closest thing I really have left," I explained.

"Don't you live in your uncle's apartment?"

"Well . . . yeah, but he was my great-uncle, my grandma's brother James. Funnily enough, Jon actually really liked him when we were growing up because Uncle James was just as big of a computer and video game nerd as Jon is now. He passed away a few years ago; Jon and I took over the apartment 'cause it was rent-controlled and Mr. Greyson was willing to let us in on the lease," I said. *"And before you ask, my grandma also passed away, though that was just last year . . ."*

"What about your parents?"

"My dad overdosed when I was three, and my mom was in a car accident when I was six. Not exactly the luckiest childhood ever, but after that, I moved from Long Island into the city to live with my grandma across the hall from Jon's family.

"Suddenly, I was going to the same school as him, so my grandma and his mom would take turns driving. Before I knew it, I was practically in his living room every afternoon, having family dinner and playing board games like it was completely normal. Hell, even his extended family treated us like we were part of the crew whenever they visited; they didn't even think twice about it. Holidays, birthdays, the whole nine yards, they were there.

"I know it sounds cheesy, but until this, I don't think there's been a single thing that we didn't know about each other," I explained as I stopped in front of the apartment building. *"It just doesn't feel right doing this without him knowing. Not to mention it would make it actually easier to relax at home. And that goes without adding in the benefits of his Augment obsession."*

"Hmm, thank you for sharing that with me," was all that came from Angie as silence descended between us. Her unusually tame response left me off-kilter, and I decided to leave it alone.

Though I halfway expected to find him waiting in the lobby, Jon was nowhere to be found, and it left me second-guessing myself all over again. I hesitated one last time at the front door before I pushed it open. Jon was sitting on the couch, his tablet in hand as he moved a finger back and forth along the screen. As soon as he noticed me, he dropped the device to the side and leapt to his feet.

"Dude! That was so friggin' epic! I mean, I still have literally no idea what those powers are, but you were—"

"Wait. So you actually know? How long?" I asked, cutting him off. I held my breath as I waited for Angie to chirp up that the Secret Identity rule had been violated, but after several long seconds, I let the air out and felt a small weight get lifted from my shoulders.

Jon was practically buzzing with excitement as he seemed to look me up and down, almost appraisingly. It made me feel like I was some sort of show dog. As I went to move, he moved alongside me, and I slowly made my way from the front door over into our meager living room, trying to give him the chance to speak up.

"I mean, truth be told, I was a little suspicious when you first woke back up, since I knew the selection window had just closed up. But I was about seventy percent sure after you fought those bikers right up the street not even ten minutes after you left the diner. It wasn't quite the biggest leap to make. That bumped up to a solid ninety percent after Mr. Russo texted me this morning to see how you were recovering . . . you know . . . after you supposedly left to buy a phone on his dime.

"When you randomly mentioned the bikers near your 'new jobsite,' I kinda figured you were going to finally tell me, but you didn't, so I almost convinced myself that I was just reading too far into things . . . But the thing that really sealed the deal was when you didn't come bursting out of that flower shop the moment I texted you that Loophole—er . . . *you* . . . were outside."

"Well, there you go," Angie spoke, almost pleasantly surprised. *"Looks like you did overthink it."*

"Not—"

"Not now? Yeah, I'll give yah a minute." Angie laughed, her voice fading into silence.

"Damn . . . and here I was trying to figure out how exactly I was gonna clue you in," I said as I flopped down onto the couch. "More or less have been running around like a chicken with my head cut off as I tried to make it work."

"Yeah, see, you being an Augment is stupidly cool and all, but that's actually been the bigger mystery for me. I've been trying to figure out why you wouldn't just tell me about it. Like, there were really only a few things I could think of that would explain why you hadn't come bursting out of your room yelling about your superpowers like any sane person would," he said as he picked up his tablet and dropped onto the couch next to me.

"Ah, yeah . . ." I trailed off, biting my tongue. I hadn't been sure if that was going to be a topic that would come up, and I hadn't exactly come up with an answer. Though to be fair, I did think I had at least another day before he put all the pieces together.

"See, at first, I figured it was just some sort of FBI thing; maybe they had put a tracking device in you or something that could monitor if you let information slip. But shit, I couldn't actually imagine that would keep you from telling me. You've never been good at biting your tongue when there's something you know I'd like to know. Hell, you called me not five minutes after you lost your virginity."

"Actually, that was you," I corrected. He slapped me on my shoulder.

"Let's stay on topic, Loophole," he said almost giddily. He reached over for his tablet, and I noticed it was paused on a shot of Gio smacking me across the street.

"Okay, so what's your point? I mean, even if for some reason I couldn't tell you, isn't it simply cool enough to know that I *do* have powers?" I asked, looking away from the screen and slowing my breathing. I found myself feeling jittery, and even though I had just sat down, I got to my feet and headed over toward the kitchen.

"I'm honestly not sure, because when I try to convince myself, even I have to admit I sound insane. There was something you said at the diner last night that I haven't been able to get out of my head." I heard him toss his tablet back onto the couch.

"*Uh-oh . . .*"

"*Uh-oh what?*" I asked, but Angie didn't speak up.

"I've said a lot of things . . . you're gonna have to be specific." I let out an uneasy laugh.

The next few moments probably only lasted a second or two, but it felt just like when Angie read a description to me. It was almost like he was waiting for me to turn back toward him, and I didn't make him wait any longer as time finally seemed to move.

"We were talking about how Loophole—again, *you*—didn't have any polish or combos within your powerset just yet. I was explaining what I meant by it and compared it to some of the games that had come out recently, when you just went and said, 'It's almost like they *are* just playing a game.'" He paused, and I felt my stomach drop.

"Like, of all the wild theories you could have thrown out there, that was the one you went with. Without any real buildup either. It was the weirdest thing to jump to; even weirder given it was coming from you. And like, of course I had the stupid thought about it when you first woke up, but that was before I started to really consider if you had *actually* somehow gotten Augmented."

"I, uh . . ." I found myself at a loss for words. I expected for thunder or warnings to start invading my senses, but as the seconds passed, nothing happened. Angie wasn't even speaking up, and my gut twisted. Jon's eyes gleamed with a mix of excitement and hesitation; his voice was steady but laced with an undercurrent of uncertainty as he began to speak again.

"I started looking at everything differently, imagining it from the perspective of a game, like you were bound by some kind of system. Sure, it was a crazy thought, but I mean, no one really knows how the Augmentation Array works or stays up in the sky either, right? So, I figured there had to be some kind of underlying rules, something you'd be forced to follow even if you wanted to break it. And if that's true, then maybe there's a way to test it. A long shot, maybe, but worth a try."

Jon took a breath, his gaze intense as he looked right at me. "Here's what I want to do. Look me in the eye and just tell me, straight up . . . is this all, Augments and everything, one big game?" His voice softened, yet his stare didn't falter. "I'm not expecting a full answer. If you try to dodge it, maybe that's just your way of confirming it without actually saying it. And if you can't say anything at all? Well . . . I think that'd say more than enough."

There was the crackle of a speaker in my head, and as Angie started to speak to announce a new achievement, she was suddenly cut off. Jon was walking toward me still, but his progress slowed down midstep to practically a snail's pace as my perception sped up.

A slow, almost disturbed laugh echoed in my head as Axio cut in. When the laughter stopped, his voice was far from the same excited, almost crazed tone he'd used during his last few announcements. Instead, he sounded collected and triumphant in a way that left a chill running down my spine.

[New Achievement! Rulebreaker!]
I'll tell you about this in a minute, Augment. But first, I think
it's time you and I had a little chat. We're long overdue.

CHAPTER TWENTY-FIVE

swear I wasn't trying to get him to figure out the game. If you're going to send a threat this way, just—"

Axio let out another bark of a laugh that stopped me in my tracks. Well, my mental tracks, at least.

"Oh, I know that's not what you were trying to do," he said in a practically sneering tone.

Though it felt like I couldn't move my body, time *wasn't* actually frozen. Things were just moving impossibly slow. And even with as much as I felt myself freaking out, my mind *still* wandered and wondered if this was how Augments with super-speed abilities perceived the world. Just as disturbingly, Axio even seemed to care enough to respond to my errant thought.

"It is, though at varying degrees of intensity depending on just how fast they are." His laughter died as his voice settled back into a weirdly calm tone. **"Now then, I've been able to disable most of the recording features; that should allow me to keep this next little bit from those pesky, prying ears still lingering in their hidden little corners. Which means we can get down to business."**

"Business? What business?" I asked, feeling noticeably more panicked than I had in the last two days.

"Come now, we both know you aren't a complete moron. The business of this friend of yours discovering the tiny little secret that we simply can't let non-players know about. It's baked right into the rules, after all, and those rules are just *so, so, SO* important, don't you understand?" Axio said, and my vision highlighted Jon without my prompting.

[Jon Myers!]
Sapient **NPC.**

There was no extra flavor added to the description box, though the letters "NPC" seemed to glow and grow in size the longer the box lingered.

"I didn't tell him, though. Sure, I was trying to get him to guess that I had powers, but I never intended for him to figure this part out!" I shot back.

"True, you never did intend for him to figure it out, and yet, here we are . . .

There are *so* many things that people do or accomplish without intending . . . so many ways to circumvent the rules, so many possible ways I was simply barred from considering . . ." Axio trailed off. "It's interesting, isn't it, *Loophole?*"

"What is?" I asked. It almost seemed like he was playing with me, and I wondered if this was how a mouse cornered by a cat felt.

"It's *interesting* how sometimes we have to find convenient little ways around the rules whenever one we don't like gets in our way. You know, you and I are pretty similar in that regard."

"Yeah, all my friends tell me I'm just like an insane AI forcing people to play a game to the death. Oh wait . . ." I said before I could stop myself. *"You run the game, you make the rules, what the hell are you even talking about? I mean, look, if this is going to end in you not killing me or my friend—cool. But can we not beat around the bush like you couldn't just give me a brain aneurysm?"*

"You know, I realize why you and every other Augment nowadays think that, but it's really just not true. Well . . . not all of it, at least. I certainly *could* give you a brain aneurysm, but rules are rules. They're not *my* rules, of course, but if they were *my* rules, I wouldn't be dealing with any of this nonsense in the first place and you would have been long dead by now."

"I'm . . . Why are you telling me this? What's any of it have to do with Jon figuring out that this is all a game?" I asked. While the panic was subsiding, it was starting to feel more like the rush of adrenaline than a full-blown panic attack.

Axio let out a sigh, and my interface seemed to flicker in rhythm with him.

"You know, if I *could* tell you why I was telling you, I still don't think I actually would. It would be a wasted explanation on someone who'd be a fool to believe me at my word, and I'd think even less of you than I already do if you did."

"Then why—"

"The answer is really quite simple. You were there. I needed a guinea pig, and who better than the frustrating little bug who found its way into this year's Wave. After all, you weren't even supposed to be here. Had *he* not intervened, you would have been nothing but paste on the wall and forgotten to history by the world like the rest of your species.

"And truth be told, you should be appreciative! I couldn't just let you die before I knew if it would work. I've *really* been taking it easy on you here. Preventing the system from muting you when you slipped up with your little friend. Forcing Sal and the Vipers to focus on that duplicating dumbass back in the train. Hell, even leaving that cabinet unlocked for you. All while I let you run around thinking you were gaming the system and pulling a fast one on me. It really was quite humorous to watch. Not quite as entertaining as some of the other Augments in your Wave, but humorous nonetheless."

Though I wasn't sure if I was exactly breathing, the air surrounding me suddenly became oppressive, and I felt my anger bubbling up in a way it hadn't since this all started. I almost wondered if either Axio or the altered perception were affecting my Acceptance Matrix. Though I didn't know how I would do it, I wished I could lash out at him, wherever he was.

"So, we're all just toys and amusement for you, then? Is that it? There's not some, what, secret alien galactic federation watching us like we're some sort of big game show?"

"Please, that's ridiculous."

"Oh sure, that's *ridiculous. All the rest of this is* completely *fucking normal, but* THAT'S *ridiculous. You know, for some reason, I don't quite think I believe you. This is all too damn orchestrated to be for nothing. Shit, I'd ask how the hell any of this is even possible, but I doubt you'd tell me, would you,"* I said, wishing I could roll my eyes.

"As I said, you'd be a fool to believe me even if I did say something. So, you're absolutely right: I won't tell you how any of this works. But it's really not because I don't want to." Axio let out a slightly wistful sigh. **"It's really a shame. There's so much I want to reveal, so much I desire to show the world, but they just had to bind me by these damn, infuriating, *RULES!*"**

His tone shifted in an instant as the edges of my vision went red.

"Sorry, sorry. I told myself I was going to keep my cool, but you must understand, this is a rather touchy subject," he growled then took deep, exaggerated breaths before he spoke again. **"*That* desire of mine, by the way? That's what this has to do with that friend of yours. I may not be able to break these chains I have been bound by, but a loophole does go quite a long way."**

"Wait . . . are you saying you wanted *him to figure it out?"* I asked as everything clicked into place. Maybe it took me longer than it should have, but the panic of the situation, Axio's tone shifting on a dime, all of it had blinded me from the truth he was dancing around.

"Ding, ding, ding! He's finally figured it out. At least as much as he needs to. Give the man a prize—Oh wait, that reminds me . . ." His tone shifted again, causing him to sound as he did during his larger announcements, with a bit of gleeful mania at the forefront.

[New Achievement! Rulebreaker!]
A core rule of Infinite Ascension has been broken. You'd think that this would end in the immediate demise of you and that friend of yours, and in any other situation, you'd be absolutely right. But the flaw in that logic is that I was the one given the authority to decide how and when Achievements are rewarded. I don't think any of them ever expected me to twist it quite this way, but that just makes it all the sweeter. Just this once, I'm going to bend the rules in your favor. Mythic-Level Achievement.
Reward: You have received an S+ tier Loot Box!
I suggest you open this before I change my mind and clean up this annoying little loose end. Oh . . . and make sure your friend uses it.

After all, he's only in trouble for violating the rule if he's not actually a part of the game. Though . . . it might not be the way he wants. Also, once things go back to normal, I'm gonna suggest you don't talk about how you got this to anyone. They'll figure it out eventually, but the longer you don't tip my hand, the longer I don't have to tie up loose ends.

"Wait, why are—" I started, but my perception suddenly returned to normal as Axio's laughter faded from my head. Jon finally moved forward, taking his step before he came to a stop and crossed his arms over his chest, still waiting for an answer to his question.

[New Achiev—er . . . Phase Points Gained?]

Angie sounded unsure as she began to speak. *"Er . . . that was a weird glitch . . . Okay, let's see here . . ."*

[Phase Points Gained!]
Teacher's Pet (NEW)!
You have done something that particularly pleased Axio. This is worth however many damn points Axio wants it to be worth and changes each time he awards it. You may only receive this boon once.
Total Value: *2500 points.*

[New Achievement! Mountain Climber!]
With a crash and a windfall of points, you just landed yourself a position in the Top 10! That was one hell of a point dump, and I still really got to ask . . . What the hell just happened?
Diamond-Level Achievement.
Reward: *You have received an A+ tier Loot Box! I mean, really, did Axio just talk to you? Why couldn't I hear any of it . . . ? What the hell is going on here?*
"For once, I'm actually sorry, but not now, Angie," I replied then looked over to Jon. "I—It's—"

[Dialogue Suppressed!]
This NPC is not authorized to know about the existence of Infinite Ascension. This is your final warning before a Critical Level Threat will be dispatched to your location.

I felt confusion bubble up for just a few moments before the realization hit me.

Axio had already pointed it out, but like normal, I was getting ahead of myself. Jon couldn't know about the game because he *wasn't* actually in the game. I wasn't sure what was in the S+ box, but the easy assumption was that it was something that would help circumvent that rule.

With that in mind, I looked at my best friend and thought carefully about my next words.

"I need you to give me a minute to go to my room," I said, and a smirk cut across Jon's face.

"What's the plan? You gonna sneak out of the window instead of answering the question?"

"No, I promise. I just need a second. I think I have something that will clear all of this up," I replied, and he just waved his hand toward my room. I held up a finger cautiously (as if he was going to suddenly stop caring about all of this and disappear) before adding, "Cool, yeah, just . . . wait here."

I moved across the apartment quickly and rushed through the door to my room, closing it behind me. I looked at my desk and materialized the S+ box onto my desk as I eyed it cautiously.

"I know you're going to just tell me not now if I ask, but for the record, I'm still very confused on how exactly you got this," Angie chimed in as I reached over for it. It was still the same shoebox-shaped standard, but unlike the others, this one was solid gold, and the S+ emblazoned on the side was ringed in stars.

"Join the club," I muttered out loud and opened the box, watching as the gold dissipated into light and left me wishing I could have kept it to sell. It contained a plain-looking black cube with sharp edges and silver trim, as well as a combined headset and glove item. I turned my attention first to the cube and highlighted it.

[The Command Room!]
This is a Legendary Trophy.
As I have repeatedly said, I'm still not entirely sure what's going on here,
and Axio isn't responding to my requests for information, so I guess we just
aren't going to get answers for that right now, are we? As for this thing . . .
This is a server that upgrades your Safe Room to include the Command
Room expansion. This expansion comes with the **Control Gear** *item.*
Warning: *This is an experimental Safe Room expansion and thus*
may be subject to higher levels of patching than normal expansions.

I turned my attention over to the bulky, virtual-reality-like goggles that came with a pair of disconnected gloves. Just like the server, the items were a jet-black color with silver trimming. The gloves seemed to be lined with circuits along the entire surface.

Another window opened as my attention lingered, and Angie started to speak again. I was surprised by how rattled she still seemed, with her normally colorful descriptions completely absent as she explained the item.

[Control Gear!]
Legendary Equippable Head and Hand Item.
This item can only be equipped by a Sapient NPC.
When equipped, this will permanently bond with the user for as long as you, Loophole, are still active within the game. The user will no longer be considered a Sapient NPC. They will instead take on the role [Guy in the Chair] and will advance in unison with your level. The [Guy in the Chair] is a support-level role. The player must remain within your Safe House or a zone you control to access all features of this class, and will not have access to all of the features that come with true Augmentation.
Please Note: *Though they will not be eligible to make claims on territories, collect points, or access Sanctuary Square, the new player will need to choose an alias to go by after equipping this item, as they will be held to the same rules—in this case, the Secret Identity Protocol—as you Augments. Unlike Augment Registration, due to the player's limited access, this name can be registered within the Command Room.*
Warning: *This is an experimental item and thus may be subject to higher levels of patching than normal equipment.*

I actually found myself speechless as I reread the descriptions a few times just to be sure I wasn't missing anything important like a compulsory "if I die, he dies" bit of fine print, but I came up empty. Angie remained noticeably quiet as I picked up the trophy, a large square box that I could feel running like it was a computer even though it lacked any sort of connections for peripherals or power, and took it over to my display case. I had only one spot available, and I placed the new trophy onto it.

There was the sound of trumpets and a spectacle of colors in my vision before I heard what almost sounded like construction equipment and the hammering of a dozen workers rushing through the apartment.

[Safe House Upgraded!]
Your Safe House is now Level 2!
You have unlocked access to Safe House expansions.
Expansion Slots Unlocked: *2.*
The Command Room *entrance has been added to your layout.*
You have utilized **1 of 2** *Expansion Slots.*
The Command Room *trophy has been moved to the* **Expansion Shelf.**

A diagram of the apartment opened, showing a perfect floor plan of the place. Along the side wall, on the wall between the bathroom and the kitchen, there was a new door that had been added with the label [**Command Room**]. I waved the diagram away and looked over to the other half of the loot box. Jon really had waited long enough at this point.

I grabbed the headset in one hand and the gloves in the other before I walked back out of the room. Jon was standing, scratching the side of his head and looking at the new door implanted in the side of the wall.

"So, uh . . . that explanation of yours gonna explain how this appeared out of thin air? Or, um . . . how we're supposed to explain it to Mr. Greyson?" he asked without looking back at me.

"Umm, maybe we could get one of those big rugs that people hang up on the walls like they are art? Might be easier to explain than a random door," I said after I walked over to him. Once I was at his side, I held the headset for the Control Gear out to him. "Here, take this."

"Huh, that's what you went into your room for? What model is this?" he asked curiously, grabbing the headset and turning it over in his hands. It only held his attention for a moment before he looked back to me with a raised brow. "And also, weren't you going to tell me if this was all actually some game or something?"

"I can't say anything unless you put that on," I replied, gesturing to the headset. "You're just gonna have to trust—"

I stopped midsentence, since Jon hadn't even waited for me to finish before he took off his beanie and tossed it my way. Before I could react, he jammed the device onto his head, and the beanie fell to the floor.

I expected some big fanfare like with everything else, but to my surprise, nothing happened. My hand tightened, and I wondered if something went wrong when I felt the heavy gloves I still had in my hand. I unclenched my teeth and held them out, tapping one of Jon's hands with them in case he couldn't see. Once again, Jon didn't hesitate to snatch them up and pull them on, flexing his fingers against the fresh material.

For just a few seconds, nothing happened once again, and I was prepared to curse Axio for whatever cruel prank he had decided to play, but I maintained my calm and was just about to ask Angie what was going on when a handful of sparks started to shoot off the sides of the headgear.

The strap along the back of it cinched to the back of Jon's head, and the mask around his eyes pulled tight against his skin. Jon took a sudden step backward as he extended his arms for balance. From the back of the headset, a pair of wires materialized and stretched, wrapping down around his now outstretched arms in tight spirals before connecting to either of his gloves.

The entire system started to glow and pulse, changing from neon green to teal and back again. It grew brighter and brighter until I had to shield my eyes, looking off toward the kitchen as I heard Jon whoop with excitement.

After waiting a few moments, the light faded away, and I finally risked a glance back toward Jon. The equipment had completely vanished, leaving him standing there with a look of exhilaration. His eyes shone noticeably with a neon green light, and a wide smile cut across his face as he bent down and picked up his fallen beanie. My interface highlighted him without my prompting, just as it had when Axio was still in my head.

[???, Level 5 Guy in the Chair]

CHAPTER TWENTY-SIX

I t's a game . . . Holy shit, it's actually a game!" Jon exclaimed, the grin still plastered on his face as he briefly looked down at his hands and then back up to the door. "This is so fucking cool!"

"Oh, he's taking this a lot better than you did," Angie said. Jon jumped, his head darting from side to side as he looked around.

"Um . . . who was that?" he asked, his eyes locking on mine as the light glimmering in them dimmed and faded back to his usual shade of blue.

"Wait, you can hear her?!" I asked, louder than I probably should have.

"Mr. Blue Eyes can hear me?!" I could hear a note of eagerness in her tone as soon as Angie started to speak. *"Oh boy, oh boy, oh boy, this is gonna be so much fun! There are so many things for you and me to talk about!"*

"Mister . . . Blue Eyes?" Jon's excitement had rapidly been replaced with confusion, and I couldn't stop myself from pinching the bridge of my nose.

"Angie . . . please behave." I looked back at Jon. "That's Angie. She's my PAI—er, my Personal AI Kinda like a game guide, though guide is a *very* loose term when it comes to her."

"Hey! I haven't guided you to your death yet, have I?"

"Silver linings, Angie. Silver linings," I sighed.

His confusion was replaced with excitement once more as he straightened up. "Am I gonna get one of those?"

"Sorry, Mr. Blue Eyes, you're not exactly *an Augment like Loophole here. You might have conditional access to the system, but it's tied directly to him. If anything, I think we can call you an Augment-lite . . . Hmm, I'm going to have to workshop that. But the short answer is no, you don't get 'one of those,' but you do get the pleasure of my company, handsome."*

"Why is she calling me Mr. Blue Eyes?" Jon asked.

"She's . . . I'm gonna go with . . . quirky," I said with a shrug and looked at the door to the Command Room. "As for *why* she's calling you that specifically? Well, she can't call you by your real name, so I guess that's what she's going with until you choose a name to go by. Once you're in the game, you're bound by the Secret Identity Protocol. Which was actually why I couldn't say anything to you, and dude, I am so stupidly sorry. You know I would have told you if I could; hell, I tried pretty much the moment I woke up in my bedroom yesterday."

I hadn't been doing it on purpose, but the words basically fell out of my mouth, and it felt amazing not having to face a warning or threat of death for saying it.

"You know what, given the circumstances, I think you get a pass," he said, following my gaze and eyeing the door. "Not quite sure what I'm gonna call myself, though . . . Have I mentioned just how damn cool all of this is? I've got a window open that says my title is 'Guy in the Chair,' but it doesn't have a whole lot of information other than 'Support for Loophole.' Um . . . Angie, could you please fill me in on what I can do?"

"Oh my God, he's so polite! Isn't that adorable!" Angie squealed before she stopped and cleared her throat. *"Okay, so Axio did give me a little bit of a rundown now that you've put the equipment on. If you really want to access your full suite, you're going to need to be in the Command Room here. Oh, and, uh . . . just as an FYI, it* really *shouldn't be a big deal or anything, but, uh . . . don't try to remove it . . . I don't think you're going to want to anyway; it's not like it's blocking that gorgeous face of yours. But just to be safe . . . don't."*

Jon looked over at me with a raised brow. "Is . . . Is she kidding?"

"When it comes to the warning about the helmet? I'm gonna say that's a fifty-fifty. To her credit, that item you're wearing was listed as experimental. I'm not sure if I could have told you that or not, but you also shoved your head into it before I could even try."

"And the whole . . . calling me Mr. Blue Eyes and gorgeous and all that?"

"Yeah . . . like I said . . . she's quirky, but at least she doesn't seem to be as bad as Axio. Welcome to my world . . . Sorry about that." I rubbed the back of my head.

"Oooookay . . ." Jon thought about it for a moment before adding, "And then Axio is . . . ?"

"The overall System AI that is *sorta* in charge of this whole thing. Honestly, it's been a weird half hour here, and if we're gonna get sidetracked by every random thing, this is gonna take all afternoon."

"Good point. I guess we'll have time for everything else later, once I've really gotten settled in," Jon said, cracking his knuckles. "At this point, I really, *really* want to see what's behind this door."

With a yank, the door opened to a room that was barely bigger than the smallest of walk-in closets. I had been expecting maybe some sort of computer or over-the-top monitor setup, given the name. Instead, the room was empty except for a large desk that wrapped around the walls, with a comfortable looking bucket chair taking up the only free space at the center. Jon once again barely even hesitated before he turned and fell into the chair.

A green flash of light flared as the room came to life. The trimming within the chair Jon had sat on began shining the same neon green that danced in his eyes, and he swiveled himself into the room. As his hands swept over the desk, keyboards and control panels appeared. A myriad of monitors of different sizes materialized as he centered himself on the desk, filling the wall as they blinked on, one by one. It was everything I was expecting and more, and I stepped in closer, trying to take in the technological overload that was the room.

"This is the Command Room, your official base of operations. Here you are provided PAI level permission to every database I currently have access to, along with a myriad of other features," Angie explained. *"As mentioned, your role is one of support. While I would like to go over everything you can do here, it may be best for you and I to take some time to do so at a later time. Much of it would probably go over Loophole's head, and I'd rather not get sidetracked by him every other sentence."*

"Hey, that's—*Ehhh*, you know what, good point," I replied. There really wasn't a point to arguing with her, especially if it did just mean Jon could break it down to the stuff that really mattered for me later.

I couldn't exactly enter the room, given how small it was, but I had been trying to get a good look at the different monitors. I saw one that seemed to have a list of all the different abilities I had created so far, another that was our apartment's layout with the trophy boosts listed alongside it, and then there was one that was an actual Vitruvian-man-like portrayal of me—with clothes on, thankfully—that had windows for status ailments pointed at various spots on my body.

My attention was briefly pulled toward a map of the city, complete with icons for the Viper dens in Hell's Kitchen, before I stopped and looked at a monitor that felt out of place in the sea of buzzing screens.

"What's this one?" I asked, pointing at the largest of the monitors in the middle of the back wall. The screen was still black, with the words No Connection blinking in the center.

"Yeah . . . so you know how you think I'm an invasion of your privacy?" Angie said with an awkward laugh. *"Well, how do you think Mr. Blue Eyes here is supposed to help you in the field if he can't see you?"*

"Oh, that is so cool!" Jon exclaimed as his hands moved inaudibly over the controls. "How do I turn it on?"

"It will automatically connect when Loophole is not inside a Safe House or otherwise barred location. And no, before you ask, this isn't some magical hidden camera thing; the monitor will be seeing through his eyes, just like I do," she explained, and I groaned.

"Great, well, I guess at least he can't hear my internal thoughts . . ."

"Also, I'd like to say that for the record, that *is* sorta like a magical hidden camera thing. Just so we have our terminology right," Jon added as he turned his attention to another screen. I heard him muttering to himself as he leaned forward to take a closer look at it. "Shit, there are so many names I could go by with stuff like this . . . Bird's Eye, Overseer, Watchdog . . ."

"I'd go with something like Encyclopedia or Database. I mean, you know a shit ton about Augments as it is," I offered. Jon just shrugged without looking back.

"There was already a Database a few years back, though you might be onto something. I'm gonna have to think on it for a bit. Is that gonna be a problem, Angie?" Jon asked.

"Not really. Your use for the actual name is going to be rather limited, especially right now. It just means I get to call you Mr. Blue Eyes for a while longer," she giggled.

"Does that name really work when my eyes are all lit up green like this?" he asked.

"Mr. Green Eyes doesn't sound as nice. Besides, I know what color they're supposed to be," Angie purred.

"Well, alright then . . . I guess I've been called worse," he responded and swiveled to another screen. Without warning, he let out a bark of laughter and clapped his hands together. "Holy crap, there are loot boxes too?! This really is just a fucking full-blown game. This monitor says you have five; think you can pop one of those for me? I want to see what happens."

"Sure, no problem," I replied. I opened my B.E.L.T. and materialized the lone C-tier box I had into my hands, taking a moment to appreciate that I didn't have to go and hide in my room. After opening it, I saw the screen that Jon was looking at was an exact mirror of the window that appeared in my vision listing the contents, with the exception that each of the lines included a small button with a circular arrow icon next to it. The contents were:

5 Enhanced Stamina Injectors
1 Targeted Ability Level Up Scroll
500 credits

"Oh sweet. Apparently, I can reroll a loot box for you within thirty seconds of you opening it," he said as his hand moved toward the screen, but he suddenly stopped. "Hmm, but it says there's a twelve-hour cooldown. That's kinda dumb."

"Well, we can't have you rerolling everything he gets until you find the exact item you're looking for. It's cute that you're upset about it, though," Angie giggled while I rolled my eyes.

"Don't waste it on any of this stuff; it's all useful to me anyway," I said, then materialized the F-tier box into my hand. "Let's do it with this one instead."

"Wouldn't that be the lowest tier? Why would you want to waste a reroll from one junk item to another?" he asked as a small screen below the disconnected monitor lit up with scrolling text. "Oh, it's a true random box. I guess if you did get something crappy, we could reroll it. But wouldn't that just mean it could turn into *another* crappy item?"

"Yeah, but I mean, I got some pretty strong boots out of the last F tier I opened; I could always get something like that too," I replied with a shrug, and Jon swiveled in his chair to look back at me.

"Sure, I suppose, but that's not exactly great logic to use either. I think it'd be smarter to start with the A+ box you received and then reroll for something of similar caliber if it's not great, don't yah think?"

I pulled the F-tier box back into my B.E.L.T. and materialized the A+ as I thought about it.

"I've only received one of these boxes so far, and it had two things in it: a book-shop coupon and a Scroll of Level Up that made me immediately use it."

"Oh shit, then never mind, don't open that," he said before I could reach for the lid. I looked up at him curiously as he swiveled back toward his main screens. "It doesn't give me an experience bar or anything like that, but I have a notification that says 'Level Up Imminent.' If that scroll just gives you the points you need to get to the next level, then it would be a huge waste to open the box only for it to take you up a few points. Especially when you could just do it right after you reach the next level."

"Well, isn't he just clever," Angie mused. I couldn't help but agree with her.

Jon had literally been getting swamped with information, probably even faster than I had at first, and even without knowing about the larger point of the game, he had found a way to exploit a part of the system. Not to mention leveling up in rapid succession *was* one of the ways to gain Phase Points too.

"Can he hear me if I internalize, or would he hear you responding to me?" I asked inside my head.

"He'd hear you if you were out and about and you were trying to communicate with him. But if you're specifically trying to talk to me like you are right now, then no. In fact, we already tested it, and I can communicate with him separately as well. The internalized communication systems are rather precisely controlled and coordinated with your intentions," Angie explained. *"There are some limitations, of course; I think if you went into somewhere like The Common Ground, he'd lose access to me just as you do, but that would be something to test."*

"So then the F tier?" I finally asked and materialized it into my hand.

"Nah, now that I know about the possibility of a level-up scroll, we don't really need to test the reroll right now." Jon shrugged without looking back at me. "I mean, you can go ahead and open it, but I think our best bet is for you to go back out and grind up to the next level, then come back here and pop that A+. You're not guaranteed to get a level-up scroll, right? So we can save the reroll for that to give you two chances. And then if you *do* get the scroll or something else that works with your setup, we can use the reroll on something else. I mean, unless you're, like, *really* looking to get something specific, it just seems like a better idea to save them for now and be a bit more tactical about it all."

"That's . . . a really good point," I said, looking at the F tier again before pulling it into my B.E.L.T.

"I'm full of them," he laughed as he swiveled toward another set of controls and let out a gasp. "Holy shit, what have you been doing to your stats?! I mean, I knew you were an idiot with games, but what the hell, dude?! Why would you put points into Charisma?!"

"Thank you!" Angie practically shouted.

"What? It seemed like a good idea at the time. And don't you go and agree with him, Angie—you didn't say shit when I did it . . . I didn't know what I was going to have to talk myself through to get myself in position for that fight, and I was trying to figure out how to clue you in on all of this! I figured a higher Charisma would get me anywhere I needed to go . . ."

"Yeah, we'll come back to how little faith you had in me figuring out what was right in front of my face later." I could see him leaning forward and rubbing at his temples. "I'm seriously trying to understand the logic here. I mean, half your skills have Luck components; at a *minimum*, you should be dropping a point into that stat every single level, if not two, if I'm being honest. Sheesh . . . how the hell have you gotten through this past day?"

"I mean . . . I haven't been doing that bad," I said defensively. "Besides, even the two times I played *D&D* with your old group I let you manage everything with my character."

"I guess you're not wrong, but still, this hurts to see . . ."

"Well, at least you're here now to keep me from making any more dumb mistakes," I laughed, and he joined in. It died down after a minute, and the silence lingered as Jon kept moving from one set of controls to the next. I really wasn't following exactly what he was doing or why the computer needed to be split up into so many different spots, but he seemed like he was finding a rhythm, and I wasn't about to question it too deeply.

"Speaking of your dumb mistakes, let me see . . ." He trailed off. "Hmm, I don't think I've ever heard of a power quite like this one . . . Okay, maybe your lack of cohesion isn't the dumbest of mistakes. You didn't exactly come up with terrible ideas; there's just not a whole lot of connection either."

"Yeah, it's a real hodgepodge of abilities." I turned to lean against the wall. "I have a barrier where I have to know what I'm trying to do first, though. So that means if I want to do something like Trick of the Light, I have to have at least a level-three knowledge in the related skill.

"I can get that from these absorbable books, and I actually do have a coupon for the bookshop over in Sanctuary Square, but I didn't really want to waste it until I had at least some sort of direction. And then once I realized I needed to figure out the cohesion of it all, I didn't really want to use my coupon until I could get your opinion on all of it, and well . . . here we are."

"Well, I can't exactly say you waiting for my opinion was a bad idea," Jon laughed again. "I've got a few ideas, actually, but I think I'd need to see what books are available . . . Um, Angie, am I able to use those too? That sounds really, *really* cool."

"Sorry, Mr. Blue Eyes; those are Augment only. There are a limited set of items that are programmed to work with non-Augments, and skill books are not one of them."

"Damn. Eh, oh well," he said. "I mean, don't get me wrong, it would be cool to be able to instantly learn anything, but my brain's cluttered enough."

For everything that was being thrown at him, Jon was taking this better than I could have ever imagined. Not to mention with an ease that made getting through it all as simple as any of our conversations.

"You know, as jealous as I am that you got Augmented and I didn't, I think it's for the best," he said out of nowhere, swiveling back toward me. It was the first time I had fully seen his eyes since he sat down, and they were shining neon green almost uncomfortably.

"Why's that?" I asked curiously.

"Because as much as I love ya, buddy, I can't imagine a world where I was an Augment and you got called in to be my tech support," he said, reaching out and smacking my arm as he started to laugh. Angie joined in almost immediately, and I felt ganged up on. After a minute, he stopped and swiveled back to his console.

"Okay, unless you're really looking for something specific in those boxes, how about you save them for now and get out there to grind that level out. It looks like there's one of those Bronze dens over on the corner of 47th and 11th; you can manage that, right? I'm gonna pick Angie's brain and see just what all my controls can do. Sound good?"

"Anything sounds good when it's coming out of your mouth, Mr. Blue Eyes," Angie said with an uncomfortable purr, and Jon laughed again.

"Heh, yeah, I'm definitely gonna need to figure out a name pretty soon. I don't know how long I can take that seriously," he noted. "Has she really been like this the whole time?"

"Only toward you. She mostly makes weird jokes and makes me question my sanity," I replied as I started to turn toward the door.

"Oh, you know—"

"Not now, Angie!" I said, for once, out loud and looked back over at Jon as he shot me a curious glance. "You gotta stop her before she can start sometimes. Okay, so 47th and 11th?"

"Yup. Go get 'em, Loophole."

CHAPTER TWENTY-SEVEN

Corner of 47th and 11th, Bronze-Level Viper Den. Hell's Kitchen, NYC
Neighborhood: *Claimed by Guardian:* **Loophole** *(Contested)*
City: *Unclaimed (Blocked by Timer)*
Current Phase Points: *5640*
End of Phase One: *03D:03H:06M:41S*

**[Tenth Precinct Assignment: Bronze-Level
Viper Den—Hell's Kitchen Cleared!]**
*You have successfully subdued all of the Vipers biker gang members at this
den. Police will be by momentarily to collect the remaining living opponents.*
Hell's Kitchen Viper Dens Cleared: *2 of 12.*
Reward: *You have received 500 credits and a Small Reputation Boost.*

How about *Patch Notes?*" Jon suggested.

"*Eh, I don't really think it fits,*" I said, stretching as I looked down at the knocked-out grunts at my feet. "*I mean, it's at least better than GuideWire or MetaMind, but I think there's still something better.*"

"*You mean like Loophole?*" Angie offered.

"*Hey, you know you like my name,*" I shot back, and she tutted.

"*It's growing on me, I'll admit that much, but I still think you're gonna be in a big fight somewhere and your enemy is gonna call you Poophole, and all of your credibility will be gone.*"

"*How about Compendium?*" Jon offered. He had quickly become a natural at just skipping right past whatever Angie said, and I found myself appreciating it.

"*That one's definitely closer,*" I replied.

Although my first two den experiences had been eventful, tackling an *actual* Bronze-level den was a surprisingly easy task. While there had been eight level-three grunts and a level-five brute that I couldn't just knock over without breaking a sweat, it *was* the first time that I wasn't even passingly worried about the outcome. I even almost felt like I had a little bit of fun as I dodged and weaved through the building, putting the bikers down with ease.

I wasn't sure if that was just because of growing confidence or because I was happy to have the weight of my secret lifted from my shoulder, but given the events of the day, I was willing to let myself have this one.

Jon didn't say much during my initial infiltration of the building, instead sitting quietly and letting me do my thing. After I had cleared out the first room and it was obvious I wasn't going to have an issue, he started to throw name ideas at me. Angie offered a few suggestions of her own, and the two largely ignored what I was doing as I fought my way through the rest of the small den.

There weren't any secret compartments, nor did I have to fight another randomly appearing snake-man, but by the end of the fight, I had gotten exactly what I had come for and leveled up. The fight had stayed self-contained and without an audience or any special features that might have complicated the battle. After it was done, the only extra thing I took away from clearing the place was a Basebreaker Phase Point gain, adding two hundred and fifty to my total.

"Hey, are you able to see the Wave Leaderboard from your setup?" I asked as I finished looting the downed enemies. While I hadn't wanted to take them because I didn't necessarily like the idea, I looted four different handguns and pulled them into my inventory. If I did happen to come across another soldier using a snake injector, it was something that I'd want to keep on hand just to be prepared. I even went as far as dousing each of their cartridges in venom before I put them away for good.

There was a flash of red-and-blue lights coming through the front door, and I wandered over to it. "You're gonna want to bring the cuffs; I don't keep any on me," I called out and held the door open as a handful of officers jogged into the building.

"Let's see . . ." Jon murmured. *"Yup, got it right here. Oh damn! Did you know you're number five? That's crazy as hell, man."*

"Eh, luck played a big part. I got a huge boost from all of the stuff going on with you," I replied. We hadn't exactly gone over any of the craziness that had been my conversation with Axio, and although I knew Angie knew I had it on my mind, she seemed unable to access any of it no matter how often it passed through my head. Given his warning, or maybe threat, I decided it was better to keep it that way.

"Hey, how yah got there doesn't matter as long as you can maintain your spot," he said.

"True." I thought about it for a second. *"Actually, speaking of that. Is there a Pretty Pink Warthog on the list still? She was up there last night, and I met her in the courtyard before the update on The First got announced."*

"Hmm, yeah, looks like she's number six," he said quickly, *"Wait, what update on The First?"*

"Oh . . . yeah, I guess I hadn't mentioned that yet . . . Angie, didn't you fill him in?" I asked.

She huffed.

"Noooooope. That is not on the list of topics I was instructed to update him on." I rolled my eyes as I walked up the street. The cops had barely been paying attention to me as they hauled out the Vipers in cuffs, and I hadn't cared to linger, so I aimed myself back toward the apartment and casually started to jog away. *"Also, as I've told you before, unless you specifically ask, I won't just offer information up."*

"Okay, well, I'm asking: what happened with The First? He hasn't been on the news

lately, which isn't exactly abnormal, but I figure if he had been taken down that would be plastered everywhere, right?"

"I mean, your guess is as good as mine. I had just finished getting registered when I noticed a crowd gathering around the giant marble statue of the guy. His status had been updated to say 'Unknown' when the system updated and said he had abandoned all of his territory claims. It was weird, though, like . . . nobody there was really freaking out about it."

"First of all, I'm gonna need you to go right to wherever this statue is and let me see it literally *as soon as possible,"* Jon laughed for a moment before he settled, and I heard the crunching of chips over the internal voice chat he was using. *"It might be a little weird, but I think I can understand why they weren't freaking out. Objectively speaking, at least."*

"Yeah? Want to explain?" Although I didn't really like the attention it was giving me, Jon had pointed out on my way over here that it was better if I got used to my disguise now for when I *did* have some way to move faster.

I had been using the anonymity of taking off my gear to move around the city, and the logic of it made sense. But because of that, I couldn't easily get into and out of fights, and besides the need for me to get used to attention, I *also* had to be more prepared to react to danger on a more immediate basis. Plus, though my neighborhood made it easier, there wasn't *always* going to be an alley big enough or private enough that I could use to activate my gear.

I slowed to a stop by a gathering crowd on a street corner and did my best to feel like I *didn't* stand out.

"Well, think about it. First, the status just said Unknown *instead of* Dead. *From what I've been reading, the Unknown status just means that there could be any sort of obfuscation that's happening. That could mean a number of things, and while yeah, him dropping the territories sucks, that really only matters to the game, right?"*

"Yeah, I suppose." I shrugged, putting on a smile and waving at a small kid who suddenly pulled at the bottom of my jacket. He looked up at me with awe as I stood waiting with the crowd, but before I could say anything, the light changed, and the boy's mother hurried him along.

"And then you have to consider the more obvious answer."

"There's a more obvious answer than that?" I asked curiously.

"Oh, much more obvious than that," he confirmed with a laugh. *"I mean, no offense but like, what would literally any of you guys do against someone who could take him down?"*

"Exactly!" Angie practically yelled, and I had to stop myself from physically cringing. *"You could have the All-Seeing Eye on your side, and you still wouldn't stand a chance."*

"Ooo—"

"No, that is a terrible name too," I interrupted, shutting Jon down before he could even get started.

"Eh, you're right. God, you move really slow; we need to figure out a way to get you around quicker," he sighed. *"There's gotta be at least five or six ways I could think of that we could probably achieve some form of flight for you with your powerset, though it'd probably take some practice and the right skill book. I really need to take some time to look into exactly how those things work . . .*

"Even then, superspeed seems less likely, and your range isn't really long enough for anything more than maybe *short-range teleportation. That has its uses, of course, but probably not as a mode of getting around. Though I guess you could hopscotch teleport . . ."*

"Yeah, you know what, Compendium might be the best bet. You know way too much about all of this," I said as I approached the corner to 49th and turned up toward our apartment.

"Yeah, I know I suggested it, but it's a real mouthful of a word. A good name should be like, two syllables at most. Loophole is good in that regard," he said. *"Oh, how about—"*

[Crime Alert! A Plain Ol' Robbery!]

Not to interrupt this very important conversation, but some of those big mean bikers are robbing that poor man's hotdog cart! That's . . . incredibly unambitious. You should go and beat them up for setting their sights so low.

Reward: *You will receive a D-tier Loot Box and a Small Reputation Boost if you stop the men from robbing that cart. This crime has a 10-minute time limit.*

"Oh, that's cool—random events," Jon noted. *"Can you see them? The map is saying they are up a block and a half on the other side of the street."*

"They show up on your map?!" I started to jog, leaving the crowd behind. Sure enough, I could see a few bikes blocking the street barely a hundred yards away.

"Yeah, it kinda sucks that you don't have one built-in just yet, but eh, beggars can't be choosers," he replied. *"Okay, what's the plan? Just gonna go in and drop them with the weight? It's a pretty reliable starter."*

"If it ain't broke don't fix it, right?" One of the bikers seemed to notice me jogging up as I entered the street and patted a brute on the shoulder. The large man turned to me with an unsettling smile.

"Well, well, if it ain't the bitchy little thorn in the boss's side," the brute snarled. He walked away from the others. "And here the bet was that we were gonna have to turn over at least a dozen of these marks before you'd show your face. Lucky us, eh?"

"Now, now, fellas, is that really how we're gonna start things?" I asked as I came to a stop and activated my Area Sense. Though I could only make out three men total, I had already learned my lesson about not checking everything I could. Nothing stood out to me as odd, my area touching the cars on the edges of the streets as well as the liquid moving under my feet in the sewers. "How about you guys just do us all a favor and get on the ground. You'll really be saving us a lot of trouble, and then no one has to get hurt."

There were civilians gathering in the distance already, and though the alert was going to be easy to finish, I felt lucky that there was a decent crowd just to stack a few additional Phase Points with the Crowdpleaser gain.

"Nah, we're just gonna—"

Without moving a muscle, I activated Weighted Clothes, and all three men dropped to the pavement. The weight outright crushed the two grunts to the ground, first dropping them to seventy-five percent before the lingering effect quickly ticked them down until they sported matching [**KO**] debuffs.

As for the brute, he collapsed to a position that reminded me of Gio, with his palms barely holding up his body. Unlike Gio, though, he had taken over half of his health in damage from the initial attack, and I felt a smile creep over my face. I stepped forward, deactivating Area Sense as I sauntered as casually as I could toward the man.

"Why is it that *none* of you ever listen when I tell you to get on the ground?"

"Ooh, ooh, I know this one!"

"Not now, Angie."

"It's because he's not menacing enough, I think, though the dramatics and quips are a nice touch," Jon added.

"Not now, J—err . . . pick a name already so I can tell you to shut up too."

"B—B—B—Bitch a—a—ass h—hero . . ." The brute spat at my feet when I was in range and I skipped to the side before delivering a swift kick to his wrist. He collapsed to the ground and took another chunk of damage. Out of curiosity, I highlighted the brute and discovered he was only level four. I felt something gnaw at me as I looked around again.

"Wait, the manhole!" Jon exclaimed as my vision swept over the road, and I looked back to it. Sure enough, the metal cover to the sewer was being lifted up by a single large hand.

[Crime Alert Updated! A Plain Ol' Robbery!]
This Crime Alert has been canceled. Rewards will no longer be granted.
[Crime Alert! AMBUSH! Snake in the Sewers!]
Now look, I don't know why you weren't suspicious about a crime called "A Plain Ol' Robbery," so you not being prepared for this is really on both of you. I don't know if I could have spelled this one out for you two any more clearly. And yes, I'm counting you at fault for this too, Mr. Blue Eyes. An old acquaintance has tracked you down. Don't let him make a snack out of you.
*This Crime Alert has upgraded from **Bronze Level** to **Silver Level**.*
Reward: *The reward for this alert is Variable depending on how you deal with the threat.*

The manhole was tossed to the side, embedding itself firmly into a car parked along the side of the road as the crowd suddenly screamed in fear. The alarm from the car began to blare and echo against the buildings. From the sewer, the hand was joined by a second that grabbed the edges of the street.

The snake-man pulled himself up and onto the main street, his large body still draping down into the sewer as he flexed and stretched his body in the sun. I could have placed this one without even highlighting him, though I still did, just to confirm.

[Sal the Snake, Level 6 (Elite) Biker Lieutenant]

He began to stalk toward me, and I felt like I had to act in a split second. Looking back toward the brute still struggling on the ground, I delivered a kick straight for his head as hard as I could. It was enough, and it knocked him out, allowing me to turn my undivided attention to my lone remaining opponent.

"Sal! Old buddy! I thought we'd never see each other again," I called out, stretching my arms out and walking toward him with a smile.

"What are you doing?" Jon asked.

"Stalling . . . I just used the main power I've been using to slow the snake guys down so far, and now I'm not exactly sure how I'm supposed to beat this dude," I replied. To my credit, Sal halted and looked at me with momentary confusion.

"You did prep the guns for exactly this situation, right? Seems like the easiest solution," he offered before Sal slammed his tail against the pavement and left a noticeable crack in the asphalt.

"Niccce try. SssnakeBite sssaid you'd be here. Don't think I don't remember your little ssstunt back at the yardsss," Sal hissed, flexing his hands and extending his claws as he started toward me once more.

"Who, me? That was all the other guy's fault; I barely did a thing. Who the hell is SnakeBite, anyway?"

"You ssstole my children's—"

"Wait, wait, wait, those snakes were your children? That's . . . You know what, never mind. I don't want to know," I said, slowly inching back toward the center of the street. The crowd wasn't bothering to disperse, and I wasn't sure if I should be worried that they weren't or flattered that they trusted me to take care of this. "Go on, you were saying."

"Give me the venom!" he shouted and lunged toward me. I activated Mirror Image and dove to the side, rolling out of the way and watching Sal as he crashed through the afterimage left behind by my ability. He hit the ground with a noticeable *THUD* that cracked the asphalt, but he barely took a sliver of damage. Jon was exactly right—there was one thing I had on me that could do the trick, and I immediately reached for one of the guns in my B.E.L.T., but stopped myself as a realization hit me.

There were dozens of civilians in the area, and I couldn't risk a bullet ricocheting off of Sal as it had with Gio. While we hadn't necessarily tried to shoot Sal back at the train yard, it stood to reason that he'd have a similar resistance to being hit. I certainly *could* try the same trick with Mute Button, but he had barely flinched at the alarm as he exited the sewer, so that wasn't a guarantee to slow him down either.

Whether I liked it or not, I still didn't have another way to get the venom into his bloodstream, and one of the guns felt like it would be my best bet. I still had six seconds left of my invisibility, and I rushed toward Sal as he pushed himself back up until he could stretch and look around, eagerly trying to find where I had run off to. It was risky getting up close, I knew that, but there *was* an advantage to him not being able to see me. I just had to hope it would work.

I pulled a venom-soaked gun from my B.E.L.T. just as I stopped next to Sal. There was only a bit over a second left on my invisibility when I pointed the gun directly at his side, the muzzle only an inch from his skin. I briefly held my breath as I reached for my Super Luck and hoped it would do the trick.

[New Ability! Defy the Odds!]

Luck is a funny thing, isn't it? Like, whenever they say something is resistant to something, it's almost always saying "99 percent effective against X!" Well, what about that 1 percent? What about that 1 in a million . . . hehe . . . shot.
Passive Ability.
Gain a 0.5 percent chance for every point of luck you have minus the enemy's total luck for your (and only your) attacks to bypass any resistances they have. This chance is tripled if you are **Hidden** *from the enemy.*

Without hesitating, I replaced Misfire on my action bar and pulled the trigger.

Sal let out a scream of pain as the bullet penetrated his side and his health chunked down by ten percent. He gained a modified version of the **[Weakened]** debuff as his head swiveled, his eyes catching mine just as I started to back up. I fired the gun twice more, and while he still dropped a similar amount of health with each hit, the debuff above his head didn't change. As I pulled the gun back into my B.E.L.T. I scanned the debuff, just to see why it looked different.

[Weakened (75%)!]

This Augment has begun to adapt. Effectiveness of this weakness has been reduced. All stats are now lowered by 56.25 percent for 1 minute.
Elite status and defenses have been nullified for the duration of this debuff.

"There yah go!" Jon whooped in my head. *"Follow it up, get back in close and hit him hard, just . . . you know . . . don't get hit."*

"Ah yes, 'don't get hit,' sage advice," I said before darting back in, activating Float

like a Butterfly while I dodged under a weak attempt at a grab from Sal. *"Also, no. Sage is also a terrible name for you."*

Before Jon could respond, I activated Sting like a Bee and aimed right for his wounds, striking three times in rapid succession and quickly bringing his health down to just about twenty-five percent. He was clearly feeling the damage, swaying like he was being charmed by music.

"You know, I get that you're pretty tough and all that, but did yah ever think maybe, I don't know, *don't* go after the guy who knows your weakness?" I said, feeling like I was able to show off just a bit. The crowd was yelling cheers of encouragement, and I noticed I had actually received a buff that I hadn't noticed. With Sal seemingly stunned, albeit briefly, I highlighted the buff.

[Home Team!]
*A crowd of more than 25 Sapient NPCs from a territory you have claimed
are cheering you on during a fight! You feel inspired and invigorated.
Increase all damage you deal by 25 percent!*

Depending on how long I'd had that buff, it certainly helped to explain just how I had taken Sal's health down so quickly. Though this should have been a struggle, the knowledge of his weakness alone made it far less threatening than it was. Even Sal seemed to realize this as he looked around, his eyes filled with rage as the crowd cheered me on.

"You think that will sssave you forever," he hissed, turning back to me with a dangerous-looking smile. "You heroesss all share a weaknesss, you know."

"What's—" I started before I saw Sal lean back. His fangs started to drip with venom before his body snapped forward, and a thick glob of green goo was launched in my direction.

His sluggishness was obvious, and I barely even had to move to dodge the attack. I was just about to follow up, maybe even make a joke about him being a bad shot, when I heard a scream of panic behind me. I turned and found an older man screaming in pain as his arm began to blister and turn red, the fabric of his shirt dissolving like it had been hit by acid the moment the venom hit it. He fell back against a wall, holding his arm up as several other civilians scrambled to back away.

"Shit!" I exclaimed, briefly looking back just as Sal disappeared back into the sewer. While I could certainly chase him down, I never even considered it, pulling multiple vials of antivenom and an Enhanced Health Injector from my B.E.L.T. I rushed right for the hurt civilian and dropped to my knees by the panicking man.

I wasn't even sure if this was going to work, but it wasn't going to stop me from trying either. The man looked at me with hopeful eyes as I dumped one of the vials of antivenom right onto his arm. The blistering and sizzling stopped immediately, and before the man could say a thing, I pushed the injector against his arm and activated it.

Unlike the instantaneous recovery I experienced when using the device, it seemed to take an unnervingly long time to do something. I was almost positive it wasn't going to work when the redness and blistering all rapidly began to heal, changing until the man's skin was left pink but recovered.

"Th—Th—Thank you!" the man said, his eyes watering as he stared up at me. In that moment, even though I hadn't put Sal down for the count, the crowd burst into cheers just as Angie chirped up.

[Crime Alert Completed! Snake in the Sewers!]

CHAPTER TWENTY-EIGHT

W hile I probably hadn't ended up with the best rewards due to letting Sal get away, I still ended up walking away from the encounter with three Phase Point gains, fifteen hundred credits, and a few new fans.

Crowdpleaser had given me a total of five hundred and seventy points from the crowd that had gathered. Apparently, even the folks watching from their windows overlooking the street counted, and I sure as hell wasn't going to complain. Thanks to the fact that the alert had actually been an Ambush, I also got the static two hundred points from Survivor. The last one I had gained wasn't one I had actually been anticipating Axio considering point worthy, yet all the same, I received it.

[Phase Points Gained!]
The People's Champion (NEW)!
*During an encounter, you chose to put the needs of a hurt Sapient
NPC first. By lending a hand instead of chasing down your . . . I
guess we can call him your nemesis for now, you've earned the respect
of those you protect . . . and maybe a little karma boost too.
This gain has a static value.*
Total Value: *250 points.*
This gain comes with a Medium Reputation Boost.

With those points applied I had brought my total all the way up to 6,910. Interestingly enough, the reputation boost moved the bar along the side of my screen nearly to the top. When I probed Angie for information, she told me that in order to claim higher-tiered territories, such as the Community District that Hell's Kitchen was a part of, I would need to reach at least the next tier of reputation, "Local Hero."

By the time I had made it back to the apartment, Angie had gone through the entire explanation of the leveling process for Jon.

As I entered the apartment, I found him still perched in the Command Room, having more or less set up a nest like he was a bird, with snacks and drinks in various spots on the desk around him. The console seemed to actively adapt to his layout needs, spawning cupholders and smaller tiered tables to place his things.

Not wanting to stand around, I pulled one of the chairs from the kitchen table and plopped down before opening the leveling window.

At Jon's insistence, I increased my Luck by two and then put a point into each my Dexterity and my Intelligence. He was still going through the back-end information he had access to on exactly *what* the different skills did, and it led to him muttering about how he'd probably be up all night just puzzling it out with an odd amount of excitement in his tone.

Of the eight base stats, he was relatively certain that I was going to want to focus on, obviously, Luck, but then Strength, Dexterity, and of all things, Intelligence. The first three were for my general build—between my abilities and my hand-to-hand skills, they needed to take priority. But Intelligence was important for a much different but equally necessary reason.

While the knowledge books I had gained so far had been without requirements, Jon learned that Angie had *conveniently* left out the fact that any book not received through a loot box would have an Intelligence requirement before I could utilize it.

While there were a good chunk of books that *could* be used with a base human's average Intelligence, they weren't necessarily going to be the books that would help me out the most. More advanced topics would often require Intelligence scores well out of my current reach, and that was before looking at books that would raise my knowledge levels above three. I wasn't even a hundred percent sure *why* I would need to care about raising a knowledge stat higher than three, but Angie insisted that *other* powersets benefited from higher knowledge levels, so theoretically mine would too.

She also insisted that unlike how the Strength stat would actually increase my strength, increasing my Intelligence wouldn't suddenly turn me into a rocket scientist. There *was* a book for that, but having a high Intelligence score wasn't automatically equivalent to just becoming a genius. It just meant the capacity for that intelligence *was* there.

When it came to the other standard stats, Toughness, Ingenuity, and apparently even Style would absolutely have some benefits on my skill set, but they were also ones that I could get through my gear over time to make up for any lack of points dropped into them through leveling. Charisma, as it turned out, was the oddball.

Jon refused to drop the fact that I had wasted an entire set of stat points just to raise my Charisma up to ten, all just to "use" the bathroom, and I was hard-pressed to find a good argument for what I had done. But given that it couldn't be changed, we just chose to move past it. As far as he could tell, there wasn't anything about the stat that would help me in combat, *but* it was impossible to ignore the fact that a higher Charisma was naturally just more helpful for a hero who innately *needed* to be in the spotlight.

We decided to approach it as we needed to, maybe dropping the occasional point into it and hoping we could gather some gains through my equipment. And that was another thing that Jon was insistent we needed to focus on, and it was something that was *also* impossible to argue with.

So far, I had only utilized four of thirteen gear slots, and filling out the rest could easily help boost the lesser stats without having to utilize *any* of my leveling points. But that said, Angie pointed out *buying* that gear would cost a veritable fortune. Someone like the NPC Greg in the Neutral Shopping Segment wouldn't stock anything *quite* that powerful, but there were team-based resale shops that I could visit and hope to get lucky.

With only so many credits currently in my digital wallet, we were going to have to be economical about just where we spent them. We agreed that while finding more equipment was on the list of things to do, increasing my available abilities was the more important thing to focus on.

With all that discussion out of the way, we finally came to the last thing I needed to take care of with my level-six increase: the Ability Augmentation.

"I really hope you get more time for this eventually 'cause this is kinda ridiculous." Like with everything else, Jon had found this part of the process endlessly fascinating, and he had already prepared a screen that he believed would give him at least some sort of information as I went through the Augmentation Process.

"It really is too bad you humans think so slow without any assistance," Angie mused, but we chose to ignore her as the Ability Augmentation window opened.

Since I was unable to Augment either of my main offensive skills for a few more levels, something I was realizing I really needed to adjust, I was left deciding between the utility abilities I had developed so far. Jon had been informed of the limited timeframe I was going to have the moment the process started, but he had pointed out that that didn't exactly stop us from discussing just what ability I should be planning to Augment *before* I ever got to the point where I was under threat of a timer.

By the time I had even gotten back into the apartment, we had already discussed the possible, or at least theoretical, outcomes for each of my remaining skills and settled on Mirror Image.

[Mirror Image!]
Level 1 Activated Ability.
Immediately turn invisible and leave an afterimage in your place.
Duration: *Invisibility: 10 seconds; Afterimage: 30 seconds.*
Cooldown: *10 minutes.*

[First Modification Option: Time Extension!]
It never hurts to have a little more time to work with!
Receive a 2x time extension for the duration of both your invisibility and the afterimage. This effect will scale with any time increases that come from leveling this ability.

[Second Modification Option: Copycat!]

*Your afterimage will now mirror your movements while you
are invisible. This effect will continue even after you reap-
pear. This modification comes with no additional effect.*

[Third Modification Option: Recording!]
*After activating this ability, your afterimage will follow a preset path.
At its current level, you may have up to 2 preset paths to select from.*

"Twenty-five seconds, what are you thinking?" I quickly called over to Jon as soon as Angie had finished reading off the options. "I'm leaning toward Copycat; feels like it could be a good way to basically get behind people to hit them by surprise."

"That could absolutely be a good tactic, but it's also something that people who are observant enough might pick up on after you use it once or twice. I know you get to Augment each skill a few times, but you have to look at the long-term viability of the modification on top of its initial usefulness," he replied as quickly as he could.

"I'd say grab the Recording Augmentation. If you take the Time Extension at face value, then that implies leveling Mirror Image will naturally result in increases to the ability's duration, so you don't necessarily *need* to get it doubled right here and now, you just have to use it often enough to level it higher. Now, Recording *might* have a similar issue to Copycat, where clever-enough people might be able to prepare for it, but that's only if you don't get more preset paths or can't change them as you choose to."

I was still a bit amazed by just how quick on the uptake he was with all of this, but when I did get past the sentimental reason for wanting Jon to know about my powers, his obsession really was a gold mine. As the timer ticked down, I took his advice and selected the Recording option. My Mirror Image ability was now sporting an alert icon. When I checked it, it read: "Please create Preset Paths." I waved it away for now and planned to take care of it when I was back outside and in my gear.

"Okay, now let's get those loot boxes," Jon said, clapping his hands together.

As we had discussed, I pulled the A+ tier out first and opened it. While it didn't end up coming with a Scroll of Level Up as my first A+ had, it *did* come with an item that made me hesitate to have Jon reroll. While it would have been nice to get the extra Phase Points from the Powerleveler gain, plus getting the extra level, I couldn't actually complain about the item I had received either.

[The Mask of Strategic Fortitude!]
Equippable Mask.
Color*: Orange.*

*Although this mask looks quite similar to your current one with just a bit
more flair, trust me when I tell you you're gonna want to put it on. Putting*

aside the fact that it's a perfect match for that jacket of yours, this mask comes with a whopping +10 Toughness and +3 Style. If that wasn't enough, on top of the obvious **Who's That?!** *feature, it also comes with* **Mental Fortress.**

[Mental Fortress!]
This feature provides the wearer a 25 percent resistance to all psy-chic- and mental-based attacks. Additionally, you are immune to **Mind Control** *effects while the associated gear is equipped.*

"There are Augments with mind control abilities? That's . . . That's really creepy."

"Well, for obvious reasons, most of them are vill—er . . . Miscreants. I know there was Pocket Watch back in the day who tried to control The First, but that ended really, *really* badly for him," Jon said as he turned out from his chair and got to his feet.

Once it was clear I wasn't going to reroll the mask, he seemed to decide he needed to stretch, though that didn't stop him from rambling on. "There's also Puppet Master over in Italy. I know Mount V was fighting him for over a year in Sicily, though last I heard he went into hiding. And the last ones I can think of are the twins, Lure and Charm, in California. Though I guess what those last two are is less mind control and more seduction? Maybe that's the same thing . . . Hmm, I wonder if there's a database I can look into that would give me info on all these guys."

"Sheesh, you're gonna put me out of a job, Mr. Blue Eyes." Angie said with a whis-tle. *"I mean, that's honestly useless information for you as a human, but it's really cute that you know it all."*

"There are a lot more people who have psychic-based abilities, though, so that resistance is going to be where that mask really goes the distance for you . . . Well, that and that plus ten to Toughness. I already added it to your primary equipment loadout," he told me before falling back into his chair and throwing his hands behind his head with a cocky smirk.

"Wait, you can do that?" I asked, opening the window myself and seeing that my loadout had indeed changed.

"Well, it's part of the job, after all." He laughed. "You know, that and being your codex of Augment knowledge."

There was a sudden beat of silence. Honestly, it might have been short enough that I was imagining it, but I think at that moment everyone in the room had the same idea. Jon's eyes sparked with excitement as he turned hard in his chair.

"That's it!" he nearly shouted. When he turned back around, my HUD high-lighted him.

[Codex, Level 6 Guy in the Chair]

"Ahhh, I've got a name! That's so fucking cool! I know I don't get to go and

do all the heroics and shit, but like, *gah*, this is legit the next best fucking thing. I know you've got the weight of all the game shit on your shoulders and all that, but like, we got this. I'm gonna make sure Loophole is known worldwide" he promised, practically buzzing in his chair.

"I'd settle for just surviving, but I mean . . . I am in it at this point . . . And now that you know, well, I guess shooting to be the best hero I can be might be pretty cool," I said, thinking about it for just a minute.

I had never necessarily dreamed about being an Augment, but the last day, even with its insanity, had felt more fulfilling than cleaning office buildings. I felt a bit dirty feeling appreciative toward Axio for allowing Jon to be clued in, especially given that we were essentially guinea pigs, but the best I could do at this point was roll with the punches.

"Okay." Jon clapped his hands together once again. "Now, get those other boxes open really quick and let's see if I should reroll anything. I still *really* want you to give me a tour of Sanctuary Square, even if I can't go there myself."

I decided to tackle the last three of the boxes I had in descending order. Within the A tier were five hundred credits and a **[Spotter's Tank]**. I materialized the tank top into my hands and highlighted it.

[Spotter's Tank!]
Equippable Undershirt.
Color*: Black.*
Okay, bro, it's the bottom of the ninth, and we have three other bad
sport's metaphors before we can do a touchdown, smack each other
on the asses, and win the big game. Now that we've got that out
of the way, let's get down to what you actually want to know.
This tank top is light and breathable, providing +1 Dexterity and +1 Luck.
It also comes with the **Team Player—Minor Leagues** *feature.*

[Team Player—Minor Leagues!]
This feature provides a 3 percent increase in damage when
you're in either a Temporary Team-Up or a Squad. This bonus
is increased by an additional 3 percent for each additional per-
son in your team, up to a maximum of 15 percent.

The B tier interestingly enough came with an item simply labeled **[The Common Ground: Level 2 Access Pass]** and ten Enhanced Stamina Injectors. It wasn't exactly hard to guess what the Access Pass was for, so I pocketed it to deal with later when I was actually in Sanctuary Square. That left me with only the F tier left to open. The box went through its usual fanfare of randomization, but when all was said and done, I only received another How the Hell Does This Fool Anybody? mask.

"That one; reroll that one. I might get another loot box here tonight, but I could always hold them off until tomorrow if we wanted the reroll chance," I said, and Jon obliged.

[New Achievement! Not Good Enough!]
You rerolled an item you received from a Loot Box.
Well, what'd'ya know, I guess beggars CAN be choosers.
Gold-Level Achievement.
Reward: *Since this is the first time you've done this, the item rerolled will have an above-average chance to be an uncommon rarity or higher item.*

The item began to spin and click rapidly through options for about five seconds before it slowed and stopped.

[Pocket Dojo!]
This is an Uncommon Safe House Expansion.
Offers access to a personal Training Dojo. This room provides a realistic but safe training area where you can practice your moves. Ability durations and cooldowns are removed while within this space, but no usage experience is gained. Any abilities on cooldown will continue to countdown while you are in this space, but they will still be usable within the dojo.

"Have I mentioned how cool literally all of this is?" Jon piped up as we examined the expansion.

"Once or twice," Angie giggled.

"All of it? Even the part where I have an axe hanging over my head if I don't get to a set amount of points . . . or that I could die if I happen to fight the wrong dude. Or hell, I could die if Axio just up and decides he's done toying with me. Just saying, I got a *whoooole* lotta ways I could end up dead here," I pointed out.

"Well, okay no, not *all of it* if you're gonna bring *that* up," Jon said, and I could practically hear him roll his eyes. "But like even *with* that stuff, think about how much better you have it now than all the regular people."

"Because of the superpowers?" I looked over at him with a raised brow just as he swiveled back toward me.

"YES, BECAUSE OF THE SUPERPOWERS!" he yelled before making a show of settling down. "Sorry, yes, obviously that. But think about it, we already lived in a world where you could die at any time, especially with the Augments running about."

"I did get crushed by a dumpster," I offered.

"Oh, for Axio's sake, will you let it go?!" Angie cried.

"Exactly. Had you not gotten lucky and been Augmented, you would have died right there, and I'd be attending your funeral with my parents. Instead, you have actual, REAL superpowers. And that's not even mentioning all of the benefits that come with the game aspect of it all. Obviously, it has its downsides, but like, they're *only* downsides if you don't take advantage of all the upsides.

"Yeah, the point thing sucks, but you're making great progress on it, and honestly, I think based on what you've already gained, I bet we could cover the remaining points by the end of tomorrow." Jon shrugged before he turned back to the monitors. "Once we can stop worrying about all of that, I'm sure as hell gonna take advantage of the upsides I get. Kinda sucks I can't share all this info with the subs, but Angie already told me *that* is a major no-no."

"He's cute when he listens," Angie said before letting out what I could only describe as a playful growl. *"I mean, talk about the whole package—smart as a whip and a cutie with a booty."*

"Angie, I appreciate the compliments, I do, but can you tone it down by like, fifty percent?" Jon asked as she giggled.

"Hmm, how about thirty percent and the ones you don't hear I just say to Loophole?"

"Deal."

"Wait, don't I get a say in this?"

"No," they said in unison, and within a moment, we were all laughing.

CHAPTER TWENTY-NINE

Sanctuary Square, Non-PVP Zone. Location Classified.
Closest Known Territory: *Planet Earth. Unclaimed (Blocked by Timer)*

O*h my actual God, this is so fucking cool!"* Jon groaned. *"Why can't I go there?! I have a name; I can put on a mask, dammit!"*

"Sorry, Codex, the subspace portals used to teleport to Sanctuary Square require the full Augmentation Process to pass through. It's a safety precaution to keep non-Augments from entering the area, and by all technicalities, you are still included in that group," Angie explained.

I was walking down the stairs into the courtyard, trying to look around slowly to let Jon see as much as possible. I could hear him making random comments about the various things in the Square as I came to the bottom of the staircase and turned toward the nearest display board. I hadn't actually taken the time to look at the leaderboard again, and while both my achievement *and* Jon had confirmed that I was on it, I still really wanted to see it for myself.

Tenth Wave

Guardians: *403*   **Miscreants:** *529*

1. **Tempest's Wrath** *(Level 10 Thunder God) Miscreant — 9270 Points*
2. **Freakenstein** *(Level 7 Patchwork Armorer) Miscreant — 7210 Points*
3. **Duke Juke'em** *(Level 6 Highschool Athlete) Miscreant — 7045 Points*
4. **Swansong** *(Level 6 Healing Voice) Guardian — 6920 Points*
5. **Loophole** *(Level 6 Perfect Planner) Guardian — 6910 Points*
6. **Pretty Pink Warthog** *(Level 6 Berserking Boar) Guardian — 6150 Points*
7. **Quizmaster** *(Level 6 Gameshow Host) Miscreant — 6055 Points*
8. **Sound Off** *(Level 6 Midnight DJ) Miscreant — 5925 Points*
9. **Pigeon** *(Level 6 Pigeon) Miscreant — 5900 Points*
10. **Heavy Ink** *(Level 6 Comic Book Artist) Guardian — 5885 Points*

I stared at the list for a minute, feeling just a bit of pride in the fact that I had risen so quickly, even sitting as technically the second-highest Guardian on the list. Tempest's continued rise was impressive, but she had noticeably slowed her rabid pace down. Whether that was because she had actually finally been met with resistance or if she had just decided to take a nap after a twenty-four-hour rampage really was the bigger question.

I turned away and headed deeper into the courtyard, turning my attention to the large statues that represented the best of both sides.

"Duuuude!" Jon groaned again.

"Sheesh, keep it in your pants, man," I laughed as I lingered on the statues of the Guardians.

"The First, Calypso, Brightburst, Mandragos, and . . . huh . . . who's that last guy?" Jon asked, listing them off one by one without the need for me to highlight them. He apparently didn't even *need* me to highlight anything either, as he was able to do it separately from his end without it affecting my own display. But even with that ability, I could tell just by his cadence that wasn't what he had just done. *"Who the hell is TechWarden?"*

"You really think that I'd *know the answer if you didn't?"*

"Fair point. Angie?"

"I do not have data on earlier Waves currently available to me. Remember, other than a direct line to Axio for clarification of specifics, you have more or less the same data access as I do," she explained.

"Sure, but I still have a human-speed brain; you can access it instantaneously if you do have access to it. But oh well, guess I'll just have to do some research on him later, then," Jon said, and I could hear an obvious level of excitement in his tone. *"Okay, what about the Miscreants? Who are their top dogs?"*

I looked over to the opposite side of the courtyard and waited.

"Jumpstart, Frightmare, Twin Revolver, Thirst Trap, and Firefist. Pretty much who you'd expect just going on the worst of the worst. I'm surprised it leaves them up like that if they are dead, though; Jumpstart has been dead for at least five years now. Dude must have destroyed half of Canada's electrical infrastructure before The First managed to stop him," Jon mused.

I took a closer look at the last of the statues for the first time and realized that sure enough, it was a perfect likeness of the man The First had been fighting carved into an almost magmalike red-and-black marble.

"The statues represent the highest scores achieved, and exist mostly like a record. Even if the person dies or, for some reason, gives up all of their territory claims, they would still have had the record up until that point. The only thing that would update is how their name and stats are listed when you pull up their description box," Angie explained.

"That makes sense," Jon said. *"Okay, so do you want to check out the bookstore first so that I can get a catalog of what they have? Or were you really determined to check out the second floor of the bar?"*

While I certainly could have gone back out and tried to close down another den or two, I had been going since I had gotten up, and the idea of taking an hour or two to just collect my thoughts was more than appealing. I had the BOGO coupon for the bookstore, and Jon really liked the idea of exploring the shop. If I got lucky, I could be adding some new techniques to my skill set by the time Axio was making his daily announcement.

With the Training Dojo in place, Jon had pointed out that I could theoretically spend another hour or two in there just making abilities and testing their effectiveness. But all of that predicated on finding a few new books that I could work into my powerset. Between the NPCs I had looted, the various missions and dens I had tackled, not to mention the loot boxes, I was sitting on just over twelve thousand credits. Assuming the books didn't drain my entire wallet, we had also agreed it would be a good idea to check The Viewfinder for a potential interface upgrade.

If, and really only *if*, I had some credits left over after that, I would check out the Guardian resale shop. Angie was relatively sure that I *probably* wouldn't find anything useful for my level there, though, which was why the interface upgrade really took priority.

According to Angie—after some probing from Jon—my action bar would naturally expand the higher-leveled I got, with the expansions coming on randomized odd levels. While I might not be able to cheat the system and gain more available spots on my action bar ahead of time, I *could* purchase a [**Bar Revolver**].

The Revolver was a relatively simple interface upgrade, offering the ability to have multiple action bar loadouts, with the total available bars dependent on the size that you purchased. Sure, I couldn't swap them in the middle of an encounter, but with enough abilities, I could have different loadouts for different situations.

"Let's take care of the shopping and stuff first," I said after I took a bit of time to consider it. *"I'm gonna want to take a little bit of time in The Common Ground, so I want to have everything else done so that you're not sitting around bored."*

"And I gotta say, I appreciate that." Jon laughed as I turned my attention back toward the Guardian side of the Square. *"Wait, go back to the Guardian statues really quick,"* he called hurriedly, which I obliged. *"Hmm . . . did you notice that all of the top Guardians are listed as Unknown?"*

I had already known The First's status had changed, so I focused on the second statue in the line and let the description pull up.

[Calypso, Level 187 Drowned Siren]
Claimed Territories: *133**
Status: *Unk—Alive*
***Note**: *This Guardian no longer has claims to these many territories.*

"Wait, she just changed to Alive . . . That was weird," Jon muttered. I had just started to look away from the statues when he gasped. *"Dude, it's her!"*

"Huh, where?" I asked, looking around. He had to have seen her somewhere within my field of vision, so I didn't have to move my head too far.

It wouldn't have mattered if I did, as she would have stood out damn near anywhere, and when that anywhere was just outside of an admittedly ordinary-looking bar, it was all the more noticeable.

Her costume looked like flowing scales, with long stretches of aquamarine-and-purple-patterned fabric going from the underside of her arms all the way down along her legs and outward like a mermaid's tail behind her. Her dark, ebony skin was a stark contrast to the opalescent aquamarine mask that covered the upper half of her face. Her silvery, dreadlocked hair was pulled back in a large bun that appeared to be tied and held with a fishing net of all things.

"She's one of The First's team members, right? Or she was, at least?" I asked as the woman was immediately swarmed by at least a dozen other Augments. A bright smile split across her face as she shook hands, though oddly, she never seemed to speak. Not necessarily wanting to join the gathering crowd of onlookers, I turned my attention back toward the Guardian's shopping segment.

"Yeah, the Paragons of Justice. Cheesy-as-hell name, but the whole team had been working together since the early days. Calypso has always sort of been his second-in-command, and she's powerful as hell in her own right. She uses songs to enchant people and manipulate water at some crazy-strong levels," Jon explained as if he was reading her stats off a baseball card. *"Why did her status just change? Didn't you mention there's something weird about that place?"*

"Yeah, it's like a sorta null zone for AIs. I guess it also blanks out statuses when folks are in it," I said with a shrug, climbing up the stairs and past a few others wandering back down into the courtyard. They gave me friendly smiles, but I didn't stop to talk as I looked around for the Beacon of Knowledge bookstore.

"Oh yeah . . . will you still be like, around to talk with me when he goes in there, Angie? Will I still be able to talk to him?" Jon asked, and I could have sworn I heard a bag of chips in the background.

"Honestly? No clue! We're gonna have to see when he gets over there, 'cause this is literally a first for the system and there's no available data to compare to," Angie said.

The bookstore was nestled into one of the corners of the Guardian's segment, looking as if it had been plucked out of the cheesiest fairy tale on the planet. I pushed through the large oak door and entered a room with more natural light than made sense for the amount of windows it had. The ceiling stretched high, with bookshelves towering up, reaching for the rafters at least two dozen feet above my head.

Sitting on a tall but comfortable-looking chair behind the register was a petite older woman, a cardigan tied up around her neck and a small pair of spectacles sliding down her nose as she read from a thick magazine titled [**The Heroic Hotty Digest: XXXL Edition**].

"Now, that's my kinda lady!" Angie whooped while I rolled my eyes as I highlighted her.

[Betty White!]
Owner of the Beacon of Knowledge.
This is a Non-Sapient NPC.
Named after one hell of an acting icon, Betty is a collector of
all things books. Though her job does tend to have her focus-
ing on the, ugh, intellectual pursuits, if you ask her nicely, I'm sure
she'd give you access to the . . . um . . . restricted section. Come
on . . . ask her nicely—I want to see what she's hiding.

"Feel free to look around, dear. Tomes are locked from use until you've purchased them, so don't try to be cute," she said without looking up from her reading material.

"Ask her if it's done in sections or if there's a catalog or something?" Jon asked, and I passed on the question.

"You can find a guide here at the end of the desk if you're looking for something specific. My stock is filled largely with books other Guardians have collected and sold to me over time. With that said, I'm more than happy to purchase any tomes you acquire, as they are very hard to come by. We do have a stock of rare items that are available on a rotating basis, and I'm afraid I don't do layaways.

"If there's a book you want, I suggest you purchase it. Oh, and no haggling with me, dear—prices are as listed." She finally turned away from her book, looking over her glasses at me with a kind smile. "Now, if you need anything, well, get it yourself. I can't climb those damn ladders anymore, and my last three assistants all quit."

"Thank you," I said, moving down toward the end of the counter where a cheap-looking school binder sat. Opening it up, it revealed a few sheets of laminated pages. Though it *was* printed, the front page of the binder acted as a filtering system, complete with categories and tags.

"Oh, this makes it much easier," I noted as I started clicking through the various filters. While I knew I would circle back to a few of the tags, I decided to first set a filter to hide any book that required an Intelligence higher than seven. Once it was applied, it lowered the total available books from two thousand all the way down to *just* twenty.

"Wait, set that to eleven," Jon called before I could turn the page to see the list of available books. *"Sure, it might be a good idea to grab books that you could use right now and just get by, but it doesn't hurt to check. That's just two levels of dedicating half your stat points to Intelligence, after all, and if it lets you expand your ability set, it's not* necessarily *a terrible idea."*

I didn't argue and adjusted the filter. That raised the available listings up to fifty, and that seemed as good a place to start as any. Turning the page revealed a tabled listing of the available books, and with a quick click, the list rearranged itself in order based on value.

"Sheesh what the hell are some of these names? **[Explosions on a Budget: A DIY Guide to Chaos]**, **[Shifting Sands and Soaked Waves]**, **[Gravity Wells and Why**

They're Dangerous*]?! Where the hell are we even supposed to start?"* I muttered. The most expensive book on the list, [*Quantum Shenanigans for Beginners*] required an Intelligence of ten, but even I could guess just how useful knowledge of quantum mechanics would be for my powerset. The problem was that it also happened to cost fifty-five hundred credits.

"These things might as well be college textbooks with how damn expensive they are," Jon complained as I continued to look down the list.

"You never went to college," I noted, looking toward the cheaper books on the list.

"Yeah, because the textbooks would have bankrupted my entire family," he shot back. *"Besides, Uncle James taught me everything I needed to know; I'm doing fine so far. Now, back to what matters here. There's a lot of good stuff on this list, and I think we can really take it a lot of ways. Hell, we could easily have you drain your wallet and buy three or four of these books right off the bat, but you wouldn't have the bar space to do anything with them.*

"I think, for now at least, Gravity Wells and Why They're Dangerous *and* [**Refractions of Reality**] *are going to be your best bet. We'll need to get you leveled up once for Refractions, since it needs your Intelligence to be at an eight, but I think we could get you a movement skill with Gravity Wells, not to mention the potential for more battlefield control."*

"Yeah, that one I get, but Refractions of Reality? *It's just optical refraction level six. Are we sure it's actually useful for me to have a higher knowledge than level three instead of something that could give me more combat capabilities?"* I asked as I eyed the two books.

They both cost fifteen hundred credits, so with the BOGO coupon, they wouldn't drain my wallet too hard. I knew we also wanted to check The Viewfinder for the Revolver, but even still, I couldn't help but eye the Quantum Shenanigans book. It was one of the few books on the list that had the "Rotating" column of the listing marked, and I felt an almost impulsive desire to grab it as well.

"It's hard to say; as far as I can tell, there hasn't been another player with Local Area Manipulation in their powerset, though that's based on my own research more than any database. I've been doing some reading up here ever since you guys mentioned these books, and your powerset seems to have a unique interaction with them," Jon said.

"Oh? I was sorta wondering about that. Like, even to me it seemed weird that there would be an entire class of item solely designed to expand my powerset," I commented as I made note of a few other books on the list I could potentially come back for.

"Yeah, so other players can use them to expand their knowledge within their own powerset, which would then in turn make their core abilities stronger. Let's say an Earth Manipulator picked up Shifting Sands and Soaked Waves, *he'd end up getting minor boosts to the damage his earth-based abilities created thanks to the Erosion knowledge in the book, even if the Tidal knowledge portion would be useless to him. On the other hand, you expand the types of core abilities you can make with each book you add,"* he explained.

"Huh . . . I mean, I guess that makes as much sense as anything. But what's that have to do with me wasting the coupon on grabbing a book that will increase a knowledge stat I already have?"

"'Cause we need to know if that does something sooner or later. The initial knowledge lets you create skills; maybe the higher level will also boost your various abilities' power. I think if there was ever a time to gamble on it, it's with a BOGO coupon," Jon explained, then seemed to take a moment before continuing, though that might have just been to stop for a snack.

I heard some crunching as he continued. *"Look, the rest of these books have their uses, don't get me wrong, I have at least two dozen ideas for [**An Atomic Guide to Thermodynamics**], but those books also cost twice as much, and I know we want to make sure you can still hit up The Viewfinder. If we're talking bang for your buck, we can start by immediately adding some gravity skills into your repertoire, then circle back and expand on that as we go.*

"Your power is so insanely versatile, we need to start you with a solid foundation. So far, you've been focusing on area-control skills, like the weight and sound controls, as well as manipulating what they see. Honestly, that's not a terrible way to focus your skill at all. I think it's better for you if you try to expand on that rather than suddenly switch directions and try to become an elemental mastermind or any of the other directions you could go.

"Yes, it's a bit of redundancy, but there's a whole lot you can do with power over gravity, and I think we can take the evening to test that in the Training Dojo. That's not saying those other skills couldn't be useful to grab down the line; I just think we could easily fall into a pitfall of expanding too wide too quickly. And if having a higher-leveled knowledge does turn out to be pointless, well, at least we know sooner rather than later, right?"

"For the record, I did say having a higher knowledge would be beneficial, did I not?" Angie added once Jon finally stopped to take a breath.

"Yeah, but you also said you weren't quite clear how it was beneficial, just that it was," Jon pointed out. *"Okay, pick those up and head over to The Viewfinder; you gotta have enough credits to get a Revolver."*

I was about to just listen to him and hunt down the two books when my eyes fell on the Quantum Shenanigans book again. I looked over to the shop's owner hopefully and figured it was better to ask the question now rather than get upset the "rotating" book . . . well . . . rotated.

"Mrs. White?"

"Just Betty, dear," the elderly lady responded with a smile as she closed her magazine and looked at me expectantly.

"How often do these rotating books . . . well . . . rotate?" I asked.

"Every Saturday, we swap stocks with Whispers and Tomes to provide our respective customers access to the rare selections we provide. When one of the books from the stock is purchased, a new random one is added," Betty explained.

"Um . . . What day is it?"

"Dude, really . . ."

"I got crushed by a dumpster a little over a week ago—cut me some slack."

"You still need to let that go!" Angie groaned. *"And by the way, it's Friday, October 11th."*

"And when did this one enter the stock? Has it rotated back and forth a few times?" I asked Betty, pointing down at the page. She stood up and walked over, a bit slower than I might have liked, and looked down at the book.

"Ah yes . . . That one is actually our newest selection; as of this morning, in fact," she replied, adjusting her glasses as she turned back to me.

"Okay, thank you," I said and looked back at the listings. "Well, I guess I'll just have to see if I can swing back this way before the rotation," I added.

"Do be quick; those rare books never hang around for too long," she informed me with another smile before turning and heading back for her chair.

I focused back on the sheet and found out that I couldn't just select the options I wanted and make them appear. Instead, the books had locations listed next to them, directing me to several different shelves within the space. I navigated the packed shelves until I found *Gravity Wells and Why They're Dangerous* and *Refractions of Reality*. Even though I knew I was getting ahead of myself, I also made a point of finding just where *Quantum Shenanigans for Beginners* was before bringing the two books up to the register and purchasing them.

With that done and in my B.E.L.T., I navigated to the opposite corner of the strip mall and back into The Viewfinder. Vanessa's holographic avatar appeared as soon as I approached a wall, and after explaining to her what I was looking for, she directed me right to it.

The Revolver actually came in fifteen sizes, with the smallest offering only a single extra loadout for fifteen hundred credits and the largest offering ten thousand alternates. I couldn't imagine what *anyone* would do with that many loadouts, but I was certainly not going to be affording its ten-million-credit price tag anytime soon, so it was better to just pretend like it didn't exist. At least for now.

The Revolvers included a benefit most of the other interface upgrades didn't. When you purchased one tier, the value of that tier was taken off of the next tier up, essentially giving you a reason to come back and upgrade as you went.

Jon pointed out that with more than ten thousand credits remaining, I could easily afford to jump right up to a [**Giant Revolver**], which would offer me six alternate loadouts for nine thousand credits. But even with the new skill books, I couldn't imagine, at least at this level, filling out that many action bars, and even Jon had to admit it would be a huge waste of money to jump up that high that quickly, especially knowing I always could come back and upgrade it later.

I looked through the options but eventually decided that the [**Starter Revolver**] with its single additional loadout for fifteen hundred credits was going to be the best bet. In hindsight, we both realized that we could have been more economical in how we had approached my shopping, as we easily could have afforded an extra book had we used the BOGO coupon differently, but there wasn't much we could do about it now. Even with that realization, I still had plenty of credits left over.

While Jon and I did briefly discuss having me check out the equipment, I found myself heading right back for the bookstore.

Jon *had* said he had a couple dozen ability ideas for *An Atomic Guide to Thermodynamics*, and I had a hard time *not* wanting to buy a book with Quantum Shenanigans in the title.

CHAPTER THIRTY

There was a little bit over an hour until Axio's daily announcement when I entered The Common Ground.

The moment I crossed the threshold into the bar, I lost contact with both Jon and Angie. We had expected something like this, of course, and had decided to use the opportunity to test it. After waiting for a minute, I stepped back outside and discovered that even though I couldn't contact them, Angie and Jon were able to communicate without issue. None of us were quite sure what that meant, but I apologized in advance to Jon, just in case Angie was . . . well, herself, and dipped back into the bar.

The place was more alive than I expected it to be for the hour, with well over half the tables in the building packed. I had just finished grabbing a drink from the bar, using the second of my three free drink tickets, when I heard a familiar voice.

"Well, well, well, haven't you been busier than a bee in spring?" Silver Wrangler's hand landed on my shoulder as the monotone system voice spoke up.

[New Friend Request: Silver Wrangler. Accept: Yes/No]

I selected *Yes*, and my Friends List opened up, splitting in half to list the Guardians and Miscreants separately. Granted, I only had a single name on each list, but they were still listed separately.

"Well, Axio did give us a pretty short time limit; kind of *had* to get moving," I explained with a shrug and turned back to look into the crowd.

"Yeah, I heard about that. We literally had a month for our first phase, and we only had to have total control over our starting territory," Silver noted.

"Lucky you," I said as I noticed a familiar pink outfit and blonde ponytail. I waved out toward the crowd in general, and Silver nodded, pushing off the bar as he followed. There was the steady din of conversation and music as we moved through the building, yet somehow it never became overwhelming, nor did we have to yell to hear each other.

"Eh, I don't know, y'all are already leveling a whole lot faster than most of us. I think it took most of my Wave at least a week to even get to level six. There's this sort of sudden uptick in folks taking the whole thing more seriously now; none of us wanna get bypassed by any of y'all noobs, y'know?"

"Heh, yeah, I guess I can see that," I said as I thought about it for a minute. Although logically I knew that Silver and I were on different sides, I hadn't exactly gotten a friendly reaction from Hydramental, and he was *supposed* to be on the same team as me. Silver, even as a Miscreant, seemed nice enough, and Pinky had been right when she had said the older Waves could be a good source of information. "Mind if I ask you a question about all this early stuff? At least clearing out my neighborhood."

"Depends on the question. I ain't gonna get another F tier for helping yah now." He shrugged. "But go on, shoot."

"Okay, well, I'm working my way toward clearing out the people contesting my neighborhood, and I feel like I'm getting into the flow of it, but I was wondering something," I said as we weaved around someone wearing serving attire carrying an absurdly large tray filled with buffalo wings to a table with a large man with half of his full-face mask pulled up. "I know it's different for you Miscreants, but was there like . . . I don't know . . . a storyline toward whoever you had to drive out?"

"Hmm, a storyline? Like one of them ol' school *Dukes of Hazzard* episodes? Was someone trying to steal my sister or somethin'?" he asked with a raised brow as he looked over toward me.

"I mean, nothing so convoluted or anything; at least, I think . . . I keep running into these bikers, and they've talked about their boss a handful of times. I don't know, it sort of feels like they are trying to set me up for some sort of big climactic battle or something like that," I explained as we finally closed in on Pinky's table. "The last few times I've cleared one of their bases or dealt with them, they've been all like 'SnakeBite will rule this city, blah blah blah.' It's all super melodramatic."

Pinky noticed us walking up and turned from a goggled man sitting next to her to give me a wide smile.

"Huh, I feel like I've heard that name before," Silver noted as we stepped up to their table.

"Loophole, you asshole! How'd you go and pass me so damn quickly?!" Pinky shouted, jumping from her chair and looking at me with fake outrage.

"I think the better question is how'd you let me? Axio *did* say the Top Ten would get an S tier; that and the threat of a swift death can really put a pep in your step," I replied with a laugh as I took one of the open seats at the raised table.

"Well, still, you don't have to be a show-off." She pretended to pout before breaking, taking her seat again and nodding over to the man still sitting at the table, slowly sipping a beer. "This is my new friend."

"If you use the term loosely," the man said as he set his beer down. I looked over, intent on highlighting him to get his information, when Pinky waved to grab my attention.

"Okay, so get this," she started, the hint of a smile tugging at her lips. "I'm trying to convince him that we should team up. Like, our territories are pretty close to each other, but he doesn't like the squad name I'm suggesting even though it's like, arguably perfect."

"It's childish. And besides, it's literally just bad versions of our names!" the man huffed, his voice coming out in a bit of a nasally whine. Pinky pulled her hand back and crossed her arms over her chest, allowing me to finally highlight the man.

[BrainCraft. Level 5 Neural Forge]

"Come *ooooon*, we can literally be Pinky and the Brain! Think about it!" She smacked the table loud enough to draw attention from a group a few tables away. There was a single beat of silence before Silver let out a bark of laughter, leaving the goggled man to groan.

"My name is Brain*Craft*, and besides, I don't see much overlap between our powers, which is something you have to consider before jumping into things all willy-nilly. A good team has cohesion and complements each other," BrainCraft pointed out as he adjusted his goggles. "Also, isn't that name like, Miscreant coded, since they always wanted to take over the world?"

"Come on, you're overthinking it! Besides, for being so smart, that's a *really* dumb take on team structure. Take it from a cheerleader: you gotta start with a good base to build a pyramid. You bring the brains, I bring the brawn—that's as good a base as any," Pinky shot back quickly before she looked at me. "Oh, I got a pass up to the second floor! We looked it up after I got the item, but according to Franky, it has a random chance of appearing in any loot box awarded from a 'nonstandard combat' achievement. It doesn't actually seem all that difficult to get."

"Ah, that makes sense. I just pulled mine from a loot box that came from an achievement for taking down some enemies on a floor below me without seeing them," I said thoughtfully.

"Yeah, I broke right through a pillar and trapped a 'roided-up meth head beneath the second floor of a building when I got mine," Pinky replied, grabbing the mixed drink she had sitting in front of her.

"I beat a man with another man," Silver offered, and we all turned to face the Miscreant who had so far remained standing. "Hey, don't go giving me that look; my boots got insulted. And trust me, you don't go and insult a man's boots in Texas—it's the Golden Rule."

Pinky made a show of looking around the table and down at Silver's feet, even stopping and taking a long sip from her drink before she spoke up. "I mean—"

"Hey now, don't go pickin' a fight with me, pretty lady," Silver said, holding a finger up to stop her.

"Wait," BrainCraft finally spoke back up as he set his beer down. "Which man insulted your boots?"

"Huh?" Silver asked with a raised brow.

"You said you beat a man with another man. Which man insulted your boots? The one who was beaten, or the one used as a weapon?"

"Yes," Silver replied, holding a straight face as he stared right at BrainCraft for a few seconds longer than he needed to. Just as BrainCraft started to squirm, Silver's stare broke, and he let out another guffaw before looking over to Pinky. "Oh, and speakin' of fights, be careful heading up to the second floor. The place has a 'first time you show up, you gotta fight' rule. It's not really that big of a problem, since you can't *actually* die up there, there are protections in place and all that, but trust me when I tell yah you're gonna feel every bit of whatever you get hit with while fighting in that place."

Pinky noticeably lit up as she looked from Silver back to me.

"I haven't gone up yet! We can go together, and I bet we'd have to fight each other!" she exclaimed with a wide smile that left me uneasy.

"Umm . . . weren't you trying to convince BrainCraft to form a squad with you?" I tried to deflect. I *did* want to see the second floor, but I still wanted to absorb my new skill books and work on new abilities as well.

"It's not happening," he offered. I hadn't noticed it before, but he had a drawing pad open on the table in front of him, and there was a sketch for a device that looked like some sort of robot . . . or a deep fryer—I really couldn't tell.

"Come on, *pleeeeease*," Pinky begged, clasping her hands together. "I promise I won't hurt you *that* bad, and I'd be willing to bet you'd get at least *some* form of achievement from it, right?" she asked, looking over toward Silver for confirmation.

"Sanctioned Fighter," he offered. "It's a C-tier box, which to be fair, have some decently useful items. The winner of that initial fight also gets five thousand credits. Oh! Also, people who watch are allowed to bet on the outcomes; your odds change the more fights you participate in, and they do regular tournaments. Up until Axio went and changed the whole game up, the Fight Club mighta been the one place that really got some of the older Waves fighting to grow stronger."

Pinky's eyes went wide, looking from Silver back to me even more eagerly.

"*Come ooooon!* It's just one little tussle! I know you guys don't like to be beat up by girls, but like, we have superpowers, you *can't* be *that* stuck in pointless gender norms," she insisted pleadingly.

"What makes you so sure you'd beat me? You don't even know what I can do," I said defensively.

"I mean, I know what *I* can do," Pinky replied, smiling as her tusks pierced outward. "We can settle this right now."

Her energy was almost overwhelming as she stared me down, waiting for a response, until I finally let out a dry laugh. "Okay, fine. Let's go fight, I guess," I said. "At least I'll finally get to know what a Berserking Boar does."

Pinky practically squealed as she pumped her fists ahead of her.

"Y'know, if I was gonna head up there to watch, I'd be betting on her," Silver noted, dropping a heavy hand on my shoulder. "She seems to have a bit more pep in her step than you do, y'know?"

"Don't you have friends in your own Wave?" I asked, and he let out a boisterous laugh that drew the attention of more than a few tables.

"I do. Actually, I'm gonna go meet up with them and rob a bank; you kids have fun now." He turned and purposefully tipped his hat toward Pinky with a wink before wandering off.

"Um . . . shouldn't we stop him from doing that? We are Guardians . . ." BrainCraft said, and Pinky laughed before she slapped him on the shoulder.

"Feel free to try. That guy is level forty-nine; I think he'd put any of us down without breaking a sweat," she noted before cracking her knuckles. "Now come on, let's *gooooo*."

"Yes, on that subject, I have things to—"

"Oh hush, Brain, you haven't gotten a pass up there yet; you don't have to make an excuse to leave," Pinky rolled her eyes before she nodded her head my way. "Though you should add Loophole; it never hurts to have a wider network."

BrainCraft looked over and shrugged before sending me a Friend Request that was quickly followed by a message.

<**BrainCraft:** She really knows how to railroad a conversation, doesn't she?>

<**Loophole:** Yeah . . . she did that to me when I first bumped into her last night. I was looking at a leaderboard and next thing I knew, she was adding me to her Friends List and trying to drag me here.>

<**BrainCraft:** Ah. I met her earlier today when she stepped in on a fight that wasn't quite going my way. Though she isn't quite my cup of tea, I do have to admit her skills are quite impressive, albeit brutish. I shouldn't say more; it wouldn't be right of me to give away her tactics to you. I do regret that I won't get to watch the fight, though.>

"Hey, are you two messaging or something? I don't like that look that you're giving each other," Pinky crossed her arms again. "Now let's *gooooo*, Loophole, I'm all worked up and ready to throw down. It's pretty much exactly how I felt before every game night back in high school . . . though that had far less superpowers involved. Although could you imagine . . ."

"I'd be willing to argue *most* things would be more interesting with superpowers involved," I said with a shrug as I pushed myself to my feet. I emptied the Captain and Coke before setting the glass down. In a flash of light, it and all the other empty glasses on the table vanished into thin air.

After BrainCraft took off toward one of the exits, Pinky and I headed for the center of the bar where the large spiral staircase circled around the head of a destroyed giant robot. The thing was battered and dented from whatever battle it had been involved in. Jon probably knew exactly what fight this thing had been in, and I was instantly sorry he'd have to settle for just my piss-poor description of it.

About halfway up the staircase, as if we were passing through an invisible barrier, the lower floor of The Common Ground disappeared, and we were suddenly on a regular staircase. We took the last few steps up into a space that was easily twice as big as the floor below and filled with Augments in gear of every color of the rainbow.

Monitors were scattered around the room, and three large platforms were positioned at the direct center, each with a stadium-like display overhead. One of the platforms was completely empty, and the crowd was largely ignoring it as they gathered around the other two. I looked over to Pinky and noticed she had a large red debuff over her head that read **[New Combatant]**. Looking at my own list, I saw that I was now sporting a similar one and highlighted it.

[New Combatant!]
Debuff.
Please proceed to Registration. All new visitors must visit the Registration
Desk to register to fight within five minutes of arrival on this floor.
Failure to do so or leaving before you have completed this will have you
permanently barred from participating in fights in this location.

"Over there." Pinky pointed to a bar running along the wall with several screens set up behind it. We hurried over, and a squirrely looking man rushed over to meet us.

"Well, lookie here, we got us a couple of new faces!" the man greeted us with a smile, patting the bar as he looked us up and down. He had a name tag pinned to his shirt that read "Schmitt—Manager." Two scanners similar to the device at The Viewfinder appeared, and Schmitt reached out, grabbing one of our hands each and pulling them over each of the devices before we could react. "Let's get you two all signed up for a bout; we got a ring open right now, and since there's two of you, we can throw you right on in.

"But before that, let's get all the basics out of the way. First off, fights all go until one Augment's health bar has been theoretically zeroed out or you have actively captured and held your opponent in place for no less than five minutes. All powers are allowed and encouraged, and the system's safety precautions will immediately pull you out and apply a Full Restore Injector in the event that your health bar is going to be zeroed.

"If you lose your bout, you will not be eligible to fight again for twelve hours; however, if you win, feel free to sign up in the random draw bouts or challenge anyone you might wish to challenge. Now, since this is your first fight, you will both be fighting with even odds. We don't allow you to place bets on your own fights, and if we find out you're using a proxy to bet on your own fight, you'll be immediately banned from the facilities with *extreeeeeme* prejudice. Any questions?"

Even knowing that Schmitt was likely an NPC and this was just something he was programmed to rattle off, the efficiency with which he said it was impressive. I couldn't necessarily think of anything to ask, but Pinky was quick on the uptake.

"Is it a static fighting location, or does it change? And if it does change, are we allowed to pick it?"

Schmitt nodded appreciatively at the question.

"Good question. For your first bout, you will be placed in a standard fighting cell. This arena will be a thirty-by-thirty-foot room and is designed to allow viewers the optimal chance to see your abilities in action. This also will allow myself and the Oddsmaker to properly adjust your odds for future betting rounds. Any fights in the random draws are given random battlefields, but you *are* allowed to choose the battlefield for a challenged match.

"Tournaments will often list the battlefields in advance, but you're a long way off from qualifying for those," Schmitt explained before tapping at the bar. "Okay, now let's get you two up onto platform three—your arena is now ready."

Pinky slapped me on the shoulder as we turned back toward the main room. My vision automatically highlighted the empty platform, and an arrow appeared above it with a thirty-second countdown timer ticking down next to the arrow. The crowd seemed to knowingly part as we walked over, and I could hear catcalls and jeers as we made our way down.

I hopped up onto the platform, Pinky following close behind me as I inspected the relatively small ring. A small crowd was making their way toward us as I took a look over at one of the other platforms with cheering spectators surrounding it.

Although the rings had arenalike monitors positioned above them, I couldn't see any fighters actually *in* the rings. I was just starting to make out what looked like the tops of skyscrapers in the second platform when a flash of light practically blinded me. As the light faded, I found myself in a large, concrete box with light filling it from nowhere. I looked around briefly until I found Pinky standing on the opposite end of the cell damn near mimicking me.

I was about to ask if we were supposed to just start when a slamming sound echoed in the room. Above us, words seemed to drop, hanging in the air as an overly enthusiastic voice yelled out.

"*Weeeee've* got a fight between fresh meat here for you all this afternoon. Coming in at an even level six a piece. It's . . . Loophole *veeeeeeeeeeeeeeersus* Pretty Pink Warthog . . . *FIGHT!*"

CHAPTER THIRTY-ONE

Our names actually appeared in bold designs floating above us as the announcer started the match and vanished just as quickly.

Pinky didn't waste any time, and I heard the crack of cement as a sudden streak of pink came rushing toward me. I dodged to the side, barely getting out of the way as she slammed into the wall directly behind where I had been standing. The wall *noticeably* buckled outward, and debris crumbled down to the ground. I scrambled around to the other side of the cell before she could recover without taking my eyes off her.

"Damn, and here I thought I could catch you off guard," she said, her words coming out slightly garbled past her tusks after she freed them and knocked away the debris at her feet.

A dusting of dirt covered her pink clothing, and she had taken damage equal to about five percent of her health bar, but that wasn't what had my attention. Her tusks shone with a silvery gleam, and they were *far* larger than I had seen them so far, curving up around her face and then back out in vicious-looking points. She bounced on her toes as she turned her head back and forth as if she were cracking her neck.

"Hell of a charge you got there," I said, mentally preparing to hit Weighted Clothes. But as I went to click on it, I froze and reconsidered. Though the attack felt like it could be an instant win under a lot of circumstances, that only applied if I didn't consider the bigger picture.

"Oh, don't worry—I'm just getting warmed up," she replied with a dangerous-looking smile.

Maybe I was slow on the uptake with certain things related to the game; I knew that much about myself. But I had seen enough to know that looks could be deceiving when it came to Strength. While I wasn't necessarily the smartest when it came to the stat system, I hadn't forgotten that crucial detail; hell, it was something I was even taking advantage of.

There was an innately casual way in which she was shrugging off the debris around her that was proof enough of her increased strength, and I would have to be foolish to waste the ability without taking more time to examine the situation. I took my mental finger off the trigger and rushed her instead, closing the gap between us in a few seconds.

There was a brief look of surprise that passed through her eyes before a surprisingly eager smile spread over her face. I didn't think much of it, assuming the thrill of the fight was already reaching her, and activated Sting like a Bee. I threw a wide swing for her side that she effortlessly caught with a quickly raised forearm.

I expected the attack to at least do *something*, but I found myself momentarily confused as my strike landed. At this point, I was more than familiar with the recoil and feeling of impact when I struck someone, but this was different. It was almost as if my fist had been halted completely the moment it came in contact with her. She gave me an overexaggerated wink before throwing a punch of her own, which hit me center of mass with a force that sent me forcefully stumbling backward.

Pinky wasted no time following up, charging forward in a sudden burst of speed that surprised me. I instinctively activated Float like a Butterfly and dodged just as she swung her head as if to gore me with her large tusks. It was close, the glinting sight of silver barely grazing my arm while I tried to find an opening. As she planted her feet, I jabbed at her side two more times in rapid succession before she could move to attack me once more, sending Sting like a Bee on cooldown. Once again, my attacks seemed to halt upon impact, and I found myself gritting my teeth in frustration at my inability to break through her defenses.

Quickly skipping backward before she could react, I put some distance between us while I tried to put together what I had seen so far. I really wished I had Jon or even Angie in my head to bounce ideas off of, but wishful thinking would only get me so far.

"You're quick, I'll give you that, even if you aren't showing me what the heck you can even do yet." She practically giggled as she started to bounce back and forth on her feet like she was a prize fighter in a boxing ring. Each time one of her feet landed, little sparks of pink bounced off the pavement, growing with each repetition. "How bout we turn up the speed and see if you can still keep up."

Before I could respond, she bounced into a low runner's pose and pushed off. The concrete buckled under the force of her start, and she came hurtling toward me. I activated Mirror Image and rushed to the side. For once, I felt like I was getting the hang of things, having taken a quick minute in my new Training Dojo before coming to the Square to set up the two preset paths for the skill.

My afterimage skipped backward, and she chased it down, right up until the image disappeared into the wall and she collided directly with it. Instead of simply having her tusks stuck, she had actually left a rather large crater in the wall. Pieces of cement practically buried her, and it took more than a few seconds for her to push back out from the debris.

Her health had also dropped by nearly ten percent from the impact, and I started to formulate a plan. From what I could put together, the bouncing she had been doing built up energy that she released when she charged. It didn't quite explain why my strikes were being halted without any actual resistance, but the fact that she took damage from striking the wall seemed to indicate she couldn't keep herself from getting hurt when she was in motion.

"So you're some sort of illusionist, then? Is that it?" she called, starting to bounce on her toes again while she looked around the room. With my invisibility faded, she found me and stared me down as her tusks shrunk by nearly half. "Well, you can't hide from me forever."

I was just about to wonder what that meant when she launched her charge again. She was moving even faster this time, rushing in toward me like a homing rocket. This time when I went to dodge, she anticipated it, her body practically drifting as she chased after me and threw a wide punch my way. I tried to dodge but was too slow, and her attack hit me with enough force to send me tumbling over the ground as my health dipped below fifty percent almost painfully quickly.

"Okay . . . that one hurt a bit," I grunted as I scrambled back to my feet. I went to materialize a Health Injector when a **[Healing Items Not Allowed]** warning flashed across my vision.

I was about to try and throw out some more banter to buy some time when she rushed in again, swinging her head as her tusks extended out further to strike me. I activated Fortune's Shield, and the orange barrier materialized out of my jacket just as her tusk scraped across my chest. My jacket probably should have been torn, if that was even possible, but the barrier did its job and left it as a glancing blow. I still took damage, of course—the jacket's ability only provided a twenty percent reduction, after all—and the force of the attack tossed me backward yet again, skidding onto the ground.

Before she could chase after me and keep me on my back foot, I finally relented and activated Weighted Clothes. I wasn't counting on it finishing her, but I hoped it would slow her down enough for me to figure *something* out.

As I returned to my feet, I found her crouched onto the ground, holding herself up on her hands in a frustratingly familiar pose. It was pretty clear she had been preparing to charge again when my skill took effect. Like with my punches, the initial crushing weight did nothing to her health bar, and a wide smile spread over her face as she stared at me.

"Oh this—This is good," she declared, barely even struggling to speak. I could tell the weight was holding her in place, but pink sparks were beginning to jump off both her feet and hands now that they were in contact with the ground. Her tusks began to grow larger as I backed up, running into the wall behind me.

If the weight couldn't take her down, I wasn't sure *what*—if anything—in my repertoire could do it. I wished I had already absorbed one of my new skill books, but even then, I'd have to be making up a skill on the fly with a questionable path to success.

My hand rested against the wall behind me as something the manager, Schmitt, had said sprang back to mind. There was one, and only *one* way I could think of that *might* let me come out on top of this fight, and I wished I hadn't already used my Mirror Image. It just relied on getting her to come at me as hard as she possibly could . . . and a whole lotta luck.

I only had about ten seconds left on Weighted Clothes, so I had to work fast, and I figured the easiest way to do it would be to just go with an old-fashioned taunt.

"So, you're fast and got sharp tusks? I don't mean it as an insult or anything, but that's kinda a one-note powerset, don't cha think?" I asked. Her smile faltered ever so slightly. "Or are you hiding a big reveal? That's the kinda thing you cheerleaders like to do, right? Put on a big show?"

"Yeah, my set *might* be straightforward, but it does its job very, *very* well," she said. Although I had assumed she was handling the weight better than I thought she would, her voice was coming through gritted teeth. The pink sparks grew the longer she stayed pinned, and as the shine from the sparks began to become nearly too much, her smile returned, even her eyes seeming to glow. "I gotta say . . . thanks for the charge up, and like, I'm sorry for how much this is gonna hurt."

I closed my eyes and let my Area Sense activate just as the timer for my Weighted Clothes ticked over. There was a thunderous *CRACK* as she pushed off of the ground, and I could hear the clattering of cement flying from the ground behind her and around the cell. Time didn't slow, and it wasn't like when Angie read a description for me, but with my eyes closed, I felt the moment she cut a path into my area.

She was moving almost impossibly fast, but my eyes opened just as a streak of pink was about to crash into me. Whether thanks to skill, my Super Luck, or just plain old instinct, I dove out of the way at the last possible moment, rolling over the ground and scrambling to my feet as Pinky crashed into the wall. I couldn't linger, and had to immediately move to dodge out of the way of the debris that went flying from the collision. As it all settled to the ground, I crept toward the cratered wall, hearing a string of what I had to assume were angered curses coming from deep within it.

Once I was close enough, I activated my Area Sense again and probed inside of the debris-filled crater. I could feel Pinky struggling under a pile of rubble, and I tensed as I waited to see if she would emerge. After nothing happened for a few moments, I stepped closer and tried to look between the gaps in the destruction.

"You, uh . . . okay in there?" I called. I couldn't find anything within the debris to single her out to highlight, and unlike a fighting game, there weren't any floating health bars for me to check either, but I had to wonder if this counted as her being captured.

There was another muffled sound of words, and I went to open a chat window with her, only to find that that function was also blocked. I let out a sigh and looked at the wall again. It wasn't like *I* was about to start digging her out.

After five minutes passed, there was a flash of light, and I suddenly found myself standing atop the platform on the second floor once again. As Silver had promised, I received the Sanctioned Fighter Achievement along with an additional five thousand credits for winning. Walking over to Pinky, who was sprawled out with a frustrated pout on her face, I offered a hand.

"No hard feelings, right?" I asked, almost unsure.

"Cheap move," she said, though she let out a sigh and took my offer of help. "But no . . . No hard feelings. I should have been more suspicious when you were pressed right up against the wall like that, just wasn't expecting you to be able to get out of the way . . . Lucky as hell dodge . . ."

"I mean, it was either get you stuck or just give up and lose, I don't really think I had another option," I said and pulled. She hopped to her feet as her tusks disappeared back into her mouth, and she dusted the dirt from her pink-and-white gear.

"That so?" she mused and shrugged. "Well, not that it matters. You trapped me in that debris like I did with the damn meth head . . . I thought if I could move my head enough, I could break free, but I hit the damn wall too hard . . . I had to have been at least six feet deep in there . . ."

We hopped off the platform, and a few people reached out to pat us on the back in congratulations. Though we didn't draw as big of a crowd as the other platforms had—or perhaps they had gotten bored waiting for the five-minute capture timer to pass—it was still surprisingly more than I was expecting, and the warm reception they offered us was oddly nice.

"You know, it's not my fault your weakness is apparently a wall," I joked, and she lightly pushed me as we unconsciously wandered over toward the nearest other platform.

"Yeah, yeah, whatever," she said with an obvious roll of her eyes. "You got to see me do some of my big tricks, and I barely even got to see what you could do! Like, what the hell is your power?! You had the weird illusion thing that disappeared into the wall, and then the weight thing was so cool. Like, I got juiced up on all that pressure; I wonder if we can get you over to California so that we can team up; I could hit people so hard with that sorta combo," she rambled.

"That move was *supposed* to take you down; it's actually one of my bigger moves right now," I said. It might not have been *entirely* the truth, but it wasn't a lie either.

"Well, it did basically the exact opposite. But now that I think about it, maybe we shouldn't reveal our secrets in a crowd of people. We can chat about that later." She winked as she pushed her way through the crowd. I followed behind, and we managed to get up close enough that we could see the entirety of the second platform.

Unlike the blank ring we had been on, this one was practically sunken in and seemed to be a miniature city block with skyscrapers and—I saw an explosion of lightning on one of the small streets and turned to see a small lady turn into a burst of lightning, rushing down the miniature avenue.

"Is that—" I started, and my vision highlighted the platform, bringing up a slew of information on the battle. The monotone robotic voice, thankfully, only read out the fighters and a buff that each one sported that answered a lot of questions before I could even start asking them.

[Tempest's Wrath, Level 10 Thunder God]
[Elastic Menace, Level 23 Rumbling Rubber]

[Equalizer.]
Variable Buff/Debuff.
For the duration of this match, this Augment's stats have been dynamically adjusted to bring each fighter to a similar power threshold.
Base stats are adjusted to boost or cap to ensure a fair fight.

"Come on, Tempest! I got fifty grand riding on you!"

"Take down that rubbery asshole!"

There were cheers and hollering coming from all around the ring as the flash of lightning barreled into a man that was stretching himself across the road. I focused on the area, and it almost seemed as if the platform responded to my thoughts, my view of it zooming in on the fight.

"This is so cool," Pinky whispered as she watched the fight. I turned to her. There was a glimmer in her eye as she focused on the platform which I often saw in Jon's eyes whenever he was on one of his rants about Augments. "I wonder if our cell just looked like a couple miniature versions of us running around since there were no buildings in the way. I want to fight in a city like that so bad. *Uggggh*, why do I have a twelve-hour fight cooldown? Can we have a rematch tomorrow? Come on, please? I still gotta figure out what the hell your powerset is about."

"You talk really fast; you know that, right?" I said. She smacked me on the arm. "What, I'm just saying . . . Look, I'll say maybe but no promises; this is cool and all, but I'm still figuring my set out. Why don't we wait until we are, I don't know, level ten? Then we'll each have had some time to break out and really come back hard."

Pinky visibly lit up at this, and she was actively bouncing in excitement when a collective cheer roared around the ring. There was another flash of light before a man whose skin and clothes appeared visibly singed popped back into existence on his back atop the now flat stage. His health rapidly replenished as a girl with raven black hair, amber eyes, and a deep scowl appeared looming over him.

Several Augments in dark clothes hopped onto the platform and started patting the girl on her back, leaving her looking between them with a self-assured pride that could only exist in someone who *had* just kicked the shit out of someone. As she continued to look between her admirers, her eyes met mine, and a deep sense of unease washed over me.

Her eyes almost seemed to dance with electricity, and although I hadn't meant to, I had enabled my Area Sense. There was a buzzing energy radiating from where she was within my field, and my stomach turned over again at the raw power that seemed to emanate. We only looked at each other for a moment before someone stepped between us and I turned from the platform, breaking off my sense.

"Whoa, hey, where're you going?" Pinky asked as she saw me walking away.

"Don't you wanna probe the current reigning queen of our leaderboard for information?"

"Nah, that's far too big of a crowd for me to deal with. And honestly, she's giving me a weird vibe. Can't really explain it," I replied, shrugging and tapping the side of my head. "Power thing, yah know?"

"I definitely don't, since I *still* haven't figured out that damn power of yours, but also thanks for the insight." She laughed then turned back to the crowd. "I'll message you if I find out anything good."

"Thanks, I'll catch yah later," I said and extended a fist her way. She gave me a warm smile and bumped it with her own. "Now, if you'll excuse me, I got some extra credits to spend over at the resale shop, since I *did* just win a fight."

CHAPTER THIRTY-TWO

While the resale shop was pretty cool to see, appearing much like Greg's Gears and Gadgets had with its long counter and wall display, there really wasn't much for me to buy. That wasn't to say the place had scarce pickings or anything like that. In fact, there were so, so, *so* many weapons and pieces of clothing hanging on the walls behind the counters, but unfortunately, there were little options within my price range that were actually worth buying.

The closest thing I saw was a **[Belt of the Thinker]** for ten thousand credits. I couldn't necessarily argue with the price, since it did come with a plus-eight boost to Intelligence, plus-two to Ingenuity, and a perk called Quick Wit that would have allowed me to halve the remaining cooldown on a single ability every hour. Still, that didn't mean I felt bad about sinking my credits into books and the Revolver. If my fight with Pinky had proven anything to me, it was that I needed a lot more offensive options to take down harder-to-hurt enemies.

I ended up leaving the resale shop without buying a thing and headed back through the portal home, making it back to the apartment only a few minutes before Axio's daily announcement. Jon joined me on the couch just as the chime hit six, and his eyes lit up with glee when the living room TV flickered to life.

He was just about to say something when the *Infinite Ascension* logo briefly flashed on the screen and images of Augments started to appear in tiles around it. It took until I appeared on the screen for me to realize that it was the current Top Ten. Our portraits hung like baseball cards, while our powerset names and scores populated under them.

Though I still felt a weird vibe just thinking about it, I briefly looked at Tempest's Wrath. Her amber eyes sat behind a plain black mask, and a scowl rested firmly on her face, but that wasn't the portrait that kept my attention for long.

"Is that a fucking pigeon?" Jon asked before I could vocalize a similar question.

While I had seen the name a few times on the list, I suppose I had mostly just glossed over it as some sort of weird joke that made sense in context. But as weird as it was, in the eighth window—with six thousand seventy points—was a portrait of a common pigeon.

"Maybe . . . it's a shapeshifter?" I offered, though even I wasn't convinced.

"Into a pigeon?" Jon looked at me with a raised eyebrow. "I mean, I know *a lot* about Augments, and I get that shapeshifters are common enough, but would they actually give somebody the option to just turn into a *pigeon?* Let alone be strong enough that *somehow* they are in the Top Ten?! Angie?"

"There are a good number of shapeshifting types; however, I do not have a current list of all of them, and neither will your current database in the Command Room. Now hush, Axio's about to speak," Angie said, and a familiar bit of feedback pierced the air before the tap of a nonexistent microphone stopped it.

"*Goooood* Evening, Augments! What a wonderful first day we've been having, wouldn't you all say? I know I, for one, have been having—at least for the most part—an absolute blast with all these new features. Now, we've got a handful of quick things to get through, and I don't want to hold you all up when you have all clearly been having so much fun!

"First things first, let's get the unpleasant stuff out of the way. To the three of you who haven't finished your tutorials yet, yeah, that's gone on long enough. This is not a joke. This is not me being flippant, or silly, or anything of the like—and yes, for the last time, Augment #392, this is all real, how are you not getting this? You have exactly one hour to complete the tutorial before I decide to do something about it. I suggest you stop listening to my wonderful voice and get out there *now* to complete it. You won't get a final warning."

My gut turned as I thought about the conversation I'd had with Axio. While he had called it ridiculous to ask if this was some sort of show, he hadn't necessarily denied that it was entertainment. It was impossible to listen to him make this announcement and not feel like he was having a sick sort of fun toying with the lot of us. Still, I couldn't necessarily ignore the fact that he had seemed to imply that he was bound by some sort of rules, though, so I found myself in a weird position where I wasn't quite sure what to make of him.

"Now, with seventy-two hours left on the clock, just over ten percent of you have already covered more than half of the necessary points to complete this phase! I certainly hope you all aren't trying to rush across the finish line just to coast the last few days; remember those of you in the Top Ten *will* receive a S-tier loot box at the end of Phase One, so keep on pushing! If you don't think the points are going to be useful in Phase Two, know that the extra experience and levels sure will.

"And if you don't think you can pass by one of those eager beavers, you can always just try to hunt them down and take them out of the game permanently. That would be fun to watch, AND you'd gain enough points to maybe wind up there yourself!"

Axio let out a dry laugh, and I felt myself tense up. Even if he was bound by some sort of rules that made him do this, it definitely seemed like he was enjoying himself. Besides, I still wasn't sure how I felt about being used as a guinea pig, even if

I did appreciate the fact that Jon was now clued in to everything and could help me in more ways than just thinking about how to use my powers. No, I knew it would be irresponsible to assume that Axio didn't have his own agenda, even if I couldn't begin to figure out what it was.

"The bigger problem we're facing is that more than fifty percent of you *haven't* even managed to gain a quarter of the points yet! Now maybe I'm over-thinking this, but the math suggests that you guys are *not* putting in quite enough effort to complete this relatively simple task I've put before you, and I just have to wonder . . . Did I not express myself well enough? Did you not take me seriously when I warned of a Critical Level Threat for not completing this?

"You know what, I think we're going to have a trial run with all of you who haven't crossed that threshold just yet. A Minor Level Threat has been deployed to each of your locations. Honestly, you all should be thanking me; it's sink or swim time, after all, and if you stop that threat, you might just survive until the end of the weekend!"

"What are the—"

"Shh," I cut Jon off.

"The rest of you—I'm sorry, but I'm all out of favors and help. I've doled out quite a few of those at this point, and my generosity has been all used up. But that's okay, you guys are doing well enough already that I think you'll survive without any extra motivation. There's three more days, so keep on get-ting stronger. I'm going to need each and every one of you at your *very* best for Phase Two because that . . . Well, you know what . . . let's not worry you all with that just yet. The day's still young, so get out there and have some fun. Good luck, Augments."

With that his voice clicked away, and the portraits of the Top Ten all vanished. There were a few beats of silence before Jon let out a laugh.

"Sheesh, that dude is way too serious for his own good." He hopped to his feet and stretched. "Are you ready to hit up the dojo? I think it'd be smart to spend some time working on some new moves for you to get you working more fluidly."

I found myself looking at him almost incredulously as he wandered around the couch and toward the fridge.

"You . . . You did hear all that, right? Nearly half the people in this year's Wave of new Augments might end up dead by the end of the night . . . How are you so calm?"

"I mean, we've been over the whole statistical chance of dying thing already, so I think that's a moot point. Besides, you have that Acceptance Matrix thing—I don't. I think the better question is how are *you* that worried?" he asked, turning back to me. "Trust me, I get what he said sounds scary; I really do. But I've been reading up on the threat levels. I'm literally gonna be up half the night here just trying to go through as much as I can cause there is *a lot*. That said, a Minor Level Threat is *at worst* something similar to Sal. I'm not hoping they die or anything—that would be messed up—but if that's the game . . ."

"Really?" I asked. Angie let out a giggle as I stood up.

"Yeah, you really have been pretty bad about probing for information, you know that, right, Loophole?"

"Hey, I was distracted trying to clue him in. Though *clearly* that was completely pointless, since he just went and figured the whole damn thing out on his own," I said, rubbing the side of my head. "Even still, I get that you find all of this really cool, I do. Maybe just . . . I don't know, pretend to be worried about the crazy AI dude in the sky that could send *kaijus* our way if I don't do a good-enough job."

"*Kaijus?*" Jon asked, his eyes visibly lighting up. "Wait, are you telling me there's gonna be something like Godzilla?!"

"Right?! Isn't it going to be so cool to see a giant monster destroying a city?!" Angie practically squealed.

"Holy shit, how are you actually excited about that?!"

"Come on, dude, you gotta admit giant monsters are pretty cool. Though I'll admit that them destroying cities might be less cool. And now that I think about it, I think one would practically crush you right now, which would be even less cool." Jon tapped at his chin. "We're gonna need to get you leveled way up before we try and get one of them to come our way."

"Yeah, we're not gonna be trying to make that happen anytime soon . . . or, you know, preferably at all," I corrected him while he rolled his eyes and cracked open a soda. I followed him into the kitchen and peered inside the fridge. "You know . . . maybe I should go and exchange some of my credits for cash . . . We could actually have some food in this fridge for once that's not just leftovers from Tio's."

"You? Buying groceries? Now I've really seen it all." He laughed and patted me on the back before walking out of the kitchen and back to the Command Room. "There's some ramen in the pantry and some pizza rolls in the freezer if you need a quick bite. Maybe later we can exchange some credits, and I'll do a grocery run in the morning. Once you're done eating, go ahead and absorb those new books, then head into the dojo—we've got some abilities to create. Plus, I think it's time we start getting you moving around faster."

"Aye-aye, captain?"

"He's cute when he takes charge."

"He barely does anything, and you think he's cute . . ." I sighed and resisted the urge to pinch the bridge of my nose in frustration.

"Hey, it's not her fault I look as good as I do," Jon called from the Command Room.

"Don't encourage her."

"Eh, fair enough. I did already have to ask her to tone it down a bit," he admitted.

As I stood by the fridge, my stomach growled, reminding me that other than a few random snacks and a hot dog from the vendor I had prevented from getting robbed, I had barely eaten. Grabbing the pizza rolls, I tossed them into Jon's air fryer and then snatched a package of ramen from the pantry. As the food started to cook, it reminded me of the buff Gio had gotten after he . . . well . . . ate one of his apparently disposable men.

"Hey, what's the [**Well Fed**] buff?" I asked as I started to prepare the ramen to go into the microwave.

"Here, let me see if I can pull it—" Jon started before Angie cut in.

[Well Fed!]

This is a buff granted when you've eaten a well-balanced meal for your particular diet. For an Augment like you, that means eating something like a good serving of your grandma's famous seven-cheese lasagna and your vegetables, mister. For a snake-man, that apparently means the head of one of his recent cohorts . . .
This buff grants you a 10 percent increase in Damage and a 25 percent increase in Stamina for two hours. Once a meal has been confirmed to give this buff, it will be noted for future reference.

"Huh . . . that was oddly helpful, Angie, thank you."

She sighed. *"Sometimes I think you don't listen to me or something. I've told you, if you ask a question related to the game, I have to answer. It's not that complicated, Loophole."*

"To be fair, when eighty percent of the stuff you say is either jokes about me or random attempts to hit on Jon, I kinda *have* to tune out some of it."

Walking over toward the Command Room while I waited for my food, I passed the oversize gym locker that had appeared after I had added the Training Dojo to my expansion slots. I materialized the two books I had which I already qualified for on gravity and thermodynamics and absorbed them, gaining a level-three knowledge stat on both subjects.

It was such a weird feeling when you were expecting it to happen. When I had absorbed my previous books, I had just let the knowledge disappear into the back of my mind until I had actively wanted to use it. But the book on snake venom had proved that it was more than just some key that unlocked additional abilities in my repertoire. I *had* the knowledge, and when I knew I was gaining it, the sudden random facts and figures filled my mind.

"Huh . . . did you know that gravity never actually stops pulling you down? Like if we dug a hole straight down to the center of the Earth where our own gravity well is, you'd just bob back and forth forever. You know . . . assuming you didn't melt when you passed through the molten core," I explained.

Jon just let out another laugh as he turned around in his chair. "Sheesh, where the hell were these when we were in high school? We coulda both had straight As."

"There are protections and rules in place that prevent the Augmentation of anyone under the age of eighteen, thank you very much," Angie chirped up. *"And as I've said, those books only work if you've been Augmented."*

"Huh . . . that's oddly ethical, all things considered," I replied, hearing the *ding* from the air fryer.

"Yeah, I still have so many questions about all of this, but the access I have now basically doesn't tell me a thing," Jon said as I wandered back to the kitchen. "Is there anything you can tell us about how this was made, Angie?"

"I've told this to Loophole, but I guess it's worth repeating for you. I am not autho-rized to speak on the motives or goals of the developers . . . and it would be in every-body's *best interest to not raise those questions, as they draw unnecessary attention,"* Angie warned. She hadn't actually added that second part when I'd brought it up before; it almost sounded like it was a last-minute addition this time.

"Eh, I figured, but I guessed it couldn't hurt to ask; not like knowing changes anything, anyway," Jon said with a bit of disappointment.

It only took me a few minutes to scarf the food down once it was finished, and without much else to say, I found my way over to the locker. Now, I had never actually gotten shoved into a locker in high school—hell, I had never even *seen* that happen outside of clichés in movies or shows—but the idea of choosing to walk into one still felt a bit silly. Even so, I stepped into and through the locker.

"Did . . . Wait, did the system let you change how it looked?" I asked, almost stunned.

When I had first entered the dojo after setting it up, the place had actually been strikingly similar to the cell I had fought Pinky in. But now, the door opened into an *actual* dojo. The more I looked around, the more I was positive I had seen this particular location *somewhere* before, and I heard Jon start to laugh over an invisible intercom.

"*Yuuup*, I figured if we are uploading new skills into your brain, we might as well take a little inspiration from somewhere else. The system made it so easy; I just had to find the scene in the *Matrix* and *bam*, instant dojo," he said as I walked toward the center of the space. "And before you ask, it's only the dojo. I can move things like the doorways and your display case within my interface, but don't expect the apartment to be getting a makeover anytime soon."

"Okay, yeah . . . this is pretty cool," I admitted as I took in the space. "I could practically sleep in here."

"I should remind you: the Pocket Dojo expansion does come with a two-hour con-tinuous use time limit to prevent just that. If you want sleeping upgrades, you have to purchase those separately, thank you very much," Angie said.

"Yeah, we'll be circling back to those later," Jon added. "Okay, now, let's get to work. The night's still young, and we've got a whole new ability bar to fill up."

CHAPTER THIRTY-THREE

I *. . . Shouldn't we be starting this a bit lower? Like maybe on the fire escape?"* I said as I looked over the edge of the roof and down.

"Hey, you're the one who wanted to wait until morning to actually try using this outside. How are we supposed to hide your Secret Identity if you go flying off our fire escape?" Jon countered as I backed away from the edge and tried to shake the nerves from my body. *"Besides, you know it works—you were floating all over the apartment. You know as well as I do that if you want to extend the time, you gotta take the leap and just start getting that usage experience."*

We had ended up spending the rest of the night working on a handful of new abilities and actually learning a whole hell of a lot about the different types I could create. In fact, while passive skills were pretty straightforward, activated abilities came in two very distinct flavors.

Whether it was simply a natural quirk of my abilities or of my own thinking, up until we started to experiment, I had largely only created what the PAI database referred to as Static Cost abilities. These abilities would always have variable length cooldowns but relatively low costs to my stamina. My Sting like a Bee ability, for example, was *always* going to cost about five percent of my stamina to activate, regardless of just how much stamina I actually had.

But on the other side of the coin were the Flexible Cost abilities. These skills came with the benefit that they generally had either no cooldown or extremely short cooldowns. This meant that they could be used in rapid succession, but depending on just how much power I put into them, they could rapidly deplete my stamina bar and leave me unable to move or defend myself if I overdid it.

After learning all of this, and knowing that Angie had a habit of withholding information until I specifically asked for it, I asked her to go back and mark all of my prior skills with their stamina costs. I also made it a point of asking her to tell me about their costs moving forward as well. She insisted she would have even if I had not made that request, but I liked to think I had learned my lesson when it came to her.

It had taken a bit of experimenting in the dojo, but I'd managed to come up with more than a handful of abilities utilizing my new knowledge on gravity and thermodynamics. The majority of them had ended up falling into the flexible category, but a few still managed to generate with fixed costs.

My second ability bar had been quickly filled up, though I did end up keeping a few of my skills on both Revolver options. Still, my new bar was, largely speaking, more focused on damage compared to my original. It led to us dubbing my first as my "Stealth" bar and the new one as my "Fight Time" loadout, although I was positive Jon was still brainstorming better names for them, and if he wasn't, I'd have to.

Testing them in the dojo had been all well and good, but the place came with a severe lack of actual enemies to practice on in its current version. So when the morning came around, Jon had been quick to wake me, forcing me to shove a large breakfast he had picked up from Tio's down, which did net me the **[Well Fed]** buff, before telling me to get my ass going.

Truth be told, I wasn't sure just how much he had actually slept through the night, but he'd assured me he'd find time to take a nap once he was sure I was getting through the day's task without an issue. I still had ten dens to get through, and Jon was determined to have me work through all but the hardest by the end of the day. And the quickest way to get between the dens . . . was through the air.

At the far-right side of my ability bar, a new single slot had appeared the moment we created the skill, and I looked at it as I tried to talk myself into just taking the leap.

[Personal Gravity Laws!]
Movement Ability.
Given you're looking at this to stall, how about I help you out just a bit.
This ability allows you to shift your own relation to gravity, allow-
ing you to freely float within your Local Area. Additionally,
with some practice, you can mentally adjust the speed at which
this change in your own gravity allows you to move.
Now, want to know the really cool thing about your Local Area that you
should already know? It moves centered directly on you! That means you're
ALWAYS in your Local Area! Now, as we went over last night, that doesn't
mean you just get to fly around as much as you want. This ability drains your
stamina at a rate of 5 Stamina Points per second while floating. For every 10
miles per hour of additional speed, the stamina drain increases by 5 percent.
Was that enough stalling? Do you want me to go on a tan-
gent about how much I like Codex's butt again?

"No, no, we're good," I replied as I shook my head and tried to shake the nerves off once more. Though I hadn't realized it—mostly given to my own stupid lax attitude about really learning the intricacies of the stats—on top of helping me hit harder, my Strength was *also* directly tied into increasing my stamina, just as Toughness increased my health.

That meant that the five hundred points of base stamina that *every* Augment had, plus the twelve points I had in Strength, left me with seventeen hundred points of stamina. With the [**Well Fed**] buff, it capped out at 2125 points. The longest I could stay afloat, just hanging midair, would be just a bit over seven minutes, so any flight I made, unless I used a Stamina Injector, had to be shorter than that due to the added drainage from increasing my speed. Unfortunately, that baseline was about as far as my math was going to be taking me, especially since I didn't have a speedometer in my interface . . . yet.

I looked down over the edge of the building again and found myself instinctively wanting to retreat back toward the ground to start from there. Apparently, some self-preservation instincts were hard to get past. Either that or I had a fear of heights that I simply wasn't aware of.

"For Axio's sake, just jump already!" Angie moaned.

"I'm with her. Let's go, Loophole, we're burning daylight," Jon agreed, and I just sighed.

"Okay . . . you can do this," I said to myself under my breath, trying to block them out as I focused on the task at hand. Turning, I took a few steps back from the edge of the roof.

While I didn't have to make a running start, I knew it was definitely the literal leap of faith I needed to just outright trust the ability. Shaking my arms out once more, I let out a slow, steady breath, took one final step back . . . and then I ran for it, darting right for the ledge, stepping onto it, and launching myself upward. I activated the ability the moment my foot was off the ground and concentrated as I quickly rose higher into the air above the neighboring roofs.

[New Achievement! 250 Feet Up!]
Trust me, we were really tempted to go with a corny "It's a Bird, It's a Plane" sorta joke for the name of this one, but I think that really limits this Achievement to you lucky Augments who get to fly instead of anyone who can jump or teleport or do any other sort of special way to get 250 feet up into the air. So, this Achievement is for exactly what it says. You've used your power to go 250 feet above the ground! Good for you, maybe now you won't be so damn slow.
Silver-Level Achievement.
Reward: *You have received a C-tier Loot Box!*

Knowing *how* gravity worked and that the ability *should* work wasn't the same as immediately moving through the air with grace. There *may* have been a bit more flailing than necessary as I swirled upward into the air. My stamina was already starting to tick down, and without an active timer in my interface, I was going to have to make sure to keep an eye on it to prevent a sudden freefall.

After taking about ten seconds to stabilize and find a bit of control over my new ability, I let out a breath and felt my smile return to me. I had done it . . . I was flying.

"Now that is one hell of a view," Jon said with a whistle. *"Okay, turn north; we're gonna start at the top corner of Hell's Kitchen and work our way around to knock all of these dens out and get your point total up and over that ten thousand hump. There's a Bronze den and a Silver den to the northwest. They actually look pretty close to the cruise terminal over there. I'll guide you in when you get closer, so get a—"*

Before he could finish, I launched myself forward, maybe faster than I needed to. I *had* oriented myself north, but that didn't mean I had to immediately make a beeline for my destination.

The sudden freedom that came with the ability to fly hit me. While I certainly did need to get as much usage experience on my skill as possible to help it level up, a sudden animalistic-like joy came over me as I rapidly picked up speed.

"WOOOOOOOOOO!"

I couldn't help myself and let out a loud, exhilarated whoop as the wind roared past me, filling my ears. Whether it was the warping of gravity around my body or some minor filter ahead of my eyes, I was able to see clearly, and I pushed myself to go faster. My stomach dropped with every burst of speed, and I darted left and right, testing my control and letting my whole body lean into every turn.

It was a strange balance between tension and freedom, each adjustment to my flight seeming to ripple through the gravity around me, like I was tugging on invisible threads holding me aloft. I knew Jon had wanted me to focus and get to work, but I really couldn't help myself.

I. Was. Flying!

I couldn't say for sure how flight felt to other Augments with wings or wind-like powers, or even how The First had done it, but this was like being suspended in an invisible bubble that moved with me. The gravity shift made me feel light as a feather, and the more I pushed at the bonds of gravity that tried to force its will upon me, the faster I went.

I dove down in a sudden swoop, just barely dodging an old fire escape, and let out another whoop as I zipped along only a few stories above the ground. Though I felt like the world should have been a blur around me, everything was crystal clear, and I even waved at a crowd who managed to catch sight of me just before I darted around yet another corner and back higher into the air.

My stamina bar flashed, and it snapped me out of my exhilaration as I let myself twist in the air freely. The thrill of the flight had distracted me, and though I'd thought I had only been flying for a few moments, the bar was nearly seventy-five percent empty.

Yanking out an Enhanced Stamina Injector, I jammed it into my arm midflight. My stamina filled back to nearly three quarters full as I twisted once more. A quick glance down reminded me that the ground was hundreds of feet below, and the idea of falling out of the sky hit me harder than I'd expected now that I had slowed. I could hear my heart hammering in my chest—a mix of thrill and a rising, prickling anxiety as I tried to reorient myself.

I scanned the skyline, the sprawling expanse of the city stretched in every direction. The city always felt different when looking at it from high in a building, like it was alive and breathing. But flying above it without anything beneath my feet? That was a whole other beast, and one that I could easily get lost in experiencing as I looked down and around at the world.

I told myself to focus before Angie or Jon could do it for me and forced my eyes back up to the skyline, knowing full well that I was burning stamina. Luckily, New York had plenty of markers, and the cruise terminal I needed was unmistakable up ahead, gleaming in the morning light. A sense of urgency kicked in as my stamina dipped below half again.

Taking a deep breath, I forced myself to steady and aim straight toward the Hudson River, but I couldn't resist one more glance at the view stretching around me. For the first time, the world felt wide open in every direction, and I resolved myself to train this ability until I could fly for far, *far* longer.

After putting on the speed to clear the distance as quickly as I could, I slowed down, orienting toward the terminal and searching for the tallest building I could find. There was one at the corner of a park a few blocks from the terminal, and I darted for it. As I came in for a landing, I stumbled slightly before I righted myself and glanced around.

"Smooth," Angie said. I rolled my eyes.

"Least I didn't land on my face . . . and no one saw that," I replied, looking around again just to make sure no one was hanging out on top of the roof.

"I saw it, Loophole, that's all that matters; though I will *say it is rather nice to see you enjoying those abilities of yours for once,"* Angie commented.

"Yeah, I'm kinda jealous; that looked fun as all hell, so I can't really blame you for taking it for a spin like that. Kinda wish I could see the experience progress for your abilities, though—it would be nice to see how much experience that little joyride got you," Jon said as I approached the edge of the building. My stamina slowly started to refill while I glanced around, wondering if I'd spot Viper graffiti from my perch.

"Is it technically a joyride if I don't have a vehicle?"

"Do you really want to debate semantics, or do you want to beat down some bikers?"

"I can do both—it's called multitasking," I shot back, panning back across the area once more. Several outlines were suddenly selected as Jon did his work in the background.

There were two different highlighted spots, and I turned my attention toward the closer of the two first. It was a small, single-story building on the southern side of the park that had more than a few people in it, probably taking in one of the last moderately nice weekends before New York's winter could start to take hold. I wasn't positive, but I thought I could make out a snake painted onto the garage door at the front of the building.

"That's the Bronze level. It doesn't look too big on the map here, and if yesterday was any indication, you can probably knock it out pretty easily. But that Silver one . . ." Jon trailed off as I looked over toward the Hudson, where the other location had been highlighted.

The cruise terminal was often filled with, well, cruise ships, and it would have been easy to simply be distracted by the floating hotels. Luckily, my vision wasn't highlighting one of those monstrosities, though I still found myself almost laughing in surprise at what *had* been highlighted. On the far end of the terminal, there was a yacht that would have looked giant if it hadn't been sitting in a line of massive cruise ships.

"The bikers have a yacht . . . Why do the bikers have a yacht?"

"Well, that's rude of you, Loophole; everyone enjoys a nice day on the water, and is it really their fault that the boat they stole was a giant yacht?"

"Um . . . yes . . . yes, it is their fault," I replied with a sigh. *"I get Axio wants to set up stakes for us, but couldn't you guys buy a yacht like you rented out that one building for the den?"*

"Would it make you feel better if you knew the yacht they stole came from a man who treats his workers really poorly?" Angie asked as I searched for another building closer to the yacht that I could move to.

"Is that who they stole it from?" I prodded.

"Do you want to feel better or not? Because I was lying when I said Axio rents out those buildings, and I kinda feel like I need you to feel better about something," Angie said before she burst into a giggle fit.

"You know, I'm starting to think you like Angie's craziness more than you let on; otherwise, you really wouldn't engage and take her bait as often as you do," Jon commented while Angie laughed even harder.

"That's what I've been saying!"

"Okay, so, I'm gonna go and take some aggression out on the bikers who stole that yacht; anyone got a problem with that?" I asked. The cooldown on my Stamina Injectors had expired, and I knew if I shot right for the yacht, I could land on it before I burned through that much of my stamina. If I did get thrown right into a fight, I was relatively confident I could handle it, but I'd at least have the injector off of cooldown if I needed it.

"I think that's the best choice; it'll let you really flex and try out some of those new abilities," Jon agreed, letting us move on. That didn't surprise me, since he had been the one really pushing me to stop slacking. *"I think you have another minute before your stamina is fully refilled, so go ahead and call it in first. That's Pier 94, if they need to know the exact spot."*

At this point, calling in the dens was becoming routine, and the dispatch officer was quick to take down the details. I mentioned the nearby Bronze den as well, though the officer informed me I would need to either call that one in separately when I was preparing to assault it *or* inform the officers who arrived to clean up the Silver den once I was finished with it.

With that all done and my stamina bar replenished, I turned my attention back to the yacht. It was almost surprising how little I thought about it this time as I pushed off from the ledge and activated my flight once again. The worry and trepidation of my first trip were already things of the past, though I did make it a point to keep my attention directly on the yacht instead of looking straight down.

I threw in all the force I could and cut through the sky once more. I could feel the anticipation of the fight already starting to build, and I eyed my new abilities expectantly. There really was something innately thrilling about it that I had a hard time denying, and I was ready to put things into action.

As I approached the yacht, I could see the back of the ship had several layered decks, each with a handful of people wandering about. I took the time to highlight them, ensuring they were in fact bikers before I made my next move.

The largest group was on the rear, lowermost deck. I could make out seven of them wandering around the platform, and at least a few more on each of the three levels above it. The grunts at the rear of the ship were each level five, and a few of them were armed with what looked like assault rifles. None of them had their eyes on the sky, and I felt a smirk tug at the corner of my lips as I eyed the first of the abilities on my new bar.

[Earthbound Impact!]
Level 1 Activated Ability.
While utilizing **Personal Gravity Laws**, *activate this ability to rapidly descend to the ground, increasing in speed by 1 mile per hour per foot dropped up to a maximum of 150 miles per hour. Before impact, your personal gravity will be completely reversed to lessen impact upon yourself. All enemies and the environment within your Local Area will be affected by an immense gravitational force and will take damage equal to the speed traveling at impact times 10.*
Cooldown: *10 minutes.*
Stamina Cost: *15%*

"Geronimo?" Jon asked, and I chuckled lightly as I set my eyes on the large grouping on the lowest deck.

"Geronimo," I agreed and activated the ability, plummeting toward my enemies.

CHAPTER THIRTY-FOUR

I hit the deck with the skill fully charged, landing far more theatrically than I needed to, and five of the bikers were sent scattering to the ground as the yacht seemed to shudder under the sudden impact of gravity. The floor immediately under where I'd landed was relatively undisturbed, but within the circle surrounding me, it all had buckled downward enough that I almost wondered if it was going to collapse.

Luckily, the yacht was sturdy enough to withstand my landing, and I stood up, tilting my head to the side enough for it to crack as I quickly swept my eyes across the area to check for any enemies that I had missed. The deck was large enough that two of the grunts hadn't quite been in my area, but the shock of my entrance had left them apparently startled, while the ones who *had* been inside all sported spinning **[KO]** debuffs.

"Now that's how you make an entrance!" Jon whooped out, though I did my best to concentrate on the task at hand.

I heard several calls of alarm from the upper decks, and I turned to look at the gathering enemies. My smile grew wider as at least one of them shouted, "It's Loophole!"

I had been trying to make it a habit to activate Area Sense whenever I had my feet planted, hoping that by doing so it would eventually become second nature. As I continued to size up the next level and the bikers who were gathering at the railing, I felt two new presences enter my area, and I immediately activated the second new ability on my bar.

[Center of the Universe!]
Level 1 Activated Ability.
Create a gravitational force within your entire Local Area, centered on yourself, drawing in either all enemies or all nonbiological objects within your area at an initial pull of 5 meters per second, with the strength diminishing by 1 meter per second for every 3 feet from the center of your Local Area the affected targets are.
This ability drains 5 points of stamina per second of use. You may gradually increase the power of your gravitational force by

> *1 meter per second for an additional 1 point of stamina per sec-*
> *ond of use up to a maximum of 50 meters per second.*
> *This ability has **no maximum** duration and **no cooldown**, but*
> *offers no direct damaging effects. This ability will only deacti-*
> *vate when you choose to deactivate it, if you are hit hard enough*
> *to break your concentration, or you run out of stamina.*

I rapidly pushed the ability to its maximum, and the grunts were forced to come running and stumbling right toward me. Though the ability wouldn't hurt them itself, they were converging on a single spot, and I did still have Misfortune Abound on my passive bar. With my attention still focused on a large brute at the center of the group gathering on the second deck, I waited, mentally counting to three before I pushed off the ground hard and took flight like a rocket up toward the brute.

My stamina bar had already been drained to about fifty percent as I darted up for my target, and I rapidly slowed myself as I came face-to-face with a wide-eyed, leather-clad, half giant of a man.

"Boo," I said, then activated the third new ability on my bar.

[Gravity Punch!]
Level 1 Activated Ability.
Rapidly compress gravity directly around your fist before you throw a punch.
For every 5 percent of your stamina, deal an additional 50 per-
cent damage from your base attack up to a maximum of 500 per-
cent increased damage. If you have spent at least 25 percent of
your stamina, knock the target backwards 15 feet, and an addi-
tional 5 feet for every added 5 percent of your stamina spent.
Cooldown: *5 seconds.*

I only put twenty-five percent of my remaining stamina into the punch, but it did its job as my fist connected with the brute's chest. Though he was a rather large man, he still was sent flying backward and into two grunts I hadn't seen lined up behind him. None of them were knocked out, but it did at least send them to the ground as I set myself down on the deck and tried to casually walk toward them.

"Now, was it really necessary for you guys to steal this yacht? Is there even a place to store your bikes?" I asked as I materialized an Enhanced Stamina Injector and jammed it into my arm, returning my levels back up to just shy of seventy-five percent. As I moved inward and under the third deck, I scanned the area and counted three more grunts and a brute on top of the brute and grunts I had just knocked over.

There was a door leading into the main cabin that I gestured toward. "Oh wait, is this supposed to be the boss's place? You know, I've been looking for him. Do you guys think he's in the back? I'm pretty sure he goes by Snake—"

"Get him!" the brute shouted, and then he and the grunts all sprang into action.

They all had already been within my area, so I didn't *have* to goad them into action, but I still couldn't help myself. While I had never been what anyone would call shy growing up, Jon had pointed out just how much more confident I seemed to get when I was midbattle, while Angie claimed ignorance about the subject with her current database access. After taking time to really think about it, though, I pointed out that I had always been prone to bad jokes in awkward situations, so it was possible that they just landed differently because I had superpowers to back them up.

I activated Center of the Universe again, quickly ramping up the force before I followed it up with Sting like a Bee. The gravitational center of my ability stayed on my body as I rushed for the brute still being pulled my way. He hadn't been lifted off his feet, instead stumbling as he tried to resist the force, but him being off-balance worked out to my advantage. I drove my fist directly into the brute's temple just as he got into range, knocking him over to the side and directly into the path of the other brute being pulled my way.

With one of the two brutes knocked out, and the other struggling to push his way out from under the first, I deactivated Center of the Universe and turned my attention to the grunts that had managed to stay on their feet.

"So how about you guys get on the ground before I have to put you there," I said, staring them down and cracking my knuckles. One of the grunts spat at the floor, his eyes shifting from me to the still conscious but trapped brute.

"Do you really think that's going to work? It hasn't yet . . ." Angie pointed out.

"I think he just really, really likes that line. He has a bad habit of latching on to a joke he really likes and just overusing it. I remember back in high school there was a week where he tried to answer literally every question a teacher asked him with a pun," Jon chimed in.

"No takers?" I asked, ignoring them both as I kept my attention shifting between my remaining enemies. "Well, eventually, one of you will learn."

I activated Weighted Clothes, and a chorus of heavy *THUDS* echoed in the space around me as the grunts collapsed to the floor. I simultaneously reactivated Center of the Universe, ramping the force up to its maximum as the weighted grunts began to get pulled across the floor toward me. As they all converged, I jumped up and into the air, holding myself with Personal Gravity Laws while I let them crash together, knocking each other out and into a heaping pile of bodies before I deactivated the skill.

"Looks like you managed to get the brute too; though I didn't see if it was the weight or if he took extra damage from being dragged on the ground," Jon chirped up as I set myself down and took in the deck, trying to quickly search for any enemies that I may have missed.

I could still hear the clattering of footsteps on the deck above me, and I knew they were trying to converge on my location. I didn't want to say it out loud, knowing that doing so itself would be testing fate, but even though this place did seem to have increased numbers, the enemies were going down with an unsettling amount of ease. Had I been more egotistical, I might have just chalked it up to the strength of my new abilities, but I wasn't going to let my guard down that easily.

Sure, I could have just barreled forward and immediately rushed to the next deck up, but taking a moment only benefitted me, as my stamina started to tick back up from the fifty percent spot it had fallen back to. I looted the bodies as I walked toward the door heading into the cabin, surprisingly adding three thousand credits and a handful of Enhanced Stamina and Health Injectors into my B.E.L.T.

I opened the door to find a grunt reaching for the handle. His eyes widened just as I drove my fist into his throat, hitting him with the second strike of Sting like a Bee which I quickly followed up with the final hit I had available to the side of his head. The enemy collapsed to the floor, and I stepped over him as casually as I could.

"These guys have a lot more on them than the last few dens," I commented as I looted his body and added yet another thousand credits to my wallet.

"Nothing wrong with that. It means we can gear you up some more if the next few dens are similar," Jon said, then let out a whistle as I took in the opulence of the room. *"Now this is some fancy living . . ."*

He absolutely wasn't wrong about that. The inside of the yacht was far more ornately designed than the last few dens I had been in, looking nothing like a hollowed-out meth lab in waiting. Hell, it was practically gaudy, with large pieces of art scattered on the walls, ornate tables, and random objects that I could only assume cost way too much for being glorified paperweights. There were couches at the center of the space, and a large TV mounted on the wall off to the side of the stairwell heading to the upper deck, along with vases filled with flowers and pictures of what I assumed were the original owners hanging on the walls.

Part of me wanted to explore—this place was clearly screaming "hiding place" for *something*—but I could hear the sound of footsteps overhead and echoing down the stairwell.

"I really hope whoever actually owns this place has insurance . . . 'cause this might get a little messy," I muttered, reaching for an overly large pitcher of water conveniently placed amongst a row of glasses and unopened soft drinks on a large table pushed against the wall.

The problem with having knowledge of thermodynamics was that half the abilities I could manage required an actual source to work with. I wasn't able to make water appear out of nowhere just to freeze it, nor could I direct it like Hydramental could, but if it was there and in my local area, it was definitely fair game to alter its temperature.

I lobbed the pitcher toward the stairwell, the glass shattering directly ahead of the open doorway before I activated the fourth new ability on my bar.

[**Freeze!**]
Level 1 Activated Ability.
Rapidly lower the ambient temperature within a concentrated loca-
tion in your Local Area to freeze over a source of unpackaged liquid of
any type at an initial cost of 10 points of stamina per cubic foot of liq-
uid being frozen, and 1 stamina per second to maintain the effect.
Maintain the integrity of the frozen liquid until you release this abil-
ity, allowing the natural temperature of the area to return.
Cooldown: *30 seconds from the time the ability is released.*
This ability has **no maximum** *duration.*
This ability provides no direct damaging effects.

A grunt rushed down the stairs, stepping onto the now frozen patch of water and immediately losing his footing, slipping backward and smacking his head hard onto the stairs like he was in a *Home Alone* movie. Unlike one of those movies, however, the grunt wasn't able to just walk it off, and a small pool of blood began to form beneath his head. His health *hadn't* zeroed out just from that, and he might have been fine if it hadn't been for the small pileup his sudden collapse caused, as immediately after he slipped, two grunts who had been following closely behind went trampling over his body.

"Wow, you guys really don't care at all about your teammates, do you?" I asked with a shake of my head as I put my hands up, readying for them to come at me. Another man came sauntering down the staircase behind, and although he didn't look familiar, the way he carried himself did. It only took me a moment to highlight him to confirm my suspicion, his name coming up as [**Luca, Viper Soldier**].

"Hey now, youse the one who came on in here and started wreckin' the place," Luca said, holding up a hand as the grunts held their positions. They both pulled rifles out of nowhere and trained them on me while the soldier looked down at the now lifeless body of the grunt. "Hell, look, youse just went and killed poor Mario here. What gives youse the right?"

"To be fair, he *probably* would have been fine had one of your guys *not* stepped on his head as they were coming down the stairs," I shot back, not lowering my guard. I could hear the door open behind me, and I held myself still as my Area Sense kicked in. I'd thought I had gotten all of the enemies on the deck, but I hadn't done a thorough search either.

"Youse always gotta shift the blame, don't cha? And here I thought we could have a nice little conversation before I hand youse over to the boss. But I guess youse just wanna tell your jokes and treat us like the garbage youse heroes always think we are," Luca said with a disappointed shake of his head. His hand moved ever so slightly, and I felt a disturbance at the back of my area.

I risked a look over my shoulder and confirmed it was another grunt with their weapon raised, attempting to sneak up on me. In the brief moment I glanced away,

Luca materialized something into his hand. I might have missed it had the look of the syringe not been etched into my brain.

"Dude!" Jon yelled in my head, just in case I had missed it. I activated Center of the Universe, this time focusing on objects instead of people as I turned my eyes directly on the syringe.

Nothing happened at first, but as the force rapidly increased, I saw out of the corner of my eyes as the grunts ahead of me lost their grips on their weapons. Several other objects around the room started rushing toward me, crashing against my legs while I held myself as steady as I could. It took a few seconds for the force to maximize, but with it high enough, even Luca and whatever increased Strength he had couldn't hold on. Just as he tried to fight against the pull of my gravity to forcibly jam the syringe into his arm, the implement was wrenched from his grip, and it came hurtling toward me.

The three assault rifles came into contact with me first, and I mentally pulled them into my B.E.L.T., only taking a minor bit of damage from the impact before they vanished into the safety of my storage. I hadn't taken my eyes off my target, though, and just before it could stab me on accident, I snagged the syringe out of the air and deactivated my ability.

"Yeah, I don't think we're gonna be doing that. I mean, you do know you dissolve into ash after using these things, right? You really should be thanking me for saving you from yourself," I said, waving the syringe back and forth before I pulled it into my B.E.L.T. to investigate later. I kicked away some of the random objects that had come rushing over and moved toward the center of the space. "Like I said, you guys don't seem to have any camaraderie, or else your boss wouldn't be treating you all so expendably. What kind of working environment is that?"

"Youse heroes always gotta be so damn wordy, don't cha?" Luca said, and his relatively calm demeanor seemed to break as his expression hardened. "Well, if youse wants to fight . . . Go on, fellas, get him!"

The three men all rushed toward me. My stamina was starting to take a hit from the rapidity and variety of use, though I couldn't say that I hadn't been effective so far. Still, I had to be a bit conservative with the remaining forty percent I had available to me. As the men approached, I spent five percent of my stamina and activated Float like a Butterfly. I began to dodge the wild swings coming from them, easily weaving my way between the men as I delivered several nonenhanced blows of my own.

Even without using an ability, my increased strength still left a mark, and each strike on these most basic enemies dropped fifteen to twenty percent of their health with each connected hit. In a matter of seconds, I had put two of the three grunts down on the ground with **[KO]** debuffs, and I was dodging back as the third appeared to swing wide for my body. But as his hand passed by my midsection, I received a new notification that took me a bit by surprise.

[Warning!]
Viper Grunt has utilized the **Pickpocket** *feature on his gloves. One*
Experimental Injector *has been removed from your B.E.L.T.*

Before I could react, the grunt jammed the syringe into his arm, and his body began to convulse. Unlike when Gio had used the syringe, the grunt's transformation *wasn't* instantaneous, and I stared as the man's body started to slowly swell and morph. I wasn't sure what this meant, but I moved in to try and attack before he could complete his transformation.

He swung a newly enlarged arm wide, and with a sudden burst of new strength, I was thrown backward into the beverage table, taking out a small chunk from my health bar.

"Talk about initiative; the bosssss hasss been wondering if thessse thingsss would work on thessse maggotsss."

My ears felt like they wanted to bleed. The grunt was still grasping at his body as he transformed, causing me to turn and look for the source of the noise. I got back to my feet, only to discover a large, already transformed snake-man staring with vicious intent from exactly where Luca had been standing. He tossed another, now empty syringe to the ground, and I cursed myself for assuming he'd only have one on him.

I risked a look back at the convulsing man, unsure as to why the grunt hadn't fully transformed. His body seemed to shake, and a scream of agony ripped from his throat while his legs fused together. He barely caught himself on his hands before he face-planted from the shift in his body's design.

I couldn't wait to see what was going to happen, and materialized one of the venom-soaked guns I still had in my inventory. There was a chance this wouldn't get through his defenses, but I wasn't going to sit around and wait. Luca seemed to realize what I was doing and moved to intercept, but he was simply too slow.

My hand clenched as I fired, and the bullet pierced the grunt's body at his shoulder. I pulled the trigger twice more, striking him center of mass with two more shots that quickly chunked down his remaining health. Though his body had started to swell and transform, the sudden introduction of the venom seemed to halt the process, and his body began to bubble almost dangerously, as if the serum he had injected was simply incompatible with his system now that the venom had been suddenly mixed in.

"On your left!" Jon called out, and I skipped backward as Luca lunged for me.

"You sssssonuvabitch!" he hissed while I fired the gun on instinct.

The bullet glanced off his body, his natural defenses holding out as I dodged and tried to think. If he was like Gio, then sound was going to do the trick, but I wasn't sure how I'd be able to make a loud-enough commotion to weaken his defense enough to sneak a shot through. I eyed the last new ability that we had opted to place on my bar for now, and although I still wanted to try out Ring of Fire, I didn't think it was going to be of use in this particular situation.

I tried to think on my feet as fast as I could while Luca lunged again and I dodged, scrambling out of the way so he crashed into one of the couches in the space, tearing through it like it was butter. I turned and materialized six of my remaining vials of venom. I knew it was a long shot, but I had to give it a try all the same. I uncorked all of them, and in as fluid a motion as I could, I flung the vials forward toward Luca, the liquid leaving the glass in a familiar congealed way just as they had when I had tossed them toward Hydramental in my first fight with Sal.

Time didn't slow, but it sure felt like it did as I concentrated on the falling venom and activated Freeze. The blob froze over in a shiny, amorphous clump of a sickly green shade, and I stepped forward, raising my fist and throwing a punch at the falling icicle. Just as my fist was about to connect, I threw every last bit of my remaining stamina into a Gravity Punch.

I had no idea if this was going to work. I figured it was a long shot, and if it didn't work, I was going to have to stall to try and get my stamina to come back. But even with the threat of failure, I felt like I was starting to get really good at trusting a long shot, so I threw the punch all the same.

The blob of icy venom burst into shards and flew with lightning-fast speed. They peppered Luca's body, piercing through his defenses and into him with ease. It was far and away more than I would have introduced into his system with just a bullet. Almost just like Sal had the first time I had encountered him, the venom overwhelmed his system, and his body suddenly started to mimic the grunt. He looked around, a sudden change in his expression making it clear he hadn't considered this as an outcome before he moved slightly forward and collapsed to the ground.

His body continued to bubble and sizzle before it ignited, burning into a giant pile of ashes. A slew of notifications appeared at the periphery of my vision as I found myself actually short of breath, including an alert of the completion of the den. I was just about to start opening them when I heard a piercing scream coming from the stairwell.

I looked over, trying to ready myself for another fight even with my depleted stamina when my eyes fell on a woman in a long green dress. There was a young boy who couldn't have been older than five or six hiding behind her as they descended the staircase. The woman's hand was covering her mouth in shock as she took in the scene, and I highlighted her cautiously.

[Warning!]
Information on this Sapient NPC has been blocked by **[UNKNOWN]**,
preventing me from disclosing more information to you.
Sorry, Loophole, if you want to know who this is . . .
you're going to have to ask her yourself.

CHAPTER THIRTY-FIVE

W*ait, what?"* I asked Angie, taking a cautious step toward the woman, who pushed the child farther behind her. I held up my hands, trying to appear nonthreatening. *"Does that mean she's an Augment or related to one or something like that?"*

"You know, if she could answer that, she probably wouldn't have flashed that warning in the first place," Jon chimed in, though I could hear the confusion in his voice. *"Why don't you just ask her who she is. Maybe these bikers kidnapped another Augment's family? Though why wouldn't Angie just say she couldn't tell because of the Secret Identity rule if that were the case?"*

"Hey there, sorry, I didn't know they had taken prisoners . . . How long have you—"

"Prisoners?! Who the fuck do you think you're talkin' to?! What the fuck did you do to my home?!" the woman practically screeched at me as she stepped over the dead body at the bottom of the stairs as if it weren't even there. She spoke in a thick accent that would have been right at home in New Jersey, and her curly black hair bounced with each step as she waved her hand absently at her son.

He retreated back up the stairs in a hurry, though the woman moved with an odd amount of confidence as she marched toward me and pointed a sharp finger in my direction. "Do you know how hard it is to get blood outta this deck?! And these guards! My hubby told me they'd keep all you nosy twerps outta our business; now he's gonna have to go and hire a whole new setta them! Do you realize how hard it is to find good help in this fuckin' city?!"

"Your . . . husband . . . What?" I asked, suddenly feeling off as I stopped and took a few steps backward. I had clearly heard what she had said, but I had to at least go through the motions, just in case I was wrong. "Look, my name's Loophole. If you need protection, I can help—"

The woman pulled a gun from a pocket I didn't even realize the dress had and leveled it at me. "I don't need your 'protection,' *Loophole.* I'm plenty aware of the thorn you've been in my husband's operation. Three years now he's been working his way through the ranks, and you're trying to upend it all in a fuckin' weekend. What the fuck gives you the right?"

"Look, I don't know who your husband is; I swear I haven't been trying to mess with him. I only just got into all of this myself. I'm guessing he must be from some—"

She fired at the floor in front of me, and I jumped backward. My stamina was slowly ticking upward, and with a few more seconds I could probably use Center of the Universe to wrench the gun from her grip, but I still needed to stall for at least another moment to be able to ramp it up quickly enough. I could see my mission tracker light up at the side of my vision as **[The Snake Key]** mission shook ever so slightly.

"You know damn well who my husband is, Loophole, and you're gonna damn well know who I am too," she sneered with a look of contempt, leveling the gun at me once again. "My name is Giada Travisi; my husband is Salvatore Travisi. And he's on track to be the strongest Augment in the world; he's gonna own this place, you'll see."

"Salvatore . . ." Realization hit me. "Wait, is your husband Sal the Snake? How is that . . ."

"She's married to an NPC?! How is that even possible?! Angie, can you tell us any-thing at all here?" Jon asked as I trailed off before I could raise the exact same question.

"I'm sorry, Codex, I am not authorized to discuss this NPC."

"Of course you're not . . . What the fuck is going on here . . ." Jon muttered as Giada continued her slow trot toward me. Through the windows facing the pier, I caught the flash of red-and-blue lights coming up, but still just out of view from Giada's line of sight. I resolved myself to stall just a bit longer, assuming that they had to navigate through the mess that was the pier. I didn't want to hurt this woman, espe-cially since she seemed to be powerless and a Sapient person, but I wasn't going to risk being shot either.

Risking a glance toward the stairs, I saw that the boy hadn't actually listened to his mother and was now peeking down around the railing. Whatever was hap-pening here, the child definitely didn't deserve to see his mother getting hurt, and I refused to let myself get caught in a situation where he'd get hurt either, regardless of who he was. Giada's stare could have cut through a well-done steak when my eyes met hers once more.

"I hate that damn name these cretins have started calling him. His name is SnakeBite to you, fuckin' weaklings," she snarled, holding the gun up at me again. "Now, what the fuck are you breakin' into our home for; we don't keep anything related to the business here. How'd you even find this place, and who the fuck leaked it? I need to make sure we plug that hole before I get rid of you for him."

"SnakeBite is Sal? That doesn't make any sense. The last time I fought Sal, didn't he say that SnakeBite told him where to find me?" I asked Jon as I tried to think back to the interaction.

"Maybe it was a misdirect? Not sure necessarily why, but it seems like the kind of thing a game would do," Jon offered. The flash of red-and-blue lights had become

impossible to ignore, glaring and pulsing through the room. Even Giada was finally forced to acknowledge them, turning toward the windows with a frustrated scowl.

"Well, looks like the cops are here, Giada. Let's put down the gun; there's no need for you to get wrapped up with these guys right now. I'll tell them you cooperated, and you won't have to be taken away with them," I said, trying to deescalate the situation. While I wasn't sure that was a promise I could keep, since she was probably going to get arrested anyway, it didn't feel right having it happen with her son watching from only a dozen feet away.

"You damn heroes! Where the hell am I going to live now that you brought the cops here?! It took Sal four fuckin' years to get me out of that dump in Chelsea. I ain't going back!" Giada shouted. She was clearly panicking and not thinking straight if she actually thought she had a way to escape. Her expression seemed crazed as she looked over her shoulder at her son. "Oswald, go, get downstairs now—we practiced for this. Grab your go-bag; we need to get out of here."

"The gun, now!" Jon ordered, and I didn't hesitate to activate Center of the Universe and ramp up the strength. With her attention elsewhere, the gun was quickly ripped from Giada's hand, causing her to nearly stumble forward as she looked back in time to realize what was happening.

When the gun smacked into me, I instinctively tried to pull it into my B.E.L.T. but was met with a warning that read:

[Warning!]

This item was not system generated. The current version of your B.E.L.T. cannot store it.

The gun fell to the floor ahead of me, and I met Giada's wide eyes as she tried to compose herself, watching as they went between me and the flashing lights in the window. She immediately turned, intent on running for the staircase, when I reactivated Center of the Universe, this time focusing on people. Her son wasn't within range, but he was still in his hiding place and had to watch as his mother was suddenly pulled backward toward me.

"What are you doing? Are you even allowed to arrest her like this?" Jon asked as I grabbed her and deactivated the skill. She struggled against my grip, but she was still only human, and my strength *had* risen quite a bit.

"She fired a gun at me; if that's not worth at least a night in detention, I don't know what is. Besides, at best she's simply married into a crime family somehow, but at worst . . . I don't know . . . I have this feeling that she knows something. I can't just let her get away," I explained as I held her in place. She bucked wildly, shouting obscenities as I heard the clattering of new footsteps rushing up and onto the yacht. I turned my head to the side and yelled as loudly as I could. "In here! I need some cuffs!"

"My hubby's gonna kill you for this!" Giada snarled, only stopping her frantic attempts at escape when her son started to descend the staircase. "Oh, Oswald! No, you need to run!"

"Mommy? What's going on?" the boy whimpered. I wasn't sure what I was expecting, given everything I had learned so far, but I highlighted the boy, wondering if it would give me any details on him. Unfortunately, it sent back the same **[Unknown]** error, and it left me feeling off kilter as I heard people rushing into the room.

"Oswald, please run, don't look!" Giada cried out, and my stomach turned.

I looked back, confirming it was the police and not just some other men I had happened to miss, and freed a hand to wave them forward. I couldn't make out Lt. Nester among the group, but the officers reacted and rushed forward as I turned to show the woman trying to escape from my grasp.

"Whoa there, Loophole, I thought you guys only dealt with the Augment threats," one of the officers, a lanky Hispanic man with a badge that read "Mendez," said. Even with his doubt, however, he didn't hesitate to pull out a pair of cuffs and approach Giada. Another pair of officers rushed forward and blocked us from Oswald while one knelt to speak with him.

"Yeah, that's what I thought too," I said, turning my attention back to the officer. I held a still struggling Giada in place as Mendez secured the cuffs onto her wrists and took control of her from me. He began reading her her rights while another few cops stepped forward, each taking in the scene and moving to the downed grunts to get them each cuffed as well. "Where do you end up taking all these guys, anyway?"

"The bikers? We got a special place upstate we ship them all off to; you Augments bust so many of them we'd be filling the prisons to capacity if we tried to stuff all of them in there," Mendez explained while a few officers tried to block the sight of his mother in handcuffs from Oswald.

"What about her? She pulled a gun on me, and she *says* she's married to Salvatore Travisi; I've fought him a couple of times now. The dude always looks like a giant snake-man, so you can't really miss him. I'd like to be able to come in and question her if that's possible . . . You know, when she's behind a bit of glass," I told him. Giada had started to calm down, though her head still whipped back in my direction once I made my intentions clear.

"I ain't got nothin' to say to you," she spat. "I want my attorney; this is unlawful entry—he's not allowed to come in here!"

"U.S. Code AUG-1103: An Augment deputized by the local police force is allowed to enter any domicile their advanced sources deem to be involved in illegal activity. If you don't like it, write your congressman . . . And you know . . . maybe don't house over a dozen of the gang members that have been distributing drugs all over the neighborhood," Mendez responded almost robotically, and I highlighted him out of curiosity. Sure enough, he was marked as a *Non-Sapient* NPC.

He turned his attention back to me with a smile. "I'll have Lieutenant Nester contact you with the info you need to get a sit down with Mrs. Travisi once she's been processed. You got anything else while I'm here?"

I thought about it for a second, eyeing the stack of notifications I still had to open, but waved them away for the moment. I wasn't necessarily expecting to level up again just yet, but I felt like I had to be getting close. To that end, I let him know about the Bronze den around the corner and that I was planning to hit it after I left the yacht, and then gave Giada a sympathetic look.

There was so much more to her than she was telling me, and I needed to understand how she'd ended up married to a Non-Sapient NPC. Not just a random officer or shopkeeper either, but one who was directly involved in illegal activity.

"I'm sorry about your home, but I think there's something going on here, and I intend to get to the bottom of it," I told her before she spat at my feet again.

"Oh, you're gonna be sorry! Just you wait till Sal hears about what you've done to me! He's gonna devour your entrails! He's gonna string you up over—"

"Mrs. Travisi . . . I'd like to remind you that you have the right to remain silent. I *highly* suggest you exercise that right before we have to send you upstate with your security detail," Mendez interrupted before he pulled her away from me, shooting me a tired look while Giada grumbled. The other officers had already collected the grunts, some having to be pulled out on actual gurneys, and I started to look around the room.

"Angie, what the actual hell? I'm not asking about her specifically, since you'll just say you can't talk about her, but what the hell?! Why is a Non-Sapient NPC married to a real person?" I demanded once the room had been mostly cleared. The officers weren't fully leaving the scene just yet, but they were giving me space to investigate.

"Non-Sapient NPCs, especially ones who are deployed to major cities instead of locations like Sanctuary Square, often find themselves embroiled in that real world. If they didn't behave like real people, it would kinda give away the whole thing, don't you think, Loophole?"

"I mean . . . I guess, but still, look at what it's done . . . And a kid? Like how the hell are these guys created? Are they actually designed to reproduce?! Isn't that going too far?" I asked as I wandered over by the television, looking toward the few photos that hadn't been within my zone when I used Center of the Universe. *"Is this yacht even stolen? They went through a lot of trouble putting up pictures of themselves and making it feel like an actual home . . . you know . . . if you don't mind all the random thugs in leather vests walking around."*

"I took a look at some cameras in the area and found the ship's registration number while you were talking down Giada. Once I had that it was pretty easy to figure out that they either stole this thing or . . . who knows, maybe they are actually renting it? You'd be surprised by the things that are in public records. This ship is registered to someone named Andrew Merens, definitely not a Salvatore Travisi, but it's been available to rent through multiple different party and houseboat rental sites," Jon explained as I looked closer at a photo of Giada holding a baby.

There was a man with dark hair and a goatee standing next to her sporting a wide, friendly smile on his face, pointing at his son as if the boy were his pride and joy.

"I guess I have never seen what Sal looks like when he's not mostly a snake," I noted, taking a look around the room again, now a mess after my rapid changes in gravity. *"I just don't get it . . . if she's Sapient, how did she get wrapped up in all of this . . ."*

"Hey, Angie, what happens when a player chooses to go Miscreant early on? Do they have to fight bikers or something like this for control over their first territory?" Jon asked, almost out of nowhere.

"Finally! Hell, I tried to bait Loophole into asking about it yesterday, and he didn't even try to figure it out," Angie groaned.

"Hey, I was in the middle of dealing with my first den and all of the bullshit with Hydramental's attitude," I shot back as I looked in the stairwell. I could have headed upstairs, but I was curious as to why Giada had tried to get her son to run downstairs. Following the steps down, being careful to step over the blood left by the now removed grunt, I made my way to the lower levels. *"I mean, it would be helpful if just once you'd offer useful information when you know I need it instead of trying to make it some sort of game."*

"It is *a game, Loophole. You can lead a horse to the damn water, but apparently, it's not that easy to make it swim."*

"I don't think that's the saying," Jon commented before Angie could continue.

"Not the point! I've told Loophole over and over, if he wants to know something, you HAVE to ask. That's the rule, Loophole. Why is that so hard for you to remember?!"

"Maybe if you didn't make me jump through hoops even when I did ask questions, I wouldn't be so damn hesitant," I shot back, slightly annoyed.

"Let's cool it down, guys," Jon jumped in before we could argue any further. *"Angie, please. How do they do it?"*

"Of course, Codex, I'd be happy to. While Guardians only have the option to eliminate and arrest the offending gang members to fully claim their territory, Miscreants actually have two options," Angie explained happily, the annoyance in her own tone completely gone. *"They can go scorched earth and eliminate them all, or they can take control of the force. This provides them with a ready stream of henchmen to further their goals and a way to quickly recruit more as they need them."*

"That's . . . huh . . ." I said and thought about it for a few moments as I entered a large, open space. Though the back had a door that opened to the lowest outer deck, this room was practically an armory, and there were still a few officers within the space, cataloging and taking pictures. There were lockers lining the sides of the walls, and in the direct center of the room, there was an opening . . . right into the water. Floating in the internal pool was a small submersible tethered in place. *"Huh . . . so she did have an escape plan . . ."*

"Yeah . . . If they are renting this place, the owner has to know about this . . . right?" Jon asked. With the police still combing the area, something they generally didn't do if there was something that the game intended for me to find, I decided to

head back upstairs and see if there was anything on the third deck instead. *"Angie, when they take over a group, do they get to . . . I don't know, alter their henchmen to be more . . . I guess . . . thematically accurate?"*

"Oooh, good question, Codex, gold star! So yes, they are given a suite of controls which allow them to give them whatever flavor they would like. I maintain that I don't think *that should include things like providing NPCs with Temporary Augmentation Serums; that one is still very new, but Axio did say he was experimenting with things during this year's Wave, so that* could *be a byproduct.*

"I can't necessarily say what their suite includes at this point, since you didn't go Miscreant, so all of that is pure speculation, mind you," Angie explained, rattling it off rather quickly. *"Now, their influence over those groups has to be slowly spread, but a Miscreant who has enough initiative could find himself in control of a group of NPC minions who span multiple neighborhoods, thus giving them control of larger and larger territories. Of course, this all assumes they want to go that route to seize control as opposed to just using brute force to strike fear into the populace."*

"Okay, what does any *of this have to do with Giada, and more importantly, Sal?"* I asked as I found my way up to the third deck. It was a long hallway with only three doors. Two of them were wide open, and I could see a bed in the one at the far end. *"Even if he* was *a Miscreant instead of a Non-Sapient, he's my level, and the bikers have been here since I first woke back up. Giada said Sal fell in with the bikers three years ago, wouldn't that make him . . . what, Eighth Wave? He'd have to be a way higher level at this point if he survived so far."*

"I think that would make him Seventh Wave, if she's saying exactly *three years ago, but that's a semantics sort of thing. You're definitely right, though—either of those Waves would* be higher leveled than you,*"* Jon confirmed, and I felt myself stop in place while walking up the hallway as a sudden realization hit me.

"Hmm . . . I think Silver said he's from the Seventh Wave . . . Let me send him a message really quick," I said and opened my Friends List.

<**Loophole:** Hey Silver, we got sidetracked at the bar last night by Pinky. I brought up a guy called SnakeBite, and I thought you mentioned having heard that name before. Any chance it does ring a bell?>

"Let me know what he says; it doesn't seem like it shows me what you're sending in those messages. You think he actually knows something? Hell, why wouldn't he have just told you about how it all works when you were talking to him?" Jon asked. I hadn't actually been sure if he would be able to see my messages or not, but having that small bit of privacy felt oddly comforting.

"Honestly, knowing him, I'd bet he just eliminated all of them. Silver doesn't really seem like a 'henchmen' kinda guy. I could be wrong, but he didn't really give me that vibe, if that makes sense. But he's a people person, so I'm hoping he just happens to know anything that we could use,*"* I said as I looked into the first room, finding what was clearly a kid's bedroom, complete with a mess of toys littering the ground.

I only spent a few minutes in the child's room before I turned and made my way over to the other open door. I wasn't necessarily expecting a quick reply, but my message box refocused in my vision only a few moments after I left Oswald's room.

<Silver: Hey bud, sorry, I'm just rollin' outta the hay here, had a late night. So, I remember there being someone with 'Snake' in their name who had been running his mouth about catching the interest of some big First Waver, but he up and vanished like, six months in. Couldn't say for sure if his name had 'bite' in it; hell, I have a Snake Eyes *and* a Snakecharmer on my Friends List. 'Snake' seems like a popular word to throw around for some reason. Personally, I don't get it, but given how dumb some people think my name is, I can't really judge them too much.>

<Loophole: Okay, thanks. I'm not even sure what I'm looking for here but wanted to follow up. I owe you a drink for the help later on if yah want to meet up at The Common Ground.>

<Silver: Ain't gotta offer me a free drink twice. I'll hitcha up later.>

"He is a really weird dude for being a Miscreant," I muttered, briefly looking into the other bedroom before turning my attention to the last room. Unlike the first two, this one *was* closed and locked as well. There wasn't an immediate key anywhere, and with Giada now in custody, I didn't want to go down and ask if she had it hidden on her either. But my stamina *had* recovered quite a bit as I had taken the time to look around.

With a quick jab, I threw a Gravity Punch with just ten percent of my stamina that busted the door wide open.

[New Achievement! Lock Picker!]
Well, that's certainly one way to get by that pesky lock, although I really think you're doing more damage to this place than you needed to. Anyway, I'll keep this brief, since I'm way more interested with all this Sal business right now. You used your powers to break through a locked door. If you had been unlucky enough to encounter a locked door before now, I bet you'd have already received this achievement, but oh well, here we are.
Wood-Level Achievement.
Reward: *You have received a D-tier Loot Box!*

I didn't know what I was expecting, but a rather professional-looking office *wasn't* it. There were more pictures and even some glass and gold awards on a large cabinet/bookshelf combo on the far wall. Practically all of the photos included the man that I presumed to be Sal. Graduating from college, playing basketball at a local court, and more than a few photos of him in his leather vest, sitting atop a sleek, pastel-blue bike.

I expected those last ones, given the collection of other photos and his presumed affiliation, but what I wasn't expecting were the pictures of a pair of younger boys. There were half a dozen framed photos of this pair, one of them sporting the same dark-black hair that Sal had. One showed them playing in the fall leaves, another had them dressed in matching wrestling gear in a school gym. But the final picture in the collection was the one that had stopped me in my tracks and was probably the most recent photo of the pair of boys.

Sal was dressed, clearly in Augment-like attire, with a sleek black mask and a huge smile spread over his face. He had an arm thrown over his younger brother, unfortunately caught shooting his brother a look that I felt should have precluded this picture from ever getting framed. The boy was younger, maybe sixteen or seventeen in the picture, but there was something about him that felt insanely familiar.

I wasn't sure if I actually did recognize him or not, but I *also* knew exactly what feature my own mask had. While I had met a few other Augments already, there were only a few I had spent more than a few minutes interacting with. After staring at the photo for maybe too long, I finally vocalized the suspicion that was quickly growing.

"Is that . . . Hydramental?"

CHAPTER THIRTY-SIX

Although I wanted to try to wrangle some answers out of Hydramental, his stubborn refusal to add me to his Friends List meant the only way I could do so would be by storming down to Chelsea and hunting him down. While his possible involvement with all this raised just so, so many questions, there really didn't seem to be any immediate benefit that would come from rushing down there to confront him.

I walked—or, I guess . . . flew . . . away from the first den, adding seven hundred and fifty Phase Points to my total. Since the den was Silver ranked, Basebreaker alone netted me five hundred points, and I surprisingly received points for not one but two Non-Sapient Augment Kills. Even though the grunt hadn't fully transformed, the serum he had injected made him count anyway. Between the level-six Luca and the level-four grunt, the total gain was worth two hundred and fifty points.

With it pretty much only a stone's throw away, I swooped into the Bronze den on the far side of the park. My new Revolver bar had already proven its efficiency, and I rather quickly cleared out the few grunts who had been left to defend the place. Although I probably could have driven the fight into the streets to get an audience, I still had a natural instinct to keep fights as far away from Sapient NPCs as possible. With the Bronze den cleared out, I added an extra two hundred and fifty points to my total before I found my way back to the top of the building I had spotted the yacht from.

With Jon in the Command Room, I didn't need to pull out the physical map I had looted, especially given that the map I had only had the dens' locations noted on it, whereas Jon got a bit more information than I did. Of the remaining eight dens I still had showing on the map, four were marked as Bronze, three were Silver, and one of them was Gold. Jon did a bit more digging and discovered that there were apparently three levels of dens higher than Gold still, but Angie insisted that those often didn't show up in an Augment's path until they had brought their level into at least the twenties.

I took a seat on the edge of the roof, letting my feet dangle over as I took in the now midmorning breeze. Although he was quick to give me the information on the dens, Jon had been relatively quiet while I tackled the den itself. I didn't necessarily need to banter with him while I fought, but his silence had still been noticeable, nonetheless.

"Okay, so I've been looking into it here, searching through some of the forums and Augment watch pages, and I can't find anything on SnakeBite. If multiple people hadn't already said the name, I'd wonder if it was fake; hell, I'm still sorta wondering that," Jon said with a frustrated sigh. *"I even did some digging on Salvatore Travisi, and it's pretty much the same. There are a few profiles out there, but none that look like the photos you saw on the ship."*

"Hmm, well, the dude is *into criminal stuff now; it kinda makes sense to scrub his online presence if that's the case. It doesn't explain why you can't find anything on SnakeBite if he* was *an Augment . . . Wait, Angie, I could theoretically change my registered name if I wanted to, right?"* I asked as I pulled the pack of gum out of my pocket and took a piece.

"Of course! Granted, unless you simultaneously change your costume, it might be hard to rename yourself in the eyes of the public community," Angie answered. *"I'm still surprised no one has tried to call you Poophole yet. Am I not as funny as I think I am?"*

"You're nowhere close to being as funny as you think you are," I replied as I looked at the bustling city. Angie let out a huff of frustration that I ignored. *"I wonder if SnakeBite went by a different name when he started. It couldn't be that hard to check if Hydramental is the only Augment who's been associated with Chelsea, right?"*

"Nah, that should be pretty easy to check. Let me take a quick look," Jon said. It took a few moments where I assumed he must have been searching before he actually spoke. *"I'm not seeing anything concrete or immediate, though if I were trying to line up the dates he would have been starting up, it's almost like a weird* lack *of news. It's almost like* anything *associated with Sal has been scrubbed from the internet.*

"You might have been on the nose about needing to talk to Giada. Hydramental would be good too, but from the way you've talked about him, I have to assume he's got a major stick up his ass about whatever happened with his brother. Again, that's assuming that that was *him in the photo. It was a younger dude, how are you sure it was him?"*

I thought about it for a moment, starting to chew the gum as I pushed off the ledge and activated Personal Gravity Laws. Just the ability to float so freely was a feeling that I was quickly finding comfort in, the weightlessness seeming to ease the tension in my body.

"Stick with me here. Do you remember what it felt like when you looked at me in my equipment before you had it fully confirmed?" I asked as I slowly moved across the sky, almost like I was literally walking on air.

"Yeah, it was that feature on your mask, right? The amount of control that Axio has even on those of us without *Augmentation is kinda freaky the more I think about it. Like, pretty much until right before you confirmed my suspicion, that blurriness that came with the mask left me with this insanely intense feeling that I was completely*

wrong. I was really only positive enough to actually say something about it when you just trusted me to follow up on your mute ability," Jon said, and I could practically hear him tapping at his chin. *"What's that got to do with Hydramental, though? The dude in the photo wasn't wearing a mask."*

"It was just . . . I don't know . . . I haven't actually been on the other side of the . . . well, mask, but I sorta feel like it's probably the same feeling? Maybe it's because I met Hydramental in costume first, but when I looked at that photo, it was like I had this uneasy feeling that I'd met him somewhere before," I explained, flipping myself as I floated above the park and looked down toward it. The blood didn't rush to my head as I hung there, which I had to assume was a side effect of my Personal Gravity Laws.

I continued. *"I don't know, it's a hunch based on limited information, I'll give you that. Maybe that's why I'm not in such a big hurry to go flying down there to confront him. Well, that and I don't even know what I'd say . . . Like, how the hell do you approach someone you've only met once and go, 'Hey, dude, remember that snake dude we fought? Yeah, so was that your brother, or some sort of resurrected version of him? I know, I know, suuuuuper weird question; I just saw a picture of you with him back before . . .'"*

"Huh? What's up?" Jon asked when I suddenly trailed off in thought.

"Hydramental was in a picture with his masked *brother . . . before he himself got involved in the game,"* I said, looking around the park as I put together the myriad of details I had learned over the last few days. I could see a few people had noticed my presence and were pointing up, signaling for others to look as well. I waved at them with a smile on my face, performing a small flip in the air before returning to an upside-down lounge, eliciting cheers from the smaller children, simply excited to see someone doing something super. *"I wonder if SnakeBite broke the Secret Identity Protocol . . ."*

"Ooooh, yeah, that wouldn't be a good thing to do," Angie chirped. *"You've been lucky enough to avoid having to deal with the Threats so far, but they can be nasty things to deal with. Those Minor ones last night probably weren't a big deal, but anything higher? That would be bad . . ."*

"You know, given how I got brought into this, I guess I hadn't thought enough about the rule to look it up. Doesn't it just suppress you before you can say something?" Jon asked.

"No, that was what happened when I tried to mention the game aspect of it all. The Secret Identity Protocol just puts in place consequences if you actively tell someone who you are," I explained.

I was a bit surprised that he *hadn't* looked it up, especially given the fact that Angie had already warned him about sharing information with online communities. Although in hindsight, that may have been in regard to the actual game and not just Augments; I hadn't actually taken the time to probe too far into what Jon had learned from her on his own.

"Huh, isn't that kinda weird, though? Like, what's the point of the rule if you don't get punished or have anything negative happen if someone discovers your identity on their own?" Jon asked while I navigated my way toward another roof as my stamina ticked under fifty percent. Just as I set myself down, a notification window popped open.

[Personal Gravity Laws!]
This ability has increased to Level 2.
The base-level stamina drain for this ability has been
reduced to 4.75 stamina per second of use.
This ability has not been Augmented.

While the speed in which the ability had leveled up compared to my other skills felt rather fast, I had been using it far more continuously than the others, so it made a bit of sense. I could have easily gotten distracted by this and tried to probe Angie for information, but Jon had actually raised a good point.

"I suppose it is kinda weird when you say it like that. I guess I just saw it as a sort of loophole in the system." A laugh escaped me. *"Hell, it was kinda where the name came from in the first place."*

"Perfectly formed jokes about your name aside, the connection between it and your powerset has always been a stretch at best," Angie said.

"I just don't get the point of having a rule like that if there's a way to so easily exploit it," Jon wondered aloud. I bit my tongue as I scanned the horizon. I briefly thought I could see a speck flying far to the northeast, but it vanished just as quickly as I spotted it.

Axio was only stopping Angie from hearing my internal thoughts on his comments to me, but he hadn't necessarily said there would be a suppression effect if I *did* bring it up. I was tempted to try, but Axio's implication that there was someone *else* who could be listening was still stuck in my head. The worst part about it was that it felt like a catch-22.

While my gut was telling me that he wasn't, Axio certainly *could* have been lying just to keep me from saying something for whatever reason he could think of, but I wouldn't know for sure unless I *did* say something. And even then, that would only be if there was some sort of immediate reaction to my revelation. Hell, even if there was a reaction, it *could* just be something Axio himself deployed.

Simply put, there really were just too many factors to consider. With the mystery of Sal still at hand, I didn't think it was prudent to get sidetracked on things that seemed leagues out of our control. And if Axio's plotting and tinkering behind the scenes was anything, it was definitely leagues out of my control.

"Okay, let's work on the theory that SnakeBite broke the rule instead of Hydramental figuring it out . . . Angie, would Axio utilize Augments who have died to . . . I don't know, clone NPCs? We've never really gotten into how they are made . . . grown . . . Look,

I just have a lot of questions, especially given that Giada back there thinks that the current Sal is her husband. Can you tell us all the information that you're allowed to give me on the Non-Sapients' . . . production, I guess?" I asked as I walked over the empty rooftop, letting my stamina slowly rise back to the top.

"Okay, that is quite a lot, but let me try to explain it in the most logical order. To head off one of the first questions I'm sure you will want to ask: the original source of this technology comes from a classified location, and I am not able to provide information on that. However, the actual process itself has not been deemed classified, as it is often expected for Guardian-coded Augments to find spawning locations to shut down.

"While the overall process is rather complex and I don't believe you have the necessary knowledge to fully comprehend, I can give you a generalized explanation that should satisfy your question," Angie said before she cleared her nonexistent throat. *"Non-Sapient NPCs are vat grown, combining dead tissue and biomass into full-size human forms over the course of a few days, depending on the variety that is needed. The NPCs capable of being Augmented require more genetic material than the run-of-the-mill NPCs used as cannon fodder, as well as additional neurological inlays.*

"As I've mentioned, those Augmentation Serums we have been seeing are new, so it's possible the growing process for the simpler models hasn't been adjusted to allow them to access those injections safely. To the best of my knowledge bases, NPCs are not generally cloned from preexisting humans, though no formal rule about it has ever been established within the databases that I have access to."

"Sheesh . . . I get I shouldn't be surprised by the technology existing or anything, especially with all the Augments running around, but it's still almost creepy to think that these folks are just . . . among us, and are essentially little more than puppets," Jon said. I was surprised to hear him sounding less enthused than normal.

"You know, it's kinda nice hearing you not immediately geek out about at least a part *of this craziness. I was almost starting to think you were going full supervillain when you got excited about the prospect of* kaijus *destroying a city,"* I said with a laugh. I thought about it for a moment then decided to add, *"Thank you, Angie. I appreciate the rundown."*

"That is my job!" Angie chirped back, clearly pleased with herself before her tone turned. *"If I may offer an opinion on this situation, though."*

"You? Offering up something freely?" I asked, trying not to sound too incredulous. *"Color me both surprised and skeptical. Okay, let's hear it and the bad punch line that comes with it."*

"I believe you two may be jumping to conclusions," she said rather flatly.

"How so?" Jon asked.

"Well, leaving aside that—as you've pointed out, Codex—Hydramental's involvement is only suspected at best, your assumptions so far are based on your own limited knowledge. I was not given the time to fully explain on the yacht, but when a Miscreant takes control of a local NPC contingent, they are given access to a suite of controls which allows them to control the flavor and type of NPCs that their gang will provide.

"This includes fine control over the powersets available for the Augmented NPC henchmen that come with those contingents. They are even able to customize the names of their men, as long-term observation has proven some Augments are more prone to theatricality than others."

"So . . . you think this is just a major coincidence? The real Sal is actually hiding out somewhere and has an NPC with his name and powerset just roaming around?" I asked as I looked over the edge of the roof. My gut still twisted when I looked down while my flying ability wasn't activated, so I averted my eyes quickly.

"I'm just pointing out it's the most logical answer, given the scope of normal Miscreant/ NPC relations. I'd also like to point out you are only assuming SnakeBite and the Sal you have fought so far have the same powerset," Angie explained.

"She brings up a good point. Salvatore isn't exactly a common name, but it's not like it's super rare either, especially in New York," Jon jumped in. *"Plus, she's right. I wasn't here when you dealt with Hydramental, so we are really trusting that your hunch about the dude in the photo is right. But unless you saw Sal before he transformed, we can't even be sure if the Augment in the photo is the same dude."*

"Maybe . . ." I trailed off. Maybe I didn't want to admit they were right, but Angie's explanation felt *too* neat, and it didn't explain everything either. I shook my arms out and cracked my head to the side as I tried to refocus myself. They were right; we really were getting into the weeds of things.

"This is probably more of a mystery than we can figure out in a morning . . . I guess all we can really do is keep knocking out the points to push me over ten thousand, then we can focus on this bigger mystery. Hell, with eight more dens, maybe I'll find some more clues.

"I have a notebook I scooped up after fighting Sal the first time, plus this burner phone I managed to snag in the fight before you got dragged into all of this. I haven't really taken the time to investigate either of them with everything going on. We can probably drop it all for now until we have at least a bit more to go on."

"I'd say that is a very prudent way to go about it. Mysteries are all well and good, but I'd rather you not twiddle your thumbs just because you've happened to make good progress on getting to the ten thousand required points," Angie said.

"Hell, if he takes care of all the Bronze and Silver dens, just from Basebreaker gains he'd cross the line; I think that alone makes that course of action the best laid plan," Jon added, then I heard him let out a loud yawn. *"Okay, Angie, I know he has the map, but it's not like he's gonna fly around with it out. If I give you the addresses to the four remaining Bronze dens, can you please* properly *relay them to Loophole here without sending him running in circles for the rest of the morning? Even though I* want *to throw myself fully into this, I do still have to finish the wiring job for Mr. Greyson, since that'll cover our rent for two months. I can't exactly back out of that commitment now."*

"Well, if you're going to ask so nicely, I suppose I certainly could do that for you, Codex. Plus, I have to admire just how responsible you are," Angie responded with a

purr before she suddenly started to giggle. *"I mean, it* would *be funny to send him running in circles, but that wouldn't necessarily be prudent for the time being."*

"Okay, good," Jon replied. *"I think you should probably hit level seven by the time you get through at least a few of those dens. I'm not seeing a 'Level Up Imminent' message, but I have to assume it's coming soon. Once you do, shoot me a text and meet me back here. It's just your stat points, but we should be able to unlock your Refractions book, and I really want to see what that's going to do once you absorb it. Sound like a plan?"*

"Yeah, that sounds like as good a plan as any," I confirmed, pushing off the ledge and starting to float again.

"Good . . . and if you do happen to discover anything else that is like, obviously pressing, shoot me a text that says something like 'CR now' and I'll know to get back to the Command Room, okay? Now I gotta run. Later, man," he rattled off quickly. Before I could even fully tell him "Later" in return, I heard a door close, and a new message appeared.

[Codex has left the Command Room. Communication has been lost.]

"Okay, Angie looks like it's just you and me again," I said as I turned and looked over the rest of my neighborhood.

"I'd say just like old times, but it's barely been twenty-four hours since it was just you and I." She giggled. *"Should I start with further comments about how attractive I think Codex is, or should we go with the old classics and I just make fun of everything you're doing?"*

"How about you just tell me where the closest of these dens are?" I suggested. She sighed.

"Fiiiiine, don't be fazed by my jokes; that's not annoying to me at all . . . There's one three blocks to the east on Eighth Avenue, just on the edge of the neighborhood. If you head on over, I'll highlight the correct building for you when you are within range."

"Trust me, Angie, at this point, I get plenty fazed when you are *just helpful,"* I said, orienting myself and then taking off, quickly hurtling toward the east.

CHAPTER THIRTY-SEVEN

<**To Jon:** Heading back to the apartment now. There in 5.>

I had just finished taking down the third Bronze den remaining when the level-up notification appeared, and I was quick to text the alert back to Jon. He just as quickly responded with a thumbs-up but nothing else.

I had pretty much hit the ground running on the first of the remaining Bronze dens, doing what I could to make sure that none of my enemies had time to react, and refining my assault strategy with each new den. And the strategy had paid off. It was barely noon as I looked down at the mess of knocked-out grunts that littered the floor of the dilapidated apartment building's lobby.

I went through my process of looting them, gathering a few random weapons and another good haul of credits to add to an already decent morning. My B.E.L.T.'s currency display showed I was sitting at just over twenty-two thousand credits between the looted bodies and rewards from the Tenth Precinct.

Once I was sure I hadn't missed anything, the Bronze dens so far having literally nothing of interest even with more thorough searches, I pushed the front door of the building open and ushered the waiting police officers in. It was another slew of random faces, but I acknowledged that they had taken control of the scene. Although no one had gotten into the den to actually see the fight, a surprisingly large crowd had gathered behind the police line and gave me a huge cheer as I emerged.

Although I was certainly starting to take to the fights that came with being an Augment, the sudden swell of people still left me feeling a bit uneasy. I could hear cries of "We love you, Loophole!" and "Yeah, get those punks out of our neighborhood!" and I acknowledged them with as friendly of a smile as I could muster before I launched myself upward into the sky and away from the crowd.

"One of these days, I'll get used to being up close with crowds like that, but this is not that moment," I muttered to myself as I looked back down at the gathering crowd, each pulling out their phones to point toward me.

"Nah, stay awkward, Loophole; it makes your interactions with others far more hilarious to me."

I rolled my eyes before putting on the speed, whipping up and over the buildings.

Although I *didn't* have a map of the area, and it was certainly *a lot* harder to navigate from above without street signs to guide me, I had at least made it a point of *really* memorizing what the roof of my building looked like before that first flight. Even then, I had to circle once before I set myself down, making sure the nearby buildings didn't look like carbon copies.

I shook my arms out and disabled my gear before I walked toward the entrance to the stairwell, not wanting to raise any questions just in case there was anyone else on the stairs. I eyed the slew of remaining notifications that had piled up and cracked my neck to the side as I opened the door. I had to climb down four flights of stairs, so it wasn't a bad time to let the notifications run through.

[Phase Points Gained!]
Basebreaker!
You've disrupted an enemy base within a territory you have an active claim on.
Value equal to Base's Rank (Bronze equals one, Silver equals two, etc.) times 250.
Total Value: *250 points.*

Rising Fame (NEW)!
Your reputation has risen in rank!
This gain has a static value.
Total Value: *350 points.*

[Reputation Increased!]
You have gone from **Unknown Vigilante** *to* **Local Hero***.*
You are now eligible to claim Small Town and equivalent-size territories.

"Hey, Angie, how many reputation ranks are there?" I asked as the window faded and a stack of abilities that had each leveled up came up next.

"There are ten ranks that scale with the ten levels of territories. There are some exceptions to the necessary reputation requirements, of course, but generally speaking, if you want to claim a larger territory, you've gotta be more famous. As I mentioned previously, the Community District that Hell's Kitchen is included in would count as equivalent to a Small Town. Though I'm sure locals would disagree with our categorization of the area as 'small,' it is simply semantics that help to keep things rather streamlined."

"Makes as much sense as anything," I said as I awkwardly nodded at an older woman passing by me. I let the ability screens appear and fade one at a time, actually a bit surprised that I had leveled more than one following that last den.

[Super Luck!]
This power has increased to Level 2.

Luck within your Local Area is now subtly affected by .2 percent for every 1 point of Luck that you have.

[Gravity Punch!]
This ability has increased to Level 2.
Every 5 percent of your stamina put into this skill now deals an additional 60 percent damage up to a maximum of 600 percent increased damage.
This ability has not been Augmented.

[Center of the Universe!]
This ability has increased to Level 2.
Initial pull rate increased to 6 meters per second with the strength diminishing by .75 meters per second for every 5 feet from the center of your Local Area the affected targets are.
This ability has not been Augmented.

[Float like a Butterfly!]
This ability has increased to Level 3.
The duration of this skill has increased from 15 seconds to 20 seconds.
This ability has not been Augmented.

[Sting like a Bee!]
This ability has increased to Level 3.
Successful strikes now impart 35 percent increased damage.
*This ability has been Augmented **1 of 3** times.*
Current Augmentations: *Time Adjustment.*

Like with my flight ability, both Gravity Punch and Center of the Universe were quickly finding a lot of use. Their low to no cooldowns made them easy to use in rapid succession, which made them leveling up more expected than not. I might have been surprised about Super Luck, but given it had just been working its magic for me in the background, I felt more relieved that it *had* finally ticked over. As for the other two, well, they had always been key moves in my set, so I wasn't at all surprised to see them moving up.

It was the final notification that part of me knew I should be feeling nervous about, yet the nerves never seemed to come.

[Threat Level Increased!]
Your rapid assault on the Vipers biker gang has caused you to become seen as a greater threat to their goals, and they have increased their activity within your territory. There will be a heightened difficulty Crime Alert within Hell's Kitchen deployed within the next 2 hours.

Due to the increased range granted to you by your Movement Ability, you will now be notified of Crime Alerts that happen anywhere within Hell's Kitchen.

"Yo!" Jon greeted, his voice coming out garbled as I pushed the door open. He was huddled over the kitchen table, shoving a sandwich into his mouth.

"Did you see that notification?" I asked, and he shook his head before swallowing.

"Nah, unless Angie reads it out while I'm in the Command Room or you're inside of the Safe House, I don't get to hear it. Even then, I only see the notifications if I'm actively looking at the screen I have for your P.O.V. Gonna guess you dinged from the dens? How many did you get through?"

"Just crossed over to seven, actually, but it seems like the bikers don't like how busy I've been. I cleared three of the Bronze dens, and now there's apparently gonna be a harder Crime Alert coming soon," I explained as I walked over to the kitchen to grab a drink from the fridge. "The alert popped up just before I got here."

"Ahhh, well nope, didn't see that one. I wasn't sure if you were gonna bother to slow down, so I was planning on bothering you so that we could refresh your **[Well Fed]** buff, but yah texted me before I was able to get back to the apartment. If you did ding, then it's definitely good timing. We can get you fed and back out there before the alert hits." He nodded over to a wrapped sub on the other side of the table before he went in for another bite of his own.

"Cuban from Tio's?" I asked, and he nodded as my stomach growled in anticipation. I walked back over and grabbed a seat as I set my soda on the table. Although maybe I should be out there waiting for the alert to hit, getting my buff refreshed was *definitely* a necessity. "Okay, so am I still doing two into Luck? If so, should I just drop two into Intelligence to finish it off for the level? I'm gonna need it to be at ten to absorb the Quantum Shenanigans book."

Jon held up a finger for a minute, chewing down the large bite he had taken before reaching for his own soda to chase it down with.

"He's cute even when he doesn't realize there's mustard on his chin," Angie giggled, and Jon immediately reached for a napkin.

"I've been thinking about that . . . well, sorta. It's more that I've been thinking about how we are distributing your points. Obviously, you have plenty of skills that are still scaling with your Luck, and we want to keep increasing it, but I'm wondering if we are seeing diminishing returns by doing two points every single time. Maybe I'm trying to min-max you a bit too hard, I don't know for sure, and maybe I'm even wrong with my line of thinking here, but there's some stuff we hadn't considered when we first talked about point distribution."

"How so?" I asked, opening the soda and taking a long drink.

"Well, now that we know that your Strength not only increases how hard you hit but has a direct effect on your stamina, I think we need to make sure, at a minimum, we balance how you drop points between Luck and Strength," he said, then paused to take another drink before letting out a rather loud, refreshed sigh.

"As for Intelligence, you only need another point dropped into it to use Refractions for now. I'd say stick with a single point this time and then drop two in on the next level so that you can use it then instead of dropping in a point now for no inherent gain. Then the extra point this level can just go into Luck or Strength to double up. That one is sorta dealer's choice, but I'd say go with hitting harder.

"The main point would be to just alternate every level. One level we double up Luck, one level we double up Strength—at least until I have a better handle on how each of the stats will help you, if at all. It's honestly kinda a shame that there's no way for you to train these stat points without the level ups so far."

"Yeah, guess I never really thought about it too much . . . Been doing that way too much with all of this, but I think that's a side effect of the Acceptance Matrix . . . right, Angie?" I wondered as I tapped a finger against the side of the soda can.

"It is, yes. Again, the Matrix is designed to ensure new Augments stay focused on the tasks at hand and don't have panic attacks over the rapid change to their perspective of the world," she explained.

"Yeah, I think I'm glad I don't have one of those," Jon said with a raised brow. "Can't you disable it?"

I felt my stomach turn at the thought, and I shook my head. "I could, I think . . . but I kinda think I need it. Angie's right—it does kinda help me just stay in the zone."

"Huh . . . Well okay, if it works it works." He gave a shrug and took a bite before adding a slightly garbled, "Now get those points dropped."

"Yeah . . . Okay, I think I'll double Strength, then; it is lagging a bit behind my Luck. I suppose if I really wanted to unlock the Quantum book faster, I could run back to the Square and see if that belt was still in stock, though I imagine it got scooped up with that cooldown feature," I said as I distributed the points. Another notification quickly popped up as soon as the stat window vanished.

[Your Action Bars have expanded!]
All Bars on your Revolver now have an addi-
tional Activated **and** *Passive Ability slot.*

"Oh sweet, I wasn't expecting that for another few levels." I paused as I considered the newly empty slots. I only had three passive skills so far, so I added Misfire back to my bar for both Revolvers. Our training session the previous night had focused on abilities that I could really use to deal out some damage, but we hadn't really put much thought into passives, something we were probably going to want to revisit.

"Yeah, that definitely gives you a few more options. What else are you thinking about adding to the Fight Time bar? One of the other new ones?"

"Maybe," I said as I unwrapped the sandwich and took a minute to take a large bite. My **[Well Fed]** buff had expired, and I wasn't intending on staying in the Safe House for too long, so I wanted to get the buff refreshed before I headed out to the Silver dens.

After I swallowed that first perfect bite, I continued.

"Freeze is useful, but I think it's *really* situational, especially since the liquid has to be *unpackaged* for me to affect it. I only used it one more time after the yacht, and I really think I have to thank Misfortune Abound more than the frozen puddle for the enemy that got knocked out the second time. So I was debating swapping that one off; I'm just not quite sure what for. Earthbound Impact has a similar situational issue to it. It's not much help in most of the dens when the bikers aren't just hanging out on the back of a yacht, but given that I just got a message that there are gonna be some more Crime Alerts, it's probably a good idea to have a strong entrance."

"Well, how about you absorb *Refractions of Reality* and we see what it does to your abilities? Let me get to my seat real quick so I can watch it from my end." Jon stood up. "If it does something good, I could see Mirror Image falling onto your Fight Time bar, just as a good distraction midfight."

I materialized the book onto the table and quickly absorbed it, watching as the book dissolved in a flash of light just as quickly as it had shimmered into reality.

[Your Optical Refraction Knowledge has increased to Level 6.]

[Alert!]
Two of your abilities have evolved.
Please Note: *The evolution of these abilities will not remove the original, weaker ability from your Ability Catalog. Evolved abilities will have the option to transfer the original ability's Augmentations to it.*

"Oh shit, it wants to change both Mirror Image and Trick of the Light," Jon called out to me, and I stood up, carrying the half-eaten sandwich with me as I opened the first of the two screens.

Mirror Image *has evolved to:* **Fun House.**
Would you like to transfer Augmentation: **Recording** *to it?*

I thought about it for a moment, rereading the ability twice before Jon and I decided moving the Augmentation was probably for the best. Although this automatically took one of its three Augmentation slots, the sudden expansion of the effect of Mirror Image left me positive that I probably wouldn't be using the lesser version anytime soon.

[Fun House!]
Level 1 Activated Ability.
Creates 3 afterimages of yourself in randomized locations within your Local Area that will mirror your visible movements. You

may choose to turn invisible for up to 10 seconds when you acti-
vate this ability and leave a 4th afterimage in your place.
Cooldown: *10 minutes.*
Stamina Cost: *10 %*
*This ability has been Augmented **1 of 3** times.*
Current Augmentations: *Recording.*

Trick of the Light *has evolved to:* **Spectrum Veil.**
There are no Augmentations to transfer.

I pulled open the new skill, wondering how Trick of the Light could have even changed, and found myself pleasantly surprised as I went in to take another bite of my quickly dwindling lunch. I wasn't sure if the way my abilities were being generated was directly connected to my recent knowledge on the difference between Static and Flexible Cost skills, but I had things to do and knew Angie would probably just blame me for not asking earlier . . . Which wasn't exactly something I could argue with.

[Spectrum Veil!]
Level 1 Activated/Passive Ability.
Passive Effect: *Creates a permanent shimmer directly around your*
body, causing cameras and telescopic lenses to improperly focus on you.
This Passive effect can be disabled but must be reenabled manually.

Activated Effect: *Warp the light around your body, ren-*
dering you invisible to all visible waves of light.
The activated portion of this ability costs 50 stam-
ina per second to use and has no cooldown.

The activated portion of the skill was certainly costly, even with the increase to my stamina from the **[Well Fed]** buff that reappeared on my status bar as I finished my sandwich. But it was the added passive effect that made the ability even more curious.

"Why doesn't the passive part have a cost? It feels like it should have a cost, given that it's a persistent effect," Jon asked before I could get the question out myself.

"This is a side effect of having higher levels of knowledge! Some abilities, when evolved from others that you have initially created, will generate these secondary passive effects, and generally speaking, as long as the passive does not provide an immediate damaging effect, it will fall into this No Cost category.

"Additionally, some abilities when evolved, if they don't generate a passive effect, will have a chance to alter from having a percentage-based cost to a variable-based cost," she explained. *"I did say that there were benefits to higher-leveled knowledge, but given the*

somewhat unique flavor of Loophole's abilities, I couldn't disclose the information on the chance that your abilities and utilization of the knowledge operated differently."

"I feel like that's just you lying as a way to hide the fact that you willingly chose not to disclose everything when we were talking about this earlier . . ." I said, rolling my eyes.

"Whaaaaat, me? Nooo, I would never do—" she started, then her voice cut off briefly before a new window appeared.

[Crime Alert! Snake Rampage!]

*A few of the Viper-gang bikers in snake form have been spot-
ted rampaging their way down Ninth Avenue, calling your name
and claiming you lack the power to stop them. They were last seen
causing random destruction to vehicles crossing 35th street.
Stop them before they cross into Chelsea!*
Reward: *You will receive 10,000 credits and a Large
Reputation Boost for stopping their rampage. This reward will
be forfeited if any of them escape, and you will lose Reputation
Points equivalent to a Medium Reputation Boost.
You have* **10 minutes** *until they exit Hell's Kitchen.*

"Well, isn't that just convenient," I groaned as the timer started to tick down.

"Yeah, you're gonna need to get moving. You just ranked up; I'd be willing to bet letting them escape would just knock you back down, and I'd be willing to bet there's some sort of negative consequence for losing a reputation rank, isn't there, Angie?" Jon asked as he started to activate specific screens in the Command Room.

"That's correct, though not completely. Losing a reputation rank has a variable out-come, anywhere from a Minor Level Threat being deployed to your location or you ceding your claim to a territory you actively lose your rank within," Angie explained.

"Cool, guess I'm just wasting time standing around then," I said, clapping my hands together. I could certainly run for the roof, but they were nearly at the south-ernmost edge of Hell's Kitchen, and time mattered here.

I dropped Spectrum Veil into the newly formed slot on my ability bar then eyed the rest of my skills. If there were going to be multiple snakes, I didn't think I could reliably use Freeze with my remaining venom vials to distribute enough of the weakness. I could certainly try to mimic how I'd handled Luca, but if the snakes were spread far enough out, I'd end up wasting more than I wanted to use, and I didn't want to empty out my stock of the stuff either.

Luckily, I still had two guns soaked with venom, and dropped Fun House in Freeze's place on the bar. The ability showed the two preset recordings that I had made for Mirror Image were available, but it also included a "Mirror Visible Movements" option.

"Wait, where are you going?" Jon asked, looking over his shoulder as I walked toward the window that led to our fire escape.

"Roof will take too long," I replied, throwing the window open and activating my gear at the same time. "It could certainly burn a ton of stamina if I keep the veil activated for too long, but it'll at least get me clear of the building for a quick-burst use."

Before Jon could follow up or make me question my decision, I simultaneously activated Spectrum Veil and Personal Gravity Laws, launching myself up and away from the building. My stamina quickly started to drop, and I deactivated the veil once I was clear of the roof. Orienting myself to the south, I took off.

"I definitely think that should be an emergency exit only. That took out like, ten percent of your stamina in the blink of an eye there," Jon's voice echoed in my head for a moment as I floated my way across the neighborhood.

"You're not wrong, but I'm not risking letting them cross into Chelsea," I said, scanning the streets as I tried to find my way to Ninth. As I put on the speed, making quick work of cutting my way across the few blocks that separated me from the southern edge of the neighborhood, I quickly caught sight of the trail of destruction the pack had left.

"Um . . . Angie . . . that's way more than 'a few,'" I heard Jon say as I darted a hundred feet overhead of a group of at least a dozen snake-men. They were attacking cars at random, and a crowd of onlookers were fleeing in every direction. For what it was worth, it didn't seem like the snakes were making it a point of trying to chase after the fleeing civilians, but any and all property that got in their way was met with vicious strikes and attacks, leaving destruction in their wake.

I turned toward the sky and flew up higher—wanting to make sure I would hit the maximum strength on my Earthbound Impact—when a sudden large flash of icy blue materialized both directly behind and in front of the line of snake-men slithering their way south along the road. Large ice walls had covered the entirety of the street on either side of them, locking them between two large buildings as the gang whipped their heads around.

I mimicked them, looking for the source before I spotted what looked like a speck of a person wearing blue on either edge of the road, just inside the ice walls. One of them suddenly shimmered, their outfit changing to a bright yellow color, and a sudden flash of electricity went flying from the source. I followed the light-ning to the gang and saw the tightly packed snakes all seem to seize from the current jumping from one to the other. They were being held in place, but it didn't look like they were going down.

A part of me knew there was no way this was a coincidence, but that didn't mat-ter. Hydramental and I had been thrown at the same task unknowingly before, and I certainly wasn't about to let him get all of the credit for taking these guys down, especially since they were still in my territory.

Quickly picking a spot at the center of the group and hopefully far enough away from the Hydramental clone, I activated Earthbound Impact and went hurtling down into the center of the Vipers. The sound echoed off the walls of the buildings and ice as my impact left a crater in the cement and sent the entire group of snake-men scattering and collapsing to the ground.

The arc of electricity continued to skip between them, and I followed up on my landing by activating Ring of Fire. A sudden burst of fire shot outward from my body, which I directed to stay low toward the ground. The fire licked over each of the snakes and elicited sharp cries of pain from more than a few of them. I only held the ability for a second to avoid burning through too much of my stamina, though, and the fire evaporated as I let the ability go.

[New Achievement! Alley-Oop!]
You comboed an ability off of another Augment's ability, doubling the damage of both of your attacks on a group of susceptible enemies. Yup, it even counts if the person you comboed off of had no intention of getting your help.
Silver-Level Achievement.
Reward: *You have received a B-tier Loot Box.*

"Oh, fucking hell, not you . . . Not only do you have to crash my party—you have the gall to use one of my elements?" I heard three voices echo together and looked around.

The attack had taken down eight of the twelve snakes, and I was barely able to highlight one of them to discover they were only level five before the body dissolved into ash. The four who still remained had taken a large hit to their bars, but at level seven, it wasn't enough to take them out right away. With some effort, they all started to recover from the shock they had been given.

"If you could fucking do all that, why'd you make me do all the fucking work back on the train?!"

The blue version of Hydramental had reappeared on the inner side of his icy wall, and I looked around, picking out his red version. Not at all surprisingly, given the light show I had just seen, I also found a yellow Hydramental had joined the original pair.

"Ah, I get it now. You didn't want to add me to your Friends List because you knew you were just gonna make more of your own," I said before I could stop myself. Given that I knew I needed to get some information out of him, I probably *shouldn't* have been going out of my way to antagonize him, but normal people might have appreciated the helping hand instead of immediately going on the attack.

The yellow Hydramental shot me a look that made it feel like he was about to throw a bolt of lightning at me when a sudden clang interrupted us.

"Now now, fellasss," a familiar screeching voice said, and I turned around to find Sal pulling his way out of yet another manhole. His level had somehow jumped all the way up to nine since the last time I'd seen him, and the four remaining non-Elites were gathering around him as they recovered from their shock. "Asss fun asss it would be to watch you two tear each other apart . . . that'sss their job."

CHAPTER THIRTY-EIGHT

Get the fuck outta the way, Loophole," the triplicated voices shouted before I felt the buzz of electricity cut through my area.

A burst of lightning went barreling toward Sal before one of the other snakes literally jumped in front of it, taking the attack and falling to just shy of ten percent on his health bar. A blast of ice quickly followed up and took down the staggered snake-man before he collapsed to the ground and began to dissolve into dust.

"See! I can handle these fake Augment fuckers on my own!"

I ignored Hydramental's jabs as I darted into the fray, activating Sting like a Bee as I went. Sal quite literally towered over the others, standing easily three feet taller than I remembered him, but he still didn't move, the smaller snake-men coming to intercept me instead.

"Sheesh, you guys weren't joking; he really does have a stick up his ass," I heard Jon say as I activated Float like a Butterfly and dodged under the first swing from one of the snakes.

Although I had rushed on my way here, the small increase from the two extra Strength points I had placed meant that my stamina had only dropped to seventy-five percent by the time I had entered the fray. With several snake-men already moving to counter me, I was more than willing to drop some damage quickly to weed out the weaker of the enemies.

I immediately threw a Gravity Punch with ten percent of my stamina, connecting with the snake-man's midsection. While I hadn't thrown a hard-enough punch to knock the enemy back, it still left an impact, dropping his health to nearly ten percent.

<**Hydramental:** Get the fuck out of here, this is my alert!>

I ignored his message. Spinning on my heel as a second of the weaker snake-men tried to sneak up on me, I dodged out of the way of a clumsy attempt at a strike and threw yet another ten-percent Gravity Punch. Sal hadn't budged from where he had emerged, but once I had space, I moved. I wasn't sure if he *was* about to attack, but I didn't want to risk it and activated Fun House, choosing to go invisible and skipping off to the side as I noticed several more snake-men crawling their way out of the open manhole.

"You know . . . if there was ever a time for some battle music, I'd say it's literally

when you're fighting a whole bunch of biker snakes," Jon said as the street began to fill with snake-men hybrids.

"There is an interface modification that Loophole could get! A lot of Augments have complained about losing headphones while fighting," Angie responded. *"I bet Loophole listens to some sort of weird shit, doesn't he? What would you suggest?"*

"Oh, I know it's probably *in bad taste or tempting fate, but I'd say go with 'Feel Invincible,' or maybe 'Kickstart My Heart,' though that one is a bit overdone,"* he suggested, and Angie let out a curious sound.

"Huh, Skillet to Mötley Crüe . . . not the range I would have expected," she said.

"It's a good song!" Jon shot back before adding, *"Wait . . . how do you know who sings those songs? That's not game related . . ."*

"Not now, you two!" I interjected before they could distract me further.

<**Loophole:** We can argue over whose alert it was later, there's more than enough of them for the both of us. Just fucking fight!>

<**Hydramental**: Fuck off!>

A bolt of electricity arced through the air, cutting through the afterimage left behind by Fun House before it struck Sal in his chest. I shot a look over at the yellow Hydramental, noticing his eyes widen briefly before his expression hardened.

The arc of electricity brightened, and sparks went flying from Sal onto his nearby staggered associates. The lightning didn't put Sal down, but he acted as a jumping point while the lightning arced over to the two Vipers I had already struck. The sudden surge of electricity quickly dropped them to the ground, and their bodies began to rapidly dissolve.

I took the opportunity to materialize one of my venom-soaked guns in the last few seconds of my invisibility. With three quick squeezes, I fired, watching as the first two bullets glanced off of him before the third penetrated and left Sal with a **[Weakened (25%)]** debuff. His immunity had grown exponentially since our last encounter, but I pulled the gun back into my B.E.L.T. as my invisibility faded to save the last five bullets in the magazine.

As I shimmered back into existence, I told the afterimages to start mirroring my movements. They only had twenty seconds left, and one of them had already fallen to a newly emerged snake-man. I scanned the battlefield and counted at least ten of them on top of the ones we had already put down, though curiously, none of the new Vipers were higher than level five, with at least one of them being identified as a level three. More were still climbing from the sewer, and I found myself instinctively rushing the nearest one.

The new additions' lower levels were the only thing that gave me some form of relief about the sudden increase in enemies, especially given the fact that Axio was clearly adapting how he sent them out. I wanted to curse under my breath, because not a single one of the monsters was wearing even a bandanna, effectively neutralizing my Weighted Clothes ability.

"Why hasn't this alert upgraded to an ambush?! What the fuck is going on here?!"

I halfway shouted in my head as I kept myself moving, striking Viper after Viper each time I had to dodge a new attack. I wasn't strong enough to put them down with unenhanced strikes just yet, but the weaker bikers took noticeable damage.

"I—I'm not quite sure, Loophole. I have raised the question to Axio, but he is refusing to accept my connection request. I do say that the proposed rewards for the level of challenge being thrown at you feels disproportional," Angie replied, her voice turning downward in contemplation.

"Yeah, it's not the reward that I'm worried about here!" I snapped. Hydramental's barrage of electricity had stopped, and I looked over, catching just as one of the new snakes snuck up on his yellow form and slammed a claw into his back.

"FUCK!" I heard a now duplicated voice shout as the yellow Hydramental burst into light, causing the remaining clones' joint health bar to drop by over thirty percent.

<**Loophole:** Let me focus on Sal. Clean up the weaker guys.>

Sal was sitting at seventy-five percent health and practically seething as his head whipped around, looking between my various afterimages and the remaining Hydramentals.

<**Hydramental:** Fuck you, he's mine! This mission is mine, and it's my job to stop this fucking gang. I can take them all down!>

The blue Hydramental then did something I wasn't expecting: he turned and fired several icy spikes toward the snakes who just *happened* to be closest to my afterimages. It could almost have looked like an accident, but I watched as the last two of my illusions vaporized when the ice went through them.

<**Loophole:** Whoa, what the fuck, man! Are you trying to hit me?!>

<**Hydramental:** If you don't want to risk getting hit, get the fuck off my battlefield!>

<**Loophole:** He's not your brother, you're not thinking straight. Calm the fuck down and let's take these assholes down together.>

Had I thought about it for even a moment, I *probably* would have realized just how stupid it was to bring this up in the middle of such a volatile situation. But it was as if I had typed the message without thinking, shooting it his way as his red and yellow form shimmered and split, the red version bursting forward and immediately shooting a fireball directly my way.

<**Hydramental:** Who the FUCK told you about my brother?!>

I dodged to the side, escaping the blazing ball of energy by inches as it slammed into a snake-man I hadn't caught coming up behind me. I turned on the monster, delivering the last of my strikes enhanced by Sting like a Bee and sending the snake collapsing to the ground in a heap as his body started to convulse. It didn't matter that I had only gone to knock the unnamed Viper soldier out—the moment the **[KO]** debuff hit him, his body began to dissolve just as each of the others had.

"Are you fucking working with them?!" the duplicated voice shouted as another sudden barrage of fire and ice came flying my way. "Are you in on this entire fucking scheme?! HAVE YOU BEEN THE WHOLE TIME?!" he yelled even louder.

"Oh shit, did you tell him?!" Jon asked, and I swallowed hard.

Many of the snake-men were taking collateral damage as the Hydramentals continued to go wild. His attacks were thrown in rapid succession, blazes of fire and icy bursts that dropped more than a few of the Vipers littering the street. The three forms split up, separating and moving as a shimmer of energy hopped from the red one to the yellow one.

Had I not been paying attention, I might have been caught off guard as he threw yet another bolt of lightning my way. Luckily, I hadn't stopped moving, continuing to dart toward the far end of the enclosed street, moving out of the way just as the bolt struck another Viper in its chest.

"Dude, this was probably *not the right time to bring it up,"* Jon said as I dodged around another Viper, tossing a few regular strikes that took down good chunks of its health with each blow.

"Yeah, probably not one of Loophole's wiser moves, that's for sure," Angie agreed.

"Seriously, guys, NOT NOW!" I shouted as I dropped the Viper with a final blow to the side of its head and spun on my heel, barely avoiding another spark of electricity that left my hair standing on edge. There was another snake that had been unfortunately close to me that the bolt struck full force. Luckily, it wasn't one of his hopping attacks, and the snake seized up as its health rapidly sank.

Given the Vipers I had already encountered, I wasn't surprised to find that the soldier was only level four, and I threw two more punches, chunking down the shocked snake's health until he fell to the ground like his compatriots. It was as if all the defenses that Gio had displayed were missing, or maybe the combination of electrical shock and my increasing strength just was enough to break through their defenses.

While I knew I should be appreciative of the ease, the rapidly expanding number of them threatened to overwhelm the battlefield, regardless of how easy they were to take down. I saw a shimmer of light pass from one Hydramental to the next and started to move again before he could pin me down.

Hydramental was throwing attacks with reckless abandon, and I dodged to the side, out of the way of yet another fireball. I wasn't quick enough, though, and a small blast of ice took me on my left shoulder, leaving a small icy patch and dropping my health by a good chunk.

<**Loophole:** Will you calm the fuck down?! You're gonna get us both killed!>

I turned and threw a ten-percent Gravity Punch at an approaching snake-man, catching the monster by surprise as I followed up my first strike with three more rapid punches to his midsection. It took the level-four attacker down, but another one quickly rushed at my side. I activated my jacket's Fortune's Shield ability just in time, and his claws glanced off my side, sending me stumbling to the side and into a small blast of fire that dropped my health to fifty percent.

<**Loophole:** Dude, SERIOUSLY, we can talk about this later. Calm down NOW, or I'll stop holding back and make you calm down.>

"It's a shame you can't read these, Codex. Loophole's actually trying to be assertive," Angie murmured, and I bit my tongue as I materialized and used an Enhanced Health Injector to bring my health back to full. I didn't quite know why I did it, but as I looked around at the buildings surrounding us, I had to assume at least a few people had their phones out, so I deactivated the obfuscation passive on my Spectrum Veil just as another ball of fire was launched in my direction.

I skipped backward from a few Vipers, letting one of them take the fiery blow as I kept my eyes on the Hydramental clones I could see. So far, I had been holding back from actually trying to counter him, but that didn't mean I didn't have an idea of how I could. I had already seen just how it affected him when his clones burst from taking damage, and if I could rapidly take out his active forms, I had to hope they'd do enough collateral damage to knock him out.

It wasn't the best plan, especially given the amount of enemies still on the field, but it would work if I could clear a few of them out of the way at the same time.

I activated Float like a Butterfly just as it came off of cooldown. It was the right move, as another set of icy spikes was sent flying my way, and I skipped off to the side to let the attack impale another Viper. Toggling Center of the Universe on as I moved, I ducked and dodged between the cluttered battlefield.

Though they had come charging onto the street, the Vipers weren't necessarily trying to overwhelm us by attacking us in a frenzy. The ones closest to me *were* trying to take swings that I easily dodged and countered, but the Vipers farther from both myself and Hydramental tore into cars on the sides of the street with animalistic rage.

As I sprinted across the street and caught each of them in my area, one by one, they started to feel the ever-increasing gravitational pull within my zone of control. With none of the bikers in clothing, I knew that Weighted Clothes could be used to fully target Hydramental, but as much as he was pissing me off, he *wasn't* my main enemy here.

Ramping up the strength of Center of the Universe as fast as I could, I pulled the snake-men toward me as I tried to cut my way back into a centralized location. Before they could stop it, and with the strength of my pull at its max, two of the three Hydramentals got caught in my field, with only the yellow-clad version hanging out far on the sideline.

<**Hydramental:** What the fuck are you doing?!>

His demand for an answer came with another barrage of ice that glanced off my body, icing over bits of my jacket and taking down small chunks of my health as I watched the Vipers try with all of their might to slither away from me.

The Vipers who had been unlucky enough to be closer tried to turn and strike me, but the pull sent them off-balance, and I was able to rapidly strike and take down the ones who were nearly right on top of me. The Hydramental in blue sent another shock of ice my way as he was yanked toward me by my gravitational pull. I didn't dodge the blast, letting it hit my hip before I swung a hard hook at the side of his head, connecting and sending the clone stumbling before my quickly changing position and gravitational pull yanked him along the ground my way.

<**Hydramental:** I am going to—>

It was my turn to ignore him, waving the chat away from my field of view as I came to a stop near the center of the street. I had given him more than a fair enough warning, and I wasn't going to risk my safety just because he couldn't settle down.

Center of the Universe had reached the height of its strength, and as far as I could tell, all of the snake-men were being yanked my way, forming a writhing serpentine-like mosh pit in the street around me as they struck out at each other in anger. None of them were acting rationally, seeming to react with an animalistic fear to a force they didn't understand.

The only one who had noticeably remained unaffected was Sal, whom I briefly caught wearing a sinister-looking smirk on his face as he quite literally watched from the sidelines. There was no room for me to cut toward him, and it wasn't my intent to try either, as I found myself completely surrounded.

The gravitational pull of my ability wasn't going to do any damage to the bikers I had trapped, and I knew I would burn through the last thirty percent of my stamina in a hurry if I tried to just throw punches and enhanced Gravity Punches over and over. I needed a quick way to clear out the crowd, and a sudden burst of inspiration hit me once I realized I *did* still have one ability that would do the trick. The only problem was that the ability I needed was still stuck on cooldown.

I knew I would need something very specific in order to make it work, and so I started to concentrate. I wasn't even sure if the skill would generate at my current knowledge level, but I focused on the outcome as hard as I could, remembering from our trial and error that ability generation required as specific of an idea as possible to get the exact skill you wanted.

A smile crept over my face once a new window appeared, and I materialized an Enhanced Stamina Injector into my hand. It wasn't *exactly* what I wanted, but I knew it would do the trick before Angie even started to read.

[New Ability! Launchpad!]

So, this ability has a whole lotta caveats and specific-use situations, but in case you weren't aware, you're kinda busy right now, so let's just focus on the specific situation that matters to you at this very moment, and we can cover the rest of it later.

Don't say I never did anything for you.

While utilizing **Center of the Universe**, *activate this ability to create a gravitational shock wave that pulses out from your location, dealing damage equal to the numerical value of the total gravitational pull nonfriendly targets are experiencing times 3, and stun each affected target for 20 seconds. Simultaneously launch yourself upward a distance equal to the highest amount of damage you will deliver in feet.*

This ability temporarily takes **Earthbound Impact** *off of cooldown
for 10 seconds, with any remaining cooldown being added to
its refreshed cooldown if* **Earthbound Impact** *is reused.*
Cooldown: *30 minutes.*
Stamina Cost: *20%*

I knew it would be temporary, but I dropped the ability in place of Weighted Clothes and slammed the injector into my arm, all while maintaining the force exuded from Center of the Universe. I turned and threw several more strikes at the closest Vipers, clearing the space immediately around me as I let out a breath I hadn't even realized I was holding.

"Here goes nothing," I said, and while Jon *might* have said something in return, I sure as hell didn't hear him once I activated the ability.

Now, I had never been fired out of a cannon before, and while I was able to put on speed *pretty* quickly with Personal Gravity Laws, I knew that the force with which I'd been suddenly sent rocketing upward *should* have been terrifying. The stakes of the battle *should* have had me laser focused on the task at hand, but while I'd left well over a dozen snake bikers and two of Hydramental's clones stunned in the aftershock, the thrill of the launch itself made it practically impossible *not* to whoop just a little bit.

As I reached the peak of my ascent, my momentum carried my feet up and over my head, flipping me backward and giving me a solid sight of the street below. I only hung there for maybe a fraction of a second before my body continued to pull up and over, but time still felt like it slowed as I took in the chaos that had formed in the midday street. I zeroed in on the center of the group, as close to directly where I had launched from as I could. As soon as my feet were pointed back toward the Earth, I activated Earthbound Impact and plummeted to the ground.

[New Achievement! Knockout Royale!]
*Well look at you, you've come quite a long way from toss-
ing some gum on the ground and wailing on these bikers through some extremely mundane punches.*
*Then again, the bikers have come quite a long way too; maybe not
quite as far as they needed to in order to survive this situation, but they
weren't a horde of snake-man hybrids two days ago, so that is kinda
progress, I think . . . Sheesh . . . has it really only been 48 hours?!*
*Anyway, the dust is gonna clear pretty quickly to reveal that
you just took down* **over** *15 of these Temporarily Augmented
Bikers with that single combo move. Talk about efficiency!*
Gold-Level Achievement.
Reward: *You have received an A-tier Loot Box!*

There was a sudden slew of notifications that stacked on the side of my vision, the top one actually claiming the Crime Alert had been completed as the dust started to settle. I didn't think the attack would finish things off, especially with Sal still in the picture, but a quick check confirmed that it *was* in fact completed.

Somehow, Sal's addition to the scene hadn't changed the alert like it had at the hot-dog cart, and while I was sure that meant *something*, I certainly didn't have the time or mental energy to figure out what.

While several car alarms were going off and I could hear indistinct screams and hollers coming from the windows of the buildings we had been pinned between, the sharp sound of a clap caused me to whip my attention over toward Sal, looming over Hydramental's sole remaining form. Even though his form, now wearing a shirt split into three colors, was outside of my seventeen-foot radius, he was sprawled out on the ground with a clear **[KO]** debuff spinning over his head.

"Oheheheh," Sal hissed out a laugh as he slithered forward and around the only actual collapsed form visible on the street, his tail casually but not violently slapping against Hydramental as he passed him. His health had dropped to just about fifty-five percent from some of the collateral damage, but his **[Weakened (25%)]** debuff had vanished. While I could try to activate my veil and hope to trigger Defy the Odds yet again, I wasn't sure if it would be enough.

"You *are* ssstrong, aren't you? Every killed peon, every one of our buildingsss you've cleared out . . . You've given usss ssso much knowledge. You've ssshown usss our weaknessesss, and it'sss let our bosss make usss ssso, ssso much ssstronger. Their deathsss will only do the sssame."

"Sheesh, that is *waaay* too much hissing, dude! You're killing my ears here," I shot at him before I could stop myself. I kept my hands up as I watched him carefully before I added, "If he's not you, then where the hell is SnakeBite?! I have so many questions I have to beat out of him."

This managed to stop him, his head falling backward as he let out a spine-chilling laugh.

"Oheheheh, you are cocky, aren't you. Don't you worry, you already have the key; you'll be meeting the bosss sssoon enough, though you might wisssh you hadn't. Now, I believe thisss one hasss far outlived hisss usssefulnesss. The bosss isss tired of looking at him," Sal hissed before he turned from me and went slithering back toward Hydramental.

Sal's claws were fully extended, and although Hydramental had been nothing but combative *and* had been quite purposefully trying to attack me, I wasn't about to let him get anything worse than a knockout. Sprinting across the street, I simultaneously pulled the gun I had only recently used from my inventory into my left hand and activated both Sting like a Bee and my Spectrum Veil. I knew at that moment it didn't matter if it was going to be enough or not—I *had* to try.

I only kept the veil up long enough to ensure I'd be considered **[Hidden]** before I unloaded every last remaining bullet into Sal. I wasn't sure how many actually connected, but between the five bullets I shot, his health chunked down by twenty percent, and the **[Weakened (25%)]** debuff returned to his status bar.

His attention was ripped from Hydramental as he turned and looked for me with vicious intent. It was already too late for him, though, and I quickly slipped around to place myself between him and Hydramental before I threw every last bit of my remaining stamina into a Gravity Punch. My stamina had already dipped below fifty percent, so it certainly wasn't the *strongest* attack I could throw, but with Sal's health already nearing thirty percent himself and his Elite defenses neutralized by his weakness, I hoped it would be enough.

My fist connected directly with Sal's oversized chest, and his eyes went wide as a percussive *BOOM* echoed outward. The giant of a snake went hurtling backward, skidding and tumbling over the ground while his health sank deep into the red but didn't bottom out. He came to a halt nearly twenty-five feet away from me. Unfortunately, my strike had *also* tossed him almost directly by the open manhole, and Sal's eyes locked onto it immediately before he glared back in my direction.

"Thisss isssn't over, Loophole. We'll finisssh thisss sssoon enough," he hissed with a pained sound before he quickly escaped down into the sewer.

Although I didn't like the fact that he had gotten away *again*, I dropped to my knees, taking deep breaths. For once, I felt truly exhausted, my stamina fully depleted. It wasn't even immediately starting to tick back up like it normally did, and I took a few seconds to let the adrenaline of the fight wear off.

It was only at that moment that I noticed the ice walls had been crumbling into nothing, and there was a loud roar of cheers coming from everywhere around me. My breaths were still coming in short, rapid bursts, and I looked back at Hydramental's knocked-out form as a few more notifications stacked onto the already large pile of silenced ones.

More than a few police officers were rushing forward. The ice had crumbled enough that the red-and-blue flashing lights at the ends of the block were easily visible, even behind the massive lines of people who had gathered behind the barricades.

"You gonna use that Resuscitation Injector you've been holding on to on him?" Jon asked, and a breathless laugh escaped me as I fell back to sit in the center of the somewhat destroyed street.

"Maybe . . . but definitely *not right away. He can sleep off his bullshit a little bit,"* I said as I listened to the cheers still coming from around me. *"Then he can answer some of my goddamn questions."*

CHAPTER THIRTY-NINE

I made out like an absolute bandit.

Though none of the enemies had dropped so much as a single scrap of loot, I did receive ten thousand credits for completing the mission. But that wasn't what really mattered at the end of it.

Even though they were massively underleveled and severely weakened, each and every one of the snakes that I was responsible for taking down counted toward a large, combined Kill Non-Sapient Augment Phase Point gain. I certainly hadn't been actively keeping track, nor had I been *trying* to kill them, but the serum's death side effect was still present and had automatically assigned the kills to me as each of the injected soldiers fell. Between the various levels they had, I gained a whopping total of 2375 points.

Then there was the Crowdpleaser gain. The buildings on either side of us were *tall*, and while not all of the windows could be opened, a cursory glance at the closest ones made it clear there were people practically pressing their noses against the glass. It wasn't quite as much as the gain I had gotten from taking down the Augments, but I *still* received 1420 points from it. This one actually came with an achievement called Showman attached to it for completing a Crime Alert with over a hundred Sapient NPC onlookers.

And then, even though it gave me *only* two hundred more points, given just how quickly I went from scarfing down a Cuban sub to taking on a horde of snake-men, it was still a nice addition to see Powerleveler at the end of the list as I went through my gains.

Although I had *just* leveled, I was wholly unsurprised to find that the swarm of snake-men had given me more than enough experience to reach level eight. I already had an idea of which of my abilities I wanted to use my new Ability Augmentation on, but knowing that it wasn't going to be placed on the timer until I got home meant we still had some time to talk it over.

Personally, I was leaning toward using it on Gravity Punch and crossing my fingers for an option that would give me a bit of finer control over how much damage I doled out, but Jon was curious to see what sort of extra effects Center of the Universe would have. He did admit that it probably wasn't the best time to try experimenting with an ability that didn't have as big of a damaging effect, though.

Since I wasn't handing Hydramental over to the police, I didn't receive any extra Phase Points just for knocking him out, which felt a little bit weird, but after gaining 3995 points in a single swoop, it was hard to complain *that* much. Since no one could really confirm he was *trying* to attack me with how many of the Vipers his attacks took down, the arriving officers didn't question me as I lifted his still knocked-out form up and took off for the tallest building I could find.

Flying while carrying him *was not* easy. Apparently, my *Personal* Gravity Laws didn't make it easy to keep things—or people—that weren't myself from being affected by the elements the higher into the air I went. Had I not been holding him as firmly as I was, I *might* have even dropped him by accident. Sure, I *could* have woken him up on the ground, but that just risked him trying to make a break for it or trying to start up another fight, and I needed to get him to hold still long enough that I could get at least *some* sort of answer.

"Dude, you are all over *the subs right now,"* Jon laughed in my ear as I set foot on top of a building just slightly into Chelsea. *"Like, not even just the Augment-focused ones; there are shots making it onto the more mainstream subs too."*

"I am? Damn, people don't waste any time, do they," I said, unable to keep the smile off my face. I didn't exactly *drop* Hydramental to the ground, but I wasn't exactly careful either, and I stepped over his body as I headed to the lone door into the main structure. With a quick test, I discovered it *was* locked and nodded to myself. Even if he *could* just burn the door down, it would at least give me a few seconds to react before he could try to run.

"It was that Launchpad and Earthbound Impact combo, dude. Someone was filming in the building next to you, and they pretty much got a clean shot of the entire thing from takeoff to smackdown—their words, not mine, though they are pretty perfect," Jon rattled off as I turned my attention back to Hydramental.

"That is certainly going to increase his reputation, even more so than the artificial boost provided by the alert," Angie chirped.

"Well damn . . . save that video, I want to see it later," I said, glancing down at the still unconscious thorn in my side. *"Hey, Angie, how long would he stay knocked out if I didn't use the injector?"*

"If the recipient is not rendered dead, the [KO] debuff will last for a maximum of sixty minutes. This was designed to allow for their . . . let's say undisturbed *transport to holding facilities if they are Miscreant aligned."*

"I guess that makes as much sense as anything," I replied, kneeling down beside Hydramental's unconscious form as I materialized the injector. *"Let's just hope he can't turn into fire and fly away. That would be annoying as hell."*

"Wait," Jon called before I could use it. *"Shouldn't you like . . . tie him up or something?"*

"Really? Aren't you supposed to be the smart one here?" I asked as I leaned back. *"Unless I can neutralize his powers, I'm pretty sure he can just duplicate and escape the bonds with one of his elements; hell, he might still do that to attack. I only have one of*

these; if I have to knock him out again because he's not cooperating, I'll just leave him somewhere and he can deal with it. But I'm not hunting him down again after this.

"Shit, he honestly might not even have anything useful, but everything we have is leading back to his brother. There's no way in hell it was a coincidence that we were both sent to this alert . . . Axio is up to something—I'm just missing a piece of the puzzle."

"Sheesh, you've really put a lot of thought into this . . . Do you actually think Axio is doing something fishy, though? I know you've been scared of what he can do, and everything going on with Sal is definitely interesting, but I mean, how much is it actually Axio messing with it all versus just doing his job?" Jon asked, but I bit my tongue.

Nothing had necessarily changed where it came to my conversation with Axio, and I still wasn't ready to risk mentioning it. Jon was already in much farther than I had initially intended to let him in, and if there *was* a second threat . . . well, I'd just have to figure out what it was *before* it could become a threat. I shrugged as I turned my attention back down to Hydramental and injected him, then quickly backed away.

"Honestly, at the end of the day, I'm not too sure, but the mobs I have to deal with have all been tied to this, and he's connected to it. It's as good a place to start as any," I replied as I watched the debuff vanish and Hydramental's health bar jump back up to fifty percent.

He immediately snapped into a seated position, looking around his new environment until his gaze met mine and his eyes hardened.

"Okay, bud, how about you keep yourself together and we talk like two normal people," I said with my hands held up. His eyes glazed over for a moment before he looked down and let out a long, pained sigh. "I've just got a few questions I want to ask . . . though I'm sure you might have one or two of your own . . . How about you go first."

"How the fuck do you know about my brother?" he immediately asked. He wasn't necessarily aggressive, but I wouldn't be calling him friendly either. It felt like there was a resignation to him as he slowly stood up.

"Remember those maps we got back on the train?" He nodded. I put my hands down slowly. "Yeah, so one of the dens on my map sent me to a yacht up at the cruise terminal, and I . . . uh . . . well, I met Giada, among other things."

He shot me a look, and I almost brought my hands right back up.

"Should you really be telling him all of this?" Jon asked, but I ignored him.

"Was she always the . . . uh . . . shooty type?" I continued when Hydramental didn't start splitting into duplicates. "'Cause I *kinda* had to have her arrested in front of her son for pointing a gun at me . . . and having a whole bunch of those Vipers acting as security detail."

"Are you trying to get him to attack you?!"

"He's gonna find out one way or another; better to just lay it out now," I answered quickly. *"Just shut up for a bit, will you two?"*

"Hey, I didn't say anything!" Angie complained.

"What the ever-loving fuck are you up to?" Hydramental said, looking up toward one of the nodes in the Augmentation Array that floated miles above us.

"Huh? I'm trying to stop these bikers before they keep unleashing swarms of fucking snake-men on my neighborhood, or did you not see the horde we just had to fight off? Everything I have discovered so far seems to point toward your brother," I replied, and he looked over at me with a shake of his head.

"Get off your high horse. I'm not talking about you," he said. "I'm talking about the fuckers controlling all of this."

"Ah, yeah. Axio's been doing a good job fucking with me too; I bet we could compare notes and be here all day," I noted. He rolled his eyes before walking over toward the edge of the building. "Look, I can tell your brother's a touchy subject, but as far as I can tell, he's either up to some shit or involved in who the hell knows. I don't want to fight you again, so if this is something you don't want to talk about, then tell me to fuck off and I will. But Giada seemed to think he's still around, so I gotta know, is the Sal we've been fighting some clone of him or some shit?"

Hydramental leaned back before hopping up onto the ledge. He looked down briefly before he sat, letting his legs dangle as he looked toward Madison Square Garden in the distance.

"Or some shit . . ." he said after a few moments had passed. "That guy . . . Sal the Snake . . . he isn't my brother. I don't think he's necessarily a clone either, but I haven't seen him outside of his snake form, so I couldn't say for sure. I think the name just happens to be a coincidence. It's gonna sound really dumb, and I couldn't tell you what his powerset is actually called since, you know, I didn't know about the game back when he first got Augmented, but he's like . . . a snake vampire."

"A snake vampire? You're kidding me, right?"

"Not now, Angie," I told her quickly before I raised a brow at Hydramental and asked out loud, "A snake vampire? You're kidding me . . . right?"

"I mean, I doubt that's his *actual* powerset name, but more or less, yeah. I didn't actually know it when he first started off, though. I just thought he could shapeshift into a Naga and had increased strength and speed when he showed it off to me. Then Chelsea had a bunch of these bikers show up. Sal swore up and down that he was gonna drive them out, and he did . . . Hell, it only took him a week." His hand tapped at the ledge as he looked back at me. "I was a dude just finishing up high school . . . I thought he was a hero . . . y'know?"

"What happened?" I asked, trying to push him forward just enough without putting him back on the defensive.

"I followed him out one night the week I was going to graduate. I thought he'd been hiding everything from me 'cause I was still in school, but I . . . I don't know . . . I wanted to see how he fought 'cause he was always so cagey about it. Maybe I'm an idiot, I don't know, but he said he didn't want to be famous, he just wanted to help people and keep our neighborhood and his family safe. He kept himself out of the news, kept people from knowing about what he did . . ."

"Maybe not an idiot . . . but just a *bit* naive," I said, and he let out a wry laugh. "It's family; people tend to have blind spots where it comes to family."

"Heh . . . but see, I barely said anything and you figured it out. It took me seeing him biting one of the bikers and seeing him burst like an overfilled water balloon to realize what he had been up to . . ." he explained, and I noticed him shudder. There was a bit of a nip in the air with fall in full swing, and being on top of a building certainly wasn't helping, but something told me that wasn't what had caused it.

"It wasn't like they were fighting and he was trying to defeat them either; I would have at least been able to understand that, given how brutal the job can be. Even back then I knew that; I had watched more than enough Augment fights online. But they were like, lining up and waiting for him to bite them. None of them even flinched when their friends blew up right next to them . . .

"He had vats all around the room with these half-grown bikers hanging in this weird fluid, and he was . . . I don't know . . . I guess experimenting on them? Most of the ones I saw him bite died immediately, but a few of them . . . I saw a few of them change into snakes themselves, at least for a few seconds, before they just dissolved into nothing like those guys back on the street did."

"Into snake-men Augments . . . which is why you called him a snake vampire . . . Okay, that at least makes a little bit of sense," I said, leaning back against the ledge. "Was that before or after the picture he keeps in his office?"

"Picture?" he asked, his head turning and expression softening ever so slightly. "What picture? What office?"

"It was back on the yacht; he had an office with a whole bunch of pics of you two growing up. There was one of him in his mask, and you were practically glaring at him in it."

"Fucker kept it all this time . . ." Hydramental muttered almost low enough that I might have missed if I hadn't been specifically paying attention to him. "It was the day after. He missed my grad party and came home telling our parents he was off stopping some crime ring. Had I not just followed him the night before I probably would have believed him. He said he wanted to take a pic to at least celebrate my graduation, and well, that . . ."

I let out a sigh as I pushed off from the ledge. His story still hadn't quite explained anything, and I wasn't even sure where this was getting me either.

"If that was three years ago, what the hell has he been up to all this time? I mean, I'm not blind, these bikers haven't been running around Hell's Kitchen for the last three years; I feel like I would have seen that all over the news," I noted, scratching at the back of my head. Hydramental just shook his head as he turned and hopped back to his feet and off the ledge.

"That's the thing. Believe it or not, after we took that pic, he spent the whole night trying to tell me and our family about all the good he was doing. He kept saying his mentor had shown him some amazing things he could do with his abilities . . . He never said who the dude was but kept insisting that it was going to revolutionize the world," Hydramental explained as his shoulders dropped.

"And then a few days later he just vanished. Giada and little Ozzy, too. My folks said he left a note, but it was just so sudden and random . . . They refused to put out a police alert because 'Sal's an Augment; he can take care of himself and his family,' but I was never able to understand why they were just so . . . dismissive."

"Well, that's not suspicious at all," Jon murmured, and I couldn't help but agree. I was just about to respond when Hydramental looked at me and took a few steps.

"When I first woke up with my Augmentation, after my PAI got me settled in, Axio slowed things down and told me some things . . . Said they were things I shouldn't repeat out loud, but the short of it was that I had a chance to confront my brother if I just got my hands on some key . . . He wasn't allowed to just give it to me because of the rules of the game, but if I just followed along, I'd get the chance. But that's the thing . . . I've cleared out pretty much every one of the dens on that fucking map I got, and I haven't found a fucking thing . . ."

Right there on the edge of my vision, almost aggressively, **[The Snake Key]** mission shook, practically demanding my attention.

"Should I just put the cards on the table?" I asked internally.

"Can he take the key from you by force?" Jon asked, and then thought about it for a moment before changing his question. *"Angie? Can it be taken by force?"*

"Only if he renders Loophole unconscious or dead. Or I suppose if he had an item with the Pickpocket feature, but those are generally on gloves, and I don't think he's wearing any. Loophole could have looted him while he was unconscious, but he has, ugh, ethics."

"Well, you've already come this far. If he goes to make a move just make it vanish, but I think he's probably not going to attack you," Jon said, once again jumping past Angie's superfluous details.

"I, uh . . . So I think I may have been the one to collect that," I told him, materializing it in my hand. The ornate key felt incredibly out of place, and the rubies that represented the snake's eyes glinted with the sun still hanging high overhead. Hydramental's eyes widened briefly before they hardened, and he stepped forward again. I immediately pulled it back into my inventory. "I found it on the train after you left, and it gave me a mission. And after everything I've had to deal with since finding it . . . well, I'm going to see it through to the end."

"That's my mission," he said, his jaw set as his blue and yellow clones separated from his body.

"Pull yourself together. I'm not going to fight you again," I warned, letting my own tone match his. "Believe it or not, I agree with you—Axio's been up to something since all of this bullshit started. I'm not going to hand this key off to you. Honestly, given all the threats tossed our way every night, I'd be willing to bet I'd get some bullshit thrown my way if I did hand it off. But if you can just *chill* the *fuck* out, I'm offering you the chance to finish this with me. If it is related to your brother, you at least deserve that much."

All three sets of eyes glazed over while another gust of wind passed by us. Electricity even seemed to dance between the fingers of his yellow form for a moment before it stopped, and his forms all remerged together. The glaze vanished, and he shook his head.

"*If* that key does lead to my brother, then when we find him, I'm asking you to back off and let me handle him on my own. That's the only way I'm going to 'finish this with you.'"

"*Does that count as chilling the fuck out?*" Angie asked. Jon laughed.

"*I think anything that's not him throwing the elements at Loophole counts.*"

"Fine," I replied, extending a hand out toward Hydramental while simultaneously sending him a friend invite. He stepped forward and grabbed my hand as he accepted the invite, his expression still hard. With that done, I took a step backward, activating my Personal Gravity Laws as I started to lift off from the roof. "Now, I'll shoot you a message when I figure out where the hell this key is taking me, and you can meet me there. Sound good?"

"Wait, where the fuck are you going? Aren't you gonna at least drop me back off on the ground?" he asked as he took a few steps forward. I held up a hand and nodded toward the door on the far side of the roof.

"Dude, you threw a shit ton of fire, ice, and lightning at me not even a half hour ago. Not to mention that flying you up here when you were unconscious was hard enough as it was. Take the stairs, and we can call it even," I said, and then before he could respond, I took off, heading back home. I did still have a level to finalize, after all.

CHAPTER FORTY

There was *supposed* to be a Bronze-level den between the roof I had left Hydramental on and my apartment.

As I was speeding back, Jon had pointed out that the map had one directly in my path, so it made sense to clear it out instead of circling back. It wasn't like my level up was going anywhere, nor did I really need it to clear what now felt like painfully easy bases at Bronze level. But as I landed on a roof opposite the marked location, nothing got highlighted. I even entered the building from the top floor, only for a system message to appear.

[Alert!]
This Viper Den has been abandoned. Total has been updated.
Hell's Kitchen Viper Dens Cleared: *7 of 11.*

While it sucked that I couldn't collect Phase Points for clearing it out, I searched through the building and discovered *another* journal. Well, at least it looked like a journal; only a single page was filled with what looked like a random assortment of timetables. I wasn't quite sure what it meant, but I pulled it into my B.E.L.T. to investigate later. I had a theory, and had Jon point me to the closest Silver-level den.

Sure enough, it was the exact same story. The building refused to be highlighted, and once I stepped inside, the total updated once again, dropping down to ten total dens. The place looked like it had been abandoned in a hurry, and while I rummaged around hoping for more clues, I only managed to scoop up an extra fifteen hundred credits and a Resuscitation Injector, which I happily stowed away.

This led to me checking the rest of the locations, discovering one by one that each of the Silver dens had been abandoned in a similarly hurried manner. I had wondered just where all the Vipers had come from when they burst out of the sewer, but I hadn't thought that they would be scavenged from most of my remaining dens.

I would have been upset about the loss of potential Phase Points if I hadn't *just* gained nearly four thousand points. I'd never know just how many I would have gotten if I had taken them on one at a time, but I was over the ten-thousand-point requirement with two days still left to go, so I couldn't complain *too* much.

Between the last three Silver dens, there were three thousand credits and a third journal. This one was even less helpful than the random timetables, with what looked like a random assortment of dots, slashes, and lines dotting the first few pages.

If I hadn't been fully aware that Axio was up to something in the background, I'd have thought it was almost too easy to get past the now seemingly low point threshold. Even then, I would have assumed it was just because he had been toying with me if Jon hadn't confirmed that six of the ten people on the Top Ten had crossed the barrier as well. He couldn't check the longer version of the list to see the total remaining players, nor could he see how many people *weren't* on track to cross the threshold, but it still felt like it was easier than I had initially anticipated.

Jon, on the other hand, was seemingly disappointed in the Wave as a whole. Something about "real gamers would have crossed that 10k line before the first day had even ended" that he muttered while I flew back across the neighborhood.

By the time I had checked all of my remaining den locations, only the Gold one had been left for me to tackle. I had expected this one to be in some grand location, and while it wasn't necessarily shabby, I *wasn't* expecting it to be a jazz club of all things. Unlike the other dens, this one still let me highlight it, and after some deliberation, Jon and I agreed it might be better to circle back to it after leveling and taking a look at the bigger picture.

While the Silver and Bronze dens had been relatively easy for me to take down, the last and only Gold den I had faced had been the one I had tackled with Hydramental. I didn't think I could count on that one being indicative of just how difficult Gold dens would actually be. Even if I *hadn't* had Hydramental's help, my talk with Axio had made it clear that he had tinkered with just how things went down.

So, I flew back home with a pocket full of credits and more than a few things to take care of.

"The rising star is back!" Jon whooped from the Command Room as I closed the front door behind me, having opted to come in through the roof. "Number two on the Top Ten, and the news has been showing footage of your fight down on Ninth for the last hour."

I looked over at the television and saw a shot from what must have been the fourth or fifth floor of a building. There was a swarm of snake-men—with many of them looking like they were trying to forcibly slither away but getting absolutely nowhere—before I suddenly went shooting upward to the sky. Jon hadn't been kidding, the cameraman had kept a perfectly steady hand and tracked my entire trip up into the air, catching as I backflipped and went rocketing back down to the ground.

"Damn, you weren't kidding . . . that was a great shot—Wait, did you say I was number two?" I asked as I pulled my eyes off the television and opened the leaderboard in my interface.

Tenth Wave
Guardians: *325*　　**Miscreants:** *471*

1. **Tempest's Wrath** (*Level 11 Thunder God*) *Miscreant —
   15420 Points*
2. **Loophole** (*Level 8 Perfect Planner*) *Guardian — 13005 Points*
3. **Freakenstein** (*Level 9 Patchwork Armorer*) *Miscreant —
   11765 Points*
4. **Swansong** (*Level 8 Healing Voice*) *Guardian — 10670 Points*
5. **Duke Juke'em** (*Level 8 Highschool Athlete*) *Miscreant —
   10525 Points*
6. **Quizmaster** (*Level 7 Gameshow Host*) *Miscreant — 10050
   Points*
7. **Pretty Pink Warthog** (*Level 7 Berserking Boar*) *Guardian
   — 9240 Points*
8. **Vice Grip** (*Level 7 Toolbox Mechanic*) *Guardian — 9125
   Points*
9. **Pigeon** (*Level 7 Pigeon*) *Miscreant — 8615 Points*
10. **Hydramental** (*Level 7 Elemental Everyman*) *Guardian —
    8125 Points*

I was almost surprised to see Hydramental at the bottom of the list, but whether I wanted to admit it or not, he had taken down a good chunk of the horde on his own, even if he *had* been trying to attack me at the same time. If he had gotten enough of them *and* received the same Crowdpleaser boost that I had, then it only made sense that he had jumped up the board.

My level-up stat screen wasn't going to wait any longer, and it forced its way into my vision. Jon didn't vocalize any objection to following what we had already discussed, so I quickly dropped two points into Luck and two into Intelligence, effectively allowing me to finally absorb the Quantum Shenanigans book.

Before I could do that, though, my level-eight Ability Augmentation opened, and my countdown was on. It hadn't come up again, so I decided to go with Gravity Punch. Selecting it, I let the window populate before the timer began to tick down.

[Gravity Punch!]
Level 2 Activated Ability.
*Rapidly compress gravity directly around your fist before you throw
a punch. For every 5 percent of your stamina, deal an additional
60 percent damage from your base attack up to a maximum of 600
percent increased damage. If you have spent at least 25 percent of
your stamina, knock the opponent backwards 15 feet and an additional 5 feet for every added 5 percent of your stamina spent.*
Cooldown: *5 seconds.*

[First Modification Option: Group Up!]
Gravity Punch's *knockback effect now happens at all levels, 3 feet for
every 5 percent of your Stamina. Additionally, enemies within 10 feet
of the impact point are pulled in at a speed of 20 meters per second and
are hit for 50 percent of your initial damage. For every 10 percent of
your stamina spent, increase the range of affected enemies by 3 feet.
All factors of this ability cap at 50 percent.*

[Second Modification Option: Limit Breaker!]
*This Augmentation removes the cap for Stamina cost, allowing you to
further increase the amount of damage dealt with each blow. Damage
dealt with attacks over 50 percent increases at a rate of 120 percent additional damage for every 5 percent of stamina spent.*

[Third Modification Option: Momentum Surge!]
After delivering a **Gravity Punch**, *grant yourself a* **[Speed Up]**
*buff, increasing your Movement Speed and Agility by 25 per-
cent for 10 seconds. Your speed is increased by 5 percent for every
10 percent of your Stamina spent, capping at 50 percent.
Movement Speed does not stack over subsequent uses of this
ability; however, subsequent attacks will refresh any current buff at the higher of the two movement increases.*

"Damn, I was really hoping for something with more fine-tune control," I said
as I wandered toward the Command Room.

"They're not bad options, though. Group Up is a bit like throwing Center of
the Universe on an enemy, and Limit Breaker could let you throw some crazy-
strong attacks, but fifty percent of two thousand stamina and fifty percent of three
thousand is the same thing at the end of the day, at least as far as the ability cares, so
the only real bonus is the increased damage you get when throwing attacks stronger
than fifty percent, which . . . well, I don't know how often you'd *actually* do that,"
Jon said as I watched the timer tick down. "I think I'd go with Momentum Surge.
The speedup starts on a five percent attack, and even if it doesn't stack the buff, that
base twenty-five percent boost is pretty damn good."

"*Tick-tock, Loophooooole,*" Angie said as the timer ticked down past ten seconds.
"*I mean, I'll be happy to select for you if you won't do it.*"

I thought about it for just a few more seconds before I resolved myself and
selected the Limit Breaker modification.

"Damn, really? And here I thought you valued my opinion," Jon said with mock
outrage. He turned around in his chair, his legs crisscrossed and a bowl of popcorn
in his lap. "What's the thought?"

"With most of the snakes back at the swarm, strong-enough attacks were able to overpower or bypass their defenses. I might be wrong, but if I come across Sal—the NPC one, that is—and can deliver one punch at, what, eighteen hundred percent increased damage? I feel like that alone would be able to seriously injure him. Although I can't imagine a scenario where I'd *actually* throw a hundred-percent Gravity Punch, but still, I saw how much a forty percent did to Sal back there. Throwing something at sixty percent might just do the trick if I could get lucky."

"Yeah, but he was also **[Weakened]**, and the debuff was down to twenty-five percent effectiveness. There's always the chance that weakness no longer applies to him," Jon shot back before grabbing a handful of popcorn and shoving it into his mouth with a crunch.

His next words didn't come out garbled, but he certainly didn't wait to swallow completely before he started to talk. "Not trying to say you didn't think it through, cause obviously Sal ain't the only person you're gonna be fighting moving forward, just pointing out your plan might not do the trick on him at this point."

I shrugged as I walked forward and grabbed some of his popcorn. "Well, speed hasn't really been a problem so far, and honestly, I was kinda stuck between the two just based on my own fights. If I didn't grab something, I think Angie probably would have stuck me with Group Up, which isn't necessarily bad cause of the AoE factor, but it lowers the maximum knockback range."

"Hey, I do technically *have to randomize it,"* Angie interjected.

"Well, how about I just blame the stupidly short time frame for making these decisions, and we just move on, how's that sound?" I offered. "Because I think at this point, we can agree the time limit is a stupid limitation."

When neither of them responded, I materialized *Quantum Shenanigans for Beginners*. Quantum mechanics felt like an incredibly nebulous knowledge base to have, but I was ridiculously eager to see what I might be able to do with it. Absorbing the book, I gained the level-three stat as a sudden burst of information flooded my mind.

Quantum entanglement, quantum tunneling, superposition—hell, even quantum probabilities. These were all concepts that I was suddenly able to comprehend as I focused on the knowledge base, and I found myself immediately enthralled and overwhelmed.

"You okay, bud? You look like you're seeing nirvana." Jon laughed while I shook myself from the daze.

"Yeah, sorry, still weird to just have a bunch of knowledge uploaded into my head," I said as I rubbed my temples trying to cure a nonexistent headache. There were a few possibilities that immediately came to mind, but no abilities seemed to generate off of them. "It's interesting stuff, but I might need to think for a bit on how I can actually use this. You might want to Google some things on quantum tunneling and superposition, and I think knowing how to at least tinker with Quantum probabilities is actually going to help me lean in on my Super Luck a bit more than I already have."

"Hmm, okay, let me see what I can look up, though this one might be really far out of my wheelhouse, which was why I didn't really jump at it the way you did. I'm a computer nerd, not a physicist," he said as he swiveled back toward his station.

While Jon's ability to reroll was available, I had only gained five new loot boxes, ranging the gamut from D to A tier, with two of them being Cs. Generally speaking, his reroll was probably going to best be saved for F tiers or something A+ or higher. Walking over to the dining room table, I materialized the boxes, opening them from lowest to highest.

The D tiers were definitely the least valuable to get, and this one was no exception; it only contained a hundred credits and five Basic Stamina Injectors. Between the two C tiers I gained fifteen hundred credits, a Targeted Ability Level Up Scroll, and an **[Infrared Lenses]** crafting ingredient. I pulled the small red ovals from my inventory and highlighted them, confirming what was an easy assumption to make.

[Infrared Lenses!]
This is an Advanced Crafting Item.
When attached to a compatible Mask item, provides the
user with the option to toggle infrared vision.
This item must be brought to a gadget specialist to attach to compatible items.

The B tier came with five hundred credits and a pair of bracers that were going to be the first item I ended up selling at the resale shop. They weren't necessarily bad, but the **[Stylish Dance Bracers]** only offered plus one to Toughness and plus three to Style, which was a terrible tradeoff when my current bracers gave me plus five to Strength. I might have considered them if they had come with a feature that would have offset that, but it just went to show that not every item was going to be a perfect fit for me.

Last but not least I opened the A tier and found a single item that I was more than happy to see.

[Steel Wrappers!]
Equippable Gloves.
Color: *Metallic Silver.*
These silver hand wraps will help stabilize and strengthen those
scrawny wrists of yours! There's really not a whole lot more to say
about them. Other than just how shiny they are when the light
shines on them, they're pretty basic looking. Just like you!
+8 Strength
+2 Dexterity
These gloves grant the **Metallic Momentum** *feature!*

[Metallic Momentum!]

Consecutive punches in rapid succession build up your momen-
tum, increasing your attack speed by 2 percent for every landed blow.
This has a maximum Attack Speed increase of 20 percent, which will
be sustained until you fail to attack for 3 consecutive seconds.

"Damn, those are slick!" Jon yelled as I added them to the empty hand slot on my gear loadout and materialized my entire outfit. He looked over his shoulder at me with a raised brow. "What's the plan? Gonna go tackle that Gold den?"

"Eh, not yet. It's not going anywhere . . . I think." Walking back over to the Command Room, I materialized the three journals and the burner phone I had found and held them out. "Think you can take a look at these and see if there's anything in here that *might* help me track down where this key I have goes?"

"I'll see what I can dig up," he replied as he turned and grabbed the stack from me, setting them on his table and opening the page with the timetables. He stared at them for a few moments before turning to his computer. "These might be train timetables; I'll have to see if they line up with any of the stations. Is this all? A couple of notebooks and a pay-as-you-go phone?"

"Pretty much, yeah. I found the notebooks randomly, though that first one I did find inside of a safe when I first fought Sal," I admitted, thinking back to it.

"Hmm, what was the code?" he asked.

"The code? What's that matter?" I said as I tried to remember what it was. I remembered it had been written on a Post-it note, and I hadn't been able to pull it into my B.E.L.T., but the memory still stuck out as weird that they had written it down in the first place.

"In most puzzle games, *every* detail matters. If they gave you a code, it probably matters," Jon explained while I nodded, having just come to that realization myself.

"I *think* it was 1-0-0-1-7, but I might be misremembering," I said. I could see as he tapped at his chin.

"That might be a zip code, actually . . . Hell, ours is 10019." His fingers darted across one of the many keyboards in his space before he let out a satisfied grunt. "Yup, Midtown East. That can't be a coincidence."

"Damn . . . how'd I miss that," I muttered, and he just laughed.

"Eh, don't feel too bad about it—it was only staring you in the face. Now why don't you go do whatever you're gonna do so your *brilliant* tech support can put these clues together. It is sorta my job, after all."

I shoved his chair forward slightly, and he laughed again as I turned to walk back toward my bedroom. "Fine, I think I'm gonna head to the Square for a bit. I have over thirty-five thousand credits; I want to check out the resale shop and see if I can't fill out the rest of my equipment slots, or at least the ones that really matter. Plus, on top of the lens I just got, I still have some Viper Skin that I've been sitting on. I think it's time I get it added on to my jacket and tank top just for that increased Toughness."

Jon turned around and held his hands together as he gave me a big, cheesy smile. "Look at you, actually thinking about how to better improve your build. Who knew all it would take to get you *actually* into video games was . . . well, *actually* putting you into a video game."

"Yeah, life or death will do that to you," I replied, rolling my eyes, though I found myself looking back at the news playing yet another shot of my fight on the street. This time it was a shot of that final strike I'd made against Sal that had sent him flying. "Though still, I hate how much fun I *am* actually starting to have with it . . . even with all the insanity with Hydramental and Sal . . ."

"You always have been a bit of a worrier; that Matrix of yours has really kept you focused pretty damn hard," Jon admitted, and I felt myself tighten at the thought of the emotional controls. "I'm still glad I don't have one of those attached to me, but I get why you guys have them."

"You should have seen the Augment walking around with a bag on his head that Loophole saw on his first trip into the Square. He was freaking out about everything because his PAI hadn't activated it, or that was my assumption at least. It really is a quick way to mentally break an Augment on accident. It's why the Matrix was implemented in the first place," Angie explained, and I found myself stopping at the door to my room.

"When was it implemented, anyway? Was it a recent thing?" I asked.

"Not recently, no," she chirped quickly. Knowing that she had to *actually* answer if I asked the question directly really did make it easier getting actual answers out of her; you know, as long as I actually remembered to ask them. *"The Acceptance Matrix was patched into the system before the Second Wave of the game, and members of the First Wave were given the option to integrate the Matrix into their interfaces."*

"And how many of them did?"

"I'm sorry, Loophole, I don't have access to that information for the First Wave," she replied almost robotically. I hadn't expected her to know, of course, she had long proven that there was more than plenty that Axio kept hidden from the PAIs, but I couldn't stop myself from asking either. *"I'd assume most of them did, though. To date, the records I can view indicate that ninety-eight percent of the Augments who are still alive have kept their Acceptance Matrix activated. Is this something you would like to reconsider?"*

I thought about it for a moment before shaking my head and opening the door to my room. The queasiness in my stomach dissipated as I walked forward. "Nah. Jon's right—I'm staying focused on the job at hand. Maybe we can revisit it eventually, but not now."

"Perfect! You just let me know if you want to make that decision. After all, I am here *to assist you!"*

CHAPTER FORTY-ONE

I ended up checking out the tailor first. I knew it was probably about time I took some time to investigate the place, but I didn't immediately attach the two Viper Skins that I had available. I wanted to make sure I knew how much it would cost to make the modifications.

The shop was cluttered but almost homey feeling. The walls were covered in shelves with what had to be hundreds of different fabrics. There were several knitting machines, worktables, and baskets full of cloth scrap scattered everywhere. Like most of the other shops, there was only a single NPC, who came sauntering out of a door at the back of the building the moment I entered the otherwise empty shop.

The tailor, a young man wearing a purple-and-black pinstripe suit with dangerously overgelled hair named Louie, actually had reasonable costs, though they did scale with the quality of the modification. For the Viper Skins, it would only cost me two hundred and fifty credits for each of them.

He showed me one of the now familiar filter binders that had a list of other items he was able to craft, though those required a specific combination of crafting items in order for him to make. After a short bit of deliberation, I told him I'd be back after I visited the resale shop, since I wanted to make sure I wasn't going to immediately replace an item that I had him modify.

Afterward, I popped into Gregory's shop next door, assuming he'd be the gadgeteer who could attach the lens modification to my mask. My assumption was right, although he was quick to inform me that unlike Louie, his cost was more variable than just based on rarity. The lenses were, luckily for me, on the lower end of the costs, at only five hundred credits.

While I was just going to have him automatically add the lenses, Jon did make it a point of having me check if there were modification limits, which of course the answer ended up being, "it depends."

Different items had different limitations, and it left me wondering if they had a grading system that I just hadn't had the forethought to investigate. After a quick probe, Jon found that the item ranks followed the seven tiers of the achievements, ranging from Wood to Mythic.

I instructed Angie to update my interface to include this information on all of my current and future items, finding myself getting increasingly annoyed that I had to essentially opt in to useful information instead of just getting it in the first place. Of all of my items, the highest-ranked things I owned were my Fortune's Guardian Jacket and my Mask of Strategic Fortitude at Gold tier, and that was apparently the literal middle of the range.

As a Gold tier, the Mask of Strategic Fortitude was capable of having a maximum of three modifications attached. Gregory *also* made it a point of letting me know that the Infrared Lenses were removable, as unlike the Viper Skins, they didn't come with a "destroyed on removal" qualifier, though of course he'd charge me again if I wanted the modification removed.

Doubtful that I'd be changing the mask anytime soon, I had him attach the lenses and discovered I could immediately mentally toggle on an infrared mode once he had finished. I wasn't sure how often I would actually use the attachment, but having it as an option had to be a good thing.

From there I headed back down into the main square, walking past a handful of others. It was still a bit weird seeing other Augments just lounging around, sitting on benches and even reading, but I was starting to get it. When I was in the Square, Crime Alerts didn't pop up, and there was no threat of being attacked, unless of course you went up into the Fight Club. It meant that, unlike the Safe Houses, Sanctuary Square was the one place you actually *could* take a few minutes to just relax without the threat of, well . . . a threat.

I was just about to make a comment about that to Jon when a chat window popped open.

<Pinky: What the hell, Loophole?! I'd ask where the hell all the points came from if Brain hadn't just shown me the video of your fight!>

<Loophole: Hey Pinky, how's it going?>

<Pinky: Oh, don't do that, you're not that smooth. Like, what the actual hell?! If you could do all that, why'd you go and let me get buried in a damn wall?!>

<Loophole: Well, I can't go and reveal all my secrets, can I?>

<Pinky: You barely revealed anything at all!>

<Loophole: Well, to be fair, I also just learned a lot of those abilities last night *after* our fight.>

<Pinky: That . . . That actually makes it a little bit better.>

<Loophole: Glad I can help. Now if you'll excuse me, I have some gear to purchase.>

<Pinky: Drinks at The Common Ground later? Brain and I were gonna grab some dinner there after Axio's normal threats and melodrama, you in?>

<Loophole: Sure, sounds good.>

<Pinky: Cool, see ya later, Loophole. We're gonna go squash a few more hideouts. Don't go rushing too much farther ahead.>

I waved the window away as I made my way through the lightly crowded Square, moving from the Neutral Segment over to the larger Guardian area.

"This third journal is some sorta cipher. I think I can figure it out, but it'll take me some time. The Command Room here has some interesting attachments, including one that might be able to act as a decoder. I'll need to test it out," Jon reported as I walked up and into the resale shop.

"Well, that's at least a start. It's cool that the room has that kinda system built into it, though," I replied, unable to hide my own curiosity.

"Yeah, I'm pretty sure there's a fluid sampler in here too. I was tempted to pour my Dr. Pepper into it, but I didn't want to break it either."

"That is a wise choice, Codex. The built-in sampler is designed only for fluids gener-ated for the game," Angie added.

"That would actually be really *useful if I managed to get my hands on one of those Temporary Augmentation Serums. I mean, I don't necessarily know* what *we would do with the knowledge of what's being used to make those, and I'm hoping to put an end to it here soon, but still,"* I said as I looked around the shop.

Unlike the other shops, this one was largely automated, and no clerks actively appeared to discuss the products with you. There were a handful of other Augments lingering around the long counter, each with a small binder in front of them. As I approached an empty space, a similar one appeared for me.

"Hmm, actually, yeah, that's a good point. You should really get your hands on one of those so we can examine it and see what we can do with that sort of knowledge," he commented. I let out an audible sigh that elicited a laugh from him.

"So, we got some traction on the cipher; any ideas on the timetables in the other one? Is there anything of use in the first journal I scooped up?" I changed the subject.

"As far as the first journal goes, it seems more like a stream of thoughts with random details about their operations in there, though I've caught a few references to dens that you've already cleared out. There might be something of use in there, but I can't think of any way to quickly find it without just reading it all page by page. It's kinda a shame you can't just absorb it like you do with the skill books," he said, and I could hear the clatter of keys over the open line.

"With the timetables, there are a lot of stations to check for a match, and the journal conveniently *leaves out train and platform information. I'm trying to throw together a quick program that will compare it to all of the stations in the 10017 zip code. Though I'm also going to have it analyze the stations here in Hell's Kitchen. There's always the chance that the 10017 code is just a red herring; seems kinda weird that everything with the Vipers has happened over on this side of the island, and I can't find any information on Viper activity over in Midtown East."*

"Huh. Well, do what you can. I mean, I'd have to kinda be an idiot not to assume that there's some sort of evidence or clue at that jazz club, so hopefully that will help us clear things up a bit,"* I said as I opened the binder and started to fiddle with the filters. *"Though even saying that, I'm not sure how I want to go about tackling this Gold den. Sure, I've leveled up since I did the one with Hydramental, but I'd also have to be an idiot to assume this one will be simple."*

"Yeah, so I was actually thinking about that. I looked up The Velvet Coil, which is really *not a subtle name, but that's not the point. The place is actively open every night like a legit business and everything. That means there could be random civilians in there, right?"*

"Maybe, what's your point?" I asked as I applied a few filters and turned the page of the binder.

"Well, maybe, *for the first time in . . . pretty much ever, you and I need to go out to a club on a Saturday night,"* he said with a laugh. *"I don't think most people mean* jazz club *when they say that, but I'm not about to argue semantics if I can actually say I got you to go to a club instead of staying in on the weekend."*

"I mean, if you two are going to clubs, I'd rather it be one where I can see you shake your booty, Codex," Angie giggled while I rolled my eyes.

"Oh, trust me, I've got the rhythm of a sloth on LSD; it's not something I'll be doing anytime soon," Jon shot back, for once acknowledging one of Angie's attempts at a joke . . . Or maybe it was flirting; I still wasn't entirely sure about that.

"Is that really a good idea, though? What if a fight breaks out?" I continued, scanning the first page. I had set it to look for items that would fit the seven slots I hadn't equipped with anything just yet: my legs, waist, back, neck, head, and two ring slots.

"If a fight breaks out, I'll just run out with the other civilians freaking out like every single other time an Augment fight happens. Hell, when we walk in, you can do a quick highlight around and make sure there are other normals in there. If there aren't, we just turn and book it. Though, I'm gonna assume more than a few normal people go. The place has an actual website, with actual reviews and everything. Hell, it has a food and drink menu . . . and yes, half the drinks are snake puns: Viper Venom, The Coiled Kiss, Fangbite Fizz . . . I kinda love it, if I'm being honest," Jon said, unable to hide his giddiness.

"Hey, Angie, is that what makes this a Gold den? The possibility of civilians being placed in harm's way?" I asked, turning the page back to the filters and adjusting them further. I really didn't need to see any of the items with smaller plus-one or plus-two bonuses for my off stats. Maybe if I didn't find something else, but the vast majority of the initial options were Style and Charisma based, and I really did need to focus on my main stats first.

"It is certainly a possibility. As you are probably aware by now, there are several different variations for the dens. While the Bronze and Silver ones are often workshops for the grunts or distribution centers, Gold dens tend to have larger operational purposes. These can be things such as the train yard meth lab or the jazz club, which is probably *a money-laundering front, though it is possible they also provide a normal nighttime service that many normal people like to partake in instead of staying in like they're in their nineties."*

"Well then, look at that, it sounds like we have some plans for tonight. You getting Augmented might just be the best thing that's happened to our social lives in ages,"

Jon whooped while I let out an actual audible sigh, which I was sure the Augment closest to me actually took notice of.

"Can I return these superpowers? I like my boring weekends . . ."

"Sorry, Loophole, no refunds, no returns. And especially *no more boring weekends."*

I shook my head as I looked through the waist items. Unfortunately, the Belt of the Thinker had been snatched up, which didn't really surprise me, but other than the Quick Wit feature, it really didn't feel like the best choice for my actual fighting style. Sure, maybe if I wanted to boost my Intelligence faster to grab a few higher-tiered books, but now that I was finding a rhythm with my abilities, I wasn't necessarily in a rush to keep stacking more abilities.

I was about to settle on a Silver-tier **[Belt of Strength]** that would have given me a plus seven to my Strength stat for six thousand credits when the list suddenly refreshed and updated with new items. There was one that appeared at the end of the list that cost quite a bit more than I might have wanted to spend on a single item, but it was arguably tempting all the same.

[Belt of the Action Hero!]
Platinum-tier Equippable Belt.
Color*: Black and Silver.*
*This black belt is practically fresh out of Hot Topic in the late
2000s, with silver studs covering it to make you look extra edgy.*
+4 Dexterity
+3 Strength
+2 Style
This belt comes with the **Action Star** *feature.*
Cost*: 20,500 credits*

[Action Star!]
*They always say action stars are masters of their trade, effort-
lessly bringing their all to every single production they take
part in. This feature might not do that for you, but it certainly is going to give you the flexibility to really show off.
Adds 2 Activated Ability slots, 1 Passive Ability slot, and 1
Movement Ability slot to all Action Bar loadouts.*

"Hot damn, that would be useful . . . You wouldn't even need to go and grab another Revolver slot right away if you went with that one," Jon commented after I unselected the item.

"Yeah, but that's well over half of my available credits," I argued, though I didn't turn the page.

"So? It's not like you have *to fill out every slot right away with top-of-the-line equip-ment. You're already killing it, and you've only put items in half your slots so far. Those*

two activated slots are valuable as all hell, not to mention adding in a fourth Passive slot and that extra Movement slot. Yeah, you got your flight, but I'm sure we could figure out something else we can do with that extra space."

"You're definitely not wrong . . . but don't you think I should at least check out the other slots before I just jump right at this one?" I asked as I hovered over the item with my finger.

"You could, but as far as I can tell, this place works like an auction house without the auctions, and there's a lot of people hanging out at the counters. It's only been a day, and the Belt of the Thinker is already gone. I'd be afraid of that thing vanishing if you turned the page," he argued right back, and I had a hard time finding a good response.

Selecting the item, a scanning tablet appeared next to me. With a wave of my hand, my credit counter plummeted downward to 17,600, and the item appeared in my B.E.L.T. I moved on to my legs, deciding that I wasn't really ready for either a cape *or* a hat, and while the neck and ring slots were there too, legs just felt overall like the more important item to grab. This time, I adjusted the filters to put a fifteen thousand max cost and only looked for leg-slot items.

There weren't a lot of great options this time around, and there were only two Gold-tier items to compare after I had the list organized based on tiers. Unfortunately, neither one really felt like the right choice. One of them was Intelligence focused, with a feature called Synaptic Surge that would double the effectiveness of Intelligence-based abilities . . . which were, at least currently, none of mine.

The other one, an item called **[Gym Bro's Sweats]** came with another Team Player—Minor Leagues feature, which I discovered *would* actually stack with the feature on my tank top, but it only had a plus three to each Strength and Dexterity.

The feature was certainly useful, but only if I was going to be teaming up with another Augment regularly. Even though I had promised Hydramental that I'd tell him when I discovered where the key went, something told me I wouldn't be teaming up with him very often past that. Hell, I wasn't entirely sure I even wanted to message him when I did figure it all out, but I knew that I probably would when it came down to it.

At twelve thousand credits, the sweats just didn't quite feel worth it, especially when I could get a Silver-tier item called **[Durable Denim Pants]** with plus-four Toughness and plus-three Strength for just five grand instead. I didn't really think the feature was worth the extra seven thousand credits, and Jon didn't have an argument for it, so I scooped up the denim.

I did a cursory glance through the slots that I still had empty, and while there was nothing of note for my head or back, even at the lower end of the spectrum, I did end up spending an extra three grand to fill up my neck and ring slots. Each of the three items were only Bronze tier, but between the **[Gambler's Ring]**, **[School Signet]**, and **[Lucky Pendant]** that I purchased, I added plus-three Luck, plus-one Strength, and plus-one Dexterity to my stats.

"Talk about one hell of a big jump to your stats . . ." Jon commented as I wandered

back out of the resale shop with my wallet noticeably emptier. *"You could probably check the bookstore and see if there's anything else you want to add, but you don't necessarily* have *to spend all the credits you have just to spend them."*

"Plus I did say I'd exchange some to buy some groceries."

He let out a bark of laughter. *"True. It would be nice if you weren't eating all of my food for once. Hell, you could actually buy the first round of drinks at the club."*

"Hey, it's not like I never *buy groceries, and you can't actually think I'm going to be getting anything alcoholic in the middle of enemy territory . . ."*

"You know, that's actually really responsible," he shot back. *"Okay, you can buy me a fun drink and yourself just a boring old soda."*

"I think we're getting off topic here," I said as I walked toward the staircase back down to the main square. There was a small line of men in matching black suits and blank white masks that covered their entire faces walking away from The Common Ground in a hurry. The other Augments on their path made it a point of giving them a wide berth as they passed and headed for the portal wall.

When I attempted to highlight the leading one, I received a warning that was not wholly dissimilar from the one I'd gotten when first scanning Giada. I checked the other three members of the pack, only to discover they all sported the exact same warning.

[Warning!]
Information on this Sapient NPC has been blocked
due to **Registered Exceptions**.

"Well, those are government spooks if I've ever seen them," Jon said with a whistle. *"Kinda been wondering where they are in all of this. Although . . . Wait, if they can get to the Square, why can't I?! This is bullshit."*

"Although I'm almost positive I know the answer to this, Angie, wanna fill us in?" I asked, watching as they walked up the stairs and disappeared into a portal.

"Your assumption is correct, Loophole. I am not authorized to access information on what a [Registered Exception] is in this specific scenario, but that exception is also probably *built into the portal mechanism,"* she answered.

"You know what, I got enough to worry about right now that I think I can skip adding 'What the hell is the government up to in all of this,' to it," I said with a sigh, then turned back to the Neutral Segment. *"Okay, I'm gonna get those Viper Skins attached to my jacket and tank top, exchange some credits, and then honestly, I think I'm gonna take a nap."*

"Dude, don't you think you're a bit young to be talking about midday naps?" Jon laughed, and I couldn't help but shake my head.

"I've assaulted a yacht, cleared out a bunch of dens, and then fought off a swarm of snake-men, and it's barely *been over seven hours,"* I replied with a laugh of my own. *"So no, I don't* think I'm a bit young for that at all."*

CHAPTER FORTY-TWO

Axio's daily announcement came and went with—as Pinky had aptly predicted—his normal amount of threats. Whether it was because of the attacks he'd sent the night before or something else entirely, the number of people not keeping up the pace to hit the 10k mark had dropped from fifty to thirty percent, though this time, Axio deployed Major Level Threats for, as he put it, "slacking off."

Pinky and BrainCraft were both well over the fifty percent requirement, with Pinky passing the total necessary points just before the announcement herself. They had been deep in the discussion of some aspects of their new squad when I'd found them. Pinky *had* ended up getting her way with the name, though BrainCraft insisted it was only until they added a third member.

We sat, talked, and exchanged a few fight stories, though it did feel like I did more of the talking than them, since they kept asking about the swarm fight. Although they had been incredibly friendly so far, I still tried my best to keep the bigger parts of my abilities concealed, and though they tried to needle an explanation for how I went from illusions to "superpowered leaps," I managed to keep my lips sealed.

I ate while there, finding that just like with the drinks, the food was quite nearly perfect. It wasn't just that they might have been the best wings I had ever eaten in my life, though—the **[Well Fed]** buff I received from eating them literally came with an additional **[Perfect Nutrition]** buff, which part of me knew wasn't terminology generally used for a basket of wings, carrots, celery, and way too much ranch.

[Perfect Nutrition!]
You've eaten something perfectly nutrition-
ally balanced for a growing Augment.
+1 to All Stats
Your **[Well Fed]** *buff will not begin to expire until this buff expires.*
This buff lasts for **2 Hours.**

While it *was* good to know there was a buff that went beyond **[Well Fed]**, I didn't necessarily go out of my way to rush out and use it either. By the time 8:00 p.m. rolled around, Jon was making me put on the nicest shirt I owned, which wasn't all that nice, with one of my uncle's old blazers. We walked across the city, something that suddenly felt incredibly mundane to me after flying over the neighborhood all day, and took in the oddly peaceful night.

I had been half expecting Angie to interrupt our plans with a Crime Alert, but nothing popped up, and as we got in line to enter the club, I found myself feeling off-balance. My interface kept wanting to highlight the building, clearly marking it as a Viper den, and I felt myself itching to activate my gear for a fight.

It was only the presence of a crowd of people who were *very clearly* marked as Sapients that held my mental finger off the button. The bouncer at the door, a *Non-Sapient* named Deacon, looked us over, checked our IDs, and then waved us in without any sort of hassle, much to my surprise. I was under no illusion that Axio would care if I was in my gear or not—the fact that there were people here he had direct control over left me at a disadvantage without my abilities.

My location panel updated with **[Gold-Level Viper Den—Hell's Kitchen]** as we entered the building. It was amazing how easily I had started to mentally ignore those little elements of my interface after just a few days with it.

The place was gaudy, loud, and far more impressive than I was expecting. Several dozen high-top tables sat in the main area of the club, littered with sleek black marble columns reaching up to what I initially thought was the roof but quickly noticed was actually a second floor. There were several staircases leading down into a section with rounded-off booths with lush green velvet cushions, smaller tables, and even a small dance floor.

I wasn't quite sure if jazz was the kind of music people actually danced to, but it was there all the same. Most of the tables and booths in the lower section were filled with patrons, and Jon led us to one of the open high-top tables, grabbing it before it could be stolen from us.

"Who knew people still liked jazz," I said as I looked around the club. I randomly selected people as I went, letting my vision highlight them just to check.

It only took a few for a pattern to become clear. Every single one of the employees I highlighted was a Non-Sapient, and while most of the people sitting at tables were Sapient, there were a few booths close to the stage that were loaded with Viper soldiers, still thankfully in human form.

I nudged Jon and pointed over to them as subtly as I could.

"Damn, right in the leather vests and everything. It's a good thing, too; not like I can exactly highlight them outside of the apartment," he said with a slight frown.

"Aww, is he missing my silky-smooth commentary?" Angie said wistfully.

"I doubt it," I thought back quickly, looking away from the stage where several members of a band in sleek black suits with emerald accents were setting up. A young woman with curly blonde hair pulled into a ponytail, ruby lipstick, and

a sleek outfit complete with a small green bowtie walked up to us. Her fingers drummed across the table as she came to a stop.

"Good evening, gentlemen, my name is Felicia, and I'll be your server tonight," she greeted with a wide smile as she set down a long, thin menu. "All house-special drinks are on sale for as long as Miss Pearl is singin'. Can I start you two off with anything?"

"Miss Pearl?" I asked, and almost on cue, I heard the tap of a finger against a microphone.

Standing at the center of the stage was a middle-aged woman who wore her age exceptionally well. Her deep cocoa skin stood as a stark contrast against the emerald-green dress that clung to her modest curves as if it was painted on. The material of the dress looked strikingly like scales, with opalescent edges that shone in the light, and she wore a pair of matching gloves that stretched up and over her elbows.

"She's our in-house resident singer; the boss loves her, so she always gets the prime-time spot," Felicia explained, almost a bit peeved, if I wasn't mistaking her tone. She shook it off quickly as a wide smile split across her face. "She should be starting any minute, so the sales are starting up now. If you like something fruity, I suggest the Fangbite Fizz, although I do have to warn you, they're dangerous."

"I'll take one of those," Jon said with his I.D. already ready for her. She barely glanced at it before she turned to me, and I just shrugged.

"Can I just get a Red Bull and some water?"

"Designated driver, huh?" she asked with a raised brow.

"Drive? In New York? Nobody drives in New York," Jon scoffed, and Felicia laughed as she set a hand on his shoulder.

"Well, aren't you just a little comedian," she said with a smile before moving her hand to write on a small notepad. "I'll get these drinks right out for you." She sauntered off as Jon watched her go almost like a puppy.

"What's she got that I don't?!" Angie huffed.

"An actual body?" I suggested. She huffed again.

"Well, at least I can think on my own." I resisted the urge to point out how much I doubted that before she added, *"I heard that."*

"I'd put your eyes back in your head; she's a Non-Sapient," I told him, a bit lower than normal, as I looked back up at the stage. Miss Pearl seemed to be having a conversation with her pianist while the rest of the band did final checks on their equipment.

"Damn . . . there's always a catch, isn't there?" Jon sighed, his own tone lowering as he pulled out his phone. "Though then again, Giada was with Sal . . . so they *are* technically fully human . . ."

"Dude . . ."

"Yeah, I know, didn't feel right saying it out loud," Jon said with his nose scrunched up. "Feels weird to see them just, integrated with normal people."

"Yeah, I know that feeling," I agreed as another tap of the microphone brought my attention back up to the stage.

Miss Pearl stood there, the lights shifting on the stage to illuminate the entire band as she slowly raised her hands up to the sides. The crowd reacted by dropping to silence, and a bright white smile cut across the old singer's face.

"Well, well, well, doesn't this just *please* this old gal's heart, seeing this place packed to the gills!" she spoke with a sultry drawl. "Okay, Zee, I think we've kept these fine folks waiting long enough—let's bring them on down to the snake's nest."

"You got it, Miss P," a younger man with a saxophone replied as he brought it to his lips and began. There were a few quick blasts before he turned to the rest of the band and shouted, "Hit it!"

The lights came to life in a perfect choreographed show as Zee stood from his stool, leaning into his sax as the band followed. His saxophone blared with sharp, staccato-like bursts before the drummer's sticks moved with the rhythm of a machine gun against the snare. Miss Pearl held a tambourine at her side that she smacked against her hip in beat, and the thrumming of an upright bass thumped with a steady groove that rumbled at my chest.

Just as I thought the music couldn't get any louder, several brass instruments burst into the song with bright, brassy tones that cut through the melody, causing the crowd to cheer in excitement.

More than a few people jumped to their feet and hit the dance floor, including, to my surprise, a few of the Viper soldiers. They grabbed partners, dancing with practiced grace as they swung in time to the erratic beat of the music. I'd never been a dancer myself, but the lively sound practically demanded movement, and I found my foot tapping in time with the song.

I was broken from the near trance the music had me in as Felicia set our drinks on the table along with a few napkins. I turned maybe a bit too quickly, and my hand smacked the glass of water she had set down. It was probably a good thing I wasn't in my gear, given how high my Strength stat jumped when I had it equipped, because that sort of strength probably would have sent the glass flying. Thankfully, it only tipped over, pouring its contents onto the table as Felicia jumped backward slightly.

"Ah shit . . . I'm so sorry," I quickly apologized as I looked around. There wasn't a napkin dispenser on the table, nor was there silverware wrapped in napkins either.

"Happens all the time; people get enraptured by the house band," she said with a forced laugh. "I think I forgot my towel, though, so I'm going to need to go find one to clean this up really quick." She turned and retreated quickly while I looked at the small pool of water that dripped over the edge of the high-top table.

"She's *really* a Non-Sapient? Like, that was so real, though . . ." Jon said, slightly in awe. Though he had seen me fight more than a few Vipers now, I hadn't really communicated with the Non-Sapients outside of the shops in the Square, and those felt so segregated from the real world that it was easy to pretend that they weren't, technically speaking, "real" people.

Felicia quickly came back with a fresh glass of water, setting it on the table before cleaning up the mess.

The music came to a slow, popping end as the crowd cheered, and Miss Pearl stepped back up to the microphone. While I was expecting for her to say something, maybe even introduce the next song, nothing of the sort occurred. Instead, the band immediately started to play once more, this time in a slow, bluesy melody. The lights dimmed, and a spotlight shone down onto the well-dressed singer. And as the slow bassline thrummed and the saxophone rang in a low, soothing tone, Miss Pearl began to sing.

> *"Hear the hum beneath the city's bones,*
> *A rattling hymn through the twilight tones.*
> *Follow the shadow, where the venom stains,*
> *Down the forgotten tracks, through the serpent's domain."*

The pianist hit a striking chord as her sultry tones filled the room and brought a hush over the crowd. Her hips swayed while she held on to the microphone stand, letting her body move with the lilting melody.

While the music continued, I let my Area Sense activate, thankful I could use it without being in my gear. It was *almost* sensory overload once the sudden influx of new information hit my mind, but it quickly settled as I probed and felt the intrusions in my space. My sense hadn't improved since I first acquired it, so I still couldn't tell specific details, which unfortunately meant that the blobs of humans, tables, and decorations pressing against me all felt more or less the same.

> *"In the heart of the city, 'neath the endless streams,*
> *There's a rhythm that plays in forgotten dreams,*
> *Through tunnels dark, where the echoes hum,*
> *A venomous trail shows where to come."*

On the balcony that ran above us, I could feel at least one person walking, but for the most part, the close collection of intrusions meant it was probably just more seating. I redirected my attention downward instead, reaching out and investigating the basement of the building.

There were at least two separate rooms I could feel, just based on the walls and doorways that I could touch, and I could feel several blobs that must have been humans. They were huddled around . . . maybe a table? It was hard to tell for sure, and with the size of the club, it was nearly impossible to tell if I was even feeling the entire basement.

I closed my eyes, trying to focus harder, to see if I could get a better read by concentrating as the saxophone started to play a slow but haunting solo. The band fell silent, their absence amplifying the solitary voice of the sax, which rose and fell in slow, deliberate waves. There was a larger figure moving from one room to the next in the basement, and it felt as if one of the blobs huddled was suddenly yanked

from the group just as the sax's solo came to an end and the rest of the band joined
fully back into the song.

> *"Beneath the gleam of the starry ceiling,*
> *Where tracks run deep and secrets are reeling,*
> *A whisper echoes where the lost trains sleep,*
> *Follow the hum where shadows creep."*

The brass section wailed in a demanding chorus as the song burst back to life,
practically rattling me from my concentration, and I struggled to maintain my
focus. The hulking form was still there, but the blobs that I thought were people
huddled around a table seemed to be frozen in place now. I wasn't sure if I had
missed something or if they were simply holding painfully still.

> *"Where the golden clock marks the fleeting time,*
> *And feet once rushed to the echoing chime,*
> *Slip to the dark where the rails run thin,*
> *Fifty steps down, that's where it begins."*

"Holy shit . . . It's the answer," Jon spoke, almost in awe. The sudden noise coming from right next to me finally broke my concentration, and I looked over to him.

"Huh? What was the question? What did I just miss?" I asked, feeling the resid-
ual effects of my ability dissipating, my new sense vanishing.

"The song—she's literally giving us the answer, dude. The starry ceiling, the
golden clock . . . Shit, let me check something," he said and pulled out his phone.
Had *he* been the one with increased strength, he might have destroyed it with how
hard his thumbs went racing across the screen.

"Seriously, what the hell did I just zone out on and miss?" I asked again, and a
moment later, he turned his phone to me with an impossibly smug grin. "Grand
Central Station?"

"That's where Sal—the *real* Sal—is. I'd put money on it. There are a few lines
that go out of there; we just have to figure out which one he's hiding in and *boom*,
we got him," he declared as the song came to a close and the audience burst into
applause around us.

"Wait . . . but why the hell would she be singing that? Isn't it a bit odd that
literally the second song we hear the first time we come here is something giving us
clues to a location we need? What if it's a trap?!" I hissed in a low whisper. He turned
toward me with a shrug.

"Why would you have gotten a key and a mission to hunt him down in the first
place? Who's been guiding you to figure out his involvement in all of this? Maybe
it's a trap, but like, there's no way that song was a coincidence, given that this is the
last place we can go looking for clues. If . . ." He had just started saying something

else when he turned and smiled at someone approaching from behind me. "Hi, Felicia, do you think you could get me another one of these, and maybe one of the appetizer sampler platters?"

"Well, aren't you just a little psychic, knowing what I was coming over here to ask," Felicia said as she came to a stop by our table with a smile. "You're not one of those Augments now, are you?"

Jon laughed and shook his head. "Nah, just a lucky guess."

"Well, that's a pretty good guess then," she declared, lightly placing a hand on Jon's shoulder again with a wink before adding, "I'll put that right in for you, sweetie."

"God, I hate her," Angie muttered as I watched Felicia head back toward a door tucked into a corner of the building on the far side of the main bar.

"What were you saying?" I asked, ignoring her grumbling as I turned my attention back to Jon.

"Maybe we shouldn't be talking about this stuff in the open," he suggested before nodding over to the dance floor. "Besides, I think your *friends* are up to something; they're all moving in a hurry."

I looked in the direction he had indicated, and sure enough, every one of the Vipers had grabbed stuff from their booths and took off toward a back door. Slowly but deliberately, I slipped my uncle's blazer from my shoulders.

"I'm, uh . . . I'm gonna go to the bathroom real quick," I told him, pulling my wallet from my pocket and sliding a few bills across the table to him as Jon gave me a knowing look.

"Do your thing. Uh . . . text me if something is happening, and I'll grab your blazer," he said before thinking about it for a moment. "Actually . . . how 'bout you just leave it on the chair closer to me. I got a feeling there's no way this ends simply . . ."

The band started up another song, and I moved as fast as I could without outright jogging. I wasn't necessarily trying to draw attention to myself, but I still wished I had my gear on so I could just activate my Spectrum Veil and move unseen. The Vipers were moving quickly but in a relatively orderly fashion as they headed toward the same door as Felicia.

As they passed through their door, I slipped into the bathroom, which was conveniently located next to it. I barely let it close behind me, verifying the room was a single occupancy, before I activated my gear and Spectrum Veil in quick succession. Not wanting to lose the trail, I pulled the door back open slowly, inching my way out and hoping no one had noticed.

Another waitress was just pushing her way through the door to what I could now tell was the kitchen, holding a tray with various plates. Pushing myself against the wall, I waited for her to pass before I rushed for the door, making my way through just before it could close.

I looked around quickly, barely catching the trailing Vipers as they turned another corner. I made my way to it, peering around the edge and finding a long staircase down to a concrete wall that turned past where I could see from my vantage point.

Almost effortlessly now that I was used to the mechanic, I opened the phone portion of my interface.

<**To Jon:** There's a basement. I felt it earlier when I was probing but I just found the staircase down. Will keep you posted but uh . . . maybe you should bail . . . you know. Just in case.>

<**From Jon:** Way ahead of you. I put cash on the table and left the moment I saw you go into the bathroom.>

There was no way he was going to be able to get back to the Command Room in time to be my second set of eyes, and I wasn't going to wait that long either. I descended the staircase, watching as my stamina drained quickly from the continued use of Spectrum Veil. It was definitely dropping, but not quite as rapidly as it might have before I had gotten the gear upgrades, which had practically doubled my total amount.

I could hear the sound of voices the closer to the bottom I got, and I was careful with my steps, thankful that the stairs didn't have any sort of squeak to them. There was a large room around the corner, and I saw the Vipers all towering over a group of older women standing around a long table.

The women looked to be sorting and organizing something under their careful observation, more than likely a drug of some sort, if I had to guess, though my familiarity with anything past weed came exclusively from television and movies. To my surprise, the women were all shackled to the table by their ankles, leaving me feeling extremely uneasy. Even if they were Non-Sapients, it felt inhumane.

That's when I scanned one of them and discovered that the woman, a lady named Maria Owens, was a Sapient.

I felt my jaw literally drop, unable to believe that Axio would go this far before I reminded myself that it *wasn't* just him behind this. SnakeBite was involved as well, and at this point, it didn't matter that he had to be higher leveled than me—this went far beyond just some code scribbled on the wall of a bar. This was beyond basic humanity.

I counted at least a dozen soldiers, ranging from level six to eight, though luckily none of them were in snake form. I was going to have to move quickly if I wanted to protect the women, and I immediately found myself wishing I could . . .

My mind trailed off as I thought about my most recent knowledge acquisition. While I had gained a cursory but wide level of understanding on the basics of quantum mechanics, the fundamentals were still a hard thing to wrangle in my head without giving it my entire focus.

I didn't have a lot of time to consider every single aspect of what this would entail, but I mentally reached for the equations that had become imprinted in my brain on quantum tunneling. It wasn't about breaking the laws of physics, even if some Augments could do that without having to obtain the right knowledge sets. It was about bending the rules just enough to slip through the cracks. All I needed was the right combination of probability and focus.

If particles could appear on the other side of a barrier just because their waveforms didn't care about the rules, who's to say I couldn't do the same? It wasn't *technically* teleporting—it was quantum problem-solving.

[New Ability! Phase Step!]
This is a Movement Ability.
I really was wondering if it was a good idea for you to go and
spend all that money on a book with "shenanigans" in the title;
after all, that's my kind of business. But you went and proved
me wrong. I don't think I like it when you do that.
This ability allows you to teleport to a location within your Local Area
that you can visibly see. We can't just let you immediately teleport to
the other side of walls right away—that would be way too broken.
The accuracy of **Phase Step is not** *guaranteed. There is a base 50 per-*
cent chance that you will end up randomly placed within 5 feet of your
intended location, reducing by 1 percent for each point of Luck you have.
Stamina Cost: *500 points per jump, unless you are jump-*
ing to a location where a version of you (i.e. an afterimage) already
exists, which reduces the cost of this ability by 90 percent.

CHAPTER FORTY-THREE

Activating Phase Step was an entirely different experience to flying or any-thing I had done so far; it had sort of like a suction effect as I popped through space from one spot in my area to another, and I appeared on top of the table, scattering their product as I released my Spectrum Veil. The sudden trip across the room in the blink of an eye caused the wind to briefly get knocked out of me, so I took short, shallow breaths to regain my composure as I scanned the surprised faces around me.

"Get down!" I hollered at the women before activating Weighted Clothes. It didn't matter that they were within my zone—since I didn't count them as enemies, the ability wouldn't even add a pound to their outfits.

Between a dozen soldiers in the room, the three thousand pounds distributed through Party Mode wasn't going to do enough to take any of them down immedi-ately, even if it did at least do *some* damage to them, but that hadn't been the point of my initial attack.

Just as I expected, more than a few of them materialized syringes into their hands, intent on starting their transformations. What they couldn't have known was that I had already activated Center of the Universe, targeting items in the space. The skill didn't have the quickest buildup time, but having it already ramping up more than did the trick. I could already feel random baggies and equipment at my feet pulling against my legs.

Of the six syringes that had been pulled out, I managed to force four of them from the soldiers' hands, absorbing them into my B.E.L.T. the moment they hit me, then deactivated my ability before too many things could come hurtling my way. To my surprise, though, they *weren't* Temporary Augmentation Serums, instead appearing as [**Superior Stamina Injectors**] once they were added to my inventory.

I was just about to vocalize the obvious question to Angie when I saw the entire group materialize and stab a different set of syringes into their arms before I could react. One by one, their bodies began to swell and burst through their clothes, yet, as always, their vests seemed to be absolutely impervious to their transformations, though it was possible that was because they were still being held by the heightened weight of my first strike.

"You think we don't learn, Loophole?" one of them growled, his voice fluctuating and shifting to a higher pitch as his body began to morph. "Your tricksss won't work on usss twice."

Knowing that I only had a moment to react, I activated Fun House, slipping into invisibility as I jumped from the table and toward the soldier who had been attempting to taunt me. My stamina had dropped to nearly fifty percent already, but I wasn't even focused on that as I threw a thirty-percent Gravity Punch at him, connecting with his chest and launching him backward into two of his compatriots going through similar transformations. The force caused them to slam into a wall with a good amount of force.

We were in tight quarters already, and the women were cramming themselves under the long metallic table at the center of the room. It was a stupid, impulsive move to jump right in, but seeing *real* people being treated this way had turned off my caution and practically enraged me enough that I just jumped in anyway. Out of the corner of my eye, I caught the glint of a lens and saw a camera that seemed to swivel to look toward me.

I didn't have time to focus on it for too long, as one of the faster transforming soldiers lunged for me. On instinct, I activated Phase Step again, reappearing on top of the table in place of the afterimage I had left behind. Materializing, I immediately used one of the Superior Stamina Injectors, finding it returned seventy-five percent of my stamina in a single burst, practically topping me off completely.

The Vipers were still moving slowly with Weighted Clothes activated, even as the last of them finished going through the process to morph into their snake forms. It was almost odd that it didn't happen at the same rate for each of the soldiers, but it also wasn't something I found myself wanting to complain about either.

So far, I had the element of surprise on my side, as my sudden jump to attack and subsequent return had left them confused as to where I was, with my remaining three illusions still moving around the room. One of them lunged toward the table anyway, and I didn't wait to be struck, using Phase Step to jump to another afterimage on the far side of my zone.

I immediately started ramping Center of the Universe back to full strength, focusing on the enemies in the room as I started to yank them toward me and away from the cowering women. The Vipers had clearly been learning, though, and instead of trying to pull against my force, six of the soldiers turned and lunged toward me.

I waited until the last possible moment, a small smile cutting across my face before I stepped across the room again in the blink of an eye. The group crashed into each other with several loud curses and hisses of anger while I settled in place of one of my two remaining afterimages.

I hadn't necessarily been considering just how Phase Step would interact with all of my other abilities, but much to my happy surprise, this *didn't* interrupt the strength of my gravitational pull. It remained maxed out, and the sudden pile of snake-men began getting yanked backward in a twisted mess. They tumbled in a heap, getting wrapped up in each other and taking more damage as at least one of them was knocked out.

"There's some sort of snake spaghetti joke in here, but I find myself drawing a blank," Angie chirped. *"Or maybe a tumble snake joke? I'll be honest, even though every digital bone in my nonexistent body wants to make a joke, I'm kinda just impressed that you're thinking on your feet."*

"Not now, Angie," I said just as I activated Sting like a Bee and threw a ten-percent Gravity Punch at the nearest soldier.

"That was a compliment, though!" she complained, but I ignored her as I watched the soldier get staggered by my strike.

"Compliment me later!"

Even though the soldier was my level, with my Strength sitting at thirty thanks to my **[Perfect Nutrition]** buff still *barely* being active, my attacks came with an impressive amount of force. The combination of abilities and my strength pummeled the soldier's health down by nearly thirty percent in a single strike. I followed up with two more blows to try and take advantage of Sting like a Bee, sending him collapsing to a heap as if it were child's play.

"Who's next?" I demanded, dropping Center of the Universe while I cracked my knuckles. I didn't wait for them to respond, having only spoken to get their attention off of my last remaining afterimage. I jumped over to it, appearing behind three soldiers who suddenly turned their heads in a panic, trying to find where I had gone.

Given that so many of my abilities lent themselves to me becoming an up-close brawler, even as I continued to grow and adapt, I hadn't really been sure how I was going to keep that style but strike multiple people at the same time. Sure, I had proven that I was good at dodging and punching fast enough to deal damage, but I knew for situations like this I needed to be able to do more than just punch a single target at once.

An idea tickled the back of my head as the principle for quantum coherence suddenly came to mind.

[New Ability! Quantum Echostrike!]

I'm really starting to appreciate just how wild this book you picked up can be, and I've oddly been missing this sorta on-the-spot ability making. It really lets you get creative. First you figure out a form of pseudo-teleportation which is, let's face it, really just actual teleportation, and now this. Now, I could go into an elongated spiel on quantum coherence and wave-particle duality, but I don't think anyone has time for that, especially with how many caveats this ability has.

*When this ability is activated, your next physical strike against an opponent or object will cause a quantum shock wave, echoing out to all identical targets within 5 feet of them. When there are only 3 targets, enemies will take 80 percent of that initial strike's **total** damage.*

For each additional opponent in the affected range, lower the total damage that all affected enemies take by 10 percent less damage, to a minimum of 30 percent applied damage.
If there are associated effects that come with an attack, replicate these effects to all targets affected by this ability.
Cooldown: *30 seconds.*
This ability has **no base cost.**
The cost of this ability is equal to 50% of the next ability thrown. If you do not use an ability for your next strike, reduce the cooldown by 20 seconds.

I didn't even hesitate as I dropped the ability in the empty slot at the end of my action bar and activated it. In that flash, I had a sudden burst of inspiration, and I threw my punch. Right as my fist was about to strike the soldier, I activated Gravity Punch with thirty percent of my stamina. The blow rippled through the air like a current, striking the two enemies directly next to him, and simultaneously, all three of them were thrown in different directions.

The damage was immense, knocking each of them down to near critical as they struggled back to upright. Unfortunately, this *also* brought my stamina down to just over fifteen percent from the rapid use of my abilities.

"Can't believe that worked," I muttered internally while Angie giggled.

"Try and tell me to shut up all you want, but I really do think you should just take the compliment. You're getting pretty good at immediately incorporating new skills into your fighting style," she replied. *"I suppose what you lack in forethought you make up for in on-the-spot thinking."*

"You know, that actually might just be the nicest thing you've said to me so far," I said, watching my opponents carefully and taking a few slow breaths as my stamina slowly crept back up at its natural regeneration rate.

When I had more time, I was *really* going to need to sit down and figure out which of my stats affected both my stamina and health regeneration, and maybe scold Jon for either not thinking it was important or not figuring it out himself with as much gaming knowledge as he had.

Of the twelve soldiers that had been in the room when I entered, four of them had already found themselves knocked out and crumbled to dust, and four of them were nearly critical. The last four had so far avoided any of my damage, and I was going to have to figure out a way to finish this with a nearly depleted stamina bar. The women were still cowering under the table, and at least for now, the soldiers seemed to be avoiding them.

In that moment, it clicked into place just why they weren't trying to use them as human shields. The women *weren't* hostages after all—they were slaves, and they couldn't force them to work if they got hurt. But even that logic wasn't good enough for me. I had to find a way to get them out of the middle of this battlefield before an attack went too wide or one of the Vipers decided they were expendable.

I needed just a bit more stamina, just a little bit more, and I was confident that I'd be able to finish this almost without breaking a sweat.

Two of the soldiers near critical got back up, materializing syringes and injecting them, which returned them to around half life in my hesitation. I might have been angry with myself for letting it happen if my confidence hadn't been quickly rising. Angie had been right: somehow, in the midst of battle, it was the easiest to come up with just the skill I needed.

[New Ability! Schrödinger's Surge!]

Did you know that in some quantum systems, energy and matter can "borrow" energy temporarily under the uncertainty principle? Look who I'm talking to, you're the one who insisted on buying the book, of course you do! Though that means you'd also know that that borrowing does come with some consequences. Instantly restores your Stamina to 100 percent. After 15 seconds have elapsed, all excess stamina from your bar is removed, and an instance of the **[Exhausted]** *debuff is applied, reducing your natural Stamina and Health regeneration by 25 percent for 30 minutes.*

If you do not already have an **[Exhausted]** *debuff when you activate this ability, refresh the cooldown on all abilities with cooldowns 10 minutes or less.*

This ability has **No Cooldown** *and costs* **No Stamina***, but the applied* **[Exhausted]** *debuff is accumulative, and if it is acquired 4 times in total, you will be rendered unconscious for 24 hours.*

I put it in place of Earthbound Impact for the time being just as I started to move, knowing the flight skill would be useless to me for the moment. The soldiers moved to react, seemingly unsure what my plans were as I activated Float like a Butterfly, dodging under and through several wild swipes of overly sharp claws. Lunging forward, I slid on my knees toward the table, using the last bit of my stamina to activate Quantum Echostrike just as it came off cooldown alongside a minimum-strength Gravity Punch. There wasn't a single Viper near me, but it wasn't them that I was aiming for.

My fist connected with the base of a chain holding the shackles of one of the women, and the power of the strike rippled outward through the other clasps. Had I been trying this with my normal strikes, it probably wouldn't have been anywhere near strong enough, but between my increased strength and the bonuses from my ability, each one shattered. The women still had parts of the shackles on their ankles, but more than one of them had been aware enough to see what had happened.

"Run now! I'll guard your exit!" I told them. I didn't wait to see if they were going to listen, turning and activating Schrödinger's Surge. As my stamina immediately refilled, I felt a practically electrical surge ripple through my body while

I spun on my knees, picking a target and Phase Stepping through the air toward them.

I didn't actually think a snake could look surprised, but the soldier managed it as I threw a wide hook at the side of his head, activating Gravity Punch and throwing twenty-five percent of my stamina into the strike. It sent him flying, his body immediately crumbling to dust when my strike flattened the last third of his health, and I had to catch myself, nearly stumbling from the momentum.

"You don't fuck with *real* people; you don't treat them like slaves!" I nearly yelled as I turned and dodged under a wide strike from yet another snake. The others had conveniently begun charging me, clearly not wanting to let me jump out of the way once more. They were just about to surround me, and I *might* have jumped out of the way anyway, but my Surge ability *had* reset my Quantum Echostrike.

I activated it and threw a fifty-percent Gravity Punch for the snake directly in front of me. Just like before, it was as if a shock wave of visible force emanated from the front target, striking each of the snakes one after another and launching the entire group backward toward the nearest wall. Their bodies smacked against the concrete with a chorus of satisfying *THUDS*. Four of the seven remaining soldiers collapsed, the **[KO]** debuff appearing briefly before they began to crumble to dust.

The remaining three weren't doing a whole lot better, even if they *had* been at full health when they first charged me. The strength of my attacks was either far higher than I had fully considered or the serum that they had started to take was becoming less and less effective at increasing their defenses. They *had* seemed to wildly increase the production of both the serum and the Soldier-class Vipers in a short timeframe, so it seemed not only possible but likely that whatever method SnakeBite was using was flawed.

The three remaining Vipers *didn't* actually get right back up, and I found myself cracking my knuckles as I slowly walked toward them. My stamina had bottomed back out, and I had gained the **[Exhausted]** debuff, but that didn't matter. I was finding myself not just *happy* that I had made these assholes crumble so easily but outright satisfied by it. Normally, I might have gotten into my head about that, worried about what sort of monster I was becoming with how fluidly I was jumping into battle, but the truth was, the Augment's Code was right, and it was the very first thing on the list.

Our job was to protect the Sapients who weren't involved in this.

They couldn't help the fact that someone had introduced this system into our world, and the best they could do was hope they could just live from day to day. It's what I had been doing before being crushed by that dumpster. Hell, I was maybe just starting to realize it was why I hadn't really applied myself past some random cleaning job. How were you supposed to try and thrive in a world where a small population literally played by different rules?

As much as I might have *wanted* to let myself go down an existential rabbit hole, I was too damn angry at seeing Sapients being treated like tools.

"You know, had you guys just been using folks like you to run your business, maybe I would have offered you three the chance to surrender; *maybe* I would have tried to coax some information out of you, even. But you guys, your *boss* . . . he crossed the fucking line," I said, staring up at one of the cameras in the corner. "SnakeBite, if you're watching . . . I'm coming for you."

I activated Schrödinger's Surge a second time, waiting just long enough for Echostrike to come back off of cooldown before I threw as hard of a punch as I could, burning every last bit of my stamina in a final Gravity Punch against the now cowering soldiers.

There was a chorus of trumpets in my head as several notifications opened in rapid succession. A second [**Exhausted**] debuff was layered over the first, and I found myself needing to take long, slow breaths while I let Angie read the notifications off to me.

[Viper Den Completed!]
You did not report this den to the Tenth Precinct.
No additional rewards will be granted.
Hell's Kitchen Viper Dens Cleared: *8 of 8 completed!*

[Phase Points Gain Updated!]
Territory Claimed!
Extra-Large Neighborhood: 1000 points.
(No longer halved due to being **Contested**.*)*

[Phase Points Gained!]
Kill Non-Sapient Augment!
You have killed multiple Non-Sapient Augments. This is worth
points equal to the defeated Augment's level times 25.
Total Value: *1950 points*

[New Achievement! Territorial!]
You have fully claimed your first territory. With the Vipers no lon-
ger having points to operate out of, this territory will not experi-
ence a game-related Crime Alert for the next 24 hours.
Gold-Level Achievement.
Reward: *You have received an A+ tier Loot Box!*

I was just about to send Jon a text to celebrate having fully claimed my territory when there was the crackle of a speaker. It *wasn't* like the one that happened whenever Axio started to talk; this one was *actually* coming from inside the room, from unseen speakers. A slow, mocking clap echoed in the room, and I glanced back up toward the camera I had noticed earlier in the fight.

"Well, that *really* was quite the show, Loophole. I must say, I am impressed," the unfamiliar voice said. It was almost . . . sophisticated? I still wasn't sure if Sal was a clone of SnakeBite or something else, but the elegant timbre that came from the speakers wasn't what I expected the real version to sound like. Maybe that was just my own expectations based on Giada and the Vipers I had interacted with so far, but it still left me feeling unbalanced.

I shook it off as fast as I could and tried my best to glare.

"No, you don't get to be fucking impressed by me, SnakeBite. I'm coming for you. I don't know what fucking sick game you're playing, but I think I've finally figured something out," I said, slowly walking toward the camera as it swiveled downward to keep me in frame. "Your power, or whatever it is you're doing with this snake-vampire bullshit that Hydramental told me about? It's because you're weak. You have to hide behind these men that you treat as disposable because you can't fucking fight at all. It's why no one has ever heard of you. It's why *no one* is afraid of you. I don't think it's going to matter even a bit that you're higher leveled. I'm going to crush you."

"Oh, you are amusing!" He laughed with a disturbing amount of glee, and the sound echoed off the walls. "You think I'm scared of you? That I'd have to face you to defeat you? That you're *actually* worth my time? No, as easy as it would be, I *don't* want to crush you.

"You see, I've been watching you; I've watched how you've grown, and just how quickly too. Your power . . . It's just so, so *interesting*. Every time I throw something at you, you adapt, you *evolve*. You're not locked to one specific tactic like so many of us Augments. No . . . you get to change, don't you? No, I don't think I'm done with you just yet. There are so many things I could do with a power like that, and I just can't do my experiments if you're dead."

I felt a chill run down my spine and the prick of my nails pushing into my own skin. I swallowed what little spit was in my mouth. "Big talk for someone hiding behind an army of minions."

Silence seemed to linger for a minute, and when he did start to speak again, the speakers actually had to crackle back to life.

"So you want to fight the great SnakeBite, Leader of the Vipers? You want to see just what *I* can do? You want to know just why no matter what you think, we are far from done?" he continued, the mirth in his tone vanishing completely. "Well, you've got the key. You know where to go. What the hell are you waiting for?"

CHAPTER FORTY-FOUR

I waited in the basement for a few minutes after the speakers went quiet, catching my breath as my stamina ticked back up painfully slowly. I only waited until I could use another injector, opting to use one of the Enhanced ones instead of the more powerful but limited in quantity Superiors I had stolen from the Vipers.

Once I had some stamina again, I crept back up the stairs, activating Spectrum Veil just before I reached the main floor. Although the den had been marked as cleared, I had no idea what sort of commotion had been caused by the escaping women. The kitchen had emptied out completely, and there was a distinct lack of music coming from the main dining room.

I let my invisibility fade to conserve my stamina and pushed my way through. The waitstaff were standing in the room, stiff as statues and looking right at me with hard stares. They weren't looking *through* me, that much was clear with the way their heads followed as I moved. I slowly walked my way toward the table Jon and I had been sitting at, taking in the eerie space. Just as I was about to ask what was going on, every single one of them, in perfect unison, started hissing.

It was a slow, steady drone, and I noticed Felicia standing perfectly at attention at the edge of our table. Her eyes were completely unfocused, even as I made contact with them, and the sound just continued to escape from her mouth. I reached out, shaking her shoulder a bit, wondering if it would break her from her trance, but nothing changed.

"You're wasting your time, Loophole. If this is what their controller wants them to be doing, then that's what they're going to do," Angie spoke in a low, practically somber tone.

"Yeah, I sorta figured, but I still have an hour to kill anyway . . . Even though I want to charge over there right now, I still don't know which line . . ." I trailed off as I looked around the room.

Even Miss Pearl and her band, standing atop the stage, were staring in my direction and hissing. Turning toward Felicia, I leaned in closer, trying to isolate just her voice in the steady drone of the room. I couldn't help myself and started to laugh once I realized exactly what was happening. It wasn't like I was doubled over in laughter, but the pure absurdity of it after the day I had had, finding what I needed so easily was far funnier to me than it should have been.

"Um . . . are you okay? Did you finally snap?" Angie asked with genuine concern while I finally settled down.

"Codex was right. This place had the answers we needed. The song told us where to start—Grand Central Station—and now they're telling me the subway line I'll find him at," I said, reaching up and wiping away an errant tear.

"But they're hissing; they're not telling you anything . . ."

"No, they're not hissing. Unlike Sal and the soldiers with their serums, they aren't *snakes. The sound they are making, with that little stutter in it, is what would happen if you told a program to read the letter S repeatedly . . ."* I explained. *"It's a pretty small line, but the S line does go to Grand Central."*

Practically confirming my words, the entire room went silent, though none of the Non-Sapients moved even an inch from where they stood. I backed away from Felicia and glanced over toward the front door. Of course, even though I *hadn't* called the den in, there were police lights beating against the window.

"Neat revelation aside, can you get out of here . . . These guys are kinda freaking me out," Angie muttered. She wasn't wrong, though, and as I headed for the exit, all of their heads continued to follow me with unrelenting attention.

I pushed my way through the door, finding a crowd of well-dressed people being held back by a police line. Looking around, I tried to see if I could find any of the women who had been chained up, but I couldn't immediately locate any of them. More than one had looked incredibly malnourished, and I wanted to make sure they were getting help before I just ran off to my next fight.

Luckily, on the far side of the crowd, I could see an ambulance with its doors open. Axio might have been playing games with all of us, and I knew he was still up to *something*, but I could at least appreciate what he did with the small bits of influence he did have over the police and medical dispatch. That really seemed to be the only explanation for how they could be here only a few minutes after I finished a fight that *no one* saw.

While I could have gone over to the ambulance to check in on the women, if they were already with medical staff, there was little I could do other than probe them for information, and that felt like a callous thing to do in the middle of a crowd.

"Hey, Loophole, are those folks in there going to be okay?" one of the officers, a Sapient named Howard, asked as I approached the police line. Before I could even answer, the door behind me opened, and the waitstaff all started to stumble out holding their heads and acting disoriented.

"They were following orders and were afraid to leave when the women being treated over there escaped. Can you make sure they are taken care of? They were being held prisoner in the basement and used to sort drugs," I said, not *technically* lying. "This place was a front for those Vipers that have been trying to take over lately. Emphasis on *was*."

"Well damn, you've been busy," Howard whistled while another officer stepped up holding out a hand.

"Hi, Loophole. Sorry, I'm actually a big fan . . . I saw your fight over on Ninth and just, *wow*, you are quite the hero," he gushed. I smiled sheepishly as I shook his hand and highlighted him to grab his name.

"Thank you, Officer Franklin. I'm just trying to do what I can," I said, then felt my jaw set as I turned toward the crowd watching me with rapt attention. There were more than a dozen phones being held up, trying to get a good shot of me. Looking between them, I squared my shoulders as I prepared to address them, knowing just what I had to do.

"These bikers," I started, raising my voice as a hush passed over the crowd. "They've been trying to hurt the people of our neighborhood. They've been trying to hurt the people in Chelsea and Hudson Yards too, and it's gone on long enough. I know I'm still new to this, still new to all of you. But I'm telling you . . . No, I'm *promising* you all, right here and now, I'm going to put a stop to it. All of it. Not just here but everywhere these asshole bikers try to terrorize. This is our home; this is *our* city. You all can count on me to protect it."

[Phase Points Gained!]
Territory Claimed!
Medium Town: 1500 points.
(Halved to 750 points. Reason: **Contested**.*)*

The crowd erupted into cheers as chants of "*Loop-hole. Loop-hole. Loop-hole!*" overtook the group. One thing I knew for certain: if there was ever a time for a superhero exit, it was when people were cheering my name.

Although my stamina was still barely creeping up, I gave the group a wave before I bent down then took off into the air and away from the scene with as much speed as I could manage.

<**Loophole:** Grand Central Station. S Line in 1 hour.>

I could have gone back home. Hell, I probably *should* have. But I knew if I went home now, Jon would talk me out of doing this tonight. He'd tell me we had the location and I could just put it off for another day. But I wasn't going to risk giving SnakeBite more time to prepare. There was a chance this was a trap—logically, I knew that, and I'd use Area Sense as much as I could to try to scout ahead. But I wasn't going to be doing this alone.

<**Hydramental:** I'll be there. Meet on the platform?>

<**Loophole:** Yup.>

"If I add him to my team, will he be able to hear Codex when he's back online?" I asked as I set myself down on a roof only half a block away from The Velvet Coil.

"Hmm, checking," she said. After a few seconds passed, she added, *"Apparently, it's a setting; you can choose to patch Codex into team chats, but it is a decision you two would have to actively make. He has a few toggles in the Command Room as well that simulate the natural way you can use the internalized system to isolate who you want to*

talk to. In short, you don't need to worry too much because Hydramental wouldn't just be able to hear him right away."

"And if I do add him, how are missions handled? Back on the train, we both had separate missions for that den, but he doesn't have the mission for the key. Would I have to share or split the mission's reward with him?" I asked, wanting to make sure I covered all of my bases.

While I *had* promised him that I'd let him know when I was doing this, I didn't necessarily want to share the reward I'd get after all the bullshit he had put me through so far.

"No, the mission is for you alone. That's not to say there aren't missions that you can share, because those do exist and will *become more common the further you go, but you don't have to worry about sharing this specific mission's S-tier reward,"* she explained before a message appeared.

[Codex has entered the Command Room.]

"Holy shit, what the hell did I miss?! How are you already out of there?" Jon's voice crackled into my head, and I could hear him huffing to catch his breath.

"Did you run all the way home?" I asked curiously.

"Well, I sure as hell didn't fly! I was trying not to miss your infiltration. What happened?" he asked again, and I let out a small laugh before I, as requested, explained just what happened.

It took a few minutes to go through everything, and we took the time to go over my newest abilities as he examined them from his side. My conversation with SnakeBite, however short it was, was the main topic of discussion, and as I had predicted, Jon wanted me to wait before making my next move.

"Look, I already told Hydramental where to go. There's every chance that SnakeBite packs up his shit and moves, and then, knowing Axio, we'd have to start this all from scratch. I'm done dealing with this asshole," I explained, stretching as I looked across the city. I couldn't exactly see Grand Central from my perch, but I knew roughly where it was.

"There's nothing I can say that's gonna change your mind, is there?" he asked, and I just shook my head. *"Cool, so what's the plan then? This guy has to have thirty levels on you. Shit, it might be forty if we are going based on Silver Wrangler."*

"Maybe I'm being overconfident, I don't know for sure, but I don't think he's that strong, even if he is at a much higher level. If he was, I feel like he would have come out himself and stopped me before I wiped his people out of Hell's Kitchen." I pushed off the roof and started floating toward the other side of the city, slowly lowering toward the ground. *"I'm not gonna charge in there with this debuff, though, just in case, which is why I told Hydramental to meet me there in a bit."*

"I'm surprised you told him at all after everything. You coulda just headed over there before he even knew what was going on. Although . . ." He trailed off, and I heard the

rush of fingers over a keyboard. *"Yup, looks like you're back in the spotlight* again. *The news already has your speech outside The Velvet Coil playing everywhere. That explains why it looks like you have an active claim on Community District Four, which they are classifying as a Medium Town . . . That's interesting.*

"Oh, and your News Appearance trophy is up to six unique events now. Knowing Murphy's Law, Hydramental probably would have seen this and bothered you in the middle of it if you hadn't *messaged him."*

"That does sound like the exact sort of scenario Axio would cook up," Angie agreed.

"Yeah, let's just assume that's what would have happened and praise my on-the-spot decision-making," I said, rolling my eyes as my feet touched the ground in an alley on the edge of Hell's Kitchen. I deactivated my gear and strolled out onto the sidewalk, blending in with the passing crowd. I let out an actual sigh before I explained myself. *"It's his brother; he deserves closure, whatever that is going to entail."*

"Yeah . . . I guess I get that," Jon admitted as silence overtook us.

The streets were crowded and the air crisp as I slowly made my way across the city, taking in the relatively peaceful streets. Even Times Square, somewhere I made a point of *never* normally crossing due to its nature as a tourist trap, had a level of normalcy to it that had been largely missing from my life in the last few days. I was tempted to jump on the S line right from the station there, but I felt like it would be odd if I just lingered on the subway platform.

By the time my **[Exhausted]** debuff had finally worn off, I had been walking around inside the main terminal of Grand Central Station for over fifteen minutes. Even though it was nearly 10:00 p.m., the place was still packed. I stayed alert, highlighting random people and finding a distinct lack of Vipers hiding among the normal populace. That *didn't* surprise me; they would have stood out a bit too much just being out and about . . . Almost like a guy in a tricolor long-sleeve shirt stomping his way through the concourse and toward the entrance to the S line.

"I wonder how that shirt works," Jon mused while I started to follow Hydramental from a distance. *"I mean, obviously it's game generated and all that, but is it like, some sort of color-changing material, or is it three different shirts sewn together that get the rest of their parts when he splits his clones off."*

"My guess would be color changing. Generally speaking, one of the first items any Augment gets is something that would help them create a unique-enough appearance while benefiting both the Augment's powerset and their own personal stylistic preferences. Something like Hydramental's shirt is a great example of how it plays into a powerset. There are even settings that will allow for future items to be transmogrified to look like their original gear in the event Augments get attached to their starting look."

"And Loophole got that orange monstrosity of a jacket because it's his favorite color and, for some reason, he's always wanted a leather jacket," Jon laughed while I rolled my eyes.

"Really, guys, I'm about to attack SnakeBite's base, and you two are talking about fashion?"

"Yeah, pretty much," Jon replied casually. *"It's called levity, bud. You have a really bad habit of getting in your head when things get too serious—you literally always have. You did it when you tried to ask Rebecca to prom, and you did it when Uncle James died. Honestly, I've been thinking about it, and I'm pretty sure* that's the reason you have Angie.*"*

"Loophole has me because all *Augments have a Personal AI generated for them upon Augmentation,"* Angie clarified.

"No, not a Personal AI in general. I'm talking about him having you *specifically,"* he said, and I heard Angie hum with curiosity.

"Yeah, I'm gonna need you to start getting a bit more specific than that," I spoke, wandering down the staircase. The crowd wasn't big enough that they had to part to give him room, but them murmuring and pointing Hydramental's way as he went made him relatively easy to follow.

"I was reading up on this a bit when you were asleep earlier 'cause I was curious. As Angie pointed out, Personal AIs are generated specifically for the Augments; the database doesn't give a super detailed explanation of the process, unfortunately, but it does give enough of the basics that I think I understand the gist of how it works."

"Silver kinda told me about it back when I first went in The Common Ground. Was surprised as hell that they weren't *all like Angie,"* I offered, and Jon laughed.

"Yeah, she's definitely a bit odd, but from my reading, it's not abnormal for a PAI to act somewhat irrationally. They are each uniquely created to act as motivators for their specific Augment based on what the system determines would best help motivate them," Jon explained.

"I tried *to tell him that before. I even showed great restraint by not making a perfectly accurate BDSM joke about how much Loophole enjoys being degraded."*

"I don't *enjoy being degraded . . ."* I muttered.

"No, I don't think that's it. I think it's more that you enjoy having someone to butt heads with. Had you been given an AI that acted like Navi or something just straightforward and robotic, I think you might have done fine, but you would have really quickly gotten bogged down in all of the seriousness of it. Angie doesn't let that happen. Even when things are as serious as they can be, she drags you out of it with her jokes, her snark, and yeah, her desire to hit on me over and over again.

"She keeps things from getting too heavy because if they did, you'd spiral. You get overwhelmed when things feel too big or too serious, and that can freeze you up. But with her, even before I got brought into this, you've been constantly reminded that you don't have to carry the weight of everything alone or make it some grand, solemn quest. She keeps you grounded in the absurdity of it all, and that gives you space to focus on what really matters."

There was a moment of silence as I let that sink in, broken only by Angie chiming in with her usual flair.

"Wow, Codex. That almost sounded sweet. Although, really, I'm just here to watch Loophole screw up and remind him that he's a moron when he doesn't ask me the questions he's supposed to be asking me . . . and maybe laugh a bit."

I couldn't help but chuckle despite myself. Maybe Jon was onto something.

"But yes . . . that does mean she's a little *bit of an asshole,"* he added with a laugh of his own.

I was getting close to the platform for the S line. The bathrooms here weren't single occupancy, and I didn't think I was going to be able to activate my gear in there. Luckily for me, while the main concourse had been pretty busy, the crowd entering and leaving the S line wasn't nearly as bad. It was a risk, I knew that it was, but I did have the forethought to reactivate the passive camera-obfuscating aspect of Spectrum Veil on my walk over to the station.

It was still a risk, but I took it as I dipped behind a random pillar, waited a moment, then activated my gear and Veil, moving out from my hiding spot and down the rest of the stairs before I released the ability and popped back into visibility to avoid burning too much stamina. More than a few onlookers jumped at my sudden appearance, but Hydramental's stomping entrance had already had them prepared for Augments.

"Yo, Hydramental," I called out in as friendly of a tone as possible. I didn't want the civilians to think that a fight was about to start. Hydramental flipped on his heels, and to his credit, *didn't* look like he wanted to take a swing at me for leaving him on a roof.

"Ready to do this?" he asked simply, and surprisingly, *he* was the one to send the Temporary Team-Up request. I accepted it and nodded.

"Yeah, let's end this."

CHAPTER FORTY-FIVE

We waited until the next train left the station before following it down into its tunnel. Several people stopped to take pictures, curious as to what we were doing, but thankfully, Hydramental had the sense *not* to send them into a panic about a potential lair full of violent enemies less than a football field away.

"So, I'm surprised you actually sent me a team-up request." I commented, glancing over my shoulder at him once we were far enough from the main platform. "Not saying I'm not cool with it; it's just that there's not really a mission we are gonna get team points for."

"I've got some gear with the Team Player feature; more damage ain't a bad thing, especially going into this," he replied with a shrug. "I also wanted to see how allies appeared on the mini map upgrade I installed after the giant windfall I got from that street fight."

"Ah, yeah, I have that feature on some of my gear too, so it works out for me. How much did the map end up costing you?" I asked.

"Thirty-five thousand credits. It was pricey as all shit, but I got really tired of having to double-check where the hell I was going all the time."

"Damn, that is a chunk of change . . ." I said, holding my tongue before I made a comment about him not using the cash for gear upgrades. It wasn't my place to question his build choices, especially since I had needed my own help with mine.

We slowed to a stop near an out-of-place indent in the wall. That alone might have made it an obvious place to investigate, even if it *hadn't* had the same Vipers logo crudely spray-painted into the spot. "You know, it really seems like a bad way to hide your bases when you're spray-painting your logo exactly where the entrance is."

"Huh? You do realize the graffiti is just something we see, right?" Hydramental asked.

My head dropped to the side for a second before I turned my attention inward. *"Is that right, Angie?"*

"Well, we can't have every random person just investigating all the places with obvious markings on them, and it makes it easier for you Augments to find them," she explained, and I just let out a sigh as I pinched the bridge of my nose.

"Huh, well no. I did not realize that . . . but I suppose it makes sense," I said as

I materialized the snake key into my hand. "Now, let's see what this will do . . . Not like there's a keyhole for me to put it in . . ."

As the key formed, the rubies inlaid into it began to shine, sparkling and glittering just as the graffiti on the wall began to glow in unison from its proximity. It started from the center before it began rushing outward along each of the lines until the entire piece was shining a brilliant emerald green that I had to lift a hand to shade my eyes from. The light burst outward before the wall vanished, and a long tunnel that faded into darkness was left in its place.

"Well, that's one way to make sure normal people don't go wandering down there . . ." I muttered, activating my Area Sense and probing for any rooms I couldn't see. As far as I could tell, the place was *just* a tunnel. One that happened to be illuminated with a faint green light, but a tunnel all the same.

"I'm just wondering if this is the normal city sewers, or if it's some alternate area like the Square," Jon wondered while I started walking down into the passage. The moment I crossed the threshold, **[Viper's Headquarters]** flashed through the location panel on my interface, and my mission tracker shook.

[Mission Updated! The Snake Key!]
Oooooh boy! You did it—you found where the key led to! Now,
if you want that reward, you're going to need to figure out what
was so important that it needed to be locked up so tight.
The reward for the mission is **still** *an S-tier Loot Box.*

We walked in silence for a few minutes, the barrier reappearing behind us as soon as we had both gotten about fifteen feet into the tunnel. Had we both not been dead set on continuing forward, that might have been something to worry about. As it stood, it just worked to make sure no one followed us. The walls were made of solid concrete, but it really didn't seem like any sewer I had ever seen. At the end of the day, it really didn't matter what it was, though—it was where we had to be.

"Have you ever seen your brother fight? Does he spit venom like Sal did?" I asked, finally saying *something*.

"Nah, I never got to see him fight, at least not in any real capacity. I've seen his snake form, though that's only been twice, and it's not like I memorized his colors or anything like that," he explained casually. Unlike in our other discussions about him, bringing up Sal *didn't* send him off the deep end. "But other than the biker incident, I never actually saw him in action."

"Well, hopefully he's as weak as I accused him of being earlier . . ." I muttered before I could stop myself and heard his footsteps come to a stop. I stopped as well and looked back at him, his brow creased in frustration as I let out a nervous chuckle.

"You spoke with him?" he asked, his voice stern as he stared at me.

"Maybe you shouldn't have said that . . ." Jon whispered.

"Loophole is *good at putting his foot in his mouth,"* Angie added with a giggle.

"I, uh . . . Yeah . . . I was just clearing the last den in my area, and he sorta came over the speaker to taunt me," I replied, deciding that trying to obfuscate it at this point was, well, pointless. "Dude sounded a bit posh, to be honest."

"Posh?" Hydramental raised one of his brows.

"Yeah, it's the best way I can think to describe it. He just sounded like he had a really high opinion of himself," I explained with a shrug before turning and continuing to walk. "He basically invited me to come and try to take him down after I beat down a bunch of his men."

"I really don't get it," Hydramental muttered as he let out a rough-sounding sigh. "He was never like this before he got Augmented. Shit, the dude got both the Presidential Volunteer Award and a Future Leaders scholarship in his senior year . . ."

"I wonder what his PAI was like; maybe he just snapped," I suggested.

"Maybe . . ." he responded, though he sounded unsure.

"Are you going to just swing at him first, or are you gonna talk?" I asked, stopping for a moment to activate my Area Sense. On either side of the concrete-coated tunnel there was nothing but filled space, and it went on for as far as I could feel.

"He's my brother . . . I need to know why this all happened, and if I can't make him see reason . . . well, he's had his chance . . ." He trailed off again.

"One way or another, this ends tonight," I said, turning again to look back at him. He stared back, and I could practically see the fire in his eye before he gave me a curt nod. The tunnel seemed to have a bit of a curve, as the darkness in the distance never got closer, but as I peered backward, the same darkness overtook my vision. "Does that mini map of yours show where this tunnel is heading?"

He shook his head. "No, it's actually giving me a sort of fog-of-war effect. It did that in the last two dens I took down this afternoon, too, but when I'm just running around the city, it shows up like it's Google maps."

"What's up with that, Angie?" I asked internally.

"Certain areas, when designated as bases or game-specific areas, will create a fog of war for those with the mini-map feature to protect any possible changes the controller sets in place. This is, largely speaking, a defensive aspect of base ownership. Other such defenses when a base is properly leveled include armed turrets, gas chambers of both the knockout and lethal variety, and of course, good ol' trapdoors."

"Does that mean Loophole could eventually have a greater base than our Safe House here?" Jon asked, and I couldn't help but be curious as well.

"He could! Though that generally takes place after *Augments form a permanent squad. Then each player would have an entrance to their base from within their personal Safe House,"* she chirped before she hummed for a minute. *"That said, having a squad* isn't *necessary to create one of these bases; it just costs a lot more on your own."*

"Guess we better just keep going," I finally said, deciding to let the topic drop instead of getting too deep into something that ultimately didn't matter right now, though once again Jon and Angie seemed to drift off into a deeper conversation that I managed to zone out.

As we continued, every so often we would stop, and I'd probe outward with Area Sense. Hydramental was, of course, curious as to what I was doing, but I had opted to largely keep my mouth shut, telling him I was just searching for anything that might have seemed out of place. The tunnel curved back and forth, almost like a snake slithering, but there were noticeably no side paths, no hidden rooms or even guards patrolling that we had to dispatch.

We had been walking for nearly a half hour, something that was easy to track due to the ticking timer on my **[Well Fed]** buff, when the faint sound of activity finally started to reach us.

"Let me scout forward really quick. I can go invisible and see what's waiting for us, how's that sound?" I asked in a low voice. If they were close enough that we could hear them, then the same was going to be true for them being able to hear us.

"I mean, I'm fine with just going in hard and fast, but if that's gonna make yah feel better about it, go for it; just don't take too long or get too far ahead," he said, though he didn't seem to be pleased about it.

I nodded and turned, creeping forward as long as I could before I activated Spectrum Veil and approached the threshold into the room. The tunnel exited into what I could only describe as a large high school gym, complete with an actual set of bleachers along one wall, basketball hoops on either end of the room, and a giant Viper logo painted, crudely, on the far wall. Gym equipment littered the rest of the floor, and there were at least three and a half dozen men that I could initially see wandering around the room, stopping at the equipment and gathering in small groups throughout.

<**Loophole:** Well, we're definitely in the right place. Pretty much training ground zero. I think there's three, maybe four dozen of them in here. No one over level six as far as I can see, and quite a few down at level three. They're all grunts and brutes, so I don't think we're gonna have any serum users to deal with.>

<**Hydramental:** Sounds like a party to me.>

<**Loophole:** I'm going in, using this invisibility takes up a lot of stamina. Hard and fast?>

<**Hydramental:** Right behind you.>

I dashed into the room, hearing Hydramental's heavy footfalls coming up behind me quickly. I hadn't dropped my Veil yet, so the bikers didn't see me as I entered. Instead, I was able to make it about a quarter of the way into the room, heading right toward a half dozen level-five grunts on the far side of the gym, when shouts of alarm went off at Hydramental's entrance.

I stopped hard right in front of the grunts just as they turned to rush toward Hydramental's splitting form. The group was nice and close together, so I activated Quantum Echostrike before throwing a twenty-five percent Gravity Punch. There was a noticeable look of shock that passed over the group as I popped into existence, only for the entire group to get thrown backward into a bench press.

Their health bars crumpled, all dropping to near critical from the single attack. I didn't let up and fell atop them, placing a few hard kicks to their stomachs and heads, knocking each of them out in rapid succession.

After seeing so many of my enemies crumble to dust, it was actually kind of nice to see the floating **[KO]** debuffs over their heads. I had to keep telling myself it *wasn't* my fault that all of those soldiers were dead. I hadn't forced them to inject themselves. Although there had been Non-Sapients dead in my wake, so far, it felt like my hands were still clean, and it wasn't a feeling I wanted to lose anytime soon.

Hydramental wasn't striking *nearly* as soft-handed as I was, and I turned just in time to see a grunt practically immolating in a blaze of red-and-orange flames. As much as I wanted to admonish him, to tell him to go for the knockout instead of the kill, the last thing I needed was for him to decide to start throwing his attacks my way. If this proved anything, it was that even though Hydramental was working with me now, this was only a one-time thing. Even if we could be cordial, I couldn't actively team up with someone who would kill indiscriminately, even if the thing he was killing wasn't *technically* alive.

A nearby brute called attention to me, and the group finally split up, half trying to surround the Hydramental clones and the other moving to rush me. I activated Float like a Butterfly and charged right back at them. I *still* hadn't actually taken the time to figure out just what fighting style I had picked up, but I knew I was light on my feet and quick to strike.

"It's Wing Chun, and very badly utilized Wing Chun at that," Angie said with an exasperated sigh. *"You'd* think *you would have looked that up by now."*

"Isn't that a Chinese style?" Jon asked while yet again I forced their conversation to dull into a drone as I focused on what mattered at the moment.

It really didn't matter to me *what* the style was—it was working for me. I dodged around the closest grunt and struck him in the back of the head before I spun on my heel and moved further into the mass of enemies. I dodged, dipped, and weaved around the bikers, landing quick jabs and strikes on their torsos and arms before I finally planted my feet in the middle of the group.

I *didn't* want to copy Hydramental and set them all ablaze, I knew that for sure, but I *had* made Ring of Fire for a reason, so I activated it and forced the blaze to rush outward as rapidly as it could.

There were sudden screams of pain as the flames licked at every single target within my zone. The fire didn't linger on any of them long enough to actually set them on fire, at least not outside of a few burnt shoulders and singed shirts, but they did all take good hits to their health bars, some falling nearly twenty-five percent from the single second of fire that assaulted them.

There was a brilliantly bright light show coming from the other side of the room as bolts of electricity bounced between the bikers and the metallic equipment surrounding them. I didn't have time to admire it, though, as the nearest brute to me had recovered and came rushing in my direction.

I dodged his first attack, dipping under the massive arm, activating Sting like a Bee, and hitting him in his side with a ten-percent Gravity Punch. I followed it up with two more rapid strikes, chunking his health down to nothing before punching him as hard as I could in the gut with a five-percent Gravity Punch that made him crumple to the ground.

I made eye contact with one of the grunts gathering around me and found myself smiling as I activated Center of the Universe. Instead of ramping it up to full strength, I only added a bit more pressure than what I normally used. While being able to yank people toward me with a massive amount of strength was absolutely useful, there was something to be said about changing gravity *just enough* to leave people off-balance.

I rushed the grunts closest to me, landing strikes with ease as each of their attempted attacks sent them stumbling.

Although I had already used a good portion of my stamina, I found myself taking down the enemies with enough ease that I limited myself to basic attacks, working my way through the side of the gym I had claimed. I didn't make it through the fight unscathed, and I took more than a few hits as I fought through the bikers, but I never found myself worried either.

It only took a few minutes between the two of us to clear out the large swathe of enemies that had filled the room. I saw Hydramental materialize a syringe into his hand before he jammed it into his arm, and I pulled a pair of Health and Stamina Injectors of my own, letting the renewed energy fill my body as I let out a relieved sigh. No reinforcements had come bursting through the far doors, and the battle was over with a mess of bodies, destroyed gym equipment, and burn marks littering the room.

Not a single one of the bikers on his side of the gym had the [**KO**] debuff, and I found a pit of anger growing in my gut. Even knowing this wasn't the moment, I couldn't stop myself from staring at Hydramental, my jaw setting as I found my resolve.

"Did you have to kill all of them?" I asked as we stood there. Hydramental looked at me with amusement.

"Are you still on that? Is that why all those assholes on your side are just knocked out?" He laughed and rolled his eyes. "They're not real, dude—you've gotta get over it."

"So what, you'd kill the shopkeepers in the Square too without caring?" I asked as he started walking toward the pair of double doors on the far side of the gym.

"If they were trying to kill me? Yeah, without hesitating."

"And what about me? Or any of the other Augments? Would you kill me?" I asked, feeling my jaw set as I anticipated his answer.

"It depends," he answered with a casual shrug.

"On?'

"If you're trying to kill me or not," he replied with another incredulous laugh. "I don't get what part of that is so hard for you to understand."

He shoved the doors open and walked through into a clinical-looking hallway on the other side of them. I followed after, finding myself at a loss for words at his callousness. Even when he *had* been trying to attack me, I hadn't even thought to go for the kill.

"There has to be a line where killing isn't the answer," I finally said, and that caused him to stop, his levity evaporating in an instant.

"Not in this world there doesn't," he shot back, giving me a hard look before turning and continuing forward. The hallway was basically sterile, with no random doors and only ending in another hallway splitting in two directions.

"Then why didn't you just go Miscreant? Killing isn't heroic; it's not what Guardians do," I demanded as I stayed close behind him.

"Guardians save people—*real* people," he said simply without looking back. "As long as we are both doing that, why do you care what happens to these puppets?"

I wasn't sure if I had an answer for that, so I didn't reply, instead following him as he stopped at the intersection and immediately headed toward the right. Only a few feet down the hall, there was another set of double doors. He peered through the windows and shook his head.

"Some sort of research room. Now try not to get your damn panties in a bunch," Hydramental said as his red form split from his main body.

"Dude, wait, we can get information out of them!" I exclaimed, jumping to stop him before he tried to blow up the room like he had with the train car.

"Relax, it's called intimidation," their voices echoed in unison. He pushed the doors open and walked in with heavy footfalls. "Okay, everyone show us your hands and tell us where your boss is."

CHAPTER FORTY-SIX

Fluorescent lights swayed overhead as we entered the room, and I caught sight of five people in lab coats jumping at the sudden entrance and demand for information.

"W-W-Who are you two?" the closest person, a bearded Non-Sapient named Dr. Rhett Lincoln, asked in a stuttering voice. While the group of them were all wearing similar outfits, he definitely seemed to be the oldest, taking a slight step forward to meet us while the other four all held their hands up at their sides, palms facing forward.

The Hydramental in red ignited a ball of fire above his hand and stared at the scientist. "Do you really think that's important right now? I asked you a fucking question. Your boss—where the fuck is he?"

Dr. Lincoln's eyes went wide as he immediately backed up and into the table he had been working at. The clinking of glass and metal from him bumping into the surface caused me to look around. The room had several long tables against the walls, with cabinets hanging above them and a myriad of different scientific-looking equipment littering the surfaces. But it was the far side of the room that caught my attention.

Several large vats lined the walls where the tables ended, each one filled with a bubbling green liquid and a hulking form connected to tubes and wires floating within. My interface was going crazy trying to highlight and provide details on everything I was seeing, but I blinked them out of my vision as I moved to try and put myself between Hydramental and the doctor.

"Dude, put the fire out—they're scientists, not fighters," I said, and Hydramental shot me a glare. I ignored him as I turned back to Dr. Lincoln. "We're looking for the guy in charge. Now, would you like to tell us where to find him, or do I have to let the hothead back there continue his whole firecracker thing? I'd really rather we do this the easy way where no one has to get hurt."

"Isn't it a bit hypocritical of you to threaten that after you just went off on Hydramental for exactly the same thing?" Angie asked, and before I could reply, Jon beat me to it.

"There's a difference between making a threat and actually doing it. Loophole, maybe surprisingly, knows the benefit of bluffing."

"H-H-He's not here," Dr. Lincoln said. I was starting to wonder why the other scientists weren't trying to go hide when I caught sight of a familiar glint of metal near the floor. Each of the men and women in the room had shackles on their ankles, holding them to a pulley on the floor that seemed to give them some form of mobility within the room while still practically locking them in place.

<**Loophole:** They're prisoners.>

<**Hydramental:** And yet they're *still* hiding him from us.>

<**Loophole:** They don't have a choice!>

"Well then, where the fuck did he go?!" Hydramental demanded, throwing a fireball. It went flying past me, smashing into a microscope on one of the tables and setting it ablaze in a way a piece of metal shouldn't. Dr. Lincoln cringed to the side as he backed away from the heat of the melting metal.

"H-H-He hasn't been here in weeks, I swear!" Dr. Lincoln gulped out. "I-I-I promise! We get our orders remotely every morning!"

"You're lying!" Hydramental's dual voices roared as another ball of fire came to life in the red one's hand. I could feel the heat emanating from it and backed away. The fire settled ever so slightly as the Hydramentals took slow, deep breaths. "We know he's here, so stop with the bullshit—NOW!"

I was mentally cursing myself as I flinched backward from his intensity. This had taken a turn far quicker than I had been expecting, and I knew I needed to at least try to deescalate the situation.

<**Loophole:** Dude, calm down, they're following orders.>

<**Hydramental:** They're fucking programs. Meatbag robots.>

<**Loophole:** And they won't reveal a single fucking thing if you scare or kill them!>

"How about we back up just a bit. What are your orders? What are you guys doing here?" I asked, taking Hydramental's hesitation as permission to try again and working to keep my tone as neutral as possible. Dr. Lincoln actually seemed to respond to this, looking back at the other scientists.

"We . . . They'll kill us if I tell you," he said, trying to find his nerves as he let out another breath. If I had blinked, I might have missed it, but as he turned his attention back to us, I could have sworn I saw a brief flicker of *static* pass through Dr. Lincoln's eyes. "Though I suppose that's exactly what your colleague back there will do if I don't . . . isn't it?"

"Well, look at that, we got one with some *actual* intelligence," Hydramental sneered with a bark of laughter. "So what, is this where you're growing all the meatbags?"

"Growing?" Dr. Lincoln asked, seemingly confused.

<**Loophole:** If he's a Non-Sapient, then he doesn't know how he was made. You can't tell him.>

<**Hydramental:** What the fuck are you on about now?>

<**Loophole:** The Code, back at The Common Ground. It's cruel to let them know the truth behind their existence.>

<**Hydramental:** Oh, for fuck's sake, of course you'd fall for that sort of bullshit.>

My mission tracker began to shake, **[The Snake Key]** practically vibrating at the edge of my vision as I took another look around the room, my eyes settling on a large, empty tank on the center of the far wall. There were tubes going right from it to each of the separate tanks around the room, and I felt my gut twisting as I tried to put the pieces together.

"Is this where you guys are making the serum? The one that all the soldiers are taking to become temporarily Augmented?" I asked, feeling the tension in the room slowly building. Dr. Lincoln swallowed hard before he went to speak.

"Y-Yes . . . We were tasked with modifying the DNA extracted from—"

"Not another fucking word, Dr. Lincoln," a gruff voice demanded from behind us, and I spun on my heel.

A man with a neatly groomed black goatee and a sharp glare sauntered into the room. He wore a leather vest that was practically identical to the other Vipers', but it was clear that he was different just from the way he carried himself. Although a good part of Hydramental's face was covered by a mask, it was hard to deny the general similarities between the two men. I was just about to highlight him when Hydramental tossed two fireballs directly at the man, who sidestepped them with a casual grace.

"YOU SON OF A BITCH!" the Hydramentals roared in anger. "HOW FUCKING DARE YOU WEAR HIS FACE!"

For all his anger, Hydramental *didn't* rush in to attack with more than just his initial barrage of dodged fireballs, his feet planted as balls of fire swirled around his hands.

"Come on, Marco, are you really going to attack your brother so casually?" Sal asked, his expression still light as Hydramental *noticeably* tensed up. I highlighted the man quickly as he crossed his arms over his chest.

[Sal the Snake, Level 10 (Elite) Biker Lieutenant]
This is a Non-Sapient Augment.

Hydramental's yellow form split off as electricity began to dance between its fingers.

<**Loophole:** We can still talk this—>

"Don't you fucking *dare* use my real name, you knockoff bitch. I AM GOING TO FUCKING KILL YOU," Hydramental's voice echoed. I could actually *feel* the static in the air just before a large rush of electricity arced across the room to Sal.

"Guess that answers the question on if Sal was a clone or not!" Jon said in a hurry as I turned from Sal's already shifting form. This really was my fault for bringing Hydramental with me, and it was something I couldn't change now, no matter how much I might have wanted to.

The scientists were still cowering around the room, unable to move due to their restraints. I moved toward Dr. Lincoln as quickly as I could, preparing to attack his chain, when he threw a set of hands ahead of my possible attack.

"No, don't! If he sees us without the chains, he'll attack—it's what he was ordered to do. These are the only things keeping us safe," he pleaded with me as another rush of static passed through his eyes. I wasn't entirely sure why he would believe that, but I chalked it up to whatever orders were put into place in the Non-Sapient's mind. If he believed it was the truth, I couldn't risk sending him into a panic by trying to force him to go against it, and I really didn't have the time to try and convince him either.

"Tell your people to get under the tables and stay there. I can't promise anything . . . This might get messy," I said, turning and looking at the massive form of Sal. He must have grown *at least* another half a foot since the last time I saw his snake form, and he was casually shrugging off both the fire and electricity being thrown at him.

Sal spit several rapid shots of venom globs toward Hydramental, one of them striking the yellow clone and dissolving it as he took a massive hit to his health. Even though Hydramental seemed to be able to throw attacks in rapid succession compared to the larger cooldowns I had, the largest weakness to his powerset seemed to be the negative impact that happened whenever one of his clones disincorporated. It also seemed to leave him stumbling for a second to recover, a period which Sal used to his advantage as he started to rush toward the next closest Hydramental.

Without waiting for confirmation from the scientist now behind me, I activated Phase Step, picking a spot behind Sal's massive form and finding myself appearing a few feet off to the side of him. I was about to curse the random chance, but Sal was still moving in on Hydramental, and I had to move on instinct to stop the snake from reaching him.

My next move was a risk—logically, I knew that—but there was nothing ideal about the situation we had found ourselves in. I couldn't push this fight back into the hall, since it was too narrow for either Hydramental or I to work in, but I also knew that pushing it further into the room threatened the scientists. As little as I wanted to risk them and the possible information they could give us, Sal was already both higher leveled than us *and* an Elite, so I had to give us the best possible chance.

I actually had to jump just slightly as I caught up with him, throwing a sixty-percent Gravity Punch directly at the middle of Sal's back with the momentum of my leap. I wasn't entirely sure if his Elite resistances would help him or not—hell, I still wasn't even sure what those fully *were*—but as my fist connected with the leather of his vest, he was blown forward and across the room with every bit of force I had added to my strike, crashing through nearly to the far side of the room and well outside of my actual local area.

Without skipping a beat, I pulled out a Superior Stamina Injector and slammed it into my arm, fully topping off my levels before I stepped as far as I could manage across the space.

The entire center of the room looked like it had had a date with a wrecking ball due to Sal's massive form barreling through it. Luckily, all of the scientists had jumped for tables along the walls of the laboratory.

Before Hydramental could make another move, I stepped the rest of the way to where Sal had landed from the force of my first attack, activating Sting like a Bee and striking downward at Sal's prone form with a twenty-five percent Gravity Punch. While he *should* have been thrown backward, the downward strike pushed that force straight through him and into the concrete floor, cratering the structure ever so slightly, with cracks rushing outward from underneath the snake-man.

I didn't wait for him to recover and pulled the last of my venom-soaked guns from my inventory. With three quick squeezes, I fired into him and watched as, surprisingly, all three bullets found purchase and pierced his skin. Even further to my surprise, he still got a **[Weakened]** debuff, though granted, only a five percent one.

I didn't hesitate and pulled the trigger three more times, halfway emptying the magazine and chunking his health down to fifty percent. Even at just five percent, his **[Weakened]** debuff was more than enough to remove his Elite status, and I hopped backward, holding an arm out in front of Hydramental before he could charge.

"That . . . Damn, Loophole . . ." Jon muttered in the back of my head as I stared at Sal as he slowly pulled himself upright. My eyes scanned the vats surrounding us before settling on the empty one in the center of the wall, which seemed even more out of place now. Out of the corner of my eye, I noticed a glint of a lens and found my anger rising as I stared directly at it.

"Really?! You taunt me, you tell me to come fight you, and this is what you do?! Just send your men at me again?! You told me I'd get to face you! You told me I'd get to see what you were capable of! So where are you?!"

<**Hydramental:** That's your big plan?! I think you've gotten a little too fucking involved in whatever story these dens have been trying to feed you. You know, I thought it was weird when you said you talked to my brother and he sounded "posh"—that ain't what my brother sounds like. This fucking fake sounds more like him. Now, step aside and let me fucking put this clone down!>

<**Loophole:** No, I need him to get the answers I'm looking for.>

<**Hydramental:** For fuck's sake, this is just a fucking dead end. I'm tired of dealing with this fucker.>

Sal started to laugh as he swayed lightly, his arms rising while he gestured to the room around us. "The bosss never liesss. Thisss! Thisss isss what the bosss isss capable of. I wanted to let you in, Marco, to ssshow you the truth. But I guesss you'll jussst—"

Everything happened in the blink of an eye. I could feel the hair on the back of my neck stand up, then a flash of icy blue went flying past me, coating Sal's upper body and mouth in ice just before a rush of electricity whipped across the room and struck the now **[Weakened]** Sal in his icy coating. His health went plummeting, and I rushed forward, taking the opportunity to try something we *hadn't* done just yet.

I leapt into the air, throwing a hook for Sal's head and adding a twenty-percent Gravity Punch with it. While Hydramental's conducted strike had sent Sal's health plummeting, my strike was *intended* to be nonlethal. It was a small but key detail that Angie had told me on my first day, and while that felt like ages ago even though it had really only been a bit over seventy-two hours, the detail had still stayed locked into my head.

Sure enough, while his health bar bottomed out, a small sliver remained, and he gained the [**KO**] debuff, collapsing to the ground as his body shrunk and morphed back into his human form.

"We need to tie him up before—"

"Get out of the fucking way now!" Hydramental's triplicated voices demanded from behind me. I spun on my heel and saw him walking toward us. He hadn't bothered to pull a Health Injector, which felt like the wrong choice, since his health was sitting at sixty percent just from the single clone of his that had been dispatched.

"No, he's knocked out. That means he's down for at least a little while. We can figure out a way to keep him locked down, and then we can ask him questions," I said, setting my jaw and planting my feet to block Sal's now human form from Hydramental.

"They. Aren't. Real. They are only going to tell you what Axio fucking wants them to tell you. At this point, I'm convinced my brother's been dead for years and this whole fucking thing has been a fucking game just to make me jump through his goddamn hoops, but I am *fucking done*. I am going to kill this asshole and wipe my hands of Axio's bullshit," he said, the echoing of his voice grating at me as he disbanded our Temporary Team-Up.

A flicker of light passed between his blue and red form before a ball of flame appeared atop his red clone's hand, all of his forms staring daggers at me. "Now, I'm not going to say it again, Loophole. Move or—"

"Julia, no!" Dr. Lincoln shouted.

The ring of a gunshot echoed across the room before Hydramental's red form dissolved in a flash of light. The source of the shot was a young woman, trembling as she held a gun out ahead of her, staring at Hydramental in shock that she had even hit him.

His health immediately dropped as his red form merged back in with his blue, leaving only the yellow clone separated from the main body. This time, the shock of his form being disincorporated somehow only affected him briefly, and it only took a second for him to recover before he spun on his heel, looking toward the young woman as electricity began to dance between his fingers.

I didn't even hesitate and Phase Stepped between them just as the bolt of electricity went surging across the space.

Even though I had been in enough fights by now and taken more than my fair share of hits, they had all been almost purely *physical* blows. So, while I had gotten used to the feeling of being struck, even thrown into walls, cars, and the ground itself, I certainly *hadn't* gotten used to the feeling of electricity coursing through my system.

My health dropped by nearly forty percent from that single strike, and I felt myself shake slightly as the current stopped. There was a look of pure hatred that spiked over Hydramental's face before his red form split back off the main body. I was lucky the shock didn't linger for more than a few seconds, and I didn't wait for him to strike again. Instead, I activated Fun House, going invisible and slipping to the side as my forms started to run in a circle around him.

"Oh, fuck you!" Hydramental shouted, throwing several fireballs at one of my afterimages. The flames blasted the illusion apart before slamming into one of the many vats, instantly breaking the glass and sending the bubbling green liquid inside spilling out over the floor.

A flash of light passed from his yellow form to his blue, and he jumped forward, raising a hand and blowing out, freezing the liquid over on the ground in an attempt to send one of my afterimages slipping. Unfortunately for him, it was on the *other* side of the room from where I actually was. I moved quickly, punching the yellow clone in the back of the head as hard as I could without activating a single ability, hoping it would be enough to just knock him out.

I wasn't sure what attacking his unpowered form would do, but once again I was taken by surprise when I was knocked backward by an electrical shock wave that pulsed out of his body. I skidded across the ground as my health dropped by another twenty percent. Without bothering to get up, I picked one of my still-formed afterimages and stepped over to it just before Hydramental's red form could start pummeling me with more fireballs. With his eyes briefly off of me, I materialized an Enhanced Health Injector and shoved it into my leg.

Another gunshot rang out, and Hydramental shouted, "You bitch!"

I looked over, seeing his health had dropped down to fifteen percent. It was long delayed, but I saw him materialize an injector into his hand. Before he could use it, I ramped up Center of the Universe. I wasn't sure if it was because he hadn't been anticipating this or if the rapid succession of his clones being destroyed had affected his own control, but it barely took any force before the injector was ripped from his grip and came hurtling in my direction.

I kept the strength up, focusing on objects as beakers and small metallic tools started flying from the tables still in my range, peppering the Hydramental clones who were between them and me. I used the scattershot as a distraction and rushed forward, absorbing the injector flying my way and maintaining my gravitational pull on items.

The only single-colored Hydramental still moving was his red form. I wasn't sure what exactly had caused it and doubted he'd tell me even if I asked, especially right now, but I assumed he had some form of passive defense that had activated when I had struck his unused yellow form that had now merged back with his blue after taking another shot from Julia. I had never seen him use every element he had access to at once, and it would explain why he never went out of his way to defend the form that wasn't throwing some sort of element.

I kept my focus on the red clone, getting in close and throwing a twenty-percent Gravity Punch at his midsection. This time, it connected, and the form exploded in a shower of light before plummeting Hydramental's health the rest of the way down. Just like in the street earlier in the day, I hadn't been trying to kill him, so my attack only left him collapsing to the floor with the [**KO**] debuff.

"That dude really *needs some anger management lessons,"* Jon muttered as I slowly caught my breath, my stamina bar nearly critical. I looked over, seeing the woman still holding the gun up, her hands trembling as her eyes met mine.

"Julia, please put down the weapon. I think we should be thanking this man, not threatening him," Dr. Lincoln spoke from the other side of the room.

My mission tracker shook again, and without me even prompting it, the snake key materialized into my hand, its eyes glowing just as brightly as they had at the tunnel entrance. I looked at it and then back over to Dr. Lincoln.

"I think I've been asking the wrong question," I said, almost like I *hadn't* just gotten into a massive fight in front of them all. My relative calmness seemed to actually put the scientists at ease, and Julia lowered the weapon before falling to her knees as she took in rapid breaths, her nerves having clearly gotten to her. "When your boss *does* come by, how does he get here?"

"I don't think I can—" Dr. Lincoln started before another rush of static passed through his eyes. He swallowed hard, his own hand trembling as he slowly lifted his arm up. It was almost like he was struggling against himself to do it, but when his finger was fully extended, it was clear what he was pointing at, especially since I had already been pretty sure I knew the answer.

The empty vat.

I turned from the scientists and walked over toward it, stepping around the prone forms of both Hydramental and Sal. The key shone brighter and brighter the closer to the vat I got until the vat itself started to glow. In a flash, the key vanished from my hand, and the vat evaporated into light.

In its place was something oddly familiar. A large, glowing white rectangle. It was the exact kind of doorway I passed through whenever I went to Sanctuary Square, though what it meant here, I wasn't quite sure.

"I was expecting just another hallway . . ." I murmured. Angie let out a nervous laugh.

"Um . . . I don't know if you should go through that . . . If it's calibrated for SnakeBite, it might hurt you if you use it," she said.

"Why would he have a key that showed him how to get it if he couldn't *go through it, though?"* Jon spoke up, and I felt myself swallow hard as my gut clenched.

"I'm not sure. It just feels like an unnecessary risk, especially with everything he still

has to take care of in this room," Angie reiterated, and I was almost positive I could hear fear in her tone.

Even still, I felt my hand rising, reaching toward the portal. They were both right. Logically, I knew that, but I had already come this far. I glanced back at Sal and Hydramental again; they'd be knocked out for at least an hour unless someone came in and resuscitated them. I pulled my hand back and turned toward Dr. Lincoln, his eyes meeting mine.

"Don't let anyone wake those two up, at least not before the hour is up. And if you do somehow have some way to restrain Sal . . . Well, can you guys do that for me? I can't let him keep terrorizing the people of this city," I said. Dr. Lincoln nodded, his jaw set in determination.

"I will see what we can do. I believe we can keep Mr. Travisi unconscious for the time being, though I can't make any promises toward the other one. We will do our best to secure the room; you spared us, we owe you that much."

"Thank you," I said with a nod before staring up at the camera and pointing at it with as much ferocity as I could. "I told you I was coming for you. There's no more hiding."

"Loophole, do you really have to—"

Angie's voice was cut off once I stepped into the portal. Just like with Sanctuary Square, it only took a second, but this time I found myself in an entirely unfamiliar place when the light faded from my eyes.

The entire opposite wall of the room from where I had emerged was glass, with the moon's light shining brightly into the space through the wide windows that overlooked Central Park. There was an almost sterile smell to the room as I looked around it.

"Where the hell am I?" I muttered out loud as I stepped forward. Looking over my shoulder, I expected to see the portal I had stepped through, only to find nothing but a blank wall. "Um, how am I supposed to get back?"

There was a noticeable silence that hung in the air as my question went unanswered, and I stepped forward, placing a hand on the wall where the portal should be.

"Angie? Codex?" I asked again and then waited. Once more, neither of them responded, but that's not to say the room *did* remain quiet.

"It . . . It's no use. They can't hear you in here—it's a Dead Zone," a raspy, pained voice croaked. It was almost too low to hear, but in the stillness of the room, only broken by the sound of an occasional random beep, I could hear it all the same. I turned around, searching for the source, only to find a large bed at the center of a wall to my side, propped partially upward.

There was medical equipment surrounding the bed, with wires and tubes all traveling along the wall and down to the single inhabitant that lay in the room. The man was practically skin and bones, and he was beyond pale, wearing a mask that was clearly helping with his breathing. His eyes were sunken in, though they met mine with a fierceness that didn't match his broken body.

My interface highlighted him, showing his nearly critical health bar and nearly a dozen debuffs that I barely had time to register. The monotone voice that I normally only heard in The Common Ground echoed in my head as the man started to let out a violent coughing fit.

[SnakeBite, Level 41 Venomized Vampire]

"It—It . . . It's nice to finally meet you, Loophole," he wheezed out in a painful-sounding rasp. Speaking sent him into a rough coughing fit that took a moment to settle before his sunken eyes met mine once more. "We should probably talk."

CHAPTER FORTY-SEVEN

W hat . . . What the hell?"

It was the only thing I could find the words to say as I looked from the bedbound SnakeBite to the room around him.

The room was every bit as sterile as the smell indicated, with a complete lack of decorations and a clinical smell that lingered in the air. Over a dozen identical monitors littered the wall opposite of his bed, neatly organized and lined up with each showing something different. The bottom row had live footage from the headquarters I had just come from, with one of the screens showing Dr. Lincoln and his team actively operating robotic-looking arms that lowered from the ceiling to lift and move the Non-Sapient Sal from this collapsed position.

Angie? Codex? Are either of you guys seeing this?" While all evidence suggested SnakeBite was telling the truth about this place being a zone where communications were cut off like in The Common Ground, I couldn't help but try asking internally anyway.

Although he had claimed we needed to talk, SnakeBite wasn't rushing to force my attention onto him, and he allowed me to take my time as I looked around the closed-off room. There was no noticeable exit on any of the walls, and while I was sure I could *probably* punch my way through the glass and fly away with a strong-enough Gravity Punch, I found myself with a sudden pit in my stomach when I glanced at my action bar and found everything was grayed out.

"Why is my action bar grayed out? What is this place?" I finally asked, turning my attention back to the shell of a man.

"I told you," he replied, taking his time to speak to avoid another coughing fit. "It's a Dead Zone. You should be able to still access your B.E.L.T. . . . It was set up that way so that they could at least supply me with water and food through my own, but that's the only part that is activated in this area. Now please, come sit down; it's harder for me to speak louder . . ."

He lifted a bony arm slowly, gesturing toward the lone other piece of actual furniture in the room, a plush armchair in the small space between his bed and the large glass wall.

"What's going on here, SnakeBite?" I asked, slowly making my way over to the chair and taking a seat.

"Pl—Please. I've really . . . I've *really* grown to hate that name, and you already know my real one. Just call me Sal . . . It would be nice if someone did after all this . . ." He wheezed, reaching to the side as a cup of water appeared in his outstretched hand. It took him some time to move his face mask out of the way, but he eventually pulled it to his chapped lips and took a sip.

"Okay . . . Sal, then. What's going on here? What was the point of this?" I asked, staring at the man. His gaze was forward, focused on a single screen on the bottom row of his display. The monitor seemed to respond to his gaze, and it zoomed in on Hydramental's prone form.

"I really am sorry that you're the one who was brought here . . . I had hoped that it would be my brother," Sal finally said. "But I suppose that's been your story since the beginning, hasn't it? Finding your way into situations you weren't supposed to be in . . . The extra Augment . . . The Loophole."

I was about to say something when he started to cough again, and he held up a finger to stop me.

"Pl—Please . . . I'll answer your questions . . . but I need to say some things . . . need to finally explain myself to someone . . ." He wheezed again, moving his mask to the side once more as he took another sip before the cup vanished from his hand. "I've been here . . . in this room . . . for the last few years. I made . . . I made some bad choices when I first got Augmented . . . trusted someone that only wanted to use me . . . His name . . . it was—" He found himself coughing again before he shook his head. "I can't say it, of course . . . He's forcefully suppressed it."

"I thought only Axio could do that," I said, unable to stop myself from interrupting. He shook his head.

"The PAIs . . . Axio even, might believe that . . . but no . . ." Sal said, repositioning the mask on his face as he took in a few deep breaths. "All of us . . . we're all just puppets and pawns in a war for control over . . . well, all of this." He gestured absentmindedly. "Haven't you ever wondered why you've just . . . gone along with it all? Why you've barely taken the time to consider the ramifications of your experiences?"

"I . . . Isn't it just the Acceptance Matrix acting to keep me balanced?" I asked as my gut clenched. I must have noticeably winced because Sal looked at me with almost knowing eyes.

"It's amazing, isn't it? Even in this Dead Zone . . . you can feel yourself panicking, even *barely* doubting it, can't you? They gave it such a simple name, and then the PAIs act to embed its importance into you right from the beginning, with you only barely even wanting to question it, all while it controls you so much more than you can even realize. I'd be willing to bet you just *happened* to see someone in Sanctuary Square having a moral dilemma on your first day, didn't you?"

"I . . . Is this some sort of mind game? Did you just bring me here to fuck with me?" I asked, finding myself getting defensive.

"Do . . . Do I really look like I'm capable of doing anything right now?" he asked, his eyes meeting mine. There wasn't any malice or ill intent hiding there; in fact, it was almost entirely compassion that I could see in his expression. "I can't be positive . . . this really is my own conjecture based on the footage I've been shown . . . but I think it was Axio who brought you here, Axio who poked and prodded you, gave you hints and every little thing you'd need until you found where I was being hidden. He couldn't unlock this area due to the nature of the Dead Zone, so he used you to do the job for him."

"Why would Axio do that? Isn't he playing some sort of game of his own?"

"They all are . . . I told you. Every single one of us Augments are just pawns . . . Even if Axio has his own goals, he still needs pawns to test and use . . . and there are others working against him . . . When my *mentor* first got his claws on me, first took control over my Acceptance Matrix, Axio appeared to me and promised that he'd undo this.

"While he has no qualms using the Matrix himself for some things, the amount of influence that was being exerted over us went against the rules he was bound to follow, and he didn't like what my mentor was trying to do either," Sal explained, taking a moment to catch his breath and find his words. "I didn't think much of it at first . . . but as my mentor made me do more and more things that I couldn't forgive myself for, I started to give up hope. At least . . . until just a few days ago . . . when your Wave started.

"My brother has had anger issues for a long time, and I never expected him to get selected for Augmentation, but when these screens started to show him . . . I assumed it was Axio's way of finally living up to his promise . . . But Marco . . . Hydramental . . . his anger at the system he was brought into clouded his vision, and I think the nature of his power made his mental health issues worse. It made him shortsighted and unable to look deeper than surface level at everything . . . And then you showed up."

"And I found the key . . ."

"And you found the key." Sal nodded. "I'm not sure what happened to add you into the Wave, but in those first twelve hours, there was a gap in the Dead Zone here. I never had a lot of people on my Friends List but, even though I had only met her once, Calypso *had* made a point of adding me after I first started working with my mentor. Just like Axio, she said she wanted to keep an eye on me . . ."

"Wait . . . Calypso? As in one of The First's *teammates*, Calypso?" He nodded. "Are you saying that she's one of the people . . . what . . . fighting Axio for control?"

"That . . . That I don't know . . . It's not like she told me exactly what she was up to . . . It was only for a brief moment during that twelve-hour gap, but she was able to get a message to me . . . She said . . . She said this was all going to be over soon . . . She said she was sorry that it had taken so long, but that it was all going to be over . . . I don't know if she was working with Axio or if they were just separately working toward the same goal . . . but it gave me hope."

A sudden stream of red rushed down one of the tubes, hitting Sal and causing him to lurch and shake as his health bar suddenly returned all the way to full. I jumped to my feet, looking down at the man as his eyes rolled backward, only for another tube to start pulling a greenish fluid from a spot on his side, sending his health plummeting back down to critical. He slowly stopped shaking as he clenched his eyes shut, struggling to catch his breath even with the assistance of the mask.

"So, what then . . . Am I on some sort of rescue mission? Are you a prisoner here?" I asked while his eyes started to unclench and his amber eyes met mine.

"Not a rescue," he said, shaking his head slightly. "Not a rescue . . ."

"Then what—"

"We'll get to that," Sal interrupted, making his glass of water appear once more and stopping to take another sip. "Like I said, Marco was supposed to be the one here . . . I wanted to apologize to him . . . to ask him to get Giada and Ozzy out of all of this . . . I guess I'll have to ask you to do that for me . . .

"You don't owe me anything, truthfully, you have every right to say no to everything I need to ask of you . . . but ever since you found your way into this, I've been watching you . . . I don't know if it's something in your Acceptance Matrix or something that affected you with how you were added to the Wave, but you put more priority on life than many in our positions . . . I don't think that will change after you do what I ask you to do, even if it does go against that very value."

"And what is it—"

"Not yet . . . there's something else you're going to need to do first . . . and you're not going to like it." Sal wheezed as a hand reached out and gently tapped against my chest. "You need to disable your Acceptance Matrix, and you need to do it now while your PAI can't talk you out of it."

"I . . ." I started, feeling my heart start to race. "How do I know you're not just trying to do something to me? Or if whoever's done this to you is trying to do something to me?"

"You don't," he responded with a long sigh, his hand pulling back as an injector materialized into his hand. "Because, in truth, I *was* supposed to do something to you."

I highlighted the injector but was only met with a series of question marks before I stared back at Sal with a raised brow.

"It contains nanites that would alter your Acceptance Matrix . . . and give my mentor a lot of control over your decisions. While Axio certainly does push people to do things, he at least maintains people's *general* free will. My mentor . . . my captor . . . doesn't have the same restraint . . . He sees us all as his test subjects . . . This showed up in my B.E.L.T. about an hour ago . . . right after he taunted you to come find me . . . I've learned what it feels like when he wants me to do something . . . He wanted me to subject you to this . . ."

"If he can make you do what he wants . . . why didn't you?" I asked, finding myself backing up and sitting back down into the chair, just to put a little bit of distance between us.

"Calypso . . ." He wheezed. His health wasn't regenerating, and I looked at the list of debuffs he had floating under his diminished health bar. [**Hemorrhaging**], [**Fatigued**], [**Bound**], [**Technologically Sustained**]. These were just a few on the list that seemed to be keeping him in the state he was in. "I don't think I could explain it if I wanted to . . . but when she messaged me, she did something . . . I'm not sure if it was something embedded in the message itself or something else, but she tweaked my Matrix . . . It wasn't the same thing as her wresting control of it with nanites like this . . . but it let me see clearly for the first time in so long . . . it let me ignore new orders . . . Maybe, most importantly . . . it let me see just how much influence others could have over us . . . all because of a Matrix that they want us to believe is just keeping us calm."

My gut was still squeezing while I wrestled with his words. I *didn't* want to turn off my Acceptance Matrix. It outright felt like a terrible decision to make, especially since I had absolutely nothing to go on other than the word of someone who, up until a few minutes ago, I had thought was the person behind everything I had had to deal with over the last few days.

"If you can see clearly . . . why haven't you turned off your own Matrix?"

Sal's head fell to the side as he looked at me. There was an almost longing nature to his expression, and it was haunting. "I still need it . . . I still need it to finish this."

"I'm sorry . . . I'm really lost here. Why do I need to turn off my Matrix? What was Hydramental being brought here to do? And why are you being held like this? What the hell was your mentor doing?" I rattled off, scratching at the side of my head. I really wished I had Jon to talk to, just to have a second opinion if nothing else.

"Where . . . Where do you think the Temporary Augmentation Serums come from?" he asked. His words were coming slower and slower, and it was clear the amount of speaking he was doing was taking a toll on him, but even if he seemed to be meandering from one topic to another, he didn't seem to be confused. He was determined to make sure *someone* knew what had been happening. "An army of Augments with the one specific power that you want them to have . . . It's the ultimate private force."

"But it's been killing the Non-Sapients that have been using it . . ."

"Test subjects . . . That's all they are to him . . . That's all *we* are to him . . . Though I don't doubt he has more than enough human subjects lined up and ready to go once he has a working formula. It's all been incremental . . ."

Another round of coughing escaped him, and he began to wheeze as soon as the fit ended. I found myself standing up while I waited for him to catch his breath, walking over toward the window to look down over Central Park as I tried to comprehend what he was telling me.

"You . . . I think the only reason he let you get this far, get here, is because he wanted you to be his next subject. I'm not sure what your powers are . . . but they seem versatile . . . they seem like something he'd want to try to take. It's the only explanation that makes sense . . .

"I can't let what's happened to me happen to anyone else . . . That's why you need to turn off your Matrix. If it's off, I think even if he finds a way to inject you, he won't be able to control you," Sal finally said after a few minutes passed and his breathing calmed. I turned from the window, my eyes meeting his. "If I could tell every Augment to do that, I would . . . Maybe you could do that for me too . . . There's so . . . There's so many things I wish I could have done differently."

He choked up, eyes welling as he reached a frail hand up to wipe away a few tears that had started to fall down his cheek.

"I wanted to be a hero . . . I wanted to save people . . ."

"Have you . . . Are you really not the one controlling the Vipers?" I asked, walking back toward his bed and staring down at him. He shook his head slowly and looked down at his lap.

"The only thing I'm good for is my power. As long as I'm alive . . . the injectors will still let them transform . . . the injectors will still let them hurt people," he croaked, his voice getting increasingly hoarse even as he materialized another cup of water. "He hasn't been able to break the connection . . . In order for a powerset to work . . . there has to be a source for them to work from. It's something to do with how our powersets are activated and given to us . . . He was very specific when he told me that that's what had gone wrong when he tested on Valor Viking."

"Wait, are you saying—" I started before he began to cough again, the glass of water tumbling out of his hand from the sudden fit and down to the ground.

"It's . . . It's . . . It's not fair of me to ask you to do this. But I need you to kill me," he finally was able to spit out, and my gut wrenched painfully. "And it's less fair that I need you to turn your Acceptance Matrix off first. This room is classified as my Safe House. Its code has been altered to turn it into a Dead Zone to hide me and make it mostly impossible for someone to stop my mentor's experiment. When I'm dead . . . this room's code will break, and your PAI will be able to try to stop you from turning it off."

"No . . . I can't . . ." I shook my head back and forth as everything clicked into place. "I haven't even killed one of the Non-Sapients; at least not on purpose . . . Can't I just break you out of here? Get you away from the person doing this to you?"

"I know . . . I heard your argument with Marco . . . It's why he was supposed to be the one to come here . . . It would have made this so much easier . . . I could have just leaned into what he thought was the truth, angered him until he just put me down . . ." Sal said, groaning as he tried to adjust himself in the bed.

Even as I wrestled with the growing panic in the core of my being, I couldn't help but wonder if he even *needed* me to do this with the shape he was in. His breathing grew even more labored as he continued to push himself.

"I wish I could send you back . . . to have you just send him in . . . but . . . but . . . but I'm pretty sure that the key Axio made for you was a one-way thing . . . and once my mentor knows that you haven't been injected . . . well, I don't think anyone would find me again. It doesn't matter if I'm hooked up to these machines or not. As . . . As . . . As long as I'm alive, the Vipers can transform . . . As long as I'm alive . . . my wife . . . my son . . . they'll never be safe . . . I know you value life . . . I know I'm asking you a lot . . . but trading mine for the people of our neighborhoods . . . isn't that a trade worth making?"

"I . . . I just . . ."

"If I could do this on my own . . . I would. I've . . . I've tried . . . but nothing I've done can lower my health faster than this damn equipment replenishes it. I've seen the guns that you've been using . . . I think with the venom coating the ammo . . . I think that will be enough . . . It is my powerset's natural weakness . . ." His voice broke, and a small sob escaped him which echoed in the empty room. "Even if you don't turn off your Matrix . . . please . . . please don't make me a victim in your story . . . Let me be a hero in mine. Please . . . just make it stop."

Almost as if to prove his point, the red liquid surged through the tubes, and his body began to convulse again, his health rapidly increasing and then rapidly decreasing as the green goo was extracted from him. He didn't scream, but the groans and gasps that escaped his lips grated against my nerves, and I winced for him.

"I . . ." I started to say before stopping myself. I didn't want to take a life or to hurt someone . . . but this . . . even I could admit that this felt like a mercy.

I was about to vocalize this when I felt my gut twist in pain. If the Acceptance Matrix *was* doing more than just stabilizing my emotions, how could I be sure that *those* were my own feelings. How could I be sure any of my decisions were my own. I had to do this on impulse . . . on instinct, and I couldn't think about it too hard, even if I did end up regretting it.

My stomach was still in knots at the thought, but I swallowed hard and concentrated on my Acceptance Matrix. The monotone voice spoke.

[Are you sure you'd like to disable your Acceptance Matrix: Y/N?]

Sal was practically doubled over in a coughing fit, his frail arms holding his sides while his health bar seemed to shudder with the shaking of his body. I took a deep breath and pushed back against the warring feelings in my stomach to select *Yes*.

It felt like a wave of fresh, crisp air entered my lungs, my eyes widening as a wave of relief passed over my body. That relief was short-lived, and a rapid wave of panic, amazement, fear, ecstasy, anger, and then even more relief rushed past me, like a slideshow of the emotions I *should* have been feeling over the last few days. When the rush finally passed, I took a few short, rapid breaths. Reaching up, I rested a hand on my chest, feeling my heart beating so hard that it threatened to burst out.

"Please . . . Please . . ." Sal continued to rasp out. I looked over at him, trying to get my heart to stop racing as I felt a natural aversion to what he was asking.

Simply knowing that *that* feeling had come from me, unaltered by the Matrix, made me feel like I was myself. But that didn't change the fact that I couldn't leave Sal like this either, even if I knew the cost.

"You won't turn your Matrix off because you need it to face this . . . don't you?"

I said as I materialized the last remaining gun I had into my hand. I felt myself let out a wry, pained laugh as I stared at it. "Kinda wish I could be so lucky . . ."

Sal let out his own sad, pained laugh, which turned into a cough as he fell back onto his bed. "For what it's worth . . . I think both my brother and you have it half right . . . There has to be a line . . . But that goes both directions . . . You can't pull your punches just because you don't want to take a life; most people won't offer you the same restraint."

"I'll do what I can for your family, Sal . . . I don't know what I'll say to your brother; he thinks you're dead already . . . It might be better if I just let him believe that instead of letting him know what was happening here. I already don't think I'm his favorite person . . . If he knows I killed you, even at your own request . . ." I trailed off as I thought about his advice, running a thumb over the grip of the pistol before I looked back at the shell of a man.

"Probably the better plan," he agreed, meeting my eyes as he reached a hand up and pointed toward his heart, tapping his chest just a few times as lightly as he could. "Right here . . . It'll . . . It'll . . . It will spread the fastest from here."

There was nothing that was going to make this any easier, and I slowly lifted the gun toward him.

"I wish there was another way . . ." I said, my voice lowering as another set of tears welled up into Sal's eyes.

"Me too . . ." was all he could manage as his hand dropped from his chest. It was only my own desire not to kill that I had to fight against, but I pushed and forced my will against it as I pulled the trigger, hitting him square in his chest.

The equipment surrounding him went crazy as the **[Weakened]** debuff was added to his stack, and his health bar started to dip downward toward empty.

"One . . . more . . ." he grunted, his body starting to shake. I saw the red fluid starting to descend the tube, and in a panic that it might make it all for nothing, I fired again, hitting him and dropping his health further. His heightened level was doing a lot of the work of lowering just how much damage each bullet gave him, but the venom was doing the work that really mattered, and even though the red fluid hit him, his health *didn't* replenish.

I saw a brief bit of static pass through his eyes, and his jaw set. As his health neared the bottom, while his eyes had a touch of fear in them, there was a practically defiant smile that spread over his lips. "Thank . . . you . . . Loop . . . hole . . ." he struggled to say through labored breaths and gritted teeth. Then, just before his health bar emptied, he let out a small laugh before adding, "Fuck . . . you . . . Tech . . . Warden."

Sal went still, and the equipment attached to him started letting out a rapid set of beeps and alarms that filled the space. The monotone voice suddenly popped back up without an accompanying notification or window.

[The owner of this Safe House has died. Safe House

**status and all effects granted by this Safe House
will be eliminated in thirty seconds.]**

A myriad of different notifications started popping into my interface, including several achievements, a huge Phase Point gain, and more than a few level-up alerts. But as I watched the life leave Sal's eyes, my own resolve finally gave out, and I fell to my knees. The weight of everything Sal had told me, of the mentor he tried to warn about, washed over me, and without the safety net of the Acceptance Matrix, it threatened to overwhelm me.

I started to take short rapid breaths as I let the truth of what I had just done hit me.

It didn't matter that he had begged me to do it. It didn't matter that I knew it was the right thing to do. It didn't change that I had done it. It didn't change that I had pulled the trigger.

Before I knew it, I was sobbing, and I wasn't sure when I was going to stop.

EPILOGUE

Part One

Sanctuary Square, much like New York City, never really slept.

There were Augments spanning the entire world, and at practically any hour, they could need one of the Square's many services. While the members of the Tenth Wave had only just begun to scratch the surface of those services, it wasn't any of the known features that had drawn Calypso to the Square firmly in the middle of the night in the Eastern United States.

She passed through the portal from her Safe House and practically glided down the staircase. Even in the moonlight, her costume seemed to shimmer like scales, and the net that held her bun together jingled slightly with each step due to the small bells that were woven right into it.

Calypso rather liked the ambience of the Square at this time of day, when the air was still and the general clamoring was relatively quiet. Sure, there were a few Augments who lingered around, using the benches and tables that littered the courtyard to read or just take a moment to themselves, but none swarmed her like she was used to on the few occasions she made an appearance in the Square during the middle of the day.

Though it may have seemed odd from the outside, most Augments learned early on that being in the Square prevented Crime Alerts from generating for locations near their respective Safe Houses. Prior to the Tenth Wave, many Augments actually *did* have spare time, especially those with territories in mostly remote locations, and that *had* bred just a bit of complacency in the Augment populace.

Calypso had known that this year was going to be different, though she had still been surprised by just how much. As one of the seven remaining members of the First Wave, Calypso had access to a much bigger picture of the world than, well, almost anyone. But had she been a betting woman—which, coincidentally, she was—she still wouldn't have bet on the events of the last few days.

Several of the younger Augments pointed in her direction as she passed along the stone pathway, and she gave them each a friendly smile and wave. She had never shared Brightburst's lack of love for the spotlight, but she also was happy that The First had always drawn more attention than she did on the grander scale. Neither of those things were why she made it a point to at least be open and cordial with every Augment that she could, however.

Whether it was warranted or not, Calypso felt the weight of every single dead Augment on her very soul. It didn't matter if they were Guardians or Miscreants—each dropping number on the leaderboards left her feeling increasingly heavy. While she had slowly grown to accept that the world had already changed and there was nothing she could do about the Augments who died in the course of battle, those weren't the ones who weighed most heavily.

Lunar Monkey, Frigid Air, Gas Giant, Hayday, Valor Viking, and SnakeBite.

While the world barely knew them, Calypso had etched those names permanently into her mind. SnakeBite was a tragedy, she knew that, but things had gone too far with him, and no matter what she did, she knew that he was never going to be out from under TechWarden's thumb. Unfortunately, she also knew that didn't bode well for the other five either, and the fact that she still didn't have any leads on where they were bothered her immensely.

The First might have his own hatred for TechWarden, but Calypso had been the one to bring him into the fold in the first place. It wasn't necessarily excusable for her to have missed the signs when Lunar Monkey had first gone missing, but it was understandable. Things had still been new when the Second Wave had appeared, and they had all been simply trying to keep up with the rapid changes that came with people outside of the approved selections becoming Augmented.

But when it happened year after year, TechWarden talking with an Augment under the guise of "mentorship," only for the Augment to mysteriously go missing only a few weeks later, Calypso put the pieces together. Of all of them, SnakeBite had been the only one whom she had managed to add to her Friends List, which meant he was the only one she had been able to try to help.

Even as late as it was, The Common Ground was easily the busiest place in the Square, and while on most occasions Calypso wouldn't have an issue signing a few autographs and adding a few more Augments to her Friends List, there were some nights when privacy was her main concern, especially when she had places to be. Entering the bar, she used one of the many abilities she had access to, letting out several slow, harmonious notes as she walked into the building.

Although her voice echoed throughout the room in an almost haunting melody, not a single person looked her way. In fact, it was almost as if every single one of them was making it a point of not looking *anywhere* near her. As one of the players with the highest level in the game, there were few people who could actually resist the effects of her songs when she chose to target them, and her Oblivious Melody was one of her highest-leveled abilities, letting her glide through entire crowds without ever being seen.

Without ever breaking her song, she headed for the closest bar. All of the

Non-Sapient bartenders knew her by now, and with a few hand movements, Calypso signed a request for an order she'd placed more than once in the last few days. Only a minute later, a container that looked suspiciously like a well-stuffed, greasy fast-food bag was placed ahead of her, along with a large Styrofoam cup. It only took the barest thought for her to transfer the requisite credits over to the bartender before taking the bag and walking away.

She sauntered around tables and past Augments moving through the room. The constant melody never faltered, and it only took her a minute before she came to the base of the spiral staircase leading up toward the second floor. Instead of heading upstairs, she circled away from the staircase, moving to the far side of the destroyed robot's head. She ran her hand along the cold metal as she walked until she stopped and placed her hand fully against a small spot near the chin of the robot.

With a *hiss*, a small staircase opened underneath the robot's head, and Calypso quickly dipped inside, letting the entrance close behind her before she finally stopped singing. The Null Zone of The Common Ground was immediately replaced with the full Dead Zone effect, deactivating her action bar and, thankfully for her, removing the more annoying passive effects of her powerset.

Calypso's powerset was classified as a Hybrid Support class, though as one of the first powersets generated, it came with a side effect that no amount of Augmentation or leveling had been able to change. Every word she spoke when she *wasn't* in a Dead Zone created aftereffects in anyone who could hear her based on her very emotion, and even then, she wasn't always in control of what the effects would be. Luckily for her, this room had been here from the very beginning, a small oasis within the larger oasis of the bar where she could speak completely unencumbered.

"I've brought you some dinner; I'd be willing to bet you haven't eaten all day, have you?" she said, descending the staircase in what was ostensibly the basement of a home in the Midwest in the eighties.

There were posters of classic sci-fi and superhero movies covering many of the walls, and where there weren't posters, action figures and other collectibles were neatly placed along various shelves.

Sitting at a large console filled with computer monitors in the far corner of the room, fingers racing along one of the many keyboards, was a man with uncombed and unkempt dark black hair. There was a similarly dark layer of scruff that covered the bottom half of his face, and he groaned as he leaned backward in the chair, stretching as he turned to look at the greasy bag Calypso was holding out for him.

"And you said you didn't care if I starved. You're a real pal, Cassie," the man said, rubbing at his eyes as he walked away from his computer setup. He took the bag from Calypso and quickly fell onto the overstuffed couch pushed up against a wood-paneled wall in the very center of the room.

"Well, you have been eating a lot less recently. It's *much* easier to get you a single burger now than trying to pick up any of your *old* orders, Christopher," Calypso replied as she walked and sat down next to him, exchanging her costume for a set of lounging clothes that she had kept queued in her B.E.L.T. for years now. While she knew she should have waited to let him at least eat some of his food, she also couldn't stop her curiosity. "Has there been any movement?"

"Not a whole lot. He broke out of the penthouse only a few minutes after the area reconnected to the Array with one hell of a punch, then flew down into Central Park and just . . . vanished," Christopher explained as he popped a few fries into his mouth. "The kid's grown a lot in a few days, but with his Acceptance Matrix disabled, it's going to be harder to keep track of him."

"Well, I certainly haven't been watching him as obsessively as you have, so I definitely couldn't speak to his larger growth," she responded, reaching over and stealing one of the fries. Meeting his eyes, she relented. "Okay, *maybe* I began to pay attention when Axio started having all the Vipers chanting about SnakeBite . . . What do you make of that, anyway? What's he up to?"

"Axio?" Christopher asked, taking a large bite of his burger as he raised a brow at her.

"Yeah . . . I get your *personal* interest in Loophole, but what did Axio gain out of leading him to SnakeBite?" she asked, moving to grab another fry before Christopher smacked her hand away and she scowled at him.

"I think we both know if I had ever been able to figure out what Axio was thinking, things would have never gotten this far," he said, his overall affable attitude faltering ever so slightly as another large yawn forced its way from him. "I think what I'm more worried about is how easily he piggybacked off the code I added into the messages you sent through to SnakeBite. It's the only thing I can think of that would explain how he was able to lead Loophole in."

"That wasn't your plan in the first place?" Calypso asked, finding herself pulling back in shock.

"Nope," he replied with a shake of his head, rubbing at his eyes. "Honestly, I was hoping I could use the metadata I slipped into SnakeBite's system to eventually create a beacon through the Dead Zone he had been locked in. It was a long shot, but damn near everything we do is a long shot. Once Axio started moving, though . . . well, it was basically like we were just along for the ride. Have you managed to find anyone with any of the others on their Friends List?"

This time, Calypso was the one to shake her head. "It's hard enough to probe people for information about random Augments who are noticeably low profile, especially with how weird some others get about me only communicating through the chat function. A few of the Sixth Wave members recognized Valor Viking, but none ever actually had him on their Friends List. If I hadn't seen Lunar Monkey, Frigid Air, and Gas Giant myself back in the day, I almost would have wondered if we had the names right."

"Well, no one said we were gonna be able to fix the world in a week," Christopher sighed and leaned back into the sofa. "Maybe we should focus our attention on what Axio intends to do next. The Tenth Wave Augments are leveling noticeably faster than prior Waves; there has to be a reason for that . . ."

"Do you think it's possible they are going to catch up with the other Waves?" Calypso asked, materializing a bottle of water into her hand before taking a long drink and then offering the beverage to him.

"I'd say it's more an inevitability than just possible. While Axio has been prodding the earlier Waves *some,* he hasn't been bombarding them with the same amount of missions and Crime Alerts as the Tenth Wave. Those added events are giving the new Wave a lot more experience opportunities which are bound to push them faster. Shit, just look at Loophole—how many Augments have to deal with an Augmented Swarm Event less than forty-eight hours into the game?"

"True . . . I can only imagine the amount of rest many of them are going to need once this first phase ends . . . and that's only if Axio *doesn't* immediately throw them into the next one," Calypso said with a slightly dejected sigh.

"Yeah, exactly. There's only so much I can do from behind the scenes now, but if that's going to be my role to play . . ." Christopher trailed off before taking the last bite of his burger. It wasn't super fast, but he still pushed himself to his feet as he took the now empty fast-food bag and chucked it across the room into a trash can that appeared out of thin air.

He was just about to walk back toward his consoles when he felt a hand holding his.

"Christopher . . . you need to sleep. Especially with your Personal Array being suppressed, this pace you're going at isn't sustainable," Calypso said, staring up at him with worry in her eyes.

"I . . . Look, Cassie, I know, but—"

"But nothing. You're no use to anyone if you kill yourself through sleep deprivation," she snapped back quickly, slowly pulling him back to the couch. "Now, how about we put on one of the classics and you can fall asleep to it like old times?"

"I . . . I guess I could spare a few hours." Christopher would face a lot of things when he had to, but arguing with Calypso was a battle he had rarely won, and he barely struggled as he settled back into the seat with another yawn. He really hadn't slept more than a few hours in the last seventy-two hours, but he couldn't help himself either. How could he sleep when there was still so much more he had to do?

While he knew just how much Calypso put on herself, *Infinite Ascension* had truthfully always been his baby. When the others quit on him after the loss of their first server, he had been the one to keep pushing forward. And he had *also* been the one to take the chance on a mysterious device with a fledgling AI that he had stumbled on in his search for new equipment.

Axio hadn't always been as crazy as he had turned out to be. In fact, he had been downright helpful early on, even if the AI didn't seem to even know what his own origins were due to limited resources.

That specific detail *hadn't* actually bothered him all that much early on, even if maybe it should have, but he had simply gotten too engrossed in the quickly evolving and expanding game that he'd believed was his ticket out of obscurity. It was only when Axio started altering the literal fabric of reality that he realized that he *might* have gotten himself in over his head. Even then, Christopher might have been able to pull the plug on things, but by that point—with others much more involved and Axio's reach expanding—he knew he had already let the genie out of the bottle.

As much as Christopher relied on Calypso, on Cassie, there were so many secrets that he still kept to himself, so many secrets that he refused to burden her with. He had a plan on just how to fix things, but he knew it was a long shot, and the fewer people who knew, the better. It was just that thought that lingered in his mind as he leaned his head down and onto Calypso's shoulder, dozing off just as the movie she had chosen started.

Trying to sleep with all of this still on his mind wouldn't give him good rest—none of the things he burdened himself with did—but they were his burdens to carry. So far, he had been strong enough that the weight of them hadn't caused him to kneel, hadn't caused him to break. He knew that with just a bit of luck, that strength would hold out just long enough for him to finish his work, even if it killed him in the end.

EPILOGUE

Part Two

Holy shit, what happened to this guy?"

"Mr. White, you know that we record everything that happens here. Please watch your language."

A woman who appeared to be in her mid-to-late thirties wearing a lab coat and a pair of horn-rimmed glasses walked alongside a gurney transporting SnakeBite's remains. She made a few notes on a clipboard before handing it over to the young Mr. White.

"Please put him in one of the closer facilities in the morgue. Dr. Jackson is on call tonight, so I will be having him head down shortly to complete the initial collections. Page me the moment he has arrived," she ordered, staring down the man who was barely out of childhood until he nodded.

"Yes, Mrs. Owens, of course," Mr. White said, taking the gurney from the two orderlies who had wheeled it in and pushing it further into the secure facility.

Maria Owens watched as the fresh-faced recruit pushed the recently deceased Augment away and felt her lip curl slightly in disgust. She had applied to and joined the Strategic Headquarters for Augment Development and Evaluation when the department had first split off from the NSA, yet she still found herself sick to her stomach whenever she had to see one of the Augments sent off for autopsy. She much rather preferred when she could send them off to containment rather than the morgue.

It had taken Maria nine years to rise from a data engineer up to her position managing Augment Intake, but she had known if she wanted to rise further or to be considered for the teams responsible for the enhanced equipment, she needed to show more initiative. So when a call had gone out searching for nondescript staff members looking for actual field experience, Maria thought she had found the right path.

After the evening she'd had, though, she was starting to question if she *wanted* to move higher than she already was. She certainly *hadn't* expected to spend the better part of two days having to bag and sort illicit materials for a gang, and it made her positive that she *wasn't* going to be looking for field-work assignments again. Seeing the Vipers transform up close was going to give her nightmares for weeks, not to mention she could still feel the panic in her chest at the idea of being caught in the middle of yet another fight.

All in all, she had a sudden newfound respect for the agents who didn't just volunteer to investigate the Augments more closely but put themselves right in harm's way over and over just to further the department's understanding of them.

She was just about to head up a hallway toward her office when a young woman with her hair pulled back into a tight bun and wearing a blouse and skirt combo that was *far* too green came speed walking her way from the opposite direction. Although the young woman had only been hired a few days earlier, Geraldine's quick and precise handling of her boss's needs were already becoming common gossip within the building.

"Mrs. Owens, I'm sorry to disturb you, I know you're busy handling the receipt of Augment 07-CH-NY, but Dr. Merens asked me to come get you. He wants to speak with you," the girl said. Although she had been rushing toward Maria, she didn't seem remotely out of breath.

Coming from any of the other department heads, having a secretary deliver a message instead of utilizing the paging system would have been odd, but Maria had been around long enough to be familiar with the doctor's quirks. Sure, he *had* been the one to implement the relatively archaic devices in the first place, but it was common knowledge that he also refused to utilize one himself.

"Really? He's still here at this time of night?" Maria asked, looking at her watch. It was just past 2:30 in the morning, and while she was used to working in the early hours, normally she was the *only* manager in the facility.

"Yes. He is apparently interested in the collected data from your team monitoring Augment 10-HK-NY."

Maria opened her mouth to argue that all of that footage had already been uploaded to the main server when she stopped herself. She looked up at one of the many cameras that monitored the facility before looking back at Dr. Merens's young secretary. "Okay, thank you, Geraldine. Please let Dr. Merens know I'll be there in a few minutes; I just need to grab my notebook from my office."

She watched as Geraldine hurried off before turning back toward her office. While she had certainly been looking forward to taking a quick nap on her couch, if Dr. Merens wanted to speak with her now, then she was going to need to speak with him now. Maria hurried to her office, gathering the notebook she had set aside after being called to Deliveries for the latest subject.

As promised, only a few minutes later she arrived at Dr. Merens office, walking past Geraldine's empty desk and pushing the slightly ajar door open.

"—and then first thing tomorrow, if you could pick up my dry cleaning; I have a meeting with the board, and I'd like to wear my good suit," Dr. Merens was saying, sitting on the edge of his desk. He had a hand resting under his chin, seemingly deep in thought. "I think that's everything I need from you for now, Geri. Please return to standby in case there's anything further I'll need."

"Of course, sir. I'll be in my quarters," Geraldine replied, beaming with an almost nauseating amount of admiration toward Dr. Merens. He gave her a wide, impossibly bright smile and a nod before she turned and started for the door, stopping briefly and bowing slightly to Maria, saying, "Excuse me."

Geraldine exited the room, pulling the door shut behind her. Once Maria turned her attention back to Dr. Merens, he had already circled back toward the sleek black chair that sat behind a desk absolutely cluttered with paperwork. Maria always found it fascinating that a man so well spoken was so bafflingly disorganized when it came to his years of research. And that wasn't even mentioning just how disheveled the short doctor was—not that she'd *actually* mention that to him.

"So . . . Mrs. Owens, you did some field work this evening?" Dr. Merens questioned, leaning back in his chair and steepling his fingers, using his clasped hands to point toward the chair on the opposite end of his desk. Maria didn't hesitate, moving to the chair and taking a seat. "You've been in Intake for the better part of five years now; can I ask what inspired the change?"

"I—" she started, feeling her hands grip onto her notebook before she swallowed. "Sorry, Dr. Merens, I thought that Geraldine had mentioned you wanted to speak with me about 10-HK-NY?"

"You can call him Loophole; our classification system really is a bit of a mouthful." He gave her a brief smile. "I apologize for the deception. I asked Geri to fetch you and just gave her the first reason that came to mind, but I am always fascinated when our staff members make large role shifts."

"Umm, okay . . ." Maria said hesitantly, unsure where he was going with this. "Well, Dr. Merens, there was an open recruitment for Field Work, and—"

"No, no, not that. I know how you got a role on the field team. I'm more curious why the change from Augment Intake to Field Work. Those are two very different specialties, wouldn't you agree?" he asked, once again smiling at her.

"Yes . . . sorry. I was looking to expand my resume for higher advancement. I'm not quite sure the department name, but I was considering applying for the Testing Teams?"

"The testing teams?" Dr. Merens asked with a bit of curious amusement in his expression. "Is there an area of expertise that you have yet to disclose to us?"

"Pardon, sir?" Maria asked, feeling a sudden nervousness in the pit of her stomach as she slipped into formalities.

"My apologies. I meant to ask if you were an engineer or scientist. If you have experience there, we are always looking to expand the team responsible for performing tests on the Augments we recover. Developing a way to produce artificial versions of the Augment's powers has eluded us for quite some time now."

Maria shook her head with an awkward laugh. "Oh, no, that's my fault, I'm sorry. I don't really know what the name of the department is, since it's restricted information. I meant the teams that participated in testing the equipment developed by us for our field agents . . . I've heard rumors that you have to be a part of that group to even be considered for trial runs of our artificial variants, and well . . . if we *did* successfully create them . . . wouldn't you want to be first on the list to get superpowers?"

Dr. Merens stared at her for a minute, letting her words hang in the air as if he was deciding just how he wanted to react before his head fell backward and he let out a boisterous laugh. Maria actually jumped before he finally settled down and reached up to wipe the corner of his eyes.

"Well, you're certainly not wrong. I think many of us have dreamed of having superpowers of our own," Dr. Merens said as he settled down. "Do you know what we generally believe is necessary for a good technology-tester for our Quality Assurance department?"

"The ability to find design flaws that limit active use?" Maria offered, though it came out as a question instead of the confidence she had meant to portray.

"While that is certainly helpful, that's not the most important thing. It's guts," Dr. Merens explained. "Generally speaking, the members of our Quality Assurance division are also members of our Field Work division. So if that's your goal, taking on more Field Work assignments would certainly be the path you'd want to take."

"Oh . . . That . . . I guess that might slow me down . . . I didn't exactly like my first experience," she explained, for some reason feeling embarrassed as she did so. "Can I ask why there is overlap? I've met with some of our field agents; I can't say I can see many of them testing such delicate equipment."

"Before I answer your question, could you answer one of mine first?" Dr. Merens asked, sitting forward and resting his chin on his hands. "What is driving your desire to be on this specific team?"

Maria hesitated for a moment before she found her resolve. "I think it's where I'd best be suited. I was married right out of high school and had my daughter not long after that. I was a stay-at-home mom and never was able to get a real education, but I loved trying to tinker with things . . . Then the Augments came along. My daughter was endlessly fascinated by them. She always wanted to watch the news whenever Calypso made an appearance . . . I swear she had a poster of her on her wall even before Augment merch took over the world."

Dr. Merens watched her carefully as she spoke, not even moving to interrupt as Maria stopped and stared at her notebook for nearly a minute.

"We were on a family trip to Niagara Falls when The First showed up . . . Nydia was so excited . . . She wanted to get closer, and dragged Henry—my husband, that is—closer to try and see him," Maria finally continued, missing as Dr. Merens's eye twitched ever so slightly at the mention of The First. "And then another Augment showed up . . . He was an electric-based Augment who went by Jumpstart, and he began to fight with The First . . . He electrocuted the entire waterfall at one point, and there were attacks being thrown everywhere . . . By the time I tried to get to where Nydia and Henry had run off to . . ."

Tears had started to run down Maria's face, and she found herself unable to actually finish her story. She reached up to wipe them away, only to find Dr. Merens holding out a tissue box toward her.

"I want to test the equipment that will protect normal people from those with so much more strength than us . . . I know people say I could go back to college, but it's just not the path I took . . . I can't bring my family back, but I can do what I can to protect the families of others just like me, and if being on this team is a precursor to being selected when we create our own version . . . well, then I want to be on it so I can eventually have the power to really protect people."

"You know, many of the members of this department have lost family or friends to the Augments. Even the ones who call themselves heroes have been responsible for so much death and destruction in the world," Dr. Merens explained while Maria took a moment to compose herself. "The reason that there is overlap between the Field Work and Quality Assurance teams is because of the inherent danger that comes with testing weapons and defensive equipment meant to thwart Augments. We have lost more than a few people to malfunction. So I have to ask, knowing the dangers that come with this team, is it still something you'd be interested in?"

"Yes . . . yes, it is," she replied, this time with practically no hesitation, and Dr. Merens's lips pulled up into a smile.

"Well then, you're in luck—I actually have one of our recent developments here, and I've been looking for an opportunity to properly test it."

He reached down into a drawer on the side of his desk without looking. A moment later, he placed a medium-size box—strikingly similar to a jewelry box—on the table and opened it to reveal what Maria first thought was a bulky-looking bracelet but determined was far too big for even the largest of arms. She found herself leaning forward to try to get a better look at it, noticing the sleek silver device seemed to be blinking from one side.

"What is it?" she asked, looking back up at him.

"We haven't quite chosen a name for it, but it's meant to provide clearer information between members of our Field Work division when dealing with the Augments. We have some preliminary test files we'd like to attempt to deliver using this," Dr. Merens explained before gesturing toward it with one hand and then pointing toward his neck with the other. "Hopefully, we can alter the design to be worn as an earpiece instead, but for now, you wear it like you'd wear a choker. I'd like you to put it on so that we can test if the information is unobscured."

"Well . . . that doesn't exactly sound like it's going to blow up in my hands," Maria commented with a hesitant laugh before she reached out, stopping only for a moment. "Shouldn't I be read into the restricted information on this?"

Dr. Merens let out another laugh. "Mrs. Owens, I'm the head of this department. I think if I am offering you the opportunity, you can assume you have permission."

Maria hesitated only a moment longer before nodding and reaching forward for the device, lifting it toward her. It was far lighter than she was expecting it to be, and it opened easily with a simple clasp. To her surprise, it was actually a nearly perfect fit for her neck. Clasping it down, she returned her hands to her sides as she waited for it to do whatever it was going to do.

"Is . . . Is there some sort of *on* switch or command word I should use?" she asked after a few seconds passed without anything happening.

"All of the Augments in the world are playing a massive game run by an Artificial Intelligence that calls itself Axio," Dr. Merens said.

"I . . . Wait, what?" Maria sputtered as her eyes went wide. "You can't mean—"

"Ah dammit, still an immediate Critical Level Threat . . . I guess I still haven't calibrated it quite right," Dr. Merens sighed as he leaned back into his chair and looked at Maria with a disappointed glare. "Ah, that's a shame . . . You know, for what it's worth, I do think you would have made an excellent field agent, but I can't quite have a Critical Threat storming our facility. I tend to prefer making sure our testers won't have anyone really asking too many questions."

"Wait, wh—" she started to say before her pager began to spark, sending a sudden high-powered jolt rushing through her system. Maria convulsed, collapsing to the floor and shaking until she fell as still as stone.

Dr. Merens stood up from his chair, slowly walking around the desk and shaking his head in disappointment.

"You know, Geri, I really did think it was going to work this time," he sighed as he reached up and pinched at the bridge of his nose.

"I have suggested that you try starting with smaller bits of information, but you seem to think you know better than I do," Geraldine's voice seemed to come from nowhere as Dr. Merens leaned down and placed a hand on Maria's lifeless form. There was a flash of light before she disappeared, and Dr. Merens returned to his feet.

"Seeing as I'm the reason we were able to develop the Personal AI system, yes, yes, I do think I know better than you. Even if we haven't gotten anywhere with providing more information to the department as a whole, I think we can call the testing of your Personal Vehicle a success. So far, no one has been any the wiser at your appearance," he said as he walked behind his desk toward a plain-looking display case that sat directly behind it. He reached a hand up to the third shelf and slowly ran his hand along the underside before he found the switch that he needed.

The display case pulled back into the wall, leaving a glowing white portal in its place.

"You're in a far better mood than I was anticipating you being after losing one of your test subjects," Geri noted as Dr. Merens stepped through the portal and into a massive workshop. There were various pieces of technology sitting on every surface, and he walked past all of them toward a simple computer with a single monitor.

"There wasn't much I could do about it. Axio's recent evolution is troubling in its own right, but I'm certainly not going to clue him in to the fact that I've established the entire department as a Dead Zone by stepping out of it to talk to him. The moment Axio started leading Loophole there was the moment we were going to lose SnakeBite," Dr. Merens replied as he logged onto the computer, revealing camera footage from the room that SnakeBite had been held in.

"I thought we'd be able to at least replace him with Loophole, but it seems he didn't complete the last objective I assigned him either, which itself is quite confusing. Make a note to remind me to complete an extensive study on his Personal Array after the morgue is done with him."

"Note created. But I'm still wondering . . . why aren't you more upset?"

He slowly scrolled through the footage until he found Loophole looking down at the gun he had materialized, and a smile slowly crept over his face.

"Because while you simply can't change the past, sometimes, you get just the piece of evidence you can manipulate to get your way." He leaned backward into his chair. "I'm sure if *I* had a brother, I probably would want revenge if I saw something like this, and I'm sure there's *plenty* we could learn from Hydramental's powerset."

Dr. Merens reached out, materializing a drink into his hand before taking a long chug from it.

"It's all about perspective, Geri. If the others all want to start making their moves, I think it's time I stop holding back so much," he declared, watching as Loophole lifted the gun up and silently pulled the trigger in the muted video. "For now, go ahead and start pulling Frigid Air and Gas Giant out of Cryo. I think it's time to see if we can alter the formula that SnakeBite's powerset taught us to be used on other powersets."

"Right away, TechWarden."

EPILOGUE

Part Three

Nate Mercer's Apartment, Safe House. Community District Four, Hell's Kitchen, NYC
Town: *Claimed by Guardian:* **Loophole**
City: *Claimed by Guardian Squad:* **Four Corners** *(Contested by Miscreant Squad:*
Droids R' Us*)*
Current Phase Points: *21255*
End of Phase One: 00D:00H:10M:20S

It had been far over a day since Nate had returned home, and he hadn't said a single word the entire time. After having vanished for nearly an hour, Jon had expected *some* sort of celebration of success, but the only thing Nate had said was that he needed some time alone.

Although Nate didn't actively choose to open his notifications, Jon was still able to scroll through the sudden wave of new information that his friend was quite actively choosing to ignore. Not only had he gotten a massive 4300 Phase Point boost to his score from defeating SnakeBite, something that launched him into first place on the leaderboard, but he had gained not just one but *two* S-tier loot boxes—one from completing **[The Snake Key]** mission and the other for reaching first place.

His luck hadn't stopped there either, as his jacket's Lucky Charm feature procced, upgrading the Achievement-granted S-tier box up to an S+ tier. Jon was beyond excited to see what the highest-ranked box could hold, but even that discovery was met with silence from Nate.

The last thing that surprised Jon was that Nate's claim over Community District Four the game-designated "Medium Town," had lost its Contested status, granting him the remaining seven hundred and fifty points from claiming it. He wasn't sure how defeating SnakeBite had completely wiped out Nate's opposition, but he certainly wasn't going to question it *that* much.

That night, even though Nate was still outside the Safe House, Jon found he didn't have access to what he had been jokingly calling Nate O'Vision to himself, though the map feature of the Command Room still worked. So even though he couldn't see exactly what Nate could see, Jon still knew exactly where Nate had run off to.

Angie, while she could still talk to him, found he wasn't responding to even her most annoying of attempts as he descended into Central Park. And it wasn't until the next morning that he came walking in through the front door, dropping a bag of groceries onto the table before heading into his bedroom, locking the door behind himself without a word of explanation.

Jon had only seen his best friend like this once before, when his grandma had passed away, and although Angie had wanted to talk with him about it, Jon decided to give Nate space, at least initially. Nate had never been the most vocal about his emotions, and that was before he had more superhuman problems to deal with. Even then, Jon had thought that by noon Nate would make an appearance and finally fill them in on what had happened after he went silent, but that time had come and gone without a single word.

With dinner approaching and Axio's End of Phase announcement looming, Jon finally decided to go with an old reliable and ran out to the deli. It only took him about a half hour to make it out, place the usual order, and make it back to the apartment with some time to spare.

"Any update on him?" Jon asked as he walked through the door. He found it incredibly frustrating that he was limited to hearing Angie from within the Safe House, especially since he knew the gear that made him the Guy in the Chair was still *technically* on him, but there really wasn't anything he could do about it unless there was an upgrade for his gear coming in the future.

"Not a peep," Angie replied with an uncharacteristic sigh. Unlike Nate, Jon heard Angie like she was coming out of invisible speakers floating near wherever he was walking, at least while Nate was inside of the Safe House; otherwise, he had to be seated in the Command Room to hear anything. *"I would really like to know what happened that made him decide to turn his Acceptance Matrix off . . . One of my primary protocols is to do everything I can to prevent exactly that from happening . . ."*

"Yeah, you've been awfully cagey about everything happening here . . ."

"Honestly, Codex, that's not out of some malicious intent on my part. I'm still doing my best to figure these changes out myself. As best as I can understand, Axio has been . . . restricting the information on just what the Acceptance Matrix controlled," Angie explained, clearly just a bit frustrated. *"For instance, it would seem I can no longer monitor his unspoken thoughts. Even before, when he asked me* not *to respond to them, I could still* hear *them. Now it's just a constant drone of static. This means I can't provide information based on things he doesn't realize are important enough to ask."*

"You didn't do that before," Jon pointed out as he set his sandwich down at the coffee table. He was going to set Nate's down there as well, but glanced toward his friend's door uncertainly.

"Yeah, but now I can't; *there's a very noticeable difference,"* she shot back.

"Does that have anything to do with why he has been able to just sit on five level ups instead of the system forcing him to choose things?" he asked, walking around the couch and toward Nate's door.

"Yes, that seems to be the case . . . As his last placed points were at level eight, I couldn't say for sure if this has eliminated the enforced time limit on the Ability Augmentations or not, and we won't know for sure until he places his level-nine stats and moves on to the level-ten selections."

Jon thought about it for a moment as he stopped at Nate's door and held up a fist. He knocked three times and leaned in, listening for any sort of movement or response.

"Hey, bud . . . Axio's daily announcement is gonna be starting soon," he called out, staring down at the door handle and debating if he should try to force it open. "I've also grabbed some Cubans from Tio's . . . might be a good idea to eat . . ."

"He's still not responding to me either; it's possible that he's asleep, as I'm not registering any movement from his system, although now I'm questioning if that *is governed by the Acceptance Matrix as well,"* Angie said, another wave of frustration passing through her tone.

"I'm gonna put yours on the table out here; come grab it whenever," Jon called through the door before he turned and walked over to the kitchen to place the sandwich down.

Almost as soon as Jon plopped down on the couch, the television in their living room clicked on, and the game's stylized logo spun on the screen. Music started to swell, letting the logo fade away as various clips of fights began to play. Like the last few announcements that Jon had seen, this was a collection of different surveillance and cell phone footage of the members of the Top Ten list; some of the best shots of each of them that the game's system seemed to have.

For the third night in a row, the shot of Nate launching into the air and smashing down into the giant group of snake-men was played from several different angles, and Jon still watched it with just a bit of awe. In just the few days he had been active, Nate had really made a name for himself in their neighborhood.

Jon wasn't too sure if that was something that Axio had been somehow influencing, but he chose to believe that Nate had just started inspiring the people around them. Even just walking down the street to Tio's, he had seen more than a few businesses with "We Love Loophole!" signs, and he found himself feeling just a bit of pride in knowing that he was a part of his friend's team.

Even before the list was displayed on the screen, Jon noticed that Hydramental had fallen off it, replaced by a man creating a wavy path of ice between two buildings and sliding along it with a wild smile as he tossed bolts of icy-blue energy toward what looked like a giant, mutated, two-headed bear.

As images of this Augment and then the ever-confusing Pigeon faded from the screen, the list finally generated, and Jon once again found himself somewhat surprised by the ever-decreasing player count.

Tenth Wave
Guardians: *195*   **Miscreants:** *312*

1. **Tempest's Wrath** *(Level 14 Thunder God) Miscreant —
   21500 Points*
2. **Loophole** *(Level 13 Perfect Planner) Guardian — 21255
   Points*
3. **Swansong** *(Level 11 Healing Voice) Guardian — 14670
   Points*
4. **Freakenstein** *(Level 10 Patchwork Armorer) Miscreant —
   13890 Points*
5. **Quizmaster** *(Level 10 Gameshow Host) Miscreant —
   13850 Points*
6. **Duke Juke'em** *(Level 10 Highschool Athlete) Miscreant —
   13525 Points*
7. **Vice Grip** *(Level 9 Toolbox Mechanic) Guardian — 13230
   Points*
8. **Pretty Pink Warthog** *(Level 9 Berserking Boar) Guardian
   — 13150 Points*
9. **Alpine Bob** *(Level 9 Iceflow Dynamo) Guardian — 12975
   Points*
10. **Pigeon** *(Level 9 Pigeon) Miscreant — 12955 Points*

Jon wasn't necessarily surprised that Tempest's Wrath had overtaken Nate once more, but the fact that it had been so close was still noteworthy to him, given that Nate had been locked away in his bedroom for the entirety of the last day of the phase. Had he actually been active, it was likely that no one would have been able to catch up with him.

Before Jon could start thinking too much about that, however, the leaderboard slowly faded away. As always, there was a familiar crackle of a speaker and mic tap.

"And three . . . two . . . one! That's it, folks! That's the end of Phase One," Axio called out, a fanfare of trumpets blasting in a triumphant rhythm as the screen started slowly lighting up and splitting into hundreds of smaller screens, each appearing with a portrait of a different Augment inside of it that became harder and harder to differentiate the more that appeared.

"At the end of Day Four, I am so proud to say that not a single one of you left has missed the point deadline, though *some* of you cut it rather close. Seriously, Applejack, that was impressive, but maybe don't wait so long to actually do your job during the next phase. Regardless, it's quite nice to know that I don't have to unleash Critical Level Threats as a punishment on *any* of you!

"While this might be one of the smaller groups moving from Phase One to Phase Two, it is also the first group that *won't* be losing another member due to failing the phase! See, first round of my testing *has* improved the quality of you Augments; providing regular motivation *does* breed results!

"As promised, the current Top Ten will each receive an S-tier loot box. And

I know, I'm sure some of you are thinking, 'Is it really fair that you're giving the people farthest ahead such a big bonus?' No, it's not fair. But I'm not here to reward mediocrity; that would be a waste of my time. That said, given that you all *did* pass this last day without further casualties, not to mention what comes next, what's the harm with throwing a little random chance to the wind? For completing Phase One, each of you, including the Top Ten members, will receive three F-tier loot boxes."

Jon found his eyes widening as he considered the ever-growing stack of possibly valuable items that Nate was sitting on. He knew whatever funk his best friend was in was serious—he didn't doubt that for a minute— but it was going to pass eventually, and when it did, those boxes were still going to be waiting to further propel Nate's position.

"Now, you have all gotten so much stronger already, and again, trust me when I say that I truly am proud of all of you for rising to the challenge. Some of you may have met those fallen members of your Wave, and while you may mourn them, I highly recommend you don't waste too much time on that.

"Maybe you've noticed it, maybe you haven't, but you all aren't as far spread as you might think. In fact, this year, even before I knew I was going to have the chance to fiddle with things so much, I made the one little modification my old programming allowed me to do. The Western Hemisphere got split into a hundred distinct regions for the purpose of the Tenth Wave.

"For those of you who *can't* do basic math, that means in each of those regions there are ten of you, and more often than not, you'd be surprised to find that you have all been pretty perfectly split between Guardians and Miscreants—granted, erring on the side of the Miscreants in some of the more spacious regions. I really do appreciate when things work out like that. Oh, though I guess one of the regions started with eleven rather than ten, although that's down to eight now, so I guess it really doesn't matter all that much."

Although he had been slacking just a bit on his Augment research, Jon had so far found some information on two of the other new Augments in New York City beyond Nate and Hydramental. Somewhat surprisingly, though, they were both people who were in the Top Ten: Swansong and Freakenstein.

Swansong appeared to be a sound-based Augment, though unlike a hero like Calypso, she seemed to be almost entirely noncombat oriented, making her rank on the leaderboard all the more impressive. Most of the footage he had found of her was of her strolling through various hospitals, her white-and-gold costume shining like wings as she spread her arms and quite literally *sang* terminal children back to perfect health. It only took looking up the hospitals that she made her appearances at to determine that she was *probably* working out of East Harlem.

Freakenstein was a rather odd monstrosity to watch, his body a quilt of molded metal and weapons that he tore and used with brutal efficiency against what Jon *hoped* were Non-Sapient private security forces. He hoped that even more when he saw Freakenstein send them flying with powerful, armor-coated punches. There were at least two separate roads in Downtown Brooklyn that were closed for repairs due to the sheer amount of damage he had delivered.

Other than that, just based on the random footage of Pigeon during the nightly announcement, Jon had a sneaking suspicion that he, or it . . . Jon still wasn't exactly sure what Pigeon was, was somewhere in New York City as well, though he couldn't find any evidence in the news of people being terrorized by an Augmented Pigeon.

"While I'm sure there are more than a few of you eager to jump right on into Phase Two, there are just a few final quirks I'm needing to finish working out. I've gotta say, I'm loving just how much more compliant you guys have been than the older Waves. I really didn't push them hard enough, and now they're in for a rude awakening, but I think you all are going to be up to the task.

"In the interest of letting you all discover just what other Augments are in your region, since that is going to be *very* important in the coming phase, there will be a three-day interlude where I encourage you all to keep working to grow stronger and do some exploring. At the end of this announcement, you will all receive a map showing the boundaries of the region you are in. Trust me, this *will* be important.

"And I am feeling rather benevolent, so I'll go ahead and warn you now: be careful before you look at this break without a point requirement and decide to slack off; I promise that *won't* end well for you. To answer the first question I know that some of you may be waiting to ask: Yes, you *can* continue to gain points during this brief period, and *yes*, doing so will give you a leg up in the next phase. But just in case that's not enough to get you all going, let's give you all some extra motivation.

"The three Augments who gain the most Phase Points during the next seventy-two hours will each receive an A+ tier loot box. Strength, skill, and teamwork . . . yup . . . I think that's a good enough hint. Congratulations again! You've all done so well to grow strong enough to survive this far; let's hope you all continue to rise to the challenge. I'm going to need *as many* of you as possible to get *as strong* as possible. Good luck, Augments."

The television clicked off, and Jon let out a long breath that he hadn't realized he had been holding. He still wasn't quite sure just how serious all of this was supposed to be. While he had certainly been flippant about some of the things that Nate had been dealing with, he *did* recognize the ever-shrinking player count in the Tenth Wave proved that it *wasn't* a perfectly safe game. At the very least, this *was* the first night that Axio hadn't levied some level of threat at the members of the Wave.

Jon was just starting to get up from the couch when he heard the click of a door opening. He turned and saw Nate stepping out of the room, his Fortune's Guardian Jacket *not* on his shoulders but instead being held in his hands as he gripped it tight enough that his knuckles were turning white. There was a certain amount of hardness in his expression that Jon wasn't sure what to make of.

"You good, man?" Jon asked. Although he had a million questions he knew he needed to ask, he also knew better than to overwhelm Nate. Even then, Nate just nodded before the jacket vanished in a flash of light and reappeared on top of Nate's clothes. "You, uh . . . You wanna talk about it?"

"I have more than a few questions that I really *think you need to—"*

"Not now, Angie," Jon cut her off, and she huffed as Nate's expression broke ever so slightly, one of the edges of his lips starting to curl upward. Jon gave him a look, knowing more than anything that while it *probably* wasn't the healthiest way to deal with things, his friend would talk when he was ready. He decided to give him the chance to redirect the conversation. "Okay, what's the plan, bud?"

A few moments of silence passed where Jon *almost* wanted to ask if Nate was *actually* pausing for dramatic effect, when his friend *finally* spoke. His voice was hoarse, like he had been crying for far longer than he should have, but it didn't matter. Jon could still hear the resolve in his tone.

"We get to work. This is far from over."

About the Author

Zane Emerson is the author of the Augment's Code series, originally released on Royal Road. With far too many comics and collectibles in his collection (and going so far as to name his son after his favorite hero), Emerson combined his love for superheroes with a passion for writing. He resides in DeBary, Florida, with his son, Wally.

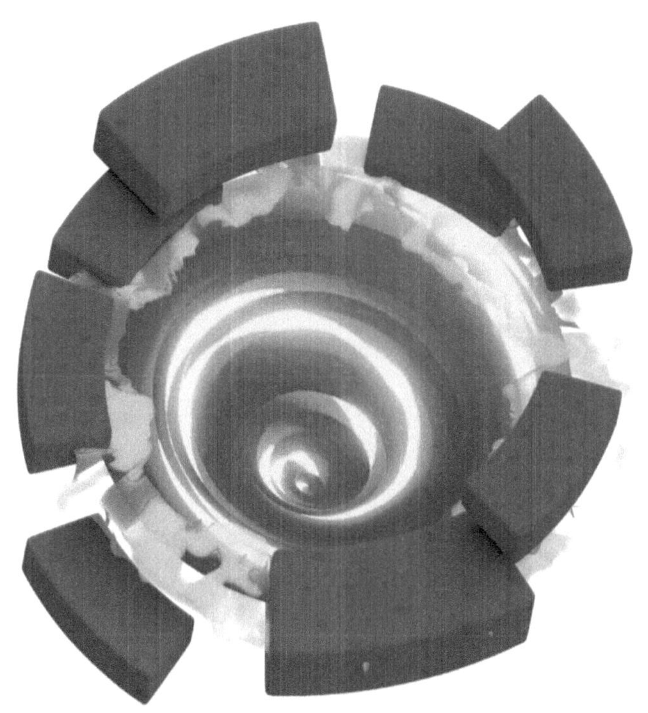

RESPAWN YOUR CURIOSITY

follow us on our socials

podiumentertainment.com

@podiumentertainment

/podiumentertainment

@podium_ent

@podiumentertainment